BAD BOY BLUES

ST. MARY'S REBELS
BOOK 0.5

SAFFRON A. KENT

This is a work of fiction. Names, characters, places, and incidents are either the product of the author's imagination or are used fictitiously, and any resemblance to actual persons living or dead, business establishments, events, or locales, is entirely coincidental.

Bad Boy Blues © 2019 by Saffron A. Kent
All rights reserved. No part of this book may be used or reproduced in any manner whatsoever without written permission of the author except in the case of brief quotations embodied in critical articles or reviews.

Cover Art by Najla Qamber Designs
Cover Model: Clauss Castro
Editing by Leanne Rabesa
Proofreading by Virginia Tesi Carey

April 2019 Edition

Published in the United States of America

OTHER BOOKS BY SAFFRON A. KENT

The Unrequited

Gods & Monsters

Medicine Man (Heartstone Series Book 1)

Dreams of 18 (Heartstone Series Book 2)

California Dreamin' (Heartstone Series Book 3)

ST. MARY'S REBELS

Bad Boy Blues (SMR book 0.5)

My Darling Arrow (SMR book 1)

The Wild Mustang & The Dancing Fairy (SMR book 1.5)

A Gorgeous Villain (SMR book 2)

These Thorn Kisses (SMR book 3)

Hey, Mister Marshall (SMR book 4)

The Hatesick Diaries (SMR book 5)

BLURB

Cleopatra Paige hates one thing in this world – just one – and his name is Zachariah Prince.
In grade school, he pulled at her pigtails. In middle school, he spread false rumors about her. And in high school, he ruined her prom.
She hates that his smirks are unfairly sexy. And she definitely loathes that his dark eyes seem to follow her everywhere. Sometimes, even in her dreams.
It doesn't matter that he's rich and popular or that he lives in a freaking mansion full of butlers and maids. He's rude and arrogant, and she wants to stay as far away from him as possible.
But unfortunately for Cleo, she lives in the same freaking mansion as Zach. Only he's the prince and she's the lowly maid who serves him.

To the brave: who stand up for what's right even when they're afraid.

To my husband: the bravest man I know.

And well, to me: This book is proof that I'm brave and that I will always, no matter what, stand up for what's right.

READER'S EXTRAS

Official Spotify Playlist

Pinterest Boards
St. Mary's School for Troubled Teenagers

Prince

Of English origin; Royal son.

Paige

Of English origin; Young servant.

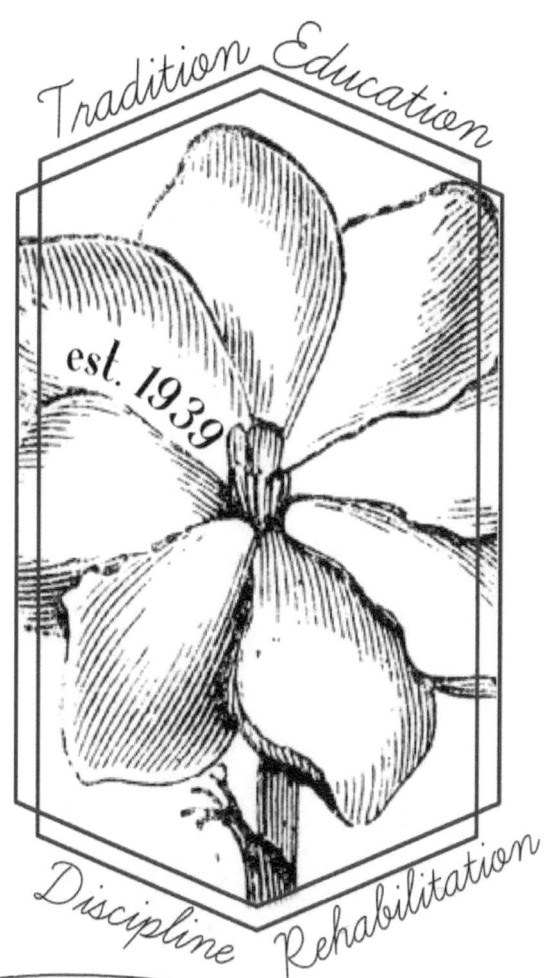

ST. MARY'S GUIDE
to Lip Lovin' for One and All:

FOR GIRLS DOOMED IN LOVE

Dream Broken Darling   I Jinx U   Teenage Decay

Good Bad Girl   Sweet Little Sweetheart   Drip Drip Gasoline

Golden Eyed Queen

FOR GIRLS BETRAYED IN LOVE

Heartbreak Juju   Crazy-Hearted Loner   Moon-Eyed Wasteland

Queen of the Bards   Sex and Candy   Train Wreck Princess

FOR GIRLS WHO DREAM

Red Addict   Pink and Shameless   Cherry Picker

Lollipop Lover   Pinky Winky Promises

FOR GIRLS WHO LOVE TROUBLE

Handmade Heaven   Cute Corruption   Troubled Sweetheart

God of a Girl   Purple Witchcraft   Young and on Fire

Wild Child Bad Child

FOR GIRLS WHO FALL FOR THE BAD

Desert Rose   She-Desperado   Watermelon Sugar

Dangerous Woman   Pink Lemonade   Glitter Glitter Baby

Chapter 1

There's a line in the town I live in.

It's invisible, this line. It's also paper-thin and razor-sharp. But it's there.

For about nineteen years, I've lived on one side of it. On the south side. It's the side with hardworking and honest people, but we don't have a lot of money. We have run-down buildings and shabby front yards and houses that creak and shake in a strong wind.

The north side is that of the rich and the powerful. It's the side with big houses, mowed lawns and expensive cars.

It's the side I absolutely hate for a variety of reasons. But I'm not getting into that right now.

I have a mission, a very important mission.

For the past six months, I've been living on the topmost corner of the north side. Not by choice, mind you. But by circumstance.

I've been calling an estate called The Pleiades my home.

It's named after the constellation of seven stars up in the sky. Probably because the palace-like mansion that sits on this estate has seven towers.

And tonight, my mission is to break into it. The mansion, I mean.

Well, to be honest, if you know the code of the service entrance, is it really breaking and entering?

I don't think so.

It's more like punching in the code and entering. Something I do every day.

The only difference is that every day I do it in broad daylight. But right now, I'm doing it under cover of darkness with my stealth mode on.

I'm wearing my black shorts, paired with a black hoodie that covers my bright blue hair, and quiet leather boots.

I'm like the night: dark and silent. Oh and hot. Temperature-wise.

Another thing to know about our town is that it's always hot. It's always muggy and humid. Summer is our perpetual weather, even in winter. Weirdly, The Pleiades is the hottest spot of all.

I'm sweating with all the black stuff that I have on. But it could also be the nervousness. It's not every night that I *punch in the code and enter* like this.

But desperate times, desperate measures.

Not to mention, I can't shake off the feeling that I'm being watched.

Stopping at the service entrance with my hand poised at the keypad, I look around for probably the tenth time since I headed out for my mission. But there's no one there. The night's dark and the lush grounds are quiet and lonesome.

Maybe paranoia comes with doing kinda shady stuff.

Sighing and turning back around, I hit the keys and enter the code. When the automatic door clicks open, I enter the small lobby-like thingy that has the stairs going down to the basement. To the servant's wing.

Slowly, I climb down, avoiding the stairs that creak lest I wake up the night staff who are probably sleeping in the on-call rooms.

I reach the landing that gives way to a wide hallway, which is illuminated by tiny nightlights. Rooms flank it on either side. On-call rooms for the sleeping staff, the staff room where we have meetings and breaks, the head housekeeper's office.

I walk slowly and without making a sound until I reach the other side of the hallway. There's another staircase that takes us to the first floor. Again, I avoid the creaking ones as I climb up.

My destination is tower three, located all the way in the east.

It takes me about seven minutes to journey through all the rooms and passages on the first floor: the ballroom, the rose room, the yellow sitting room, the private dining room and whatnot.

Then I come upon the sprawling stairs that will take me to tower three, where the guest wing is. As I climb up yet again, I thrust my hands in my pockets to see if I still have my weapon.

Yup, it's there.

I feel the edges of the pouch and smile in the darkness.

Now that I'm so close to my destination, I can't wait. I *literally* can't wait.

My feet are faster and my breaths are coming out in pants. I'm swimming in adrenaline. I feel alive. Like I have more than one life in me. More than one heart and two sets of lungs.

Calm down, Cleo.

I can't slip up now and have someone bust me. Not when I'm *so close* to my goal.

Finally, *finally*, after all the traveling and walking and climbing, I reach it. The exact guest room I was looking for.

"Okay." I puff out a breath and glance from side to side. "You're so dead, you fucker."

I fish the keys that will get me into the room out from my pocket.

The tiny silver-colored key.

Okay, so yeah, this might be a little against the law. Like, maybe ten percent against it.

The keys in my pocket don't belong to me. I swiped them from Mrs. Stewart, the head housekeeper's, office right after my shift ended.

But hey, I plan to give them back tomorrow so this is more like borrowing. I'll have to, actually; she's weird about keys. But that's beside the point.

The point is that I'm not a thief; I'm a borrower.

Biting my lip, I insert the key in the lock and it turns easily. The click that comes as I open the door is loud. Or maybe it sounds that way to me and I swallow, freezing in my spot.

God, please. I'm so close.

I need to do this. This needs to happen. This is my only chance.

Glancing up and down the darkened hallway once again, I count the seconds but nothing stirs. The mansion is still asleep and quiet, much like the night outside. There isn't any indication of movements from the inside either. Meaning he's asleep too. Totally oblivious of what's going to happen to him.

Opening the door only far enough so I can fit through, I creep inside. The room is cool, courtesy of the AC. The night lamp is on and it throws the sleeping body on the bed into light.

Mr. Grayson.

A fifty-year-old guest who flew out to see the famous apple orchards of The Pleiades and take the grand tour of towers six and seven. They are more like a museum and are open for public display.

Yeah, The Pleiades is kind of a big deal for our town.

Half of it is preserved, and privileged people from all over the world come to see the beautiful architecture of it. Throw in a world-famous golf course or two and they're happy as a peach. I hear that the tour alone costs more than what I make in a year working on the cleaning staff.

The other half of this mansion is where the Princes live, the oldest family of this town. In fact, they are the founders of this town with a line.

They built The Pleiades a long time ago and have lived here for centuries.

A guy once lived here too.

A guy with jet black hair and jet black eyes. A guy I haven't seen in three years, ever since he abruptly went away.

A guy I don't like to think about.

Anyway, enough history lesson. It's showtime.

I've been in this guest room a hundred times before so I know where everything is. Namely, the closet that holds my prize.

Softly, I tiptoe toward it, keeping my eyes on the sleeping man. He hasn't stirred yet. Probably drunk off his ass.

I open the closet door and there it is: his freshly-pressed suit for tomorrow.

I wish I could fist-pump right now but that might be too risky. So I fish out my weapon, the itch powder, and open the lapels of his suit jacket. Glancing at Mr. Grayson one last time, I sprinkle the powder all over the fabric, especially on his pants.

He's so not going to know what hit him.

Biting my lip once again, I try to keep my gleeful laughter under wraps. I'm not out of the woods yet. I need to get back to my cottage undetected or Mrs. Stewart will wake up to the best news ever: Cleopatra Paige was finally caught breaking a rule and it's time to fire her.

She's not a huge fan of me or my blue hair or my blue lipstick *or* my leather boots. Basically, she hates my guts and she won't hesitate to fire me if I step even one toe out of line. And right now, I'm so far past the line that I can't even see it.

With my mission completed, I creep back out of Mr. Grayson's room and shut the door quietly. Then, I'm retracing my steps, climbing down, walking, traveling all the way back to the servant's wing.

With any luck, I'll be back in my cottage before the clock strikes midnight and when I come to work tomorrow, Mr. Grayson will be reduced to a monkey who scratches his own balls.

You're awesome, Cleo. You're fucking awesome.

I grin.

Just as I'm about to step on the stairs that will take me up to the service entrance, I hear a rustle behind me and my name is whisper-shouted.

"Cleo!"

I gasp and my fingers fumble on the wooden bannister.

"Cleo."

I scrunch my eyes closed and bow my head. Sighing, I face the caller. It's Maggie, the head cook.

She has her arms akimbo and her lips pursed as she watches me with accusing eyes. "What did you do?"

"Nothing."

She looks me up and down, probably noticing my stealth mode and somehow, her gaze falls on the pockets of my hoodie. "What do you have in there?"

I pat them and realize there's a bulge where I stuck the itch powder and the key in. "Nothing," I repeat.

Even I don't believe myself, and I'm an excellent liar.

"Give it here."

Time to up my game.

"Maggie, there's nothing in my pockets, okay? I came in because I thought I left my phone in the staff room. But I didn't. So yeah. Nothing in my pockets. Not up to any mischief or anything."

I spread my palms in mock surrender as I finish my nonchalant speech.

Maggie watches me for a beat. Her stare is making me nervous, or rather more nervous than I already was.

"I watched you grow up, you know. I know when you're lying, Cleopatra Paige."

"I'm not –"

"Come on. Let's go to the kitchen."

With that, she turns to her right and walks into the hallway that breaks off right before the stairs where I'm standing.

Damn it.

Not exactly what I had in mind when I broke into the mansion tonight. Whipping off my hood so my long, wavy hair can breathe, I follow her.

The kitchen at The Pleiades can probably fit the cottage that I live in three times over. It's a large circular room with industrial lights and steel countertops. It's more or less like the kitchen of a very posh restaurant, complete with a walk-in freezer and high-end grills and whatnot.

Maggie gestures at me to take a seat in a nook with a little dining table by the window, overlooking the night.

She's in her robe, meaning she was on call tonight, and I know that she's a light sleeper. Just my luck.

I watch her as she scurries back and forth, collecting dishes and forks, and getting the blueberry pie out of the little fridge off to the side.

Maggie is super cute. Short and plump with a mop of curly honey blonde hair, peppered with gray.

She cuts us each a piece and sets one of the dishes in front of me before taking a seat.

"Eat," she tells me, her motherly face stern.

I shoot her a small smile. She knows how much I love blueberry pie – actually, I love all sweet things – and she always makes sure to save a few pieces for me.

Sliding the dish close to me, I dig in. "Thanks."

She grunts and my smile gets bigger.

Maggie points a finger at me. "Don't. Don't you smile at me. You're not off the hook yet."

I bite my lip to keep from smiling and mouth *sorry*.

She cuts a piece of her own pie. "Now, is this about that guest, Mr. Grayson?"

I gulp the bite I had in my mouth and Maggie raises her eyebrows.

Clearing my throat, I whisper, "Maybe."

"I told you to stay out of that."

"Stay out of it?" I ask in disbelief. "Do you even know me? I can't stay out of it. I won't stay out of it. He groped Grace. *Groped* her. He practically groped me." I gesture to my boobs. "And you don't grope these without consequences."

Grace is one of the girls on the cleaning staff. She's shy and doesn't like confrontation. So when I caught her crying in the staff room, I forced her to spill her story. Apparently, Mr. Grayson has been harassing her, making lewd comments and patting her butt whenever she walks by.

Motherfucking asshole.

A couple days ago when I felt a brush across my chest while I served him breakfast in bed, I thought I'd imagined it. But Grace's story had me re-evaluating things.

So I acted. Someone had to.

Maggie studies me shrewdly and I feel my cheeks flushing with warmth.

"And that's the only reason?" she asks.

"Yeah." I shift in my seat. "What else could it be?"

Shrugging, she eats a bite of her pie. "I don't know. Maybe something to do with the fact that you hate this job."

"I don't hate this job."

"Really?"

I slide the pie away. "Yes. I mean, do I like cleaning up vomit when the guests go wild and finding used condoms on the floor? No, I don't. Do I like dusting off the windows or mopping up the floor until I can see my face on the tiles? Nope. But it's a job and you know I need it. I need it more than anything else in the world right now."

Maggie was the one who got this job for me.

In our town, if you don't go to college, you most probably go here. You work on the cleaning staff or on the cooking staff or whatever staff you seem fit to work on.

My parents were the select few who had other jobs. My dad used to paint houses and my mom used to tutor kids sometimes.

College was never an option for me; I'm not into books and all. But neither was working at The Pleiades.

I wanted to travel the world like my mom used to say when I was little. I wanted to explore it and see what I liked. See where my passion was. I wanted to find myself.

Pity flashes through Maggie's eyes and I look away. If I don't, I might start crying and that's the last thing I want tonight.

Tonight was about tit for tat. It was about the adventure, the rush of it all. Tonight was about feeling alive.

"You know, you don't have to do this. This job. You could pack up right now and leave this town. Just like you planned. Just get in your car. The blue car that you love so much." She smiles. "Take a road trip. Send me postcards. No one's going to blame you, Cleo."

Okay, first of all: I can't just get in my car. I can't.

I won't.

My blue car that I used to love so much, the car that I spray-painted myself with my dad, scares me now. I can't touch it. I won't touch it. Because every time I do, I can't sleep for days. I get nightmares. Sometimes I throw up, get dizzy, claustrophobic.

But I can't tell her that. Because she'll say the same thing that she's been saying for the past year.

You need to see someone, Cleo. Talk to someone.

"I can't," I whisper, threading my fingers together. "I need this job. I *need* to get my house back."

My old house. The house I grew up in.

The bank took it away last year because of my dad's debts. After a lot of pleading, they gave me a second chance, along with a time limit to come up with the money. I only have about four more months to gather it and I need this job to get me there.

"Your parents wouldn't have wanted this for you."

"Well they're not here, are they?"

I was trying to be snappish. But I guess, I sounded more... forlorn, like the orphan that I am.

Sighing, Maggie sits back. "Fine. I can't make you do anything that you don't want to do."

My chest feels heavy but I still manage a trembling smile.

"But," Maggie says, sternly. "I don't want you inside the mansion after your shift's over. Do you understand?"

I straighten my spine. "Yes."

"No matter what happens. No matter how tempting it is to take revenge. You're not a vigilante."

"You mean like Wonder Woman?" I grin.

"It's not funny."

I shake my head seriously. "It's not."

Maggie nods in approval. "You will not set your foot inside this place if you're not working. I don't even want to think about what would've happened if someone else had found you loitering around instead of me. So no more nightly excursions."

"Got it."

Maggie looks me over. My navy blue lipstick, my blue hair and my black attire.

I'm used to such looks from people. Back on the south side, no one cared. But here, on the other side of town, people look at me with judgement. My blue, wavy, messy hair is the first indication that I'm not sophisticated enough. My navy blue lipstick means I don't know a thing about fashion.

But coming from Maggie, it kind of hurts. It makes me self-conscious.

"It's not a secret that you don't follow the rules and Nora doesn't like you very much for it."

Nora is Mrs. Stewart aka Mrs. S and yup, she hates me.

"That's putting it mildly."

"It is. You can still quit and leave this town but since you don't want to, let's not flaunt how much we don't care about the rules in her face. Let's not try to get fired."

"I wasn't trying to –"

"Save it."

I go quiet and tuck a strand of my hair behind my ear as Maggie continues, "Now, empty your pockets and give me whatever you had in there."

Looking at her for a few seconds, I decide to just hand her all my goods. I fish out the pack of itch powder and the key and put them on the table.

Shaking her head, Maggie takes them into her possession. "Cleo. Cleo. Cleo." She sighs. "What am I going to do with you?"

"Love me, maybe?"

Maggie chuckles. "Finish your pie and go home."

Twenty minutes later and a lot of turning around to see if I'm still being followed, I'm in my cottage.

Servants' cottages are located a little farther away from the main house. There are about five or six cottages in total, arranged in a semi-circle with woods at our backs.

I live in the smallest one with my best friend, Tina.

We've been BFFs ever since we were kids. A few guys stole her pink bike and I punched them to get it back.

Like me, Tina's on the cleaning staff. College wasn't for her either but unlike me, she always planned to come work at The Pleiades.

My room has a twin bed, a small dresser and an even smaller closet. The walls are white in color, which I'm not such a fan of.

When I first moved in, I thought I'd paint it blue with my dad's paintbrushes; I saved a couple of his brushes among other things from my old house. But then I realized, I didn't want to make it blue.

This isn't home.

The north side, The Pleiades, they are not home. They are not my safe place. These are not my people.

My people – the people I can really call mine – are dead.

They've been dead for a year and I wonder how long it takes for the grief to go away and an orphan to not feel like one.

I put on my mom's nightie, made of cotton and lace, and blue. My mom was a huge fan of the color blue. In fact, she had blue hair like me.

I'm just getting under the covers when something flashes in my peripheral vision.

It's a falling star.

I scramble up on the bed and clutch the bars on the window. When I was little, my mom and I would always make it a point to wish upon a shooting star, if we saw one together. It was just one of the things we did.

And like always, I close my eyes and make a wish.

Please let me get my house back.

When I open my lids, the star's gone like it wasn't even there. Strangely, it makes me sad.

But then, a second later, I don't have the time to be sad.

Everything inside me comes to a screeching halt when I notice something else in my peripheral vision.

It comes and goes so quickly. Quicker even than a shooting star, that I could've imagined it.

But no. I saw it.

I saw the corner of a shoulder. A flash of an elbow. A long, muscular thigh encased in dark jeans.

Someone walking down the dirt path that cuts through the woods.

The feeling of being watched that I've been experiencing all night comes back in full force. In fact, it brings on other things.

Things that I'd forgotten about.

Mad rush of my heart. The tightness in my chest like my lungs are starving for air. And those... butterflies in my stomach, with sharp, blade-like wings.

"Oh my God," I whisper.

It's not possible, right? He's not here. He went away three years ago.

I mean, I *know* that shoulder. I'm familiar with that elbow and that thigh. I've seen them almost every day ever since I was ten. I've watched them grow up and get bigger and stronger with age.

I could pick them out from a line-up, even if I were sleepwalking.

I could pick them out even though I haven't seen them, seen *him*, in three years.

Then, I'm jumping out of my bed and dashing to the front door of the cottage. I throw it open and run outside in my bare feet.

The ground is hot and hard even through the grass that surrounds our front yard. But I don't care about any of those things.

I care about what I saw.

But again, there's no one as far as the eye can see. The night's just the same as it was half an hour ago when I walked back to my cottage.

I look around, up and down, side to side.

Did I imagine him?

But *why* would I imagine him? Why would I imagine the guy I've hated for almost a decade?

Is this what it feels like when you lose your mind?

Maybe my parents' death is affecting me in all the wrong ways.

A few seconds later, I'm back inside, in my bed, under the covers.

I close my eyes to go to sleep but all I can see is that shoulder and that elbow and *him*.

Chapter 2

"**B**lue!"

There's only one person on this earth who calls me that.

Three years ago, his voice used to be rough and low. Grumbling. I'm sure years must've matured it even more. Not that I care about it.

I don't.

And neither do I care about what I saw last night. I think I made him up. It was a dream or something. A figment of my imagination.

Anyway, *this* voice is high and giggly, kind of cutesy. It belongs to my five-year-old neighbor, Arthur. We all call him Art and he calls me Blue.

So maybe there are two people who call me by that name.

I stop and turn around to find him running toward me. He has his backpack on his shoulders and he's grinning at me.

I grin back. "Hey, big guy."

Panting, he comes to a stop and I get down on my knees. He has blond hair and green eyes, and a perpetual cowlicky thing on the back of his head.

"Look!" He shows me his fist. "Did I do it right?"

I've been teaching him how to make a fist and, yup, he completely nailed it.

"It looks perfect."

He beams. "Yay!"

Smiling, I pat at his cowlick. "You're gonna destroy them."

"You think?" he asks.

Art looks at me with such hope that my heart squeezes.

"Duh. Just don't back down, okay? Always remember, we're the underdogs. But contrary to what people think, underdogs are not weak. We fight back. In fact, we fight the hardest. People underestimate us and you know what, let them. That's their biggest mistake. And don't ever let anyone tell you otherwise, my friend."

He smiles and nods enthusiastically. "Okay!"

Art and I, we were destined to become friends. Like me, he's an orphan too. Although his parents died when he was only two. Ever since then, he's lived here on The Pleiades with his grandma, Doris, who's also on the cleaning staff.

But other than that, the most important thing that links me to this five-year-old adorable and shy boy is the fact that we're both the bullied. At least, I once was.

Art's a little small for his age, so some kids at his school are giving him trouble for it. They push him around and threaten him, making him cry and turning school generally miserable.

Fuck them.

Bullies are cowards. They can't stand on their own two feet so they hide behind empty threats. All they need to set them straight is a little pushback and I've been teaching Art how to do that. Since I have a little experience in that area.

We fist-pump and I stand. "I love you. I gotta run. But I'll see you tonight, okay?"

He nods. "Is it pancake night?"

Since Doris is getting on in age, I help out with Art whenever I can. Tonight I'm babysitting him and since it's Monday, we're doing breakfast for dinner.

"You bet!"

After saying my goodbye, I'm running toward the main house where our daily meeting is going to start in about ten minutes.

Like last night, I punch in the code to the service entrance and get inside. Even from the top of the stairs, I can hear the hustle and bustle of the staff.

There are people coming in and out of the kitchen, the staff room. Women wear gray dresses with white trim on the collars and sleeves like me, and men wear white shirts with black pants. Our uniform here at The Pleiades.

There's giggling and talking and even shoving. The entire house is awake and hard at work.

I climb down the stairs, call out *hello*s and *hi*s, until I reach the staff room. People are already sitting down and Tina, who went in earlier than me because she has no problem waking up early, is saving a seat for me.

As soon as I sit down, Mrs. S walks in and Tina leans over to whisper, "Right on time. Who would've thought?"

I'm kind of famous or infamous for being late so I just flip her the bird under the table; I've been busted before for doing it in plain sight.

Tina simply giggles.

Mrs. S takes her seat at the head of the table and everyone falls silent. There's coffee and tea and cookies in the middle – courtesy of Maggie and her staff – and together with the long dining table and straight spines and serious faces, this could be a scene from Downton Abbey.

"Good morning, everyone," Mrs. S greets us, looking around, her eyes stopping on me. "Very glad to see everyone in here and on time."

I smile. Though it might have looked like a grimace.

"So, today, we have a little change of plans."

Mrs. S is smiling and I don't have a very good feeling about this. If she's happy, then that means something is wrong. She's never happy and neither does she let anyone else be happy. Namely, me.

"Today's a special day." She keeps smiling and my frown gets bigger. "To celebrate this unplanned but special occasion, Mr. and Mrs. Prince are having a party. I know that it's a little short notice but I want most of you in the ballroom. I want every inch of that place clean and polished before the decorators get here. I've assigned some of you to work with them and I don't want any mistakes or complaints, got it?"

She pins everyone with a glare until we all nod.

"Tonight has to go smoothly. It's probably the most important event you'll ever work on here at The Pleiades. Well, one of the most important ones, at least."

Okay, she's killing us and she knows it. Her eyes are gleeful and filled with joy. I've never seen her like this before, all excited and cheerful. And she isn't even telling us about her so-called special day.

"Isn't any of you going to ask me what's the occasion?"

"Will you fire us if we do?" I mutter under my breath and Tina snorts.

Mrs. S glares in our direction but thankfully, Leslie, one of the girls on the staff, asks her about it.

Mrs. S turns her attention away and smiles. "Today's the day that I, among some others who have been working here for decades, have been eagerly waiting for." At this, Maggie and a few other senior staff members beam. "I'm so very pleased to say that tonight's party is in honor of the Prince who's returning to The Pleiades after three years. Our very own, Master Zach."

Master Zach.

I can see her mouth moving but I can't hear her. Her voice seems to be coming out of a tunnel or from somewhere deep down and far away.

Suddenly, all I can do is feel.

The racing heart, the savage butterflies in my belly. The tightness in my chest.

Shakily, I run my eyes around. Everyone is calm and focused. Mrs. S is still talking but all I can hear is his name.

Zach.

He's back.

It was him, wasn't it?

I saw him last night, or rather, caught a glimpse of him before he disappeared. It wasn't a dream or my imagination.

I didn't make him up.

Oh God.

"I'm sorry. What'd you just say?" I burst out, loudly and effectively bringing all the eyes in the room to me.

Mrs. S stares at me. Hard.

I know she doesn't like to be interrupted, especially when she's giving out instructions left and right. But fuck it.

"How long have you worked here, Cleopatra?" she asks, instead.

I take a deep breath. It doesn't help. I'm still as shaken up as I was the moment I heard his name.

"Listen, I know I'm being rude and everything and you hate being interrupted but you don't understand." I clear my throat and slide to the edge of my seat. "Did you just say that Zach is coming back because I think you did. And that's just impossible, right? Because last I checked, he left. Abruptly. And I thought that he wasn't coming back. I thought that maybe his parents *finally* cut all ties with him. You know, because he was just so... out of control. I mean..." I wave my hand in the air and I have a feeling that I'm waving them a little too fast. "I never bought the whole going to Oxford scenario."

I air-quote *going to Oxford*. "I never believed that he went to Oxford. But that's okay. I don't care about that. What I care about is…" I thread my fingers together on the table, digging my elbows into the wood and leaning forward. "What did you just say?"

My legs are jiggling and I hate that just the thought of him returning has reduced me to this.

This jittery, shaky, mess of a girl.

Angry and violent.

A girl who couldn't decide if she wanted to hide to avoid confrontation and getting sent into detention yet again or punch him in the face like she did when she was ten and he was twelve.

"Cleopatra, I don't know what's gotten into you today. But I'm going to overlook it because you've been dealing with a lot. Although I will say this – if you don't get your erratic behavior under control and see someone…"

There it is.

"I'll have no hesitation in letting you go. Is that clear?"

Beside me, I feel Tina's grimace. I can even feel Maggie shaking her head.

I press my hands together and force my legs to stay still. It's a good thing my heart is an organ, firmly caged within the ribs. Because if it weren't, it would be exploding out of my chest and lying a pulpy mess on the floor.

"Crystal," I say with difficulty.

"And Cleopatra?"

"Yes?"

"It's Mr. Prince to you. Don't forget your place."

I grit my teeth, grind them, *smash* them.

"I won't."

Zachariah Prince.

I met him when I was ten and he was twelve.

In fact, I met him my very first day at St. Patrick's. It's a posh school for posh kids on the north side of town.

At the time, I was probably the only one from the south side to go there. My parents were very proud. They wanted the best for me and so, they worked very hard to get me into that school.

I never had any high hopes of St. Patrick's, to be honest. I would've been happy to just go to my regular school on the south side with Tina and all my other friends.

Anyway, whatever I was expecting to happen on my first day, it wasn't even remotely close to what actually did.

I got caught stealing, or rather *borrowing*, carrot sticks, from a girl at lunch. It wasn't my fault. I was hungry and they had this long list of prescribed snacks that kids could bring. All of it was some bullshit, healthy stuff that didn't do anything to curb my hunger.

So I improvised.

And got caught and sent to detention.

Where I met him.

The guy who'd become my bully for the next however many years I was to go to that stupid school – St. Patrick's has both middle and high school wings.

When girls my age were falling in love with cute boys, I was falling in hate with Zach. When boys were asking them out on dates, carrying their backpacks, opening their doors, Zach and his minions were pushing me through them.

They were tripping me in the hallways, spilling drinks on my uniform and my homework. They were hiding my blue car and sending me hints on my phone as to where it could be.

Not to mention, they were Photoshopping my face on every cheese commercial that they could find on the internet, and calling me Thunder Thighs, Jiggly Lump, Lard Ass. You know, because I love eating and I'm not exactly a delicate flower when it comes to my body.

And while his minions were doing his dirty work, Zach would simply stand there and stare at me. Sometimes he'd smirk. Especially when I fought back.

Oh yeah, I fought back.

I wasn't helpless. I was far from it.

In fact, I punched him in the face a day after I met him because they'd slashed my books and scattered the pages all over the hallway.

My dad always taught me to stand up for myself and I did.

Countless times.

I'd break into *their* lockers and steal *their* homework. I used to key *their* cars. One time, I even got into this big fight with one of the girls in his inner circle because she hid my clothes after a gym class and sent boys into the locker room to gawk at me. It became a whole big thing at school.

For years, I've plotted ways to murder them.

To murder Zach.

I would have too, if he hadn't gone away. But now he's back and I'm acting like I'm in school again.

I'm looking left and right, walking very, very slowly lest I slip on something. Something like a banana peel, deliberately planted so I'd step on it and so people could laugh at my ungainly, curvy, jiggling body.

I'm jumping every time someone calls my name. Someone laughs and I tighten my muscles and narrow my eyes, preparing myself for the punch line, which I definitely think involves me. I'm flexing my fists, remembering the right technique to make one like I've been teaching Art. I'm thinking up ways in which I can fight back.

I'm drowning in anger and hate and I haven't even seen him yet.

Gah.

So in order to regroup and act like an adult, I've shut myself up in the service closet by the kitchen. The party's on and I'm supposed to serve champagne, instead of drinking it myself and sitting on a large mopping bucket.

But whatever.

They'll survive without me. A lot of the cleaning and cooking staff are serving tonight, including me. I used to be a waitress back on the south side and I need the extra cash, so I always volunteer for such events.

Suddenly, the closet rumbles and shakes, making me yelp. Dust falls from the ceiling and the tray full of champagne flutes set on the floor vibrates.

Someone's knocking at the door.

"Cleo."

My tensed shoulders sag at the familiarity of the voice. It's Tina.

I press a hand to my heaving chest, lean over and unlock the door, letting her enter. In contrast to me, her blonde hair looks put-together and she looks very polished in her uniform. I'm pretty sure my mascara has smudged with the nervous sweat and I've already chewed off my lipstick.

"What are you doing in here?" she asks, her expression concerned in the meager light of the yellow bulb.

"Trying to regroup myself."

"By hiding?"

"Hey, don't judge."

"Fine. I'm sorry."

Tina takes a seat beside me on an upturned bucket. "You okay?"

I shake my head.

"You drunk?"

I bring two fingers together. "Maybe a little."

She nods, as if she understands. "Grace says thank you."

I smile. "Yeah?"

"Yup. Mr. Grayson was all red by the time he left. He couldn't keep his hands off his crotch."

Laughing, we high-five.

A few beats of silence. Then, "It's really happening, isn't it?" I swallow. "This isn't a nightmare or anything?"

Tina shrugs. "I could pinch you, if you like."

"I pinched myself a dozen times. So yeah, I think it's real." My elbows dig into my thighs. "I think he's really back."

I can feel it.

That's the whole problem, actually. That I can feel it. Feel *him*.

I know he's out there, in that ballroom that I almost broke my back cleaning. He's probably mingling with people, namely his minions. He's drinking, laughing, *smirking* like he doesn't have a care in the world.

Like his coming back didn't ruin everything.

Mr. Prince.

Is that what I'm supposed to call him now? While I strip his bedsheets and take out his fucking trash?

I nod. "What if he picks up where he left off?" I blurt out my biggest fear, wringing my hands. "What if he tries to do something... bad? Get me fired or something? What if I can't get my house back? I have so much more to lose now. This isn't prank wars or whatever."

"Look, calm down. You don't know what's going to happen," Tina explains, grasping my hands. "And you won't know unless you go outside and face the situation. People say he's visiting for a few days. Maybe he won't notice you. It's a big house. How many times have you seen Mr. and Mrs. Prince? Not many, I bet. Besides, if you keep hiding and don't work the floor, Mrs. S will fire you anyway."

I sigh. She's right.

"God, I hate him."

"I know. That's all you ever talked about when he was here."

"Well, duh. He freaking ruined every second of my life while he was here. He even ruined my prom."

God, the prom.

The worst memory of my entire existence.

I was so happy that night. All dressed up in my navy blue skater prom dress with my leather boots. My make-up was all dark and heavy. I basically looked like a badass Cinderella ready to lose it. Her virginity, I mean.

I drove to school and waited for my boyfriend, Neal. He was new in town and from the south side and as soon as I saw his hipster glasses and suspenders, I knew he was my soul mate.

But he never showed up.

Instead of him, I got a text on my phone – typical of Zach and his minions – with Neal's picture sucking face with a girl at a party at The Pleiades.

I drove to said party, and laid it to him. Not Neal. Zach.

I laid it to Zach. It was pretty shitty, all the things I said to him. But all of them were true.

"Well, you know, Neal didn't have to go," Tina offers.

I whip my gaze to her. "Don't you think I know that? Of course I know that. Of course I know that Neal didn't have to go. But the fact that *he* – Zach – invited him in the first place, bugs the fuck out of me, okay? He did it on purpose. They weren't even friends. He did it to hurt me and because Neal was such an idiot, my first and only boyfriend was getting a lap dance from a girl who didn't even go to our school. All on prom night."

We're silent for a few more seconds.

"I'm glad we stole all his suspenders." Tina snorts.

I snort too. "Can you believe he had them in like, every color?"

"Oh my God. He had them in neon yellow, too."

"Oh God, yes." I laugh and look up at the ceiling, shaking my head.

"How could you go out with him, Cleo? Like, how?"

"I don't know. I just…" I sigh. "I guess I just wanted to see what it felt like."

"What?"

"Falling in love." I swallow. "All I've ever done is hate him. Zach, I mean. All I've done is be angry and hateful. I just wanted to see what it felt like to be in love with a guy."

"That's fair, I guess." She sighs too. "Are you ready to go back out there?"

I have no option but to nod and stand up. I can't stay here all night like a coward. I need this job. I have a goal. I can't let him keep me from that.

"Okay, let's go."

The party is happening in the ballroom, located in tower one.

The space is large and never-ending with high cathedral ceilings and vintage Victorian decor. Every corner is filled with intricate arrangements of flowers and tea-light candles. It's super understated for me but whatever floats their boat, I guess.

I've been making rounds of the floor, serving champagne for the past couple of hours, and so far, I haven't seen Zach.

I know he's here, though. I know it. Somewhere, amongst all the slick suits and designer dresses, lurks the guy who's haunted my thoughts ever since I met him.

A man sporting a tuxedo calls for me as I pass him and his group of friends by. I turn to them with my plastic *fuck you* smile in place and present them the tray. Without stopping their conversation or even sparing me a glance, they each pick up a flute.

Or at least, I think they do.

I'm not looking at them or even paying them any attention. They are inconsequential. Invisible. They don't exist for me.

Nothing does except him.

Because the moment I turned, the crowd in front of me parted like some useless, catastrophic miracle and I saw him.

Zach.

He's here.

The boy I hate, the boy I've always hated, is back. And he's standing just ten feet away from me.

God, ten feet is not enough distance between us. Nope. It's close. It's real close. We need an ocean between us. A continent. A whole planet. An entire galaxy, maybe.

As it is, I can see him clearly.

I can see every angle of his face.

The sharp peaks of his cheekbones, the slant of his jaw, his strong forehead. Even his eyelashes, how thick and dark they are. How all together, he has to be the most beautiful guy I've ever seen. Such a delusion, his beauty.

His meanness comes forth in his size. In the veins of his neck and the way he comports himself. All silent and watching and intense and big.

And Jesus Christ, he's gotten bigger. He's taller than I remember. Broader too.

Was he this huge three years ago? This... beautiful, with slick, black hair and full lips?

His shoulders look massive. Even from ten feet away, I can see his chest straining against the dark t-shirt that he has on. His entire body seems to be bursting out of his clothes: black leather jacket and blue jeans.

The clothes that are completely wrong for this occasion. The clothes that only Zach is wearing. The rest of the people are in expensive, formal attire.

And just like that, he sticks out.

He screams rebel. Bad boy. He screams that he doesn't give a fuck.

He didn't three years ago and he doesn't now.

My chest is buzzing, probably the butterflies, and also with something else. Something that feels like loss.

I've never thought about it too much but Zach and I, we could be... a bit alike.

We always ended up in detention together. Our uniforms were always disheveled by the end of the day, like we couldn't wait to get out of there.

And from what I could gather, Zach hated going to school just as much as I did.

I mean, I did my homework, got okay grades, but I didn't like it. Zach was the same. He was a grade above me, and rumor had it that he was held back a year and that he was flunking every subject.

In my weakest moments when I'd cry in my pillow, thinking about going back to St. Patrick's the next day, I'd imagine a life where Zach and I were friends. A life where he wouldn't pick on me and I wouldn't hate him.

But it was all wishful thinking, obviously.

He did pick on me and I did hate him.

I hate him even now as he throws a smirk at someone to his right.

Bastard.

I hate that smirk. It's so unfair that it's beautiful and sexy.

He'd never change.

A hand flashes in front of my eyes and I yelp, almost losing my grip on the tray.

"Aren't you supposed to go away once you've served?" says the man who called for me, his eyebrows arched up in an arrogant fashion.

"Yeah, we don't need anything right now," the other man in the group says as he sips his champagne.

The third man chimes in, "We'll call if we do."

The only woman in the group, decked out in a silver gown, mumbles, "Don't hold your breath, though."

I'm only half listening to them and their condescending comments. Actually, I'm glad they interrupted my ogling.

I need to get away from Zach. Now that I know where he is, I can keep an eye on him and stay out of his sight. I don't want him to see me. I don't want him to know that I work here now. Or at least, hold on to this secret for as long as possible.

Apologizing to the group, I take a step back.

I'm on the verge of getting away unscathed when something makes me look up and my gaze clashes with his.

Damn it.

I knew it. I fucking knew that he'd find me.

There's a thing between us, see.

This *thing* makes us aware of each other. It doesn't matter where we are. In the school hallway, in the empty detention room, or in a crowded ballroom.

Somehow, he's always been able to find me and I've always been able to find him.

Maybe this is how hate works, mysteriously and annoyingly.

With his champagne glass poised at his mouth, Zach is watching me with his black demon eyes. Like he used to.

Like he never stopped. He never went away. Last three years never happened. It's still prom night. I'm still sixteen and he's eighteen. I'm still waiting for my boyfriend to show up while Zach's laughing behind my back because he's about to ruin all my dreams of love.

And on Monday when I go to school, I'll find out that Zach's gone. He's left town abruptly and people are buzzing with shock and gossip.

Except right now, the ache in my belly is sharper and my heart has stopped along with the butterflies that have become frozen, trapped because of his focus on me.

"Oh Christ, what would it take for you to go away? Are you waiting for a tip or something?"

This time the man's voice startles me so much that there's no saving the tray. It slides right out of my hand and I watch it crash to the floor in horror.

There's shrieking, gasping and jumping as the delicate flutes shatter against the marble, spilling bubbles everywhere. Some of them get on the shoes of the man who flagged me down. They were Italian loafers, no less. This piece of information is given by the woman in the silver gown.

A small crowd is gathering around me. There are murmurs and laughter. I can't say who's the one doing it. Because my eyes are glued to the broken glasses, the upturned tray.

"I'm so sorry," I whisper to no one in particular, my eyes filling with tears of embarrassment.

Standing has become such a chore and I wince as soon as my bony knees hit the floor. My hands stick out to catch my balance. But they accidentally land on the puddle of liquid, splashing it on the sleeves of my very white blouse.

That's the least of my worries, though.

Because as soon as my palm connected with the sticky floor, I felt a piercing stab of pain go through my fingers and wrist.

"Oh, fuck."

Did I just cut myself?

A gash runs straight down the middle of my left palm. I'm so shocked as to what even happened in the past twenty seconds that all I can do is stare at the red droplets oozing out of the cut.

In all my years of waiting tables, I've never dropped a tray. My old boss used to call me a natural.

So what the fuck just happened?

All of a sudden, my thoughts shut down when I feel someone take my hand in theirs.

It's big, the hand. Dusky. So dusky and bronzed that my skin looks even paler.

Maybe it's the shock but I'm kind of entranced by the look of my small hand trapped in a large one. The blood on my skin is brilliant red but compared to the bronze fingers that are curled around me, everything looks dull.

"You're gonna need bandages."

The voice. *His* voice. It's soft and low.

It's exactly as I remember it but with a rougher edge. An edge that wasn't there before. His voice is probably the only voice that I can recognize out of a thousand voices, even from far away, even after years.

God, it's awful. It's fucking terrible.

Why do I know so much about him?

Why is he touching me? He's never touched me before.

With suspended breaths, I look up at him, ready to tell him to get away from me and snatch my hand back. But all I can focus on is that his hands are not the only things that are bronzed.

For some reason, I hadn't noticed it before. But his face has become darker as well. Tanned.

"Don't," I say, somehow finding my voice.

With his face still dipped, he lifts his eyes up to me. He studies me for a beat and I squirm under his intense scrutiny.

"Don't what?"

I swallow against the impact of his voice. It hits me in the chest and I wince slightly.

Of course, he notices.

And maybe to mess with me even more, he rubs his thumb over the pad of my palm. The touch is gentle, not more than a whisper of his skin over mine.

But it's the only thing that I can focus on.

I snatch my hand back and fist it. "Don't touch me." Then I add, to make it super clear, "Ever."

Chapter 3

He's darker now. That's all I can think about. In combination with his rougher voice and his bigger body, his tanned skin makes him look ruthless.

More ruthless than before.

More ruthless than what he used to look like, standing in front of his locker, or at the school gates, or sitting at the largest and loudest table at the cafeteria. Or riding his bike down the highway.

I'm not sure I like that. Actually, I'm pretty sure that I don't like it. As if he wasn't intimidating enough. As if my palms didn't itch enough to slap the arrogant look off his face.

Damn it.

Why did he come back?

Everything was fine. Everything was normal. I'd gotten used to not hiding or looking over my shoulder and being mellow all the time and not plotting mayhem and murder. I'd gotten used to my curvy body and how my thighs jiggle when I walk.

The only reason I took this job was because I thought he wasn't coming back.

I know people said that he went to go to Oxford University like every other Prince in their family. But I never believed it.

Zach hated school. He was so much of a rulebreaker and a rebel that it's laughable to even think that he'd walk in his ancestors' footsteps.

Not to mention the way he left. So abruptly. Kind of like in the dead of night. He didn't even graduate high school.

I knew that when he left, he didn't go to Oxford and he wasn't planning on coming back.

But I guess I was wrong about one of those things.

He *is* back.

After the dramatic fiasco in the ballroom, a couple of staff members escorted me out. Tina helped me clean up the wound and told me to take it easy. I'd been rattled all day and something was bound to happen. I don't think Mrs. S would be as forgiving, though.

But I can't think of that right now. I can't think of what tomorrow will bring now that Zach knows I'm here, at The Pleiades.

They put me on kitchen duty after I so thoroughly embarrassed myself. It's hot and sticky in there – I don't know how Maggie does it – and I need a little break.

So I step outside through the service entrance and try to just breathe.

The night air isn't much better and my uniform for the event, white blouse and tight black skirt, clings to my sweaty body but I don't care. Anything is better than being cooped up in that kitchen.

I toe off my two-inch-heeled Mary Janes and unravel my braid, followed by the top two buttons of my blouse. I fan the fabric, trying to get some air going, and lean against the wall, closing my eyes.

"Are you okay?"

The rumbly voice makes me jump.

"Jesus. Fuck," I almost shriek.

At first, I don't see anything other than the dark outline of bushes and trees in the distance. But then I notice a cloud of smoke and whip myself in the direction it's coming from.

Him.

Zach is leaning against the brick wall, his foot propped up. A cigarette hangs from his lips and he doesn't have his jacket on, leaving him in his dark t-shirt that shows off his bulging biceps.

Oh jeez.

He isn't even flexing them and they look menacing.

"You scared the fuck out of me," I accuse.

An intricate-looking Victorian lantern lends enough light that I can see him. His face is turned toward me and I can't escape the sheer grandness of his features. Sharp and cutting with a square jaw and high cheekbones, complete with dark velvet hair.

"I can see that," he comments.

Then his corded chest swells out like a giant wave as he takes in a drag before sending the smoke out in the night.

"So are you?" he asks, looking at me again.

I creep closer to the wall and take a small step back, away from him. "Am I what?"

My only concern is to get out of here. I'd be turning back and running. But experience has taught me to never leave my back exposed and open. So I keep walking backward, slowly.

"Are you okay?"

My bare feet get caught up in my abandoned Mary Janes but I catch myself from stumbling. "What?"

In typical fashion, he remains silent and smoking. And staring.

That's what Zach does: he stares. Like his eyes are a microscope and I'm a bug or an interesting specimen that he wants to study. That he's been wanting to study for years or squash under his boots.

"Did you just..." I squint at him. "Ask me if I'm okay?"

"Sounds like it."

Three years.

I'm seeing him after three fucking years and this is what he asks me.

After everything, after all the pranks and the things he's put me through, is he really asking me that? Like I'm some kind of a stranger that he happened to find on the street, and now he's enquiring about the fucking weather.

"Why?"

"Why what?"

"Why are you asking?"

His eyes go to where my injured hand is, fisted against the wall. My cut starts to throb. I feel the gash heating up, as if all my blood is rushing to it just because he mentioned it.

That's when I remember that he touched me.

I can't believe he *touched* me.

At that moment, I was so shocked that I couldn't register anything about the touch. But now I remember that his skin was warm – somehow, warmer than anyone else's. And it was rough and scrape-y, his palm. As if he has more fate lines than anyone else I know.

He motions with his chin. "That needs a bandage."

I open my sweaty, heated fist. "It's fine."

"It was a deep cut."

"You'd like that, wouldn't you?"

"I'd like what?"

"For it to be a deep cut."

Again, he doesn't say anything to that, simply keeps his eyes on me.

Over the years, I've learned that this is his intimidation tactic. Going all quiet and intense so the other person is forced to fill the silence.

I'm not falling for it.

I'm not falling for anything he's planned. I would think that even this meeting was a set-up, if I hadn't spontaneously thought of stepping out.

He's done this before, actually. His minions locked me inside Mr. Philips', our history teacher, office after giving me a fake message that he was waiting for me. I was stuck inside that room for two whole hours until the cleaning crew came in and unlocked the door.

Asshole.

"Are you aware that you're walking backward?" he asks at last, turning toward me, propped against the wall on his arm.

I realize that he's right. I *have* been walking backward. "What's it to you?"

"You can't do that."

I scoff. "Yeah? Why? Are you going to stop me?"

He shakes his head slowly. "No, but if you keep going then the potted plant behind you will."

My eyes go wide, and I come to a jerky halt.

He's right.

There are potted plants flanking both sides of the service entrance and I feel the brush of the leaves against my back. If I'd kept going, I would've stumbled into them or maybe even fallen.

"I knew that," I lie.

"Sure," he says with an amused voice that gets my back up; it's an old reflex.

There's something about him, you know. Some quality, some kind of provocation that lights my skin on fire.

"I didn't need you to tell me that," I insist.

"Got it," he replies flippantly.

Even though I take offense at his tone, I decide to stay quiet. I promise myself that I won't say anything.

I don't. For about six seconds. Then, "What the fuck are you doing here?"

Back in this town. Back in my life. Back in my fucking head.

"Getting fresh air."

"Right. And you had to pick this spot?"

"Yes."

Then he has the nerve to twitch those cancer-breathing lips before taking another drag and tilting his face up. A growl surges up in my throat but it's cut short by what he says next.

"I forgot that you could see the stars up here," he murmurs.

His voice almost sounds like a low, satisfied sigh. Like the sight of stars is something he hasn't had in a long time.

While he seems at peace, his words are playing havoc on my body.

They halt my breath and make my heart race. They awaken the butterflies.

I remember the falling star from last night. I remember the wish I made, and now, he's here. A potential danger to everything I've been working toward for the past few months.

"And you couldn't see the stars where you came from?" I ask.

Zach looks away from the sky and at me. "No."

Monosyllabic answers.

Great.

They're designed to stoke curiosity. Rationally, I'm aware of that. Irrationally, I'm wondering about his whereabouts for the past three years.

"Ooo-kay." I nod, hardly believing him. "Where did you go off to again?"

Silently, he studies me. "Why? Did you miss me?"

"Oh yeah, definitely. Like I miss getting shot in the head."

Zach smirks, his black eyes glittering. "You know, I wasn't real sure about coming back. But if it makes you happy, then I'm all for it."

"Sarcasm." I raise my eyebrows. "Gotta love it."

"I aim to please," he says, making the goose bumps wake up on my flesh.

I ignore that and get to the real question that's been nagging me all day. I don't care where he went, all I care about is why he came back and when he's going to go away again.

"Why *did* you come back?"

I'd think my question got lost in the wind with the way he remains silent. But that's another special thing about our town with a line. Even the air is dead. Nothing moves, just like him. His face is blank. Expressionless. But there's something in his eyes, his stare.

It's burning, like that cigarette trapped between his lips.

Then, that stare moves. His lashes flicker as he takes in the loose curls of my hair. I have an urge to reach up and touch them, but I resist it. I fist the fabric of my skirt to keep my hands occupied.

"Still blue, huh?"

I raise my chin. "Always."

His lips twitch as he repeats on a whisper, "Always."

I don't know why he's looking at my hair like that, with such intensity. Maybe he's thinking up something mean to say. Whatever the reason, he doesn't stop and when his lashes dip, I forget about the question I asked him.

What were we even talking about?

"Do you still use blue glitter pens?"

I used to, back in school. I was the poster child for the color blue. Blue backpack, blue clothes, blue glitter pens, and, when I grew up, blue hair.

I nod. "Yes."

He nods back, looking... nostalgic. "Of course you do."

I should say something. I really should. But I'm in a trance. I think this is what being hypnotized feels like.

Right now, all I can do is track his stare as it slides down the line of my throat, which feels jam-packed with rocks, making it difficult to swallow. When he comes down to my chest, I realize that the last time he saw me, I was a C cup. I'm a D now.

I have every intention to tell him to stop ogling. Asshole pervert. I don't want him to stare at me. I don't want him to make my skin shiver.

But my words won't come out. They are stuck to the back of my mouth and my teeth are gritted.

God, make him stop.

But he keeps taking me in. My tucked-in waist, rounded hips and thighs, my bare toes. My curvy body that has only grown in his absence.

"Why did you come back?" I ask again. This time with a desperation that wasn't there before.

He brings his gaze back to mine, and through the cigarette in his mouth, says, "Maybe *I* missed *you*."

Forcing myself to break his stare, I look down. My Mary Janes are lying on the ground, one on its side and the other some distance away from it. Abandoned. Marooned and astray. Kind of like me, right now.

I need to get away.

Shaking my head, I bend down and pick up my shoes. "I'm leaving."

"Nice uniform, by the way."

I stop.

Hugging my shoes to my chest, I return his stare. His jaw is clamped. I can see the tic in his facial muscles.

Is he pissed off that I work for his family now?

Tough luck.

As if I like this arrangement. As if I'd ever set foot inside the house where he grew up.

"Thank you," I say, smiling falsely and smoothing a hand down my skirt. "I think so, too."

Zach looks away from me as he lets his finished blunt fall to the ground and crushes it under his boots.

"Never thought doing dishes and mopping floors were part of your life goals."

I knew he was going to say something insulting. He's Zach.

But still, I flinch.

Life goals.

What does he know about goals and ambitions? What does he know about what happens when they're snatched away from you in one blink?

Even though it stings, I keep my voice calm and casual. "Well, you don't know everything about me now, do you? And it's called a job. That's how responsible people buy stuff."

"Responsible, huh?"

"Yes."

Straightening up and away from the wall, Zach comes to his full height. Cocking his head to the side, he asks as if he's so curious, "What else do responsible people do? Besides changing bedsheets for a job and breaking and entering into their place of work."

My eyes widen. "It was... you."

Oh God.

So, he *is* an asshole pervert. He was watching me last night.

"It was. You were cute in your little black outfit. Stupid but cute. Did you really think no one would recognize you?" He chuckles. "As cute as you were, I hate to break it to you though. You've got no future in espionage. You're a little too..." He looks me up and down. "Visible for that. So maybe it's good that you get to change sheets and mop floors. Gotta keep your options open."

And there it is. A little dig at my body along with other insults.

Nothing has changed, has it? He's still the same. Only now, I'm more vulnerable. I have more to lose. Like my job and eventually, my house.

"Thanks for your concern about my career choices."

"Don't mention it."

"Right. I wouldn't expect you to understand," I say, because I really can't stop myself. "I wouldn't expect someone like you, who's gone through life riding on his daddy's shoulders, completely wasted and high, to understand what it's like for the rest of us."

I stand tall under his scrutiny. I stand tall and firm, even though I'm quaking inside when he takes a step toward me. Then another and another. Until he's so close to me that I can smell him.

Cigarette and blueberry pie, like the ones Maggie bakes.

Two things I never thought would go together but somehow do and I don't like that. Not one bit.

Zach's face is in the shadows now. But the sky and the stars provide enough light that I can see his eyes and his mouth when he says, "Yeah, maybe not. But I do understand one thing."

Clutching my shoes tightly to my chest, I go for bravado. "What's that?"

"If you want to keep this job, you're gonna have to keep me happy," he drawls.

His threat lingers between us, heavy and dark, just like him.

The soft leaves brushing against the nape of my neck suddenly start to feel sharp-edged and dangerous.

"I'm not your personal slave, if that's what you think my job is," I tell him, trying to hold on to the last remnants of my courage.

He leans down and his scent becomes so thick, so pervasive that my lips part. His stare falls to them before he looks me in the eyes. "I think your job is whatever I want it to be."

Zach fills my entire vision. His dark t-shirt, his broad shoulders. I can't see anything beyond him. It makes my heart pound faster. With fear. With hate.

So much so that I can't stop myself from sneering, "You haven't changed a bit, have you? I bet you still think you own the world."

He shakes his head, slowly, dangerously. Hypnotically. "I don't give a fuck about the world. But I do own you."

Fully knowing that it might make my situation worse, I scoff. "You'll *never* own me. Not now. Not ever."

"Is that a challenge, Blue?"

Blue.

How can one word have such a drastic effect? It makes my inside tumble. My chest quivers as *Blue* slides down my throat as if I've inhaled it like a drug.

"It's a promise."

Zach scans my face, as if he's memorizing my features. As if he plans to dream of me tonight.

I let him.

I let him memorize it, soak it in, so when he sees me behind his closed eyelids, he understands that I'm not kidding. That no matter what I'm not going to play his games. That somehow, I'm going to find a way to put this all to an end.

Getting my house back is too important to me.

"If we're making promises, then let me tell you one thing," he whispers, low and rough. "*If* I want you to be my slave, you'll be falling to the ground so fast that your knees will bleed along with your palm. So don't tempt me. I'm very easily tempted."

Chapter 4

The Dark Prince

Night sky.

I have a thing for it. A blue so deep that it's almost black and the cluster of stars, trying to light it up.

It's impossible, but I do appreciate their determination and that they come out night after night only to fail.

The first few months away from this town were hard because I couldn't see the night sky. It's practically impossible to see it in the city. Probably that's why no one sleeps in New York. They don't have a sky to call their own.

But even then, the lack of sleep, the fact that the world was an unknown void for me, I never thought of coming back.

Because nothing's worth coming back here. Not then and not even now.

Three years and not one thing has changed. This town still smells like shit and a fuck-ton of bad memories. The wide walls, the big architecture, miles and miles of estate that foolish people pay premium dollar to tour.

It all makes me feel small. Tiny, worthless.

The Pleiades, my birthplace, has always made me feel how much I don't belong here.

I'm in my old room. It's done in dark shades, gray and black. Everything looks polished and fresh. They probably spent an entire day cleaning it up, thinking I'd be staying.

But I'm not.

I know what freedom feels like, tastes like. I know that freedom is riding my bike down a never-ending highway. Freedom is the wind in my face.

Freedom is the knowledge that at the end of the day, I don't have to come back to a place I was trapped in for eighteen fucking years.

I'm shoving my clothes inside my backpack when I hear a knock at my door. I'd let it go but I'm going there anyway.

Besides, I have a feeling who it might be, and I need to set her straight once and for all.

Zipping up my bag and slinging it over my shoulder, I cross the room and open the door. Nora, Mrs. Stewart to everyone else, stands there, carrying a tray of food. She looks at me, followed by the backpack on my shoulder, and her lips purse in disappointment.

She lifts the tray and says, "I brought you food."

"I can grab something on the road."

"So, you're leaving then?"

"Yes."

She's silent for a heartbeat before saying, "Tests come back next week."

I clench my jaw. "Call me with them."

Her silence at my casual answer stretches longer than before. I know what it means. It means she's prepping her comeback. That's the thing with Nora. She thinks that just because she's been working for my family ever since I was born, she has some kind of liberty to lecture me. Like I'm her kid or something.

For the most part, I let her think that. Maybe as a gratitude for all the times she snuck food into my room, or put me to sleep or dried off my tears that I was too proud to acknowledge myself when no one else was allowed to have any contact with me. But if she knows what's good for her, she'll keep her mouth shut.

"Nothing's changed, you know," she begins softly, or rather it would be soft if her expression wasn't stern and her voice didn't sound like it belonged to a school principal. "In fact, things have gotten worse. If you thought your leaving would solve everything, then you were wrong. It didn't happen. He's still the same and she still makes excuses for him. Most of the staff don't know what's going on. But the ones who do, we're not allowed to talk about it."

Ah, so she's going with emotional blackmail.

"Got it," I say, going the casual route.

"Your mother loves your father very much."

Jesus.

She doesn't know when to stop, does she?

I look at the floor, trying to hold on to my patience. I'm not very good with it. Never have been. Not even at the best of times, and this isn't the best time.

"All right, here's the deal," I begin, telling it how it is. "I rode my bike most of the night last night to get to this piece-of-shit town. I'm running on very little sleep. My father's reaction on seeing me for the first time in three years was to ask if I finally came to my senses and crawled back to apologize and ask for money. All my mom said to me was that if I was planning on staying then I needed to play nice and not upset my dad. I needed to show up at the party, drink champagne, smile at people I don't give a fuck about. All just to show the world how happy they are to have me back."

I pinch the bridge of my nose. "I should've left the moment she came out with the party plan. Anything to make my dad look good. But like an idiot, I stayed. And now I'm cagey. I'm impatient and I'm this close to going on a fucking warpath. So stop talking and let me pass."

Does Nora listen to it? No.

She gives me the stink-eye, holds onto her tray like a shield and continues like she never heard me. "And you love your mother very much. That's why it took one phone call, just one, for you to get back. And that's why you didn't leave when you should have."

I grit my teeth and look at the ceiling for a second. "You're fired."

She cracks a smile. "Okay. But unfortunately, you won't be here tomorrow to see if your dismissal took or not. So at least let me get to the point."

"And what the fuck would that be?"

"My point is that no matter how much you deny it or outright reject it, we're designed to love our parents. That's just how it is. It's unfortunate. Some people don't deserve our love but that doesn't mean it will go away."

"Well, I was designed differently. Now, I gotta go."

Finally, my words register with her. Her face crumples and I feel a twinge in my chest. I ignore it. It's not my fault she put her faith in me. I can't take the fall for people's mistakes.

Nodding, she says, "I just want you to know that I called you because I didn't want you to regret not being with her. Years later, I didn't want you to look back and question your choices made with anger."

"I won't." I don't know why but I go ahead and add, "I'm not gonna stay in a place where I'm not welcome. I did that for the first eighteen years of my life and it wasn't pretty. Besides, she doesn't need me."

"I know. I know you have bad memories here. I know you don't owe your mother or your father anything. But as I said, it's unfortunate. We're destined to love the people who give us life. I knew you'd want to be here as her son. Not because she needs you. With all due respect, I don't care what she needs. I only care about you."

Sometimes when she says these things, I wonder if it's because she really cares for me or is it because she gets paid for it.

I shake my head and grit my teeth. Even so, the question comes out, "Who's been taking care of her?"

"I am. Along with a couple of other staff members."

"And Dad? What's he doing all day?"

She shrugs. "Meetings. Work. He doesn't want to acknowledge it."

I smile bitterly. "Like always."

"At least stay until the tests come back," she urges again.

"I fucking hate this place."

"You're going to hate yourself more if you don't stay. I don't want you to hate yourself. You do that plenty anyway." I go to say something but she cuts me off. "If you still don't like it, no one is capable of stopping you, Master Zach."

"Zach," I snap. "If you want me to stay here, just call me Zach. And no one can know why I'm staying. I don't want it plastered all over."

"That you're a good son?"

"Don't test me."

"Understood."

I sigh and letting go of the door, I walk back to the bed. My backpack falls to the floor. "And leave the tray."

Suddenly, I'm ravenous.

I stare hard at the sky that, for all intents and purposes, should be black. It's fucking midnight. But it looks blue.

Dark, dark blue.

I hear Nora setting the tray down and then retreating from the room. Just as she's about to close the door, I turn around and ask her, "What's she doing here?"

Nora frowns. "Who?"

My nostrils flare as I take in a deep breath. My body feels tight, wound up. I need to get out of here, even if I'm not *going* anywhere.

"Cleopatra Paige."

I don't think I've ever said her full name out loud and I don't think I will after this, either.

Her name's like her.

Loud and dramatic and a fucking handful. Or mouthful. Whatever.

I can see Nora's confusion but she still replies, "She works for me. She's on the cleaning staff. Is this about what happened at the party? She's never done anything like this before. In fact, she's experienced. She used to work –"

"At the diner on the south side. I know. How long has she been working here?"

"About six months." Looking at me shrewdly, she adds, "She actually lives right here. In one of the cottages."

My fists snap close. "Why? What happened to her house?"

Maybe it's the intensity in my voice or maybe it's my rigid stance, but Nora takes a second to look me over. And I don't like that.

"She lost it."

"Excuse me?"

"Last year. Along with her parents," she explains. "Maggie, she made a case for her and I took her on. She has nowhere to go."

I don't think I've ever clenched my teeth so hard. I'm about to fucking smash them with the force.

She has nowhere to go.

Nowhere. To go.

And she came to the worst place in this town.

"She's not my best employee. She's loud and I don't get the whole messy blue hair thing but she's been doing okay. Should I be aware of something?"

Her voice reaches me through a tunnel, a deep and dark tunnel, and somehow I manage to answer her. "No."

"It looks like you know her."

"I don't."

"But –"

I let my anger show on my face. "I think you should go."

Nodding slowly, she leaves.

As soon as the door is shut, I pick up the keys to my bike.

For three years, I was free. Free of this place. Free of my parents. Free of all the things that they made me feel: anger, hatred, loneliness.

But apparently, I'm back and there's one very important difference.

She lives here too, the girl with blue hair. The girl who bore the brunt of all my hatred and who I haven't stopped thinking about since I saw her the first time when I was twelve.

And if I had known that, I never would've come back.

Because I don't want anything to do with her and I'm pretty sure she doesn't want anything to do with me.

Chapter 5

He came to me in my dreams last night. Like he used to be back at St. Patrick's. As I tossed and turned on the bed, in a state of half-wakefulness, I realized I've seen Zach grow up.

I've seen him as a smart-ass middle schooler with spiky hair and a wrinkled and dirty uniform who always ended up in detention. Even though at that age he was shorter than all the teachers, he'd still tower over them with his *fuck you* attitude.

And then, he grew taller. He literally shot up overnight and got bigger than everyone else. Practically everyone had to tilt their neck up to look at him and meanwhile, he barely spared them a glance.

I saw him as he was in the school hallways. Large and careless. Rulebreaker with his tie flipped over his shoulder and the top two buttons of his uniform shirt loosened. He never had his books with him. He'd be empty-handed, always. Like his memo got lost in the mail that it was supposed to be a school and you were supposed to carry textbooks.

And then, I saw him watching me.

He'd watch me get humiliated with a blank face. Sometimes when I fought back and called out insults, his lips would twitch. Sometimes they'd stretch and he'd smirk. Like I was put on this earth to be his amusement.

I saw him on his bike. His hair and tie flying in the wind and the smoke coming out of his mouth courtesy of his cigarette. The revving of his bike is engraved in my brain.

So yeah, last night, I saw flashes of his life, entwined with mine.

I was glad when the morning came and I had to wake up.

As I run to work, I'm actually looking forward to a day filled with menial tasks. Just so I don't think about him and that he's back.

He's really, *really* back. And he knows that I'm here.

I'm so inside my head that I don't watch where I'm going and right at the entrance of the staff room, I bump into someone.

"Hey, you okay?"

It's Ryan. He's from my old neighborhood, and I've known him all my life. He's worked at The Pleiades as a chauffeur for about two years now.

I clutch the fabric of his suit jacket on his bicep. "Whoops." I chuckle. "Sorry. I guess I didn't see where I was going."

He smiles. He's only a couple of years older than me and I've always thought that his presence is comforting.

"It's okay." He steadies me. "Are you feeling okay? You know, after what happened last night."

At his reminder, the cut on my palm pulses like someone is sticking their finger right in the center of the wound.

I fist my injured palm at my side and shoot Ryan a bright smile. "No, I'm okay. I don't know what happened last night. Stress, maybe. But I'm feeling awesome right now."

"I'm glad to hear that," he says, smiling warmly.

"Okay, I'm gonna go. Can't piss off Mrs. S twice in a row."

I'm already moving past him when he stops me.

"Cleo, I, uh." He scratches his forehead. "I was wondering if you'd like to, uh, go on a date with me."

"What?" I squeak.

"Date. With me? If you'd like to go?"

Did he just ask me out on a date?

Me?

Cleopatra Paige? The blue-haired, weird, goth girl.

It's happened only one other time, with Neal, and I was the one who asked him out on a date. And well, we all know how that turned out.

"Cleo?"

"Yeah. Sorry. I just, um, you want to go on a date with me?"

He chuckles self-consciously. "Well, yeah. If you don't, then –"

"No. I mean, it's not that I don't *want* to. I've always thought you're hot and –" I widen my eyes because holy fuck, what am I saying?

It's not that I'm lying, though.

If I'm being honest, I've always had a little crush on him. Especially while we were growing up. Tina and me, we both did. We'd take turns marrying him when we played together. He was just so cute and his smile used to make me feel all warm and fuzzy.

Ryan chuckles again but the sound has lost its embarrassed quality. "And?"

"I just..." I shake my head, feeling flushed. "I never realized that you wanted to. Go on a date, that is."

Shrugging, he runs his hands along his hair. "I've always wanted to but I never had the courage to ask you before. And with everything that happened last year, I didn't want to put any pressure on you."

What happened last year is a weight I always carry around. And even though I'm heavier for it, people treat me like I'm the most fragile, delicate thing ever.

Blinking my eyes, I clear my throat. "Yeah. I don't think I can. I like you, but I can't. It's just that... I don't think I'm ready. And with all the work and you know, I can't."

"I understand," Ryan nods and there's a slight twinge in my heart.

He reaches out and runs a thumb over my jaw.

"I won't give up though," he says with a twinkle in his eyes. "Now that I know you think I'm hot."

With that promise, he leaves and all I can do is watch him go.

And then, I smile.

His thumb was soft and smooth. The only place I felt it was where he touched me, on my jaw.

Ryan's touch was exactly what a touch should be: warm and fleeting. It didn't radiate out to any other part of my body. It wasn't consuming.

Not like *his* touch, scorching and electric. Something I'll think about for days to come.

Still smiling, I walk inside the staff room and take a seat beside Tina. Mrs. S is yet to come and so everyone's talking. Well, mostly gossiping, and of course, the topic of conversation is Zach.

Leslie, one of the maids, is extremely happy that he's back. "I can't believe how hot he's become. Did you see that body?" She waves a hand over her face. "Man, oh man. I want him."

Tina shushes her. "Keep your voice down, would you? If Mrs. S hears you, you'll be on toilet scrubbing duty for the rest of the month."

So Mrs. S has a rule: no sleeping with the masters of the mansion or the people they fraternize with. She says it's bad for her reputation. We won't be a clichéd house, where maids have affairs and end up pregnant.

I've only worked here for a few months but one of the girls got fired for sleeping with a guest who was here on the tour. I wasn't there but rumor has it that Mrs. S caught them red-handed, doing it in one of the guest rooms in tower three.

Leslie waves her hand. "She isn't here. Besides, there are ways to get around her. You don't think everyone follows the rules, do you?"

Leslie is loud and fun and even though she's a terrible gossip, I've always liked her. I just don't believe everything that comes out of her mouth. But seeing that she's talking about the guy who more or less ruined my entire education experience, I come up with a plan.

Nothing diabolical, just something fun. And I'm going to save Leslie a lot of heartbreak in the process.

"You don't want to break the rules for him, trust me," I tell her, leaning over so only she and Tina can hear me.

"What do you mean?" Leslie asks, interest written all over her pretty face.

I look left then right before focusing on her. "So, last night, at the party? There was this girl talking to one of her friends. And she was saying that when she tried to hook up with Zach earlier, he had a little problem."

"No way," Leslie breathes.

I nod and hold my finger up before folding it down. "And you know what, I don't think that was the first time either."

Leslie's eyes go wide. "What do you mean?"

"I mean, I went to school with that guy." *Unfortunately.* "I know things."

Tina snorts. "Really?"

She knows I'm lying.

Leslie grabs my hand in excitement. "Are you serious? What things?"

I smirk. "Look, it could be just gossip. But back in school, I heard a rumor that he, you know, couldn't perform, per se. So he had to take like, a pill or something."

Leslie gasps.

Tina snorts again.

"I mean, listen, I don't believe that blue pill thing. I think it was an exaggeration but... the not-performing thing could be true. But who knows? Gossip is gossip."

Leslie nods. "Makes sense. Gossip *is* gossip. Such a shame though, if it's true. That guy is fine."

I sit back in my seat, satisfied and smiling. "Oh yeah, definitely."

Tina shakes her head at me and I shrug. By the end of the day, everyone on the staff will know of Zach's little problem. Whether they believe it or not, they're going to wonder and that's all I care about.

Fuck you, Zach.

We all go quiet when Mrs. S enters and starts firing off instructions like always. One of the girls is sick so I volunteer to take up her duties. It's good. The more I work, the better. They'll compensate me for the extra time and I'll be that much closer to my goal.

But ten minutes later when the meeting is dismissed and we're supposed to go about our duties, my triumphant smile courtesy of my little revenge and extra work melts off my face.

Because one of the duties that I so enthusiastically took over is to clean the room of my former bully.

Chapter 6

The prince of The Pleiades lives in tower two.

I've been to his room before, of course. My first time in there, I went a little crazy. I snooped inside his closet and all his drawers. Not that I found anything interesting. He'd been gone for a couple of years by then and his room was empty besides the furniture. Except for dust bunnies, there wasn't anything interesting in there.

I wonder what I'll find now that he's back. Not that I care but still.

It's nearly lunchtime; I'm done cleaning the other rooms in the tower. Except his. I've been avoiding it so far but I can't. Not anymore. I have to do it.

I push the cart with all my cleaning supplies and laundry bag, along with fresh towels and sheets, and go to his door. His room is located at the end of a gleaming corridor made of Italian marble and adorned with paintings made by expensive, foreign hands. There's a tall window – which is a pain in the ass to clean – tucked away in the corner, overlooking a courtyard with a water fountain.

I press my ear to the door but don't hear any sounds.

Actually, I'm kind of hoping that he isn't here. Maybe after last night's party, he met up with his minions and got trashed, and is now sleeping off his high somewhere. He's been known to do that. Every Monday he used to either cut school or come to his classes after lunch, all hungover and sleepy.

Whatever the case, I'm not going to know unless I knock.

Grimacing, I raise my fist and do it.

Nothing.

Puffing out a breath, I knock again. No response.

Oh my God. Could it be? Could I be so lucky that he isn't in there?

I can't control the grin that overcomes my face. Fist-pumping the air, I get out my key and slide it into the lock. The lock gives easily and I push the door open. Maybe I'll be done before he returns and I won't have to see his handsome but cruel face.

The first thing I notice when I step inside is that it's bright. Glaring bright. I have to put up my hand to avoid the sunrays blasting through the windows.

Zach's room has the biggest ones of all the rooms in this place. They go from floor to ceiling and take up an entire wall.

The first time I was here, I was astounded by the sheer size of them. It's almost like a glass wall. You can see the woods spanning the property. You can see the entire sky through it.

And the best part? There's an alcove extending into the window, sticking out separate from the architecture of the room. The sides and the bottom of the alcove are glass, as well. So when you step into it, it's like walking on air.

As much as I hate him, I love the room he grew up in.

I step out of the glare of the sun and slowly, the bright spots behind my eyes go away. I'd be relieved that I can see but I'm not.

Because as soon as my eyes adjust, they fall on the giant bed. Which is currently occupied.

By a sleeping Zach.

I press a fist over my mouth to keep myself from shrieking out. I even lock my knees so I don't make any sudden moves and wake him up.

Why didn't I think of this before? Why didn't it occur to me that he might be sleeping?

I'm an idiot. That's why.

Oh, and another question: why the hell does he sleep with no shirt on?

I can see him. Like, really fucking *see* him.

He's sprawled on his stomach, both his arms flung above him. One over the pillow and the other seems to be under. The gray sheet that he has on only covers his lower body, leaving his back exposed and bare.

I wasn't wrong last night. He *has* grown and has become tan.

Even though I haven't ever seen him without his shirt, I can still tell that those grooves on his shoulders where they meet his biceps, weren't there before. The bulges of his arms have grown as well, making them look like tight waves of water. Not to mention, his back is a freaking study of taut planes and ridges that move when he breathes.

Jesus Christ.

It's so unfair, right? That someone so breath-stealing can be so rotten.

I don't know how he can sleep with that sun glaring down at him but I'm going to count my blessings and leave.

But I don't leave like I should. Like the policy is to not disturb when the occupant of the room is sleeping.

Because my eyes land on his backpack and his clothes from last night. They are lying in a heap at the foot of his bed.

Without volition, I move toward them.

The backpack's black and it's open. Going to my knees, I widen the gap and look inside. His clothes smell of fresh laundry but they are all wrinkled up and shoved inside, as if in haste. Kind of like how I'd do it, sloppily and messily.

In the next compartment, I find his wallet, keys, some toiletries and a book.

A *book*?

I pull it out without thought.

Zach isn't into reading and stuff like that. Nope. He's not the kind of asshole where he's all tough on the outside but secretly harbors love for the written word.

I've seen him tearing out pages from a textbook and making planes out of them, sitting on bleachers. One time he tore a book in two because a teacher asked him about homework. Granted, I only heard about that but I believe it.

So why would he have a book inside his bag? A book about the stars. *Written in the Stars.*

I forgot that you could see the stars up here.

I flick through the pages. There are constellations, described and drawn, along with their origin and the stories behind them. It's clean and crisp. Almost untouched, but somehow, I have a feeling that it's not. Not really.

Zach has touched these pages. But that doesn't make sense.

I always thought that stargazing and watching the sky is something that poets and philosophers do. People who have depth.

Zachariah Prince is no poet nor a thinker. He has no depth. All he is is a rich, bored guy who amuses himself by tormenting others, namely me.

But then, I come to the end of the book and all my thoughts get channeled into the fact that it's a library book. It's overdue and it's from New York. NYPL: New York Public Library.

I was right.

He wasn't in the UK, going to Oxford. I don't know how but I can say for sure that he's been in New York for the past three years.

I glance at him. He's still sleeping heavily, probably dreamlessly too. I wish that I could ask him about the city, about all the places he's seen.

But I can't because I hate him and he thinks I'm a plaything.

Such a fucking waste.

I quickly look through the rest of his stuff and a good thing too. Because I hit the jackpot with the pack of cigarettes. A double pack, at that.

His stash, maybe?

Staring at the Marlboros, I smirk. He has no idea what's coming.

I clutch it in my hands and stand up, ready to get out of here. But then, I hear a sound. The worst sound in the world. Worse than a bomb blast.

A grunt.

Then, a groan.

"Fuck."

Another grunt.

"Jesus Christ."

My mind has completely shut down. I watch his back on the bed and there's movement, rustling.

He's waking up.

Oh my God, he's waking up.

He couldn't have kept sleeping for five more seconds? Because five more seconds and I would've been out of here.

I stand frozen in the middle of his room as I lose my ability to think.

What the fuck do I do now?

Suddenly, my legs move. But instead of taking me to the door, they take me into his bathroom and before I can even comprehend what's happening, I hop into the bathtub off to the side, and I pull the shower curtain shut.

It's one of those opaque ones that completely hides you and thank God for that. Then, I plaster myself against the wall and press my free hand over my mouth. In the other hand, I have the double pack of Marlboros that I stole.

I hear bare footsteps and a couple more grunts. To my horror, those sounds are walking closer.

Oh God.

He's coming toward the bathroom.

Toward *me*.

Why the fuck did I think it would be a good idea to hide inside his bathtub? I wasn't doing anything illegal – well, if you don't count stealing his cancer sticks and going through his stuff. I could've easily gone away through the door.

Now, everything is way, *way* worse than it needed to be.

Apparently, not worse enough because there comes a hiss. A distinct sound of something – a thick stream – hitting the ceramic, followed by a sigh.

I take it back. *This* is the worst sound in the world. Zach, peeing.

Why? Why is this happening to me?

Hysterically I think, if he's sleepy and his aim isn't on point and *if* he gets something out of the bowl, I'm not cleaning it up.

No.

Nuh-huh. I'll quit my job before I… do *that*.

An eternity later, I hear the flush of the toilet and the rush of the tap opening. Oh, thank God. He's done.

What are the chances that he'll go away now? And go back to sleep like before, no less?

Zero.

Zero chance of that happening because a microsecond later, the curtain rips open and I come face to face with the guy I've been trying to avoid ever since I was ten.

"What the fuck are you doing?" he thunders – I don't know how he manages that since he just woke up but still, the sound echoes in my chest.

His arm is stretched out wide, strangling the curtain with his grip, and for a few moments, all I can do is stare at his face.

It's clenched tight, every little line, every taut muscle on display. He's anger personified with his ticking jaw and gritted teeth.

I'm supposed to answer him; I know that.

But my tongue is swollen.

I stare at the five o'clock shadow on his square, killer jaw. Dark, enticing skin. Spiky, messy hair. Black eyes dripping with rage.

And veins.

God, he has so many veins, running just under his skin. One of them goes down his taut neck. It bumps over his collarbone and then disappears beneath his muscled pecs.

His chest is massive and the curves of it make a tight valley that then changes into the ridges of his abdomen. I go to count those ridges; I'm pretty sure that he's got a six-pack. Could be eight too.

But I get sidetracked by the fact that he's not wearing anything.

He's naked.

Naked.

"Oh my God!" I squeak, clenching my eyes shut.

"How did you get in here?"

"Oh my God. Oh my God," I chant, trying to dissolve into the tiles my spine is stuck to. "You're naked. I thought you'd at least have your pants on."

"What the fuck. Are you doing?" he growls, this time slowly.

"Why were you sleeping naked?" I snap. "Who sleeps naked?"

"People who wanna rub one out whenever the mood strikes."

My breathing ceases at his drawled reply.

Rub one out.

He means... rubbing his *thing* out. Right? Masturbation.

The thing that's on full display right now. A few feet away from me. Within touching distance. Is this the punishment for making up that lie about him?

No. No. No.

"Open your goddamn eyes," Zach seethes, breaking my internal chant.

I grit my teeth. "Put on some *goddamn* pants."

"Not until you tell me what the fuck you're doing, hiding in my bathtub."

I can't believe this is happening to me.

I can't believe I'm trapped inside a bathtub, with a naked Zach glaring at me.

But I need to woman up. I need to open my eyes, get this over with and leave. From now on, I'm not volunteering to take up anyone's duties. At least, not without knowing what they entail.

Slowly, I open my eyes and make sure to keep them only on his face. "I wasn't hiding."

He shoots me a long stare. "If you're in there to take a shower, then I hate to break it to you, but that's not how you do it."

"What?"

He gestures to my clothes, looking up and down my body. "You're supposed to take them off. And not only because it makes rubbing one out easier."

"What?"

This time my *what* is higher in cadence. I shrink into the wall some more. Although I don't think I'm going anywhere.

Zach puts his other arm out and splays it wide on the wall. Leaning toward me, he says in a raspy tone, "Rubbing one out. Haven't you ever done that in a shower?"

"Of course I have."

Oh man.

Wrong thing to say. So completely, *utterly* wrong.

The tightness of his face melts away and his eyes shine with mirth. Before he can comment over my slipped-out careless reply, I almost shout, "Don't. Don't say a word. I don't want to hear it, okay?"

His jet-black eyes flick back and forth over my face. "Kind of uptight, aren't you? For someone hiding in my bathtub." Throwing me a lopsided smile, he rasps in a low voice, "Tell you what. I'll turn around and you can do whatever you do to make yourself..." One final sweep of my features and then, "Loose."

Loose.

Right.

Can I murder him? I mean, how bad can prison be, really? They give you free food and a bed to sleep on.

Puffing out an angry breath that widens his smirk, I snap, "Real classy. I'm here to do my job, you idiot. Taking out your trash and changing your bedsheets. My life goals, remember?"

His smirk is replaced by a sharpened edge of his jaw. I guess he's still angry about the fact that I work here.

Join the club, asshole.

"And yet, my sheets aren't changed and the trash is still in the trashcan."

I narrow my eyes at him. Well, because he's right. I didn't clean. I *snooped*.

"I don't remember letting you in," he goes on.

"I knocked. You didn't open."

"That still doesn't explain how you got in."

I have this grave urge to shift from one foot to another as if I did something wrong, which I kinda did. "I had the key."

"I want it back."

"What?"

"The key. I don't want you in my space."

He's right. He really doesn't. I'm a snoop. But hello? After everything he's done to me over the years, I have the freaking right to look through his stuff.

"Trust me, being in your *space* is the last thing I want. Who knows what prank you'll play on me?"

"Prank."

That word in my mouth didn't sound nearly as dangerous as it does in his. It's the way his lips and his tongue molded around the word and gave it a life. A dangerous kind of life, and suddenly, I'm bombarded with all these ideas. Of what he can do to me.

Swallowing, I look at the curl of his biceps. They are huge.

He could crush me, if he wanted. He could wrap his large arms around me, restrain me with his body, cover me and hide me under him. And it would take days for someone to find me.

"Yes." I clear my throat, my eyes still stuck to his rippling muscles, as my lungs are running out of air. "If you're thinking of locking me up in here, I'll have you know that they're looking for me. My friend, she knows I'm up here and if I don't show up for lunch, she's going to call 911."

"Good to know."

His mocking tone makes me look away and at his face. "I'm not kidding."

I kinda am but he doesn't need to know that. If I don't show up for lunch, Tina will think I'm still finishing up my duties. No one's coming for me.

"Neither am I," he says. "Now, if you're done fucking around, I want the key back."

"I can't give you the key," I say, exasperatedly. "You know Mrs. Stewart? She's my boss and she's freaking weird about them."

"I don't care."

Asshole.

I clutch my sides, as if protecting the keys inside my pocket. "I'm not getting fired because you have privacy issues."

As soon as I say it, I realize what this is. My worst fear is coming true. This is all a ploy to get me fired.

I knew it.

Boring his eyes into me, he leans closer. He's practically hanging over me, like a dark shadow.

"Getting you fired is the last thing on my mind. Where would be the fun in that?" he says, reading my thoughts and making me breathless.

Thoughtless.

"Besides, if I want, *I* can fire you right now. In case you forgot the conversation we had last night, you do as I say. I'm the boss of your boss." He extends his arm. "Give me the fucking keys."

He didn't look as threatening then as he does in the light of day. Could be because last night, we were out in the open and right now, we're here, so fucking close to each other.

With his *thing* in between us.

Like a puppet, I look at his arm. My gaze hooks on to something that wasn't there before.

It's a tattoo, a sentence running along one side of his wrist: *I can cross the line.*

"You never had that in school..." I trail off.

"Give me the fucking keys before I take them," he grits out, ignoring my asinine sentence.

I whip my eyes up at him. His frown is fierce. Scary.

Biting my lip, I fish the keys out of my pocket and drop them onto his open palm. But that's not the only thing I drop. As I take a deep breath of relief thinking that now he'll let me go, my other fist opens, as well.

And out comes the double pack of Marlboros that I stole from him.

Zach looks down at it, and then up at me. I must look like a trapped animal, all wide eyes and panting breaths.

A frisson of current flashes across his eyes. "Are you stealing from me, Blue?"

"No."

"No?"

I shake my head, panicked. "N-no."

Zach looks at my hair. It's messily braided and pushed away from my face because Mrs. S doesn't like loose strands.

"So are you saying that some things do change? You're not a thief anymore?"

My heart bangs in my chest at the mention of the word *thief*.

He and his minions used to call me that back in school. In fact, Zach started calling me that the very first day we met in detention. All because I borrowed someone's carrot sticks without asking. I replaced them the next day. Not that anyone cares about that.

I lick my sweaty lips. "No, I wasn't stealing."

Keeping his eyes on me, he tosses the keys over his shoulder. They land somewhere on the floor with a clatter that makes me flinch.

Somehow, having both his hands free has tipped the situation from terrible to catastrophic.

"Do you know what happens to little thieves like you?" he asks, softly, running his eyes up and down my body again.

A body that's exploding. My skin is flushed and riddled with goose bumps. They are so sharp that it's painful.

"I told you I wasn't stealing," I repeat but with a little more heat.

He ignores me, all bunched up and tall. "They get punished."

Oh man, is he growing right in front of my eyes?

I scoff and pretend to be brave. "What is this? Your kinky fantasy? Am I supposed to call you sir now?"

At this, Zach steps inside the bathtub and I barely, *barely*, manage to not squeak. He's bringing his dangerous, naked bulk even closer to me.

Don't look at his thing.

"Maybe," he replies to my earlier question. "A little respect would go a long way. Since it looks like your fate is in my hands."

"If you come any closer, I'm going to scream," I warn him.

"Yeah?"

"I'm not joking. And then, I'm going to sue your ass for sexual harassment." I nod for good measure. "That's right, asshole. I know my rights."

Or I will. As soon as I get out of here, I'm googling the shit out of this.

Zach cocks his head to the side, still advancing toward me. "Do you wanna know what I'm gonna do to *your* ass?"

Jesus.

I stick my hand out, careful not to touch him. "Can you just stop with the sexual innuendos? I wasn't stealing, okay? I was just trying to make your life a little difficult."

Zach stops, comes to a sudden halt in his tracks. "What?"

I admit, "I was going to flush them down the toilet. That's it." When he keeps silent, I glance at him. "It's only fair. After everything you've done to me."

He remains silent but watching.

There's no expression on his face. Nothing but pure intensity, and I can't look at him. He's too close. Too large.

Too naked.

His smell and the heat of his skin surround me like two strong arms and I can't break their hold.

When I feel him leaning toward me, I snap my eyes up at him. My heart's in my throat, ready to fly out of it as I realize that any second he might touch me.

Again.

Oh my God, he's going to touch me.

I'm about to scream when a great rush of water rains down on my head like some heavy weight. It takes a second for me to understand what has happened.

Zach just turned on the shower. With me inside the bathtub. Fully clothed and all.

"W-what –"

Cutting off my garbled words, he orders, "Get out."

He doesn't need to tell me twice.

Shuddering and stumbling, I jump out of the bathtub. My boots slosh with water and I barely manage to stay upright on the slippery floor. Water sluices down my hair and my face and my uniform is almost completely drenched.

"Here."

At his voice, I turn around, outraged and furious, ready to give him a piece of my mind. But Zach throws something at me and on instinct, I catch it.

"Don't forget to take these."

Speechless, I stare at him.

"Now get the fuck out. I don't wanna see your face for however long I'm here for, got it?"

Then he pulls the curtain shut, leaving me in a wet, clinging dress, clutching a double pack of Marlboro cigarettes.

Chapter 7

He's staring at me.

And working out. But mostly staring.

I was on my way up to the main house for the daily morning meeting when I was stopped by Grace and we started chatting. As usual, Tina was already gone before I even woke up.

Two seconds into the conversation, I realized a presence. Like when the air is so heavy and saturated, and you know that the sun is going to scorch the earth today.

The air seemed full and brimming but I knew it wasn't the sun.

It was him.

Anyway, right now, he's by the pool, doing push-ups. In nothing but a pair of black track pants as he watches me talk with Grace.

What's his aversion to clothes? Why can't he work out in a shirt or something? Why does he have to put his... sculpted muscles on display?

People who wanna rub one out.

I shake my head and dismiss his crass words. But I can't dismiss what's happening in front of me.

With every rep, his arms strain and bulge, and I think that any time those veins of his will pop out of his skin.

Whatever. I don't care.

Neither do I care about the fact that he's glistening, and I can see every ripple and groove of his shoulders and back. Even the drops of sweat that are pooling in those ridges.

Why's he working out in this heat, anyway? The main house has a big gym, for God's sake.

"Hey, do you want to walk and talk?" I interrupt Grace, loudly, looking away from him.

She looks at me like I've lost my mind. "Okay. But we do have some time before the meeting."

"I know. Let's just go. Let's impress Mrs. S with how early we can arrive."

Grace smiles. She has light brown hair and kind, brown eyes. "It's because of him, isn't it?"

I begin walking and with every step, I feel like my thighs are shaking even more than usual. My entire body is bouncing more than it usually does.

It's him. He makes me conscious of my figure. I thought I'd forgotten all the mean things his minions would say to me when my boobs started growing back in the ninth grade.

But that's the thing about bullying, isn't it?

You never forget. Never. You might pretend that everything's okay now. That it doesn't affect you anymore, their little insults and jeers. That years might have dulled their effect.

But he's bringing it all back for me.

"Who's him?" I ask her nonchalantly.

"The new Mr. Prince."

Mr. Prince sounds super weird. I only ever think of him as Zach, the asshole.

I decide to walk faster and not think about what *that* is doing to my body. The sooner I'm out of his sight, the better. "Nope."

She chuckles. "Okay. Don't tell me. But just so you know, he was staring at you."

I try to swallow, push saliva down my throat, but it's like my heart's stuck there and it won't budge.

I know he was staring at me. He still is. I can feel his eyes on my back as I keep walking away, trying not to be self-conscious in my own skin.

Maybe he's not even thinking about my less than perfect body. Maybe he's thinking about how best to spoil my day like he did yesterday, when he doused me with water and ruined my uniform.

I had to run back to the cottage and hunt down my back-up. By the time I was presentable again, the lunch hour was over and I had to go clean the windows.

I was almost dead by the time I was off for the day.

"I don't care," I say.

"Got it." Then she shrugs. "It's against the rules, anyway."

"What is?"

"You know, consorting with the people we serve."

She air-quotes the word *serve*.

I burst out laughing. "Oh my God, you're adorable." I side-hug her. "There'll be *zero* consorting where the new Mr. Prince is concerned. Believe you me."

No one hates him more than I do.

As soon as we come down the stairs of the service entrance, I smell pie. Grace walks toward the staff room while I make a beeline toward the kitchen. I need a piece of pie after all that staring.

Before I even make it inside the kitchen, I squeal, "Maggie! I love you, you know that? How did you know I wanted pie this morning? You have no idea how shitty my week's been –"

My words get stuck inside my mouth when I find *him*, of all people, in the kitchen.

How did he even get in here this fast? Wasn't he just outside?

Zach is sitting in the nook and Maggie is fussing over him like he's a little kid. He has a piece of my pie in front of him and he's just taken a bite out of it when I barge in.

He's still sweaty from his workout. But thankfully, he's put on a shirt. Or rather a vest-like t-shirt with sweaty patches that puts his biceps on display.

"Cleo." Maggie beams at me. "Sit."

I don't. I stay standing at the threshold, cursing the fates. Is this what my life is going to be like from now until he leaves? Seeing him everywhere?

I don't wanna see your face for however long I'm here for.

Then why the fuck is he in the servant's wing?

I glare at him and he returns it with a cool look.

"Cleo?"

"Huh?" I look at Maggie. "Sorry. I just kinda checked out."

"Did I hear you say something about a shitty week?" Maggie is cutting up a piece of pie and plating it, probably for me.

With my eyes on Zach, I nod. "Yup. Super shitty."

His lips twitch.

"Why? What happened?" she asks.

I narrow my eyes at him, then. "Bedbugs."

"What?"

"Uh-huh. They came back."

"Came back? What do you mean? I thought we called in the exterminators last time."

So another thing about our town: we have bedbugs, both on the south side and the north. It's probably all the heat. And a couple of months ago, we had a big break out at The Pleiades. Mrs. S freaked the fuck out.

"I know. I thought the same." I shake my head slowly. "I thought they were gone for good. But the fucking bastards came back."

Zach lowers his fork and chews slowly as he stares at me.

His eyes are hot and they move like they did the night he came back. They stop at my breasts for a few seconds before going down and pausing at my belly.

I'm all covered from top to bottom, but his eyes make me feel... unclothed. They make me sweat. I'm very aware of the droplets sliding down my spine and even my stomach. I swear with the way he's watching me, he can see that drop plopping into my belly button.

"Oh my. Nora is going to be very unhappy," Maggie says and puts down my pie right opposite to Zach. "Come, sit. Master Zach is just having breakfast."

I look at her and decide, why not. Why should I let go of my pie just because *Master Zach* is here?

Walking to the table, I reply to Maggie, "I bet. I'm unhappy too. In fact, I'm outraged." I reach the table and slide the chair out. Staring at Zach, I say, "Freaking blood-sucking leeches."

Then I dig into my pie and hear a soft chuckle.

Bedbugs.

It would've been a wonderful little prank.

Not to mention, I know a guy on the south side that could've gotten me some. For the right price, he could get anything. But his fee was a little high this time around: me. He wanted to hook up with me.

As if.

I'm not that desperate to make Zach's life difficult yet, thank you very much.

So I have a new plan and I'm executing it right now.

I have the night shift at the main house tonight, meaning I'll be sleeping in one of those on-call rooms, and it's the perfect opportunity. Even though I'm exhausted after a full-day shift and then babysitting Art until Doris was home, I'm doing this.

I'm in the kitchen, which is illuminated by the usual night lights. And in my hand is a bottle of laxative. I bought it from the store when Tina and I went grocery shopping.

For the past three days, Maggie's been making Zach's favorite things – all of them sweet and all of them my favorite too – and so, he's been eating his breakfast in the kitchen. Which means, he does a little eating and a lot of staring at me, ruining my mojo.

It's time for a little payback.

God, I love payback.

I have it on good authority that Maggie has made English-style fruit custard for Zach. Well, she told me. And it's in a white container that I fish out and set down on the counter.

I hate to waste good food so I dip a finger in it and taste the yummy goodness before it's gone forever.

I moan. It's the tastiest thing I've ever put inside my mouth. Too bad it has to be ruined.

Opening the bottle of laxative, I dump some in the custard and then stir it with a spoon. Perfect.

"This is for ruining my uniform that day, asshole. And for all the things that came before," I whisper to the bowl before putting it back.

Just as I turn around though, I hear a squeal, which makes *me* squeal and I slap my hand at the wall by the fridge to turn on the light.

The room gets flooded with a glare and it takes a moment for me to take in the person who caused all the ruckus.

It's a face I haven't seen in a couple of years. It's a face I never even liked to begin with. It makes sense that I'd see it now that Zach is back.

It's Ashley Howard.

There were rumors that Zach and Ashley were an item and that their families wanted them to get married in the future. Maybe they will. They both deserve each other. Ashley Howard is to Zachariah Prince what Bellatrix Lestrange was to Lord Voldemort.

She was the one who hid my clothes and sent boys into the locker room that one time.

Right now, her eyes are wide and she has a wine bottle in her hands. "Cleopatra?"

I sigh. "One and only."

She walks closer. I'm wearing a blue nightgown; well, I'm wearing *the* blue nightgown, with the lacy neckline and hem. It belonged to my mom. I have a robe on over it, but it's not tied and I'm regretting that.

"I heard you were working here." She smiles as she comes to stand before me. "I guess the rumors were right."

"I guess so."

Ashley has a tight black dress on and she looks a little unsteady on her feet. Probably courtesy of the wine bottle in her hands. Her blonde hair's tied up in an intricate knot that I can never, not in a thousand years, copy and her high heels give her an edge over my bare feet.

Looking me up and down, she checks me out. Not in a sexual way but more in a way that my figure is something to look down upon.

"You haven't changed a bit, have you?"

I stand up tall. "And neither do I intend to."

See, it's easy to say these things.

I've said these things to her plenty of times. But that doesn't mean her digs at my body didn't make a home inside of me. For a long time while I was going to St. Patrick's, I'd feel ashamed of my figure, even though I knew I shouldn't have.

And since Zach came back, those insecurities have come rushing back.

"So you're what..." She takes a sip of her wine straight from the bottle. "The maid? Like, you clean and take out the trash kind of thing?"

I blush and tighten my fists.

Granted, I don't like this job but there's no shame in doing it. This wasn't my plan but it's okay. There's an honor in honest work.

Like there's no shame in having curves.

I hold my head high, defiantly. "Yes. *That* kind of thing. So what are you doing these days?"

She giggles and waves an arm down her front. "Partying." Then, soberly, "I'm in college."

I widen my eyes in mock excitement. "No way. You got into college." I clap my hands. "So why aren't you in college right now?"

Ashley kind of glares but her tipsiness is making it a little difficult. "Because Zach's here. Oh! I guess Zach's your boss now. So what d'you call him? Mr. Prince?"

There it is again. That stupid name that people want me to address him with.

"No. I call him asshole."

This time her glare's perfect, like it used to be.

"Since you're here, why don't you fetch me a glass for this?" She gestures to the bottle.

Right. The maid jokes.

"I'm off duty. Why don't you help yourself for once?"

I try to leave but she stops me. She watches me a beat and I'm about to tell her to back off when I feel something. Something chilly and liquid splashing down my chest. It's her wine.

She's spilling her wine down my front with a malicious smile.

I'm frozen, completely paralytic.

I can't believe she's dousing me, my mom's nightgown, in red wine.

When the bottle is empty, she cocks her head to the side. "I wish I could help myself but I'm kind of clumsy. And looks like I'm out of wine too."

I can't say anything. Not yet.

Not when I can feel the thick droplets of wine sluicing down my chest.

"I'd say sorry about that." Ashley motions to the red stain that's slowly seeping into the fabric. "But I think it gives you good color. I don't think blue's your thing at all."

To prove her point, she looks at my hair. It's loose and falling down my back like my mom's used to when she was alive and she'd come into my room to tuck me in for the night.

"Yeah, blue's not your color."

I breathe deep but all it does is move my chest, making the droplets slide down faster. The nightie is stuck to my skin, heavy and clammy, and my heart's gaining speed. It's pounding like it's insane.

She turns around and sets the wine bottle on the island. "Maybe try something else for a change. Like, I don't know, going back to your normal hair color and eating less. And yeah, wearing something that's not so very eighties."

That's it.

That's the final straw.

A growl rises up in my throat and I take a step toward her. I see a flash of her eyes widening before a voice booms in the room.

"What the fuck is going on?"

His voice.

It's rough and invades the air around us.

I whip my eyes over to where he's standing at the threshold. As soon as our gazes clash, he moves toward me.

In the background, I can hear rustles and more movements. Footsteps. I guess we woke up the on-call staff. But I don't care about that. And neither do I care about the fact that Ashley skips over to him and winds her talon-like hands around his bicep.

"What the hell's happening?" he asks again with a deep frown.

I raise my chin. "Why don't you ask your girlfriend?"

Ashley goes to say something but Zach throws her a look and her mouth closes. "What the fuck are you doing here?"

Ashley pouts. "I swear your house is so fucking confusing. I got lost."

"It helps if you're sober," Zach says, seriously. Angrily, even.

But she chuckles like a moron, or rather like a drunk moron.

Seriously, how cliché can you get?

"And then." She turns to me, looking at the red stain on my nightie. "Then, I found her."

Zach focuses on me, his eyes roving over my face. "Are you okay?"

It's a simple question but I can't seem to answer. I stand there, staring at him like I've forgotten all the words.

Maybe because his voice had turned intimate and low when he asked the question. Or it could be because this is the second time he's asked me that. This surreal question. Like he cares about what happens to me.

Before I can gather my wits, Ashley begins talking and she tells him how disrespectful I've been toward her, and that I should be fired for insubordination.

When she stops, Zach's eyes move lower, and for the first time tonight, I realize that my mom's nightie is light and made of cotton. And it has a plunging neckline and Zach can see all of that.

"What happened to your dress?" he asks.

I snap my robe closed, hiding my nightie. I don't want him to look at my ruined clothes. His stare makes everything worse, stickier.

"Doesn't matter. I have work tomorrow and I need to go sleep."

And I need my mom and dad to come back.

I should leave now that it's all over but my legs won't move. They are trapped by the sudden thought in my head.

Usually, I'm good with burying everything inside and doing what needs to be done. I'm good with putting a date on my fucked-upness. Delaying dealing with it until I get my house back.

But standing here, in front of the guy who's always tormented me and *liked* it, I feel so alone. I never told my parents about the bullying and the pranks but now, the choice has been taken away from me. I couldn't tell them even if I wanted to.

They are not here anymore.

There's no one to save me. From the world.

From him.

"Are you crying?" he asks with a frown.

At his question, I realize that yes, I am. And just like that my tears turn into something hot. Something like anger because what the fuck am I doing, showing weakness in front of him.

"No, I'm not," I tell him in a clear, stern voice. "I don't cry. Especially not in front of people who don't give a fuck."

He said that to me once, actually.

Didn't your mom teach you to not cry in front of people who don't give a fuck?

Even though it was years ago, I can see he remembers it, too. He knows what I'm talking about. It's in the way he's looking down at me, with such intensity.

Such... connection.

Like we share something.

I hate that.

I hate that we share a history. I hate that he'll always be a part of my life. He'll always own a corner of my soul.

"Is it the dress?" he asks.

This is the moment when Ashley chimes in, "Oh please, don't be a baby. It was an honest mistake and it's only a dress." Then, she mutters under her breath, "And not a very good one at that."

The growl that's been building up inside me finally escapes.

"What'd you just say?" I narrow my eyes because I've had it with her.

I've fucking had it with everyone. I'm going to fucking rearrange her face.

She flinches at my question. "Excuse me?"

I think I hear gasps.

I was right. The staff members are up and about and they're probably watching this altercation right now. But no one dares to enter the kitchen. Maybe because *Mr. Prince* is here.

Fuck it. I don't care who's watching; I'm not backing down.

I take a threatening step toward her. "Say it again. I dare you."

Ashley moves back. "You've lost your mind."

I laugh. "And you're so going to lose your teeth right now."

With that, I launch myself at her, or try to.

But suddenly, Zach is holding me hostage. His fingers are wrapped around my biceps and my body is flush with his.

"That's enough."

Even through the shocked shrieks and gasps of people around me – definitely everyone's watching – I hear his low growl. It inflames my anger.

"Let go of me."

"Not until you've calmed down."

I struggle against his hold but all he does is clench his jaw and flex his grip around my arms. "I swear to God, Zach, let me go or I'll scream this fucking house down."

His black eyes flash. "That's the second time you've threatened me with it. Keep it up and I'll give you a real reason to scream."

Zach appears menacing, glaring down at me. His words highlight the fact that he's bigger and stronger than he was three years ago. Every muscle in his body is bunched up and stacked, fraught with power. And my front is smashed with his.

I swallow. In real fear.

No one would dare step forward if he decides to do something. Not a single person. Servants don't have power over the rich.

"Let me go," I say with clenched teeth.

His impossibly thick eyelashes flicker as he studies my face, my neck – I will the rapidly beating vein on the side of it to slow down, to not show fear – and then, finally, his eyes settle on my chest. Thankfully, it's covered with the robe.

He lets me go and I take a stumbling step back. My biceps have lost feeling under the force of his grip and I wish I could reach up and rub my nerves awake but what he says next stops me.

"I'll have your dress replaced."

My breath gets stuck in my throat, and almost becomes a hiccup. Did he just *casually* say that he'll replace the only thing I have left of my dead mother?

"You'll have it replaced," I respond in a flat voice.

"It shouldn't be that hard to find a replacement."

His lips barely move when he says it. It's so unimportant to him that his body doesn't even put the effort into the words.

I'm aware that he doesn't know the importance of my *dress*. He doesn't know that this was my mom's or how I cling to it every night, foolishly searching for her warmth, her presence. The fabric doesn't even smell like her anymore; I've washed it too many times.

I foolishly think that if I have something of hers with me, touching my skin, she isn't really gone. She's here, watching over me.

Zach doesn't know any of that. And neither does Ashley.

But would they really care, even if they did? Would it really bother them, make them feel guilty that they ruined the last thing that meant the world to me?

"So here's the thing, Zach, unless you can magically bring back dead people, it's going to be very hard to find a replacement," I say with a throat full of so many emotions that I'm drowning in them.

"It belonged to my mom. She died last year in a car crash. My dad, too. They were on their way back from their anniversary dinner. My dad thought it'd be a nice treat for my mom. Seeing as how he never took her anywhere because we didn't have the money. I'm sure you know that because you and your minions wouldn't let me forget it.

"You wouldn't let me forget that I come from the other side of the line. The trashy side. But anyway, he'd gotten a great job, my dad, painting a church in the next town, and he thought why not? Why don't I take her out and do something nice for her? So they went. But they never came back."

I'd helped Dad plan the whole thing. Besides, I had good news of my own. I was going to tell them that after graduation, I was leaving on a cross-country road trip. My mom would've been ecstatic. She always wanted to get out of this town but never could. So in a way, I was fulfilling her dream.

"They died because my dad wanted to give her something special. Something she never had and something you guys take for granted," I continue with fisted hands and stinging eyes. "Something that most of you don't deserve. Because you never lift a finger to earn anything. You don't even change your own sheets. You can't even put your laundry in the basket and somehow, people like you get to rule the whole world."

I take a deep breath and look into his black eyes. They are shimmering, penetrating, and if I let them, they'll suck me in and drown me.

"So I don't want you to replace it because you can't. All I want you to do is let me go so I can get a good night's sleep and get back to working for you so you get to be a big bully and potentially ruin lives."

I have no idea where I even got the energy to say all those things. And why I even bothered to tell him this.

But whatever. I said it and now, I need to go cry in my pillow.

As I step away from them in my sticky dress, I look up and find everyone watching me. There's Grace and Leslie. There's Maggie too. They are all looking at me with pity.

Mrs. S is nowhere in sight. But I'm sure news will travel and she'll come to know tomorrow.

Maybe I'm really fired after this.

But I can't seem to care. I want to lie down. I feel heavy like my wet dress. A little dead too, I guess.

They let me go without a word and when I reach my room for the night, I curl up and hug the pillow, crying into it.

Chapter 8

The Dark Prince

There's a little bottle on the counter.

Leaving Ashley behind, I go and pick it up. Laxative. It probably belongs to *her*. Sighing, I bow my head before pocketing it.

"Get lost," I tell Ashley.

"What?" she asks, confused.

I turn around and face her. "Get lost."

"But Zach –"

"Get the fuck out."

"Are you doing this because of her?" Ashley asks, looking up at me with pleading eyes.

There was a time when my dad wanted me to marry her. That was reason enough for me to just fuck her, steal her virginity in a cheap motel room, and leave her sleeping on the bed.

Just to spite my dad. *Anything* to spite my dad.

But I underestimated the blonde, virgin princess. She never really left. She hung around, year after year, watched me fuck other girls. Always others, never her.

I never understood why but I think I do now.

She loves me. In her own way, she was giving me the time to sow my wild oats. She still thinks we'll end up together one day.

Poor Ashley.

"This isn't St. Patrick's anymore," I say.

"What's that supposed to mean?"

"It means stop being a bitch and grow the fuck up."

Her eyes flash fire. "Excuse me?"

I shake my head. "Jesus, how much have you had to drink?"

Ashley draws back as if I slapped her. I might as well have. Drinking used to be my way of coping three years ago – not sure if I'm allowed to preach about it. That and my bike.

"Are you... are you taking her side?" she almost shrieks as a reply. "Did you see how she was? She was going to attack me."

"And I'm thinking I shouldn't have stopped her."

Ashley is hurt. Her bee-stung lips tremble. "Why did you, then?"

"She would've gotten fired and you're not worth it."

An actual tear slides down her cheek.

It's not that I deliberately want to hurt Ashley. She hasn't done anything that she wouldn't have done back in school.

It's just that I don't want anything to do with her or the old crowd or all the things we did back at school.

"Ashley, look –"

"You've changed," she cuts me off, looking at me like I've grown two heads or something. "I can't believe after all those years, you'd defend her. *Her*. Cleopatra. Do you even remember how much we hated her? How she didn't belong with us? The way she talked back? And she's not better now. She's a freaking maid. A maid, Zach. Nothing about her has changed."

Yeah, nothing about her has changed.

Blue is still the same. Loud, spunky... bright. Brimming with so much life that it's hard to look at her.

But still I looked.

I watched her get humiliated for years. I watched her get pushed around, get insulted, laughed at.

For years, I was her bully.

I'm not a fan of words or letters or anything. Never have been.

But *bully* is the word I hate the most. I hate it so much that it might be a living, breathing person.

A person I want to strangle and choke the life out of.

"I'm not defending her. I've never defended her," I say to Ashley. "I'm just letting you know how things are."

"What did they do to you at Oxford?" Ashley muses.

"That's the thing. I never was at Oxford. I've never been to the UK. I was in New York, crashing on strangers' couches."

And realizing that the world is a much bigger place than my dad had me believe. A place where people look at me like I'm worth something, even though I'm only a high school dropout.

My dad will shit a brick when he hears of this, that I outed the secret. The prodigal son wasn't at Oxford but squatting in buildings like a homeless bum.

You're not trying hard enough, Zach.

You really are dumb, aren't you?

You'll never amount to anything if you can't even spell your name right.

But that's nothing new, is it? He's been shitting bricks ever since he found out his perfect little son has long, deep cracks.

I know the staff's still here, watching everything. At The Pleiades, it's hard to keep secrets. I make eye contact with a brown-haired, mousy one. "Escort her out. She's a little too drunk to walk on her own."

Ashley calls out my name and I spin around to face her one last time.

"Don't ever come here uninvited. And don't harass the staff. You're not gonna like how I react the next time. Just a fair warning."

With that, I leave.

I thrust my hand down my pocket and wrap my fingers around the bottle of laxative. I have a headache coming on; I need a fucking cigarette.

But guess what? I can't have any. Because someone stole them from me.

My fingers tighten around the bottle in frustration.

Fucking thief.

Chapter 9

I don't get fired.

Mrs. S hears about my nightly adventures, however. She lets me go with a warning. It's a shock but I guess I know the reason.

Pity.

Pity is the reason. I see it reflected in everyone's eyes. Maggie, Leslie, Grace, even Ryan. They all have been giving me sad, sympathetic smiles.

It's like my parents died all over again and I have to go to the morgue to identify their bodies. And then, it's like the bank took away my house again because of all the debt and missed payments. Now, I have weeks of begging to do until they give me another chance to somehow make a partial payment.

It's history repeating without actually repeating itself.

So I'm happy just to be sent on my daily duties. Only Tina's assigned to work alongside me and in order to shift the pity, I tell her about Ryan's asking me out.

"What the fuck is wrong with you?"

And that's her reaction when I tell her that I refused to go out with him.

"Nothing." I shrug, pushing the cleaning cart as we walk down one of the hallways in tower two. "Nothing's wrong with me. I can't go."

"It's not even a question, Cleo," she says, stopping and putting her hands on her hips.

"Do you know you look like a mom when you do that?" I ask.

She folds her arms across her chest, then, throwing me a stern look.

"Not helping the mom situation there," I sing-song and resume pushing the cart.

She sticks her hand out and grabs the handle, halting our progress again. "You have to go. You're going."

Sighing, I roll my eyes. "I can't. I don't have the time."

"I'm sorry, what?"

"I work all day and then..."

"Then what?"

"Doris might need me to babysit Art. She's old and she gets tired easily. Plus I'm giving Art punching lessons. Do you know he's getting bullied at his school?" I shake my head. "Seriously. What's wrong with the world? How do these people, these *fucking bullies*, even sleep at night? Do they think it's okay to torment people? Is it okay to scare them? Does it make them feel bigger? Like, seriously? God! World's fucked up, Tina. Sometimes I think I should go and put the fear of God in those kids. Trust me –"

"Stop talking."

"What?"

Tina puts her hands on my shoulders. "Just stop. You're not going to put the fear of God in children, okay? Take a deep breath."

"What?"

"Do it."

"Fine. Here." One deep breath later, "You happy?"

"Not particularly. But I think this will do. Now, repeat after me: My name is Cleo and I'm going to live my life."

When I purse my lips at her she glares at me.

"My name is Cleo," I parrot the words. "And I'm going to live my life."

"And I'm going to try to find happiness for myself."

I grit my teeth. "And I'm going to try to find happiness for myself. But. I can't go." When it looks like she's going to protest, I almost shout, "You know why."

"Why?"

"Are you seriously asking me this?"

"Yes."

"I can't go because." I look at the ceiling. "I can't get into a car."

"Okay?"

"What's wrong with you? I cannot get into a car. I throw up, remember? I get claustrophobic. I can't... My parents died in a car crash. I haven't touched my car, the car that I used to freaking love, in a year now. How do you think I'm going to get to this date? Ryan's going to want to pick me up and I just can't."

Tina's looking at me like I'm crazy. "That's not even." She throws up her hands. "That's not even an excuse. Take the bus."

Legit point.

"But –"

"No. No buts. You're going out with Ryan. End of discussion."

"I –"

"Look, you can't stop living, Cleo. You can't. Remember what you told me about Neal? Why you went out with him in the first place?"

I stubbornly remain silent.

"You went out with him because you wanted to know what it felt like. What it felt like to be in love with a boy. Because all you ever felt for a guy was hate. Look what happened last night, Cleo. You blew up. You have so much anger and sadness inside you because of what happened to you at St. Patrick's. You need to move on."

Tears fill my eyes and I don't know how to stop them.

"Ever since Zach came back, you've been jumpy. You've been consumed by him. All you ever do is think about him and what he's going to do to you. What *you* can do to *him*. He's the only thing on your mind."

She's right.

The guy I hate is the only thing on my mind. He's the first thing I think about when I open my eyes in the morning. He's the last thing I see when I close them. He doesn't even leave me alone in my dreams.

It's worse than what it was at St. Patrick's. When school was over, I got to cross the line and go back home. That invisible line between the south side and the north protected me from him.

But now I live where he lives.

There's this constant awareness of him being around. My heart's always ready to pound at the slightest smell of him. The butterflies are flapping their sharp wings, making me bleed on the inside. My lungs are always on the verge of losing air.

I'm obsessed with him, with the way I hate him, with the way he makes me feel.

"I don't know..."

"I'm not blaming you," Tina says. "I never blamed you. He's the asshole. He's the bad guy in this situation. The bully. But don't you think it's time to just let it go? Don't let him win, Cleo. Don't let him ruin even the slightest chance you have of finding love or even going on an awesome date. Ryan is amazing. Your parents loved him, remember? Go. Live your life. You deserve happiness. You deserve to dull the pain. You deserve to fall in love."

I do.

I certainly, *certainly* do.

When Zach left, I could've dated. Not that people were asking me out on dates at St. Patrick's but still. He wasn't there to ruin it for me. I could've kissed and made out, even lost my virginity. I could've done all those things but I never did. For some reason, it never even entered my mind.

But Tina's right. Again.

I deserve to fall in love and find out what my parents had. They were so in love with each other. Like disgustingly in love, and I always thought that one day I'd find someone to be crazy in love with too.

Smiling, I wipe off my tears and nod. But before I can say anything, my gaze falls on him.

The guy we've been talking about.

Somehow, I forgot that this is where his room is. Which is stupid because we were going to do the windows right by it.

Zach's leaning against the doorjamb with his arms folded across his chest, his eyes on me.

He's sweaty and the only article of clothing on his body is a pair of track pants. They hang so low that they show more than they hide. Namely, that deep V of his sculpted pelvis. But the worst and most disturbing thing is a hint of the dark tuft of hair that disappears under the waistband.

I don't want to think where it leads and how long he's been standing there or if he heard any of the conversation Tina and I had.

And neither do I want to think about the piece of gossip that traveled this morning, alongside my midnight meltdown.

He was so scary, I swear. And then, he looked at me and said escort her out; she's drunk. *Oh and you can't forget the last thing he said to her:* don't come back here uninvited. *It was the most perfect moment. He was perfect. He totally defended you, Cleo.*

Grace, who rarely gossips or gets animated about anything, was telling everyone about it at the morning meeting – *animatedly* – and all I could do was listen to it as I grew breathless.

He defended me. My bully defended me.

It's impossible. I don't believe it.

But I can't stop myself from growing breathless again. Because he's walking toward me.

Slow, loose steps.

I would think his walk was casual. But his eyes, which are trained on me, make everything predatory.

Something from deep within me makes me take a step back like I'm really his prey. A good, little prey, running away from the predator like I should.

Tina notices my distractedness and turns around to see what's causing it. She grabs hold of my arm to stop me from stepping back but I tell her to leave.

"What?"

"You should go," I tell her again, looking away from Zach, who's still advancing on me, and at her. "I can handle this."

"But Cleo –"

"I'll be fine."

Zach's hovering over us now, or rather me. He hasn't spared Tina a glance but he addresses her, still staring at me. "She's right. She'll be fine. Get lost."

Tina swallows as he looks up at him. "If you do something –"

"Bedbugs," he rasps. "I need to talk to her about bedbugs. Now, beat it."

I swallow too but for Tina's sake, I give her a small smile. "Go have a break. I'll come get you in a bit."

With one last look at the both of us, Tina leaves.

And then, it's just me and him.

Zach resumes his advancing and I resume moving back.

Why do I keep moving back like I'm afraid of him? Like I can't take him on.

Finally, I hit the wall.

My spine feels the rough, cool bricks and I look to my right. The corridor is deserted. This isn't as isolated as the bathtub was but it still feels like a dark, shady alley.

Zach comes to a stop right in front of me, his ropy muscles all magnified and somehow, more enhanced than a few days ago when I saw him naked. He puts both his arms on either side of my head, looming over me.

He's so close that I can see the sweat glistening on his brow. "What do you want?"

"Your dress," he says and I claw my nails at the wall. "Is it going to be okay?"

I wasn't expecting this. I wasn't expecting him to talk about my ruined nightie.

It was the most perfect moment. He was perfect. He totally defended you, Cleo.

"Nightie," I tell him in a voice that matches his, for some reason. Then, I clear my throat. "It's called a nightie. And kinda. I mean, I'm looking into it. Red wine stains are almost impossible to get out."

Zach acknowledges the statement with a subtle nod of his head and a lazy sweep of his eyes over my face. "Maggie should know what to do."

Oh yeah, I thought of that too. She's good with home remedies and stuff. But I'm not going to share my plan with him.

Why are we even having this conversation?

"Ashley," I blurt out instead. "I, uh, I heard that you sent her away. Grace was happy about it."

"I don't know a Grace."

"She works for you. For your family. She's the one you told to escort your girlfriend out."

"She's not my girlfriend." Then, a moment later, "She wishes, though."

God, the arrogance. Like every girl on this planet wants to be with him.

Not me, though.

Never me.

"Why?"

"Why what?"

Why is she not your girlfriend?

"Why did you send her away?" I ask, squeakily. "I-I mean, it's great that you did. She's a grade-A bitch. No offense to your choice of company or anything." I hold up my finger. "Actually, on second thought, I *was* trying to be offensive.

So yeah, you should take offense. Anyway, I'm happy about it. You know, that you sent her away. Like Grace and everyone else. Not that it matters that I'm happy. I mean, why would it? I think, it's actually the opposite. It's like... my unhappiness is what you live for, right?"

Gosh, I have no idea where I'm going with this. What am I saying? All I know is that my heart's beating really fast and he's super close and somehow, all I can hear right now is Grace's voice.

Zach holds his silence and I wonder how he can do that when my words have a life of their own.

"No."

"What?"

"I don't live for you. Nothing about you matters to me," he replies after a few seconds.

"Right. Of course. I knew that."

He totally defended you, Cleo.

He did not. Grace doesn't know anything.

I scan Zach's hard face, angled jaw, the flicks of his hair brushing against his eyebrows. For the first time I notice that he looks... pale. Kind of haggard, sweaty, even. His cheekbones have a sunken look and his stubble is thicker, like he didn't have the time to shave this morning or he simply forgot.

"Do you... are you sick?"

"You worried about me?"

I scoff. "No. I'm just..."

"You're just what?"

There's a bite in his voice and it gets my back up. "I'm just wondering if you have a fever. And if you do, then is it contagious because I don't want to catch anything from you. You're a little too close to me."

At this, he gets even closer. As if he's crossing the threshold, the line, just to scare me.

My glance jerks to his right hand. The hand he uses the most and the one where his tattoo is. I read the script running down his wrist. *I can cross the line.*

But suddenly, that hand is gone from the wall and I whip my gaze back to him. He fishes something out of his pockets.

"No, Blue. It's not contagious. What I have is because of you."

I focus on the object he's holding and dear God, it's the laxative.

My eyes go wide when I understand his meaning. He fell for it. He fell for my prank and that's why he looks like this. Pale and sweaty and clammy.

"I…"

"I found it on the counter last night. Belongs to you, doesn't it?"

I jerk out a nod.

"Another way to get back at me."

I go to nod but then stop. Did he say he found it last night?

If he did, then why did he… eat it? Why did he eat the custard? That was the only thing in that fridge I could've put it in because that was the only thing meant for him. And for me, too.

"Why did you eat the custard?" I ask, confused. "If you knew… about my prank."

His answer is a tight clench of his jaw.

Then something else occurs to me. He hasn't smoked in a while. I haven't seen him with a cigarette ever since I took his pack. Not that I keep tabs on him but still. Even now, his smell is… un-smoky.

"Wait a second. Are you…" I shake my head because this is *bizarre*. "Have you not been smoking? Why would you not smoke?"

This is the very first time I don't understand him. I don't understand his motivations, his actions.

All these years, it's been simple. He was rich and bored and bad. And I was the new girl from the other side of the line. He and his friends bullied me because they could. Because no one would lift a finger and because I was on their turf.

Why would he deliberately hurt himself though?

"I…"

I trail off again because I literally have nothing to say. My mind is blank.

Actually, no.

I'm lying. My mind isn't blank. It's flooded with stupid, crazy thoughts.

Thoughts like… maybe he did it for me.

He hurt himself. On purpose.

He hurt himself because *I* wanted him to hurt.

Zach lowers himself over me some more, making my jumbled thoughts go away.

Okay, thank God. Because it's the craziest thing I've ever thought. Zach doesn't care what I want. He never has.

Crazy with a capital c.

There's no touching between us, nope. But the weight of his chest inches apart from mine still feels crushing. It still halts my breaths.

"You're getting brave, aren't you?" he asks, instead of answering my earlier question.

"What?"

"But there's a very thin line between being brave and being stupid."

A barely-leashed threat lingers in his tone. A threat that steals my voice.

He cocks his head to the side and licks his lips. "You don't wanna cross that line. You don't wanna be stupid and steal my stuff or run your mouth off about my dick."

Oh God, I'd forgotten about my careless, harmless little joke.

He *knows*.

How does he know?

"There are no secrets in this house. Not from me. Do you understand?"

"I –"

"Shh." He puts his finger on my navy-blue painted lips. "Don't talk. Just listen. I've been real nice to you. Real patient. I've been giving you passes because I can't change history. I can't change what happened at St. Patrick's and if these little, childish games make you happy, then you can have your fun. I can *allow* you to have your fun."

He lowers his eyes to look at my lips, which I realize are parted. I'm breathing onto his finger, misting it up as he continues, "But it's getting a little annoying now. People who annoy me, make me angry. And you really don't wanna make me angry, do you?"

I'm frozen.

He presses his finger into the plumpness of my lips, flattening my mouth, pushing against my teeth, probably smudging my lipstick.

"Be a good girl, Blue, and shake your head."

I don't. I can't.

He's never been this close to me. If I thought the bathtub was close, then I was crazy. This is close. This is hovering and looming. This is the definition of the word pervasive.

He's everywhere.

His smell, his breaths, his voice, his heat and his skin. So much skin.

Then his whole hand captures my jaw, all while his finger is still on my parted lips. He puts pressure on my chin and forces me, *makes* me shake my head.

"Good. That's good," he murmurs. "I told you the first night I came back: don't tempt me. Stay out of my way and I'll stay out of yours."

His soft tone hits me in the stomach. Right in the indentation of my navel, and I suck in a breath.

Zach notices.

He notices my heaving chest. I bet he also notices how my breasts are punching the fabric. They feel heavy to me. Heavy and dangling and... ripe.

God, and sweaty. Just like his torso, all ridged and corrugated with muscles.

It's like we're both suspended in this moment. Him with his eyes on my chest and me with my eyes on his face.

It's wrong and it shouldn't happen but it is happening and I want it to stop.

A second later, it does when a sound travels from down the hallway. I hear footsteps bounding, approaching. Someone is climbing the stairs.

The weird paralysis of my body breaks and my palms slip on the wall. Zach looks up at me, at his hand that's still wrapped around my jaw.

"Let me go." I look toward the stairs at the end of the hallway.

His reaction, however, is completely opposite to mine.

Amused, he says, "I don't like your tone."

My heart's in my throat, my legs are shaking. "You're joking, right?"

"Are you laughing?"

I grit my teeth. "Whoever it is, I don't want them to see me like this. With you, okay? I can't have anyone think that we have something going on."

Zach frowns as if he's genuinely bemused. "But we do have something going on."

I throw another glance toward the stairs, wanting to push him off, physically. But I don't want to touch him. Especially when he's not wearing a shirt. I'm afraid to touch his skin.

"What?"

His eyes bore into mine. The blackness of them reaches out and almost consumes me. "You think about me all the time. I'm the only thought in your head. I make your heart beat faster, don't I? I make your chest feel tight. You shiver when I'm close. Your pulse is fluttering on your neck. Tell me, did it flutter when he asked you out?"

I gasp; the bastard overheard everything.

Damn it.

And he's right. He's so fucking right but I don't have the time to argue with him.

Zach chuckles humorlessly. "No secrets, remember?" He shakes his head once, slowly. "You wanna fall in love, huh? Let me tell you something about love, Blue. It hurts. Remember when you cut your palm and it was bleeding? It's like that. Only the cut is in your heart and the blood never stops. In love, you bleed forever. Do you wanna bleed forever, Blue? I bet your heart is real fragile. I bet it cuts easily."

Every part of my body is attuned to his words, especially my heart. The thing that bleeds in love, according to him. It's beating like crazy.

Crazy, crazy, crazy. Like me. Why am I not pushing him away?

The sounds and laughter are growing closer and finally I get enough sense to say something. "Let me go."

He smirks. "Say please."

I fist my hands. "Please."

"That wasn't so hard, was it?" Getting serious, he continues, "And Blue? A town can handle only one bully and this town's already got one."

Something flashes on his face quick like lightning. "Don't be a bully, Blue. Don't be like me."

He tightens his grip on my jaw once more before letting me go and moving away.

Just then, a couple of maintenance guys come into view. They barely pay Zach and me any attention as they walk in another direction.

Deflating, I grab hold of the cart and get out of there.

chaqter 10

It feels like the prom.

Tonight's date with Ryan.

I'm wearing my dark blue dress with white polka dots and pockets. It's strapless and hugs my body tightly before ending mid-thigh. It's a kind of dress that I always have to push myself to wear because I think my curves are super visible.

But whatever. I'm wearing it and I have paired it with borrowed blue sandals from Tina.

I told Ryan that I'd meet him right outside the restaurant he picked for us. He was bummed that he wouldn't get to drive me over but I'm saving that conversation for another time. Fourth or fifth date, maybe.

And now, I'm waiting in front of the restaurant like I was waiting for Neal at prom.

Actually, I don't think this is like prom at all. Ryan would never cancel on me like Neal did.

In fact, we've been trying to find time to go out for the past few days. But Ryan's been super busy and I've been working night shifts a lot, along with the day shifts; there's a new party coming in for a tour of the towers and the grounds, and Mrs. S was going ballistic.

Although that doesn't mean that we don't see each other every day or steal some time to talk between jobs.

He's just so sweet. Exactly like I imagined. Kind and caring. We haven't had a kiss yet – I guess we're waiting for the official date – but he's kissed my cheek. He has run his finger down my cheek as well. Both of those things were nice and warm, typical of him.

Sometimes though, he looks at me with pity, which bugs me. But I guess, after my meltdown in the kitchen with Ashley, I can't really blame him. I bet his pity will go away after a while. Everyone else's will too.

For now, I'm kind of excited. It's been a long time since I was on a date. I'm excited to get to know him, see him smile, have him touch me. Kiss me.

Besides, Tina, as always, was right. My parents would definitely have approved.

Right on time, Ryan pulls up at the curb and gets out of the car. I smile at him but then, my smile vanishes when I see a pained look on his face.

He approaches me and pulls me to the side, away from the entrance of the restaurant, where we can't be overheard by the patrons going in and out.

"What's up?" I ask, feeling apprehensive.

He grimaces. "I hate to do this but I'm going to have to take a rain check."

"Oh."

He rubs his hand up and down my arm. "I was already in my car, ready to drive over when I got called into work. So I thought I should tell you."

Ryan's distress is obvious, and it makes me feel a little better. He isn't abandoning me like my first boyfriend. He has a genuine reason.

"It sucks. But I get it. I mean, we've been so busy with everything for the last few days, so." I shrug.

Ryan gives me a penetrating look that makes me blush. "It sucks, yeah."

"You could've called, you know." I mock-punch his shoulder. "You didn't have to come all the way here just to tell me that."

Smiling, he does what he's been doing often: he thumbs my cheek, softly and smoothly.

"I wanted to see you," he says. "You look beautiful."

Blushing even more, I say, "Thank you."

Then I check him out with lowered lashes. He dressed up for the date, too. He has a black suit jacket on and a sage green shirt. "You look nice too."

His eyes heat up. "Next time, I promise that we'll go. No one will ruin it for us. Not even Mr. Prince."

What?

"I thought, uh, that Mr. Prince was out of town. When did he come back?"

He left the next day after Zach's welcome party on a business trip or something. If he was back, we would've heard about it.

Ryan chuckles. "I tend to forget that we have two Mr. Princes now. I'm talking about the other one. The new one. Zachariah. Zach. Whatever they're calling him. He said he had a short-notice meeting."

"Zach. They call him Zach," I tell him mechanically, as the earlier warmth in my chest slowly goes away.

Ever since I had my chat with Tina and Zach cornered me in the hallway a few days ago, I've maintained my distance.

Every morning on my way to work I see him working out by the pool, shirtless. I feel his stare across the expanse of ground that separates us but I make it a point to never stare back. I make it a point to not see how his muscles ripple and how sun spotlights every drop of sweat that he sheds.

I also make it a point to never go into the kitchen in the morning because Zach's always there, getting fussed over by Maggie.

A couple of times I saw him getting out of tower one, where Mr. and Mrs. Prince's bedroom is located – junior members of the staff, such as me, aren't allowed in their suite. He looked agitated, angry, but as soon as our eyes clashed, I looked away.

Most nights, I hear the roar of his bike as he leaves the estate to go wherever he goes. Again, I make it a point not to think about it. Along with other things like how he sent Ashley away and how he made himself sick with the custard. How he hasn't smoked in a while.

Don't be like me.

What does that mean? I make it a point not to wonder.

As the days passed, I thought that he meant what he said. If I left him alone, he'd leave me alone too. I'd go back to trying to save up for my house and he'd do whatever he came here to do. I thought that maybe now that we've grown up, things really changed.

"Didn't you go to school with him?"

Ryan's question brings me out of my head and I nod. "Yeah."

People have been asking me that since the first night he came back.

Didn't you go to school together?

How was he back in school?

Do you know why he left? Why he came back?

Has he always been this sexy, this good looking?

"Were you..." Ryan pauses. "Were you guys friends?"

"No. No, we weren't friends," I tell Ryan, waiting for the familiar anger against Zach to rise up in me.

Familiar heat and the sense of injustice and the urge to punch him for ruining this for me.

Nothing changed, right?

Zach did ruin my date. He said there were no secrets from him. So he probably figured out that tonight Ryan was taking me out.

This is *exactly* like prom.

But unlike prom, unlike all the years at St. Patrick's, I don't have the need to get even. All I feel is empty.

Exhausted, tired. Scared.

I feel scared. I feel like for years, I've hated Zach with such intensity that he's consumed every thought in my head. He's taken up all the spaces in my body that I have nothing left to give. Nothing left to feel.

Maybe I hate him so much that I'll never be able to love anyone. I'll never have what my parents had.

"Okay, well, I'll see you," Ryan says.

He asks me if he can drop me off anywhere, maybe at The Pleiades, but I decline. Finally, with a soft kiss on my cheek, he drives away.

And I start walking north. Toward the mansion where *he* lives.

Chapter 11

I'm in Zach's room.

I walked for hours to get here.

I walked for miles in my blue sandals that gnawed on my feet. I have blisters on my heels and my skin tore open, oozing blood.

But I kept putting one foot in front of the other. I kept bleeding and sweating in the heat until I reached The Pleiades. Instead of going to the cottage, I walked toward the main house and got in through the service entrance.

If someone had found me wandering the hallways, in a dark blue dress, with bloody feet, I don't know what I would've said to them. Maggie would've been pissed. Mrs. S would've come to know and I could've been fired. But I didn't care about that. I didn't care about the job or the house I'm trying to get back.

Good thing too because I didn't encounter anyone on my way to his room.

His door was locked.

After the whole debacle of him dousing me in water and taking away my keys, Mrs. S said that we weren't allowed in Zach's room, unless he was the one letting us in. But there was no hesitation in me when I used the pin in my hair to break in.

And now, here I am. Dizzy and tired and probably as pale as a ghost.

Maybe he's out on his bike right now, doing what he does this time of night. But I'll wait for him to come back.

I don't know what I'll do when he does come back or why I came into his room in the middle of the night. I'm pretty sure tomorrow, all of this will look crazy and unhinged. But for now, I don't know what else to do or where else to go.

I look around his room. It appears the same from days ago when I stupidly hid in his bathtub.

But there are subtle differences. A few of his clothes are scattered on the dresser. His backpack is on the black leather couch, directly opposite from his king-sized bed. His empty mattress holds the shape of his body and rumpled dark sheets.

And then, there's his book, sitting on the nightstand.

Still in my sandals, I round the side of the bed and limp over to it. The cover of the book is all white, with the title written in bright blue.

Last time I flicked through it, but tonight I take the time to read what's inside. There's a story behind almost every constellation, and soon I'm flying through the pages.

I don't remember sitting on the bed but I am. Right on the edge as I read the love story of Perseus and Andromeda. Apparently, the night sky is full of them, love stories. That's where the term comes from: a love written in the stars.

Again, I don't remember taking off my sandals and lying down but I am. I'm on my side, facing the big window as I keep on reading. The sheets feel warm like a cocoon, and even if I didn't already know that this is where Zach sleeps, I'd smell him and figure it out.

Blueberry pie and clean musk.

Last thing I remember before closing my eyes and drowning in his quicksand of a bed is turning the page and thinking that there's no way I can sleep in *his* room.

Turns out, I was wrong.

I did sleep. God knows for how long and God knows what woke me up with a jerk. But I'm awake now and sort of dizzy and foggy.

I take in the room; it's dark. The overhead lights have been switched off. I swallow in fear. And then, my eyes fall on a shadow. A big, black shadow in the shape of the guy I've come seeking.

He's sitting in a chair, in the glass alcove, overlooking the sky and stars and age-old love stories.

The only light in the room is the glow of the lamp, ripping his body in two: dark and light.

I can see his elbow propped up on the arm of the chair and his gorgeous soft lips lightly wrapped around his finger. He's contemplating as he watches me sleep.

Slowly, awareness seeps into my brain and I prop myself up. Apparently, the book I was reading was tucked under my cheek and my movements cause it to fall.

It does with a thud and we both watch it. Me, with a grimace and him, with a blank look.

I'm about to get off the bed when he speaks, "You know…"

I whip my eyes in his direction.

He's leaning forward now, his fingers threaded between his spread thighs as he says, "When I was little, I used to have trouble falling asleep. So, Maggie used to tell me stories. About the stars, because I'd lie there and watch them."

He points to where I was lying with the tip of his chin. "She told me a story once about Orion. According to the legend, he was a hunter and one day, he meets these sisters and falls in love with them. He spends years chasing after them, trying to win them over. But Zeus finds out about it and decides to put a stop to it. So he turns the sisters into doves. And they fly away and leave Orion and his undying love behind. Do you know what happened to them?"

Zach's voice is soft, softer than I've ever heard. A lullaby, and he's telling me a story.

And I'm here, sitting on his bed, listening to it not only with my ears but with every part of my body. I'm listening to his every word as if his are the last words I'll ever hear.

It's like a dream.

I clutch the sheet that I don't even remember putting on myself. "No."

"The sisters are now a constellation up in the sky called Pleiades. They are seven stars. Though, you can only see six of them for some reason."

The Pleiades. This mansion with seven towers.

"The Prince who built this place decades and decades ago must've been into stars," Zach murmurs, reading my thoughts.

And probably, *this* Prince gets his love for stars from his ancestors.

"And Orion," I whisper. "What happened to him?"

"He's a constellation too. And centuries later, every night, he still chases after them across the sky. He's probably going to chase after them till the end of time."

There's a smile on his lips. In the darkness I can't tell if it's real or not but it still has an effect on me.

An effect that makes me whisper, "It's a beautiful story."

"You think so?"

I nod. "Yes. Loving someone so much that you become immortal like a star. So you could love them forever. Yeah, it's beautiful."

It's something I want. So, so badly.

It's something that I'm afraid I'll never have. Because of him. Because of how much I hate him, the guy who told me the most breathtaking tale of love.

The guy who thinks love makes you bleed.

Zach's smile widens and morphs into a chuckle. He sits back and throws out a laugh. A rusty, harsh laugh. "I told you that story, Blue, because it's the most pathetic thing I've ever heard. I remember laughing the first time I heard it. And the reason I keep going back to it is because it makes me believe in how shitty and miserable love is. How lonely."

I don't even know why he thinks that. But I can see that it's something he believes in with his very soul. With every fiber of his being and with every dark thought in his head.

"Love isn't misery," I say finally, because I have to say something. "It's not shitty. It's not lonely. It doesn't make you bleed. And if it does, well then, it's not love. My parents were in love and they weren't miserable. They were happy. Love is good. It's... magic. It's supposed to make your life easier, better."

Zach studies me for a few heartbeats, his fingers on his mouth again. "I didn't think it was possible but *that* was the most pathetic thing I've ever heard." I narrow my eyes at him but he keeps going, "Besides, it's been a thousand years of chasing and the guy can't take a hint and apparently, neither can you."

Thrusting the sheets aside, I stand.

Only, I forgot about the blisters and the pain, and I stumble. "Fuck."

I would've probably fallen on the floor if not for a strong grip around my arm. His fingers flex on my bare skin when he looks at my feet. "What the fuck happened?"

My toes have splotches and ugly looking boils around them, and I'm sure my skin must be ripped on the bottom and in the nook where my foot meets my ankle.

Ugh.

Stupid blue sandals.

Before I can answer him, he comes down on his knees. Those fingers of his vanish from around my arm and grip my left ankle. I have no choice but to hold on to his shoulders, his very hard and curved shoulders that ripple under his threadbare t-shirt as he moves my foot this way and that.

"What are you doing?" I ask his bowed head.

His finger traces the arch of my foot and my toes wiggle. "How'd you get these?"

I try to extricate my leg but his grasp tightens. "It doesn't matter. I –"

"They're bleeding. Insanely," he snaps, as if I'm an imbecile.

As if I haven't noticed.

I fist his t-shirt to keep my balance. "I know. I can see *and* feel, thank you very much. And it's not my fault that they're bleeding. It's yours."

He looks up. "What?"

"Yes. I've been walking for miles because I wanted to see you. So it's your fault."

It's irrational but at the same time, it makes complete sense to me.

"Why?"

"Why what?"

"Why didn't you call a cab or something?"

I sigh sharply at the look on his face. He knows the answer. He probably overheard it the other day when I was talking to Tina.

"You know why," I tell him with gritted teeth. "Now, let my ankle go."

There's a clench in his jaw and finally, he comes to his feet. Sighing, I wiggle my toes on the hardwood floor in freedom.

"Let's go," he says.

"Go where?"

He tips his chin forward. "To the bathroom."

"What?" I lean back from him like he's making a play to grab me. "Why?"

"So I can murder you and dump your body," he deadpans. "It'll be easier to clean all that blood up in the bathroom."

I scoff. "Funny. You wouldn't murder me."

"Wouldn't I?" he says softly.

"No. Because if I die, you can't torture me."

He shoots me a long look. "You know this is breaking and entering, don't you? I remember locking my door. So either let me dress your wounds or I'm calling the cops on you."

"Did you hear yourself?" I ask, exasperatedly. "Are you saying if I don't let you *take care of me*, you'll have me arrested?"

Still staring at me, he gets out his phone from his back pocket. "Since it's Saturday, you won't make bail until Monday. You'll definitely be fired and on top of that, to come up with bail money, you'll have to dip into your savings – savings that I hear you were keeping aside to make a payment on your old house."

"You're a psychopath, you know that?"

"It's your choice," he says, coolly.

"Fine. You want to *dress my wounds*? Be my guest. I don't even care. I've gone crazy, anyway. I've completely lost my mind because I'm here. I came into your room like an idiot. So yeah."

Muttering to myself, I start to limp in the direction of the bathroom but a hiss escapes me when blisters pop with the pressure.

Behind me, Zach curses and I barely suppress a shriek when he lifts me in his arms, bridal-style, and strides over to the bathroom. I have very little choice but to fist his shirt and coil my hand around his neck.

The whole thing is over in less than five seconds and the next thing I know, he's sitting me down on the marble countertop of his sink. I'm on the side, my legs dangling.

I think I should say something, show my stance that I'm against him picking me up like this. But my breaths are still shaken up and my feet are still throbbing, and I can't form words.

A second later, Zach sits in front of me, on the closed toilet seat, and spreads out the first-aid box right next to me on the counter.

Then he circles his large fingers around my ankle once again and puts my foot on his thigh.

I suck in a breath at how hard it is, the muscles there. It's like putting my foot up on a rock. A very warm rock.

The smell of antiseptic fills the space as Zach dabs some on a cotton ball with deft, expert movements.

"You didn't have a meeting, did you?" I ask, instead of focusing on very weird feelings he's invoking in me by his gentle ministrations.

With easy flicks of his hand, Zach cleans the cuts on my toes. My foot jerks with the sting but he holds it in place. "Nope."

I curl my fingers at the edge of the counter. "You made it up."

He finishes up with one foot and switches over to the next. He treats it the same way. Carefully cleans the area, dabs at the blood and puts the band-aid on.

Throwing away the soiled cotton balls, he shuts the first aid box and stands, making himself taller and intimidating. "I did."

I want to stand too, so we can be on equal footing, but he doesn't give me space. He's crowding me and I crane my neck up to look at him.

"So you could ruin my date," I conclude.

"Was this your first date with him?"

His eyes move over my features and I squirm in my seat. "Why?"

"Because he looked broken up about it." He scans my rumpled blue curls and I tuck a strand behind my ear. "Like he wanted to be with you rather than driving me around for no reason."

"Of course he wanted to be with me. What did you think? We had a date, you idiot. We'd been planning to go out for days."

"Yeah, about that. Why didn't you?" he asks, casually.

"There was no time. Jobs, remember? We both have one," I snap.

His eyes drop to my mouth before coming back up to my eyes. I feel like I'm going to explode. I'm hot and sweaty and tired, and I'm breathing way too fast.

"Do you like him?" he asks, looking cool and relaxed.

"What difference does it make?"

"Do you?"

I dig my nails into the counter. "Yes. I like him. I've always liked him. I've liked him since I was a kid. Since before I met you, and I've been looking forward to this date for days now. I wanted to go out with him. I wanted to have a good time." I know I'm saying these things but they sound weird to me, like I'm trying to convince myself as much as him.

Even so, I forge ahead. "I guess that's why you ruined it, didn't you? Because it would've killed your fun if I did one thing that made me happy."

"He wouldn't have made you happy."

"I'm sorry?"

"And neither would Neal. Your taste in men sucks."

"What?"

He scratches his jaw and looks me up and down. "But then again, maybe you like going out with assholes. Guys who cheat on you. Guys who don't put you first."

Then he comes even closer to me. I'm so stunned by what he's saying that I don't even protest when he splays his palms on the counter on either side of my body and hangs over me.

"Is that what you want from life, Blue? A guy who doesn't care about you. A guy who doesn't do anything and everything to be with you," he whispers. "You should thank me. I did you a favor. I saved you."

His whispered words are causing a ruckus in my chest. Can whispers do that? Aren't they supposed to be soft? How can they do mean things to my heart, then?

"The only thing you need to save me from is you," I whisper.

His features rearrange themselves into something even more unreadable. Something hard like granite and sharp like glass before he rasps, "Believe me, I'm trying."

A pain shoots up in my chest and I realize it's my heart.

Maybe it's bleeding. Maybe the butterflies that he created in me a long time ago are slashing it with their savage wings.

In love, you bleed forever.

I wonder if in hate, you bleed forever too.

Somehow, my hands move. They uncurl from around the marble edge and I put them on his chest. With all my strength, I try to push him away, but he stays put. "Then try harder. Leave me alone."

I don't want to bleed.

"Leave you alone, huh?"

"Yes. You said if I stayed out of your way, you'd stay out of mine. You promised."

"But you're not out of my way, are you, Blue?" he throws in, his palms still on either side of me. "You broke into my room in the middle of the night. It's a felony, remember? You broke the law to be in my way."

I fist his shirt, every bone, every muscle in my body throbbing with fear and with something else I can't name. "Do you want to know why I broke the law to *break* into your room? Because I'm tired and I'm exhausted and I don't know what else to do. I don't know where to go, who to talk to. I don't want to dress up for a date and have you ruin it over and over."

I push at his chest again as I continue, "I came here to *be in your way* because I want you to leave me alone. I came here because I want you to keep your promise. You were right. This town already has its bully and it's not me. I don't want it to be me. I don't want to be like you. I don't want you to consume me. I don't want you in my thoughts. And I'll do anything, *anything* at all including tolerating your presence for a while if it sets me free for good. Do you understand that?"

I watch something crackle over his face. Dangerous and hot.

On fire.

The flames of which radiate outward and lick my body.

"Anything, huh?"

A tremble passes through me at his low, *criminal* tone. A tone that's darker than his eyes, those thick eyelashes. Darker than the midnight velvet strands of his hair.

Zach's eyes drop down to my lips.

My mouth is throbbing like my feet. Maybe his stare has the power to bruise it.

His gaze slides down along my throat and settles on my breasts, the throb sliding down, too.

Before I can even form words, Zach shifts. His hands wrap around my waist and he orders, "Spread your legs."

"What?"

Looking back into my eyes, he shakes his head once. "You want me to stay away from you, don't you? You want me to keep my promise? And you'll do anything for it?"

Is he... implying what I *think* he's implying?

When I keep looking at him with a frown, he squeezes my waist hard. Harder than I had anticipated, and I whimper.

"Answer me. You'll do *anything* to save yourself from me, yeah?"

I nod. Wordlessly. Like a little, plastic, brainless doll.

"Then let's see how much you wanna be saved. Show me how much you hate me, Blue. Spread your fucking legs."

I get a serious case of shivers at his low tone. I'm not sure if my thighs drop open themselves or he powers his way between them.

But suddenly, he's here.

Between my thighs.

"You're an a-asshole," I stumble over my words, raking my nails over his chest, panting slightly at the bulk of him.

"Heard you the first thousand times before."

Zach's hands travel down from my waist, smooth down my dress, and the throb follows. My skin beats like my bleeding heart.

He keeps going until he reaches the hem of my dress, just above my knees. In the silence of the bathroom, my harsh breaths are the only sound. I couldn't stop them, even if I wanted to. I need extra air, extra oxygen to be able to survive this.

His bronzed hands get under the skirt and all I can see are his wrists, one of them with the tattoo peeking out.

The feel of his callused fingers makes me whip my eyes up at him. Only to find him watching his hands on me, as well. Something about that is so... needy. As if he has to look with his own eyes before believing that he's touching me.

Touching the tender skin of my thighs, making me squirm.

"Zach..."

He lifts his eyes up to me. "Are you a virgin?"

My thighs shake at the intimacy of his question. At the expanse of his broad chest that's filling up my entire vision.

"What?"

"Your cherry. Do you have it?"

I should push him away. I can end this whole thing now. I can just jump down from the counter and take off. I don't care if he ruins my dates, uses me for his amusement.

I don't care. It's okay. I don't want to date or fall in love or anything even remotely that.

As long as I don't feel this way. Heavy and panting and so, so lazy yet so awake and throbbing.

But my mouth opens and I answer his question, instead. "No."

His thumb moves in circles, hot and rough against my soft skin, as he says, "You're lying."

I am.

"I'm not," I reply, fighting against the effect of his circling thumbs.

Why is it hypnotic?

It's making me drowsy.

His skin is flayed and half peeled-off in places – probably from the bike – and every circle he makes feels scrape-y, full of friction.

Zach's mouth stretches into a lazy smile. "But you blush like one."

Then he moves again. Putting pressure on my thighs, he slides me down the counter until my ass almost hangs over the edge. He hitches up my calves around his waist and my ankles cross at the small of his back, just over his tight butt.

I thought his thumbs were driving me insane but the scratch of his jeans along my thighs turns every breath into something... erotic.

Before I can dwell on that, Zach grabs my face.

His hands are so large that they span my entire cheek, going up to my messy hair. "So, if I shove your panties aside and stick my finger inside you, I won't find that tiny little piece of flesh that proves you're untouched?"

I shudder at the graphic picture he's painted.

Inside me. His finger.

Fingers that are tangled up in my hair right now. Fingers that are rough and raw.

I shake my head. Only I don't know what I'm shaking it for. Am I telling him he can't do it? Or answering his question?

"I won't, huh?" He takes it as a reply. "I won't find it."

"No."

Why am I lying?

His fingers in my hair tighten. "Who took it?"

"What?"

"Who. Took it?"

"Who took what?"

"Your cherry. Who did you give it to?"

My lips part under his hovering ones. When did we get this close? Not touching but breathing over each other's skin.

Grabbing his wrists, I find my voice. "None of your business."

His black eyes are swirling. "When'd it happen?"

"After you left."

His smile is cold. "Did it hurt?"

I jerk out a nod.

"It did. Was he big?"

"Stop. Please."

"Was he big or not?" He squeezes my cheeks, his fingers curled around my hair in a vise-grip. "Did he stretch you out, Blue? Or is your pussy tight as fuck for me?"

I have no idea what's happening. I literally have *no idea* why he's asking these questions.

All I know is that I'm flushed and shaking and quivering.

Everything inside me is... in chaos. The pounding of my heart, all the extra air that I'm sucking in, the tug in my stomach.

It's like an earthquake.

I'm a victim of an earthquake. I'm a victim of him.

"He stretched... he stretched me out," I whisper, looking at him with foggy eyes.

Except, aren't victims supposed to be in pain? Aren't they supposed to be either lifeless or close to it?

I'm none of those things.

I'm alive. I have more life in me than anyone else on this earth.

Zach swallows, his own eyes appearing glassy like mine.

"Don't lie to me, Blue," he rasps, clutching my hair with mean fingers.

I jerk when he says my name. Well, the name he gave to me. The name that I've always, *always* loved in secret. In fact, I never even acknowledged it to myself.

I'm acknowledging it now.

Maybe because Zach not only says it, he makes me *taste* it. I never thought you could taste a name, especially not your own. But mine tastes... musky and spicy.

As if it were a truth serum, words slip out of my mouth before I can stop them. "You'll find it. The... thing. Inside of me."

His lips part too and he expels a pent-up breath. I take in his air, filling my body with what was once in his.

"Zach, I –"

My words cut off when he moves away from my lips. A moment later, I feel him on my neck. He's nosing the line of my throat.

I grip his biceps. "A-are you smelling me?"

"Yeah," he groans.

I flinch and my neck bends sideways. I'm nothing in the face of his aggression right now. The way he's sniffing my neck, like he's snorting a line of cocaine. I'm nothing in the face of that need.

Need of a junkie.

"Why?"

"Because you smell nice. Like sugar."

And sugar is his favorite thing in the world. He's eating up my scent.

God.

I arch my back when he gets to the triangle of my throat, and I take a deep sniff of my own. What I smell is exactly what I fell asleep to, in his bed.

His blueberry pie and musky scent.

"Y-you smell good too," I blurt out, then clench my eyes shut in embarrassment.

Zach lifts his head and I have to open my lids when I feel his panting breaths over my lips.

He looks drugged up, I swear.

His pupils are wide, swirling like he really just took a hit of something potent, a narcotic that jacks up your heartbeat and sends you into the stratosphere.

"Do you know what else I'll find?" he rasps, his fingers touching the pulse on my neck.

"What?"

"If I touch your pussy right now. Do you know what I'll find?"

The P word is even more intimate than the V word and I can't stop myself from arching my back even more and fisting his shirt.

And neither can I stop my pussy from clenching, opening and closing like a mouth. "No."

Zach rubs our lips together. "Wet. I'll find it wet. And swollen and slippery and fucking horny."

Slippery.

I'm slippery.

I can feel it. The moisture, sticking to my panties.

"I can smell you from here. Your pussy's wet, Blue. She's so fucking wet. She's leaking. For me. She wants me. She doesn't hate me, does she?" he says, pouring his words down my throat, jamming it with them.

He's right.

He is.

I can smell myself too. I smell spicy and musky, just like my name.

And then, I see myself.

Sprawled around him. My dress is hiked up to the tops of my thighs, my pale skin is glistening under the light. I'm holding on to his shoulders like he's going to save me from everything bad in the world.

When *he* is everything bad in the world.

In *my* world. Him.

But what shocks me more than anything is that he's... hard. His dick is hard and it's pressed up against the most intimate part of me.

The bulge in his jeans is right up at my wet panties and I *like* the weight of it, the heat of it.

"I don't. I don't... want to..."

Finally, Zach stops and looks into my eyes and a tear breaks free, streaming down my cheek.

His thumb wipes off that tear with such tenderness that a few more shake loose and follow its path.

"You don't wanna feel this way, do you?"

I shake my head. "No. Not for you. N-not for someone who..." I swallow as the words rip out from somewhere very, very deep inside of me. "Someone who makes me hate. Someone who doesn't let me move on and let go. You change me. I don't know how you do that but you change me into a worse version of myself."

Something goes off in my chest, then. A bomb of memories.

Memories of that night three years ago when I said all sorts of things to him: the prom night.

You know how in love, you become a better person? You make me a worse person, Zach. I've never hated anyone the way I hate you. You're nothing but a big, fucking bully. That's all you'll ever be. I'll never forgive you for what you did tonight. For all the things you've done before. I'll hate you till the day I die...

Zach breathes through his nose, clenching his teeth. "Yeah. I do, don't I? So next time when I tell you to stay away from me, you do that. If I look at you, you look the other way. If you see me walking down the corridor, turn around and take a different route. Because the next time I see you in front of me, I'll take it as an invitation. If you keep throwing yourself at me, I'll snatch you up. And I'll make you pay for it on your goddamn back."

Zach rips his touch away and steps back.

I snap my thighs closed and jump down from the counter. My tears won't stop falling and the last thing I see is the agitated plow of his hand through his hair.

Then, I'm running away from him. From his room. From the place he grew up in. The place with seven towers and a glass window that you can see the stars through.

I tear open all my bandaged wounds as I run and run. For miles and hours. Until I reach the house that *I* grew up in.

I make my way in through an open window in the kitchen and climb the rickety stairs up to my room.

Then I curl up on the floor and sob.

chaqter 12

T he Dark Prince

When I was about seven, I made my parents a card for their anniversary.

I don't know what I was thinking, but I guess I wanted to impress them. I wanted to show them that I was normal, like any other kid.

I wanted them to be proud of me.

But I guess that was too much to ask.

My dad took one look at the card and his face scrunched up. I remember him crumpling it in his hands and throwing it in the fire.

"You'll always be an illiterate freak, won't you?"

I didn't know the meaning of *illiterate* but from his expression and the way he chugged down the whiskey in his glass in one go, made me think that it wasn't a good thing.

I remember my mother barging in and trying to console him. "It's okay, Ben. We have the best tutors. With practice, by this time next year, you won't even know –"

"That he's defective?" My dad clenched his teeth. "Maybe it's you. Maybe I shouldn't have married you. Because I know it isn't me. I know *I* am not making him slow. It didn't take me that long to learn how to write."

I watched my mom cry at that, and then my dad turned to me. "Go to your room and stay there. No food for you until you can spell your fucking name right."

I don't remember much after that. I remember screaming – my parents fighting, and I know Nora snuck some food into my room later that night.

She loved the card I'd made. She even told me that she loved me.

I never said it back. I never said *I love you too*. Something made me clam up. Maybe the fact that she was looking at me with pity, or it could be that I never believed her.

Even though by that age, I understood that that was what you did, when someone said *I love you*.

That was why I had it on the card.

On the card, I'd written *I love you, Mom and Dad,* along with my full name; I'd been practicing a lot, getting the hang of the letters just right.

I was expecting them to say it back to me, but I guess I messed up the letters and there went my *I love you too*.

In my defense, I was seven. I was pathetic. I was still trying to win my dad's approval by trying harder, being good, making stupid cards.

I'm not anymore.

I don't need love. I don't need acceptance or approval. I reject them before they can ever reject me.

But Blue's different. She's still naïve. She thinks love is this amazing, magical thing. She wants to fall in it.

It's funny how people forget that it's called *falling* in love. There's a reason for that. You fall and you break your fucking leg and you bleed. That's what love is. Bleeding, cutting yourself open on purpose.

It's a weakness to be that crazy, that you'll hurt yourself for someone else. Or that you'll love someone despite how much they've hurt you.

But whatever.

She's not my problem.

Though I will admit that I acted foolishly tonight. I knew it was a mistake. The moment I made up an excuse to ruin her date.

Honestly, I have no clue why I did that. Maybe I was just doing her a favor. That Ryan guy isn't for her. He isn't man enough to be with her.

But maybe I should've let them go. Maybe Blue needs a little heartbreak in her life to get the real picture.

I look at the bed where I found her asleep, her blue hair sprawled out on my pillow.

And then, there are her sandals: also blue and caked with tiny droplets of her blood. There are little indentations where her toes and her heel dug into the cheap plastic.

Fuck.

No wonder she was bleeding. And she's going to bleed even more because she ran away from here barefoot.

Gritting my teeth, I crush her sandals in my hands and stride over to the closet. Opening the door, I throw them in and shut it back with a bang.

My cock is hard as fuck. Harder than it's ever been.

I jump into the shower and try to clean off the feel of her. I try to clean off her scent, her softness.

And when the memory of her becomes too much, I pull at my cock.

I hear her words in my head: *I don't want to... Not by someone who makes me hate.*

Tears have never been my thing. But still, I jerk off to her.

I beat it, pull it, tug it, until I'm spraying cum all over the tiled wall, thinking about her blue hair and her sugar smell.

Fuck.

Fucking fuck.

Fuck.

Bracing my hands on the wall that wears my cum and breathing deep, I clench my eyes closed. Probably in regret. But then, I shut it down.

She hates me anyway.

One more crime against her wouldn't matter.

Chapter 13

"How did it even start?" Tina asks.

I look up from where I'm mixing dry ingredients for baking cupcakes for Art's bake sale. I suck at baking but Doris is sick and I volunteered to help. So I'm helping, or at least trying to.

"What is *it*?" I ask.

"This whole thing between you and Zach. Like, what happened? Why does he torture *you*, of all people?"

I go back to flicking the flour. "Because he's mean. And rich, and that gives him the right to do anything he wants."

This isn't something new. I've told this to her a thousand times. She's heard me cry and bitch about it for years. I don't know why she's at it again, though.

"Do you remember the very first time you met?"

I stop mixing; it's already *incorporated* more than the recipe called for.

The first time.

I hardly remember any of it, except that it was my first day of school and I was hungry enough to *borrow* carrot sticks and then, I met him in the detention room.

Although, I do remember that he was looking out the window, staring at a water fountain, and his uniform was as messed up and wrinkled as mine. I remember this utter longing to talk to him, the only boy who looked like me: dirty and untidy.

I remember this tug in my stomach. This flapping and fluttering. At the time I thought, I was so hungry that my tummy was making weird noises. But later, I realized that they were the butterflies, and that tug was the miserable connection between us.

Anyway, when I did talk to him, he turned out to be a complete jerk who called me a thief, smirking, looking me up and down like I was a reject or something. I got angry at that, and I might have said something back.

But again, I don't remember.

"Not really. I mean, I was like, ten and in detention. The only thing that jumps out is that he was super arrogant and rude and I hated him."

Tina drums her fingers on her chin. "I wish I remembered what you told me."

"Why are we talking about this again?"

"Because enough is enough." She slaps a hand on the island. "We need to go talk to him."

"What? No."

"Yes. Are you going to wait for him to leave and then go on dates? Or have fun and live your life?" She shakes her head. "You can't wait on anyone, Cleo. You can't be scared of him. He needs to learn his lesson. Forget about letting go. You were right. Justice is the answer."

"It's not. We're not going anywhere and I'm not afraid of him."

I'm not. Not really.

I'm afraid of myself. Of the things *I* am capable of.

Last night was exactly like prom. Even the words I used were the same.

That's what he does to me. He pushes my buttons. He pushes them and pushes them and I become something entirely different.

Don't be like me.

After I ran away yesterday, I spent the night at my old house. I couldn't sleep, not like I'd slept in Zach's bed but I lay there, curled up and crying until the morning came. I had enough presence of mind to carry a phone in the pocket of my dress and text Tina that I was spending the night at my parents' house.

I did tell her things. But not everything. Not about my stupidity in breaking into his room. Not about what transpired between us.

And how I responded.

How I became... all turned on and *Jesus Christ*, wet.

I was wet. For Zach.

"Why not?" she asks, after a while.

I sigh. "Because I said so, okay? Leave it alone."

She props her hands on her hips and looks at me suspiciously. "Why do I think you're hiding something from me?"

With a jumping heart, I lie, "I'm not. You're paranoid. Now let's get these cupcakes done, okay?"

She keeps giving me the look but I don't pay her much attention from where I'm measuring the wet ingredients.

"Jeez, stop staring at me. You're going to make me screw up," I snap a few moments later.

"Whatever. Making cupcakes is the stupidest idea, by the way. Brownies. Make brownies. They are square and therefore, easier."

She's right but I'm not going to tell her that.

By the time we finish with the cupcakes, it's dinnertime and I tell Tina to order pizza and decide to go get Art.

He's been playing outside for a couple of hours now. Along with making cupcakes for the bake sale, I told Doris I'd keep an eye on him while she got some rest. So Art spent the entire afternoon with me, and we watched a Batman movie.

"Art," I call as soon as I step outside into the muggy heat but get no response.

He's not where I left him in the yard, with his bicycle and all those toys he likes to play with; the car type thingy that he can drive and his fire truck and whatnot. I swear, half of his things are at our place.

I call out his name a second time. Nothing again.

My heart thuds in a sickening beat.

I know he must be nearby. I know that. Sometimes he likes to go around the back and play in the woods. I've played with him there myself.

But why isn't he answering? He answers. He *always* answers.

Despite my still-throbbing feet, I take off running, thinking that he must be out back.

He has to be. Where would he go? This is a safe place; he's been playing out here for ages, even before I came along.

He's fine.

I'll turn the corner and I'll find him playing in the woods. He'll grin at me shyly and tell me that he wants me to play with him. He'll show me the fort he built with his toys and rocks like he did one time. I'll ruffle his hair because I can't resist when he's being my snuggle-bug, and then we'll go eat pizza.

But he's not there.

"Art!" I call out again. "Where are you?"

I keep going further, even though I've never known him to go this far out. Doris once told me that he's shy. He never goes to places he doesn't recognize. When I first started babysitting him, she said, *He's a fairly easy kid. You won't have any problems with him.*

And I never have.

But now I've lost him somehow.

I keep calling out his name but I still don't get an answer.

"Oh God, oh God, oh God," I mutter, bending, placing my hands on my knees.

Where did he go?

"Art!" I shriek like a madwoman. "Come back here!"

Then suddenly, someone's shaking me.

"What's happening? I could hear you from the house," Tina asks, gripping my arms.

I see her through the sheen of tears.

"I c-can't find Art. I can't..." I wheeze. "I can't find him. Oh my God, I've lost him, Tina. I've lost him."

"Okay, calm down. Relax. We're gonna look for him together. He must be somewhere around here," Tina says.

I nod. "O-okay."

Then a long shadow approaches us and my focus shifts.

It's Zach. He's striding over, his steps long and determined.

I don't know what happens to me but I let go of Tina and my legs start moving. I run toward him, like I ran yesterday when he ruined my date.

I almost smash into him but he stops me, steadies me with his hands and stares at me with a frown. "What happened?"

I clutch his wrists. "Doris, one of the maids, s-she has a grandkid, Art. I was supposed to watch him. I-I always watch him. He was playing outside and I was keeping an eye on him but then I forgot because I had to... I had to make cupcakes for his bake sale. And when I went to find him he wasn't there. I d-don't know where he went, Zach. I think I lost him. I don't –"

He squeezes my biceps. "Hey, he's okay. He's fine. I'll find him."

I look at his face, all focused and harsh. And he's leaning over me with his entire body. He's hiding the sun behind his massive shoulders and corded back.

And I know why I ran to him just now.

Zach is big and strong and... and he's capable. He knows this place. I *know* he'll find Art.

I know it.

"He's a good kid. He's just so small and tiny and what if he's hurt? I don't... He just vanished. How can he vanish, Zach?"

He stiffens at my words, his fingers becoming rigid on my flesh. Before I can ask him what's going on, he lets me go and takes off running toward the woods.

I follow.

It's hard to keep up with him. My feet are screaming with pain and his strides are long. But I keep going. I think Tina's behind me, but I can't be sure.

We go deep into the woods, deeper than ever, before Zach comes to a stop and kneels on the ground.

Here, the ground is covered with dead, dried leaves and the trees form a canopy up above. There's very little sunlight and everything is colder.

I don't like it.

As I get closer to Zach, I realize he's looking down at something.

It's a hole in the ground.

I fall on my knees beside him, the leaves crunching beneath my knees. But I don't care about that because it's a ten-foot drop and Art is at the bottom of it.

"Art!" I scream, almost toppling in myself.

But Zach pulls me from the edge, with his arms around my waist.

"No, no, no. I have to go get him. It's my fault. I wasn't doing my job. I've got to –"

He squeezes my waist, kneeling beside me. "No, I'll go get him."

I fist his t-shirt. "Why isn't he moving? Tell me why he's not moving."

Zach frames my face with his hands and applies pressure, making me look at him. "Because he's unconscious. It's a high drop. He's fine."

"B-but –"

"He's breathing, Blue. I checked."

My watery eyes run over his face. Frantically. Crazily. Like I can't get enough of his sharp, angled features. Like I'll never get enough.

"J-just bring him back. Please," I whisper, water clogging my eyes and my throat.

His nostrils flare as he studies my features, and he nods. "You stay where you are."

I nod back.

He lets me go, and gets to work.

His hands pat the ground, as if looking for something under the leaves. A few pats later, he finds it.

It's a long thick root, buried under the fallen foliage, connected to a huge tree that I didn't even notice until now. The root is thick and sturdy and looks to be going down into the hole.

As Zach grips it, probably trying to use it as a rope, I hear thudding footsteps approaching.

Tina's kneeling beside me. "Are you okay? Did we find him?"

"Yeah. He's in there." I motion with my chin.

Zach turns his focus on Tina. "I want you to go and get me a rope. And bring a staff member back with you."

Nodding, Tina squeezes my shoulders. "I'll be right back."

With that, she whirls around and runs back.

Using the root, Zach lowers himself into the hole, and I crawl over to the edge, looking down. Art's still unconscious and my body starts shaking.

Oh God.

How did I fuck up so bad? I'm never babysitting him again. Ever.

But then, I watch Art's tiny chest move. Up and down. In a rhythm.

He's breathing.

Thank God.

Just like Zach said.

Who's almost at the end of the hanging, sturdy root, which only goes down midway. Before I can stop myself, I call out, "Be careful."

Zach looks up at my words and I bite my lip.

I shouldn't have said that. I mean, it's a little too personal and nice. I'm supposed to hate him, right?

But I just thought... I had the right to say it.

And I'm not taking it back.

"Please," I say, crouched on my hands and knees, peeking down at him, with sweaty hair curtained around my flushed face.

His dark eyes don't give anything away but he jerks out a nod. Then he looks down and lets go of his purchase.

I suck in a breath when he lands on the ground, by Art's feet. It was smooth and effortless.

He kneels beside Art and my voice breaks as I ask, "Is he okay?"

Zach picks Art up in his arms. That's effortless, too. And smooth and gentle as he cradles his head.

I couldn't stop crying, even if I wanted to; I don't want to.

I don't want to stop crying because everything is swollen inside of me, raw and shaken up. And Zach's entire hand covers Art's head as he probably looks for an injury. He pats Art's head slowly, almost like a caress and I have to dig my nails into the ground to keep steady.

Still staring at Art with a careful frown, Zach says, "He's fine. He's got a bump on the back of his head. But he's gonna be okay."

I press a fist on my mouth to stop all the sobs from coming out.

"Are y-you okay?" I ask, and the way Zach's head jerks up makes me believe that it was the wrong thing to say.

Fuck it.

I'm not afraid of him. What am I right now is super emotional and almost unhinged. I don't care if my concern is such a suffering to him.

Zach's answer is a black frown and silence.

Soon, Tina's back with the rope and she's brought a couple other staff members, including Ryan, with her.

"Where's Zach?" she asks as she stops beside me.

"Down there."

Ryan kneels on my other side, concern evident on his face. "You okay?"

"Yeah."

In a terse tone, Zach instructs Ryan and the others to throw him the rope and explains what to do. Five minutes later, he's out and Art's in my arms.

"Oh, Art, I'm so so sorry." I hug him, smelling his hair, kissing his forehead.

I feel the bump on the back of his head and realize that he needs a doctor. I've been so focused on him getting out, I haven't even wondered how long he was in there.

"We need to go to the hospital," I tell the group huddled beside me.

"Yeah, I'll get the car ready, let's go," Ryan says, getting up on his feet.

"Someone needs to tell Doris," one of the staff members says.

Cradling Art, I manage to stand, as well.

Doris. Yup. Someone needs to tell her how badly I fucked up when I was supposed to watch her grandkid.

And let's not forget the car.

Tina goes to say something, probably about my one-year-old phobia of cars, but I shake my head once to tell her to shut up.

I can handle it.

Car's the perfect solution. How else would we get there? Bus isn't an option. It'll take way longer to get there and Art needs the medical attention now.

Ryan cradles my cheek in that gentle way of his. "Hey, everything is going to be fine. It wasn't your fault. These things happen. Art's going to be fine."

I squeeze Art's shoulders, smooshing him to my chest, and nod. "Yeah, okay, thanks. Let's –"

"I've called the doctor. He'll be here in a few." Zach's voice breaks through my panicky thoughts.

He's standing away from the group and I watch his eyes as they look at where Ryan is touching me. "No need to go anywhere." Then he orders a staff member, "And get someone to close up that hole."

With that, he turns away, leaving.

There are leaves clinging to his jeans, his boots, mud caked on the sleeves of his shirt, even his elbows and arms.

He's retreating, going away, after saving Art and even me. With Art in my arms, heavy and unconscious, I go after him.

"Wait. Zach."

He comes to a pause but doesn't turn around. I keep going until I come to stand before him. Somehow, he got a little dirt on the side of his jaw, too. I have a very strong, potent urge to reach up and wipe it off.

"What?" he bites out.

"I... How did you know about the hole? How did you know Art could be down there?"

The sun doesn't move and neither does the air. It's all still and hot but oddly, Zach's face, his entire body turns shadowed.

Darkness slashes his features, his demeanor, like last night when he sat in that chair of his, with the entire galaxy at his back.

"Zach –"

His gruff words cut me off. "Because I've been down there."

At first I think I haven't heard him clearly. But when the rigid look of his face doesn't go away, I realize that I have.

I have heard him clearly.

Clutching Art to my chest even tighter, I ask, "When?"

He clamps his jaw before saying, "A long time ago."

And then, he spins around and leaves.

Chapter 14

The Dark Prince

I was ten when I fell into that hole.

By then, I'd stopped making silly cards or trying to improve myself or be better. Just so they'd love me back.

By then, I'd learned to sneak out of the main house and roam free on the grounds. I had an entire plan set up to run away as soon as I figured out how to make money and save up enough to survive on my own. Although the way it came about – me, moving out – wasn't how I expected it to be.

I was down in the hole for hours. For the entire night, actually.

I remember trying to get out on my own, grabbing onto the roots and heaving myself up. I also remember falling on my ass a lot.

When I got tired, I remember lying there and watching the sky. I thought no one would ever find me. No one would even bother to look, definitely not my parents.

When I stopped trying to win their approval, they stopped bothering themselves with me. They handed me over to nannies, tutors, maids, whoever they could find to pawn their kid off to. They paid them enough money not to open their mouths about my disability.

My dad didn't want the world to know that his son was anything less than perfect. And neither did he want to waste his time on an imperfect kid.

And my mom? Well, my mom never wanted a kid to begin with. She didn't want anything to interfere with her parties and her carefree, rich life. Ironically, it was my dad who wanted a child. So when my mom gave him an imperfect one, she did everything she could to make up for the fact, including neglecting said child.

I remember wanting to cry down in that hole. Crying for my mom, my dad, even. I remember making deals with God that I'd try harder. I wouldn't run my tutors off. I'd spend time practicing lessons. I wouldn't be deliberately difficult and stir up shit.

Just get me out of this hole.

But then, I also remember stopping myself and getting angry. I thought, why the fuck should I try? Nothing is ever good enough for them. No matter how much I practiced, my dad would find a flaw and bash me over it.

I went to sleep, debating and exhausted.

It was Nora who found me the next day. She'd sent out a search party when she went into my room to wake me up for school.

For two days I was in bed; I'd sprained my ankle. And for two days, Maggie and Nora were the ones who took care of me.

When they told my parents, my dad's reaction was to pretend it never happened. And my mom's reaction was to say, "Why do you keep making waves, Zach? Why can't you be a good, quiet boy? You've always made things difficult for me."

Yeah, Mom. I was lying in a fucking hole the entire night and things are difficult for you.

I think she was counting on me falling to my death or something. Although she'd never say anything crass like that, but disappointment was pretty fucking clear on her face.

Yeah, I'm a huge fucking disappointment. For everyone.

Not for *her*, though.

Blue never acted disappointed in me because she's always assumed the worst. She's always looked at me with disgust and hate.

It's comforting. Familiar. It's how everyone in my life has looked at me, if we count out Nora and Maggie. But then, they're getting paid, aren't they, to be nice to me.

What isn't comforting is the way Blue looked at me today when I found that kid and pulled him out of the hole.

Today she looked at me like I moved the stars.

It hurt.

It still does.

I never thought it would. Never thought that naïve, innocent, *warm* look in her eyes would be so glaring and harsh.

Never thought it would make me angry.

It made me want to remind her who I was.

But it also made me want to grab her and kiss the fuck out of those blue-painted lips.

And that can never happen.

She won't let it.

Chapter 15

Everyone thinks he's the prince.

The savior. The hero.

They haven't stopped talking about how he pulled Art out from the hole. Everywhere I turn, someone is talking about the new Mr. Prince.

The cooking staff fawns over him when he goes to eat breakfast. Grace claims that he smiled at her while they were passing each other by in the hallway. Doris calls him *my good boy*.

"I handed him the bottle," Leslie breathes to a group of us standing by the stairs in the servant's wing, going upstairs to the first floor. "He was working out by the pool and I was coming out of the pool house, you know. He was like, *hey, excuse me? Can you hand me that bottle of water?* I had a fresh bottle of water." I roll my eyes at that obvious statement, but she goes on, "I did and…" She pauses to sigh. "Our fingers touched."

"Really?" Grace's eyes are wide.

"Yes. Oh my God, his *fingers*. They were just so warm."

I grit my teeth. I know all about his fingers. I know how warm they are, how rough, how the pads are callused and scraped.

I know what they feel like when they're on my thighs, in my hair, on my pulse.

I *know*.

As they talk and talk like they know him, I admit that I'm kind of jealous. It's been a week since he rescued Art and I haven't had a chance to talk to him.

Not even once.

It's not as if we're friends or anything, that I can casually walk up to him and say, *hey*. In fact, up until a few days ago, I was praying for him to leave. Although now I'm thinking, what if he leaves and I don't get to say something?

It's not that I don't see him. We live in the same place. Of course I see him.

And I mostly see him with Art.

Since Art's accident, I've apologized to Doris a thousand times. She's pretty chill about it but I can't get rid of the guilt. I've said sorry to Art too but again, he doesn't mind.

These days, he's pretty happy actually. Courtesy of Zach.

I've seen them together numerous times. Mostly, they're by the pool and I see them while going back from my shift. I deliberately walk slowly just to watch them together. Sometimes Zach works out – he works out twice a day; it's crazy – and he lets Art be his spotter. Art counts his reps and claps when he's done and tries to imitate him.

One time I saw Zach lying on the ground with Art in his arms, straight up. Grunting, he lowered Art, who laughed like he'd never seen anything funnier. Then, Zach raised him in the air again, like he was doing bench presses. Only instead of weights, he had Art.

I think my knees trembled at the sight.

I never knew Zach could be so… sweet and sexy at the same time.

A few times, I've walked up to them to pick up Art on my way back because Doris still somehow wants me to watch him while she's working.

But Zach and I, we don't talk. He doesn't even look at me. Sometimes it feels like he can't stand the sight of me. And I don't understand why. I don't understand why it bugs me.

The only person who isn't a fan of Zach's is Tina. She hates him, and that's saying something.

"God, I can't believe how everyone's so crazy about him. Can't you see, people? He's the devil. Fine, he saved Art. But what about all the other things he's done? What about them? People can be so stupid."

"You sound like me," I tell her while dusting the library in tower two one day.

"You know, I'm glad you're moving on and all. But you need to be more upset about this." Then she gasps. "You know what would be the best thing ever? You should go out with Ryan. That'll show him."

"Oh, here's another great idea: why don't *you* go out with Ryan? You used to like him as much as me."

She goes quiet and it takes me about ten seconds to figure out why. And when I do, my squeal is loud. I mean, really loud.

"Oh my God, you like him," I shout, poking her shoulder with my duster. "God, Tina. Why didn't you say anything?"

"I don't like him." She rubs her shoulder. "I mean, I used to like him but not anymore."

"Either stop lying or stop blushing. You like him and you're going out with him."

"I'm –"

"And I'm dressing you up."

"No way."

"Yup."

Tina looks at me guiltily. "But I don't –"

"Look, Ryan's great but..." I repeat what Zach said to me that night in his bathroom while he was dressing my wounds. "But he wouldn't have made me happy."

I promised Maggie that I wouldn't break into the main house under any circumstances.

Not to mention, the suite I want to break into belongs to the guy who told me to stay away from him.

But I'm not much of a rule-follower. Besides, I deliberately left my phone in the staff room on the off-chance that it might come to this. If someone catches me, I have a perfect excuse.

So I'm in my stealth mode again. Black hoodie, black shorts and quiet leather boots.

Okay, in my defense, I've tried everything else. It's the dead of the night and I can't sleep. I should be tired after a full day's work but I'm not. I even read the books I bought on astronomy; apparently, I'm into reading these days.

And stargazing.

Every night for the past week, I've searched for Orion. I looked it up on the internet. It's a winter constellation, supposed to be only visible from January to March.

It's winter here – although, all we ever feel is the heat – but I can never see it.

I'm very quietly walking to the door of our cottage when I see a flash of black in my peripheral vision.

I dash to the window and open an inch of the drapes. Someone's walking across the yard. More stumbling than walking. It's a drunk walk.

And it's Zach.

Oh my God, what are the chances?

What is he doing here?

As I press my palm on the window, he turns and looks directly at my cottage. I'm not sure if he can see me peeking at him through the drapes, but he's frowning at the window, like he's mad.

Frantically, I look around at the other cottages. They are dark and sleepy. But what if someone wakes up and finds him here?

What is he *thinking*?

A second later, he falls to the ground and all my thoughts vanish. I'm running out the door before I can stop myself. I practically fall beside his sprawled form.

"Zach? You okay?"

Turns out, I shouldn't have bothered. Because he opens his eyes and they look clear and alert. "Why wouldn't I be?"

I sit back on my heels. "Because you just fell. Just like that. Under my window."

He shrugs. And then frowns as he takes me in. "What are you wearing?"

I look down at myself, my black hoodie and my shorts. "What?"

"Were you planning on breaking the law again?"

I swallow and fist my hands on my knees. "No."

Yes.

His lopsided smile is slow to come and that's how I know he's a little drunk. That and his boozy, musky smell.

Zach looks away from me and toward the sky.

A few seconds pass in silence and I stare at him like a lovesick fool.

I am a fool, in any case. Because I was going to break the law just so I could talk to him. The guy who's made me cry countless times. The guy who's repeatedly insulted me, hurt me and tormented me.

My bully.

"What are you doing?" I ask.

"Watching the stars."

I look at the cottages again. They're still dark, without a hint of movement. "Why are you watching them from practically under my window?"

He shrugs again.

Now that I'm close to him, I don't know what to do. I don't want to go away but I don't know how to stay, either.

"Watch them from your room up in tower two, okay? Get up."

Finally, he focuses on me, his eyes both shadowed and bright from the moonlight. Which kind of looks buttery and yellow when it touches his skin.

"Do I look like I can get up?"

He goes back to staring at the sky. His breaths are unhurried, lazy almost, like he's soaking up the night one puff of air at a time.

Even sprawled like this, he looks powerful. As if he's the only guy in this whole wide world. The rest of us are inconsequential.

Or maybe it's not power. It's the loneliness.

Has he always been lonely? I can't remember. My hatred for him was so strong that I never paid attention to anything below the surface.

Sighing, I get up and offer him my hand. "Come on. Let's get you away from here."

Zach carefully observes my hand for at least ten seconds before taking it in sluggish movements. Our hands clasp, mine clammy with all the nervous sweat and his hot and dry.

And scratchy.

Swallowing, I tighten my fingers around his and pull him with all my strength. He doesn't even budge. He lies there, staring up at me, as if he couldn't care less about the whole thing.

Staring back at him, I pull again.

Not even a twitch.

But then, I feel him curling his fingers around mine tightly. And before I can even gasp, he yanks me down.

My breath is knocked out as soon as I make contact with his hard body.

"What the..." I squeak in shock.

Zach grunts, his head bumping against the ground. "Fuck, you're heavy, Blue."

I try to scramble off. "Jerk."

It only makes him laugh and tighten his hold around me. "Relax. I could carry you in my sleep with one hand."

I stiffen over him. "Are you kidding?"

A small smile is still playing on his lips as he shakes his head once. "Cross my heart."

Then, he goes and does it.

He makes a little cross on the left side of his chest with his long finger, and I feel it on *my* chest. The rough pad of his finger dragging lines like I'm making a promise too. Only I don't know what I'm promising.

"And hope to die?" I breathe out.

One slow nod. "Yeah."

His whispers are deadly. They are.

And so are his eyes.

I'm finding out that I don't care though. I'm relieved they're on me after such a long time.

"You never look at me anymore," I blurt out.

"Because it hurts."

His words make me flinch, even though there wasn't any meanness in them. They held a kind of emotion I've never gotten from him before.

It resembles a weird mixture of torture and desperation.

It makes me breathless and shivery for some reason. A little sad for him, too.

"Why does it hurt?" I ask.

His arms wind around my waist and his legs go on either side of me, sort of cradling me into his body. My knees are digging into the grass and so are my elbows but that barely registers, seeing how I'm flung over him.

"Because you look at me like…"

"Like what?"

"Like you don't hate me anymore."

My heart's banging in my chest. He must feel it. He must feel my heart knocking on his chest through mine.

"I do," I'm compelled to whisper.

And for some reason, I don't want to even *think* about how I'm lying right now.

"Good."

His raspy voice makes the butterflies take flight in my stomach. There are so many of them and they are so wild that if they want, they could fly me away with them.

"You're going to die soon, you know," I whisper lamely.

Slowly, amusement comes to line his features. "Am I?"

"Yes," I explain. "Cross my heart and hope to die? You're dying. Because you lied."

"Lied about what?"

I don't know why I'm going back to his comment but I am. Maybe because I need a reminder of how things have been between us, for years.

How I shouldn't want this.

"I'm not an idiot. I know I'm heavy. I have a pretty good memory of all the things your minions called me back in school. All the times they made fun of my thighs and my waist and my chest. I remember all of that."

"I remember that too."

"Of course, *you* never said anything. You just watched. You let them say and do all those horrible things to me."

"I never stopped them," he whispers, his palms splaying open on the small of my back, that flash of an expression flickering through his features again. The one that I saw when he told me to not be like him.

His low words paired with that expression start up an ache in my belly. It's not a gentle ache either. Nothing Zach causes in me, in my body, is ever gentle.

I shake my head. "No, you didn't."

But then, something occurs to me. Or more like, hits me in the chest, almost making me gasp.

"I wanted you to," I say quickly. "I-I wanted you to stop them. That's why I…"

It's my turn to trail off because I don't even know how to say it. How to say the words that I'm about to say.

"That's why you what?"

"That's why I'd always…" I pause to prepare myself. "I always looked at you. Whenever they said or did mean things to me, I'd always stare at you."

Why would I look at him when I knew and when he proved over and over that he wouldn't help me, that he wouldn't stop them? Why would my eyes find him in my most miserable moments?

"It's stupid, isn't it? Me looking at you and expecting you to help me? When I knew you were behind all the pranks in the first place."

That expression on his face flickers again and for the life of me, I can't figure out what it is.

"Stupid, yeah," he says with a clenched jaw.

Weirdly, I want to touch that jaw and see how it feels.

"But that isn't true now, is it? You, uh, defended me that night. You sent Ashley away," I breathe out.

His features tighten. Those hands on the small of my back tighten too and I know – I just *know* – that he wouldn't admit to it.

He wouldn't admit to defending me or coming to my rescue.

"Did you find someone else?" I jump topics and ask.

He frowns. "Find someone else where?"

"In New York?" His frown deepens and I explain, "You shouldn't have blurted out your secret to a room full of maids if you didn't want it to travel everywhere. Besides, I already knew you weren't at Oxford. Such a stupid lie. Like you'd ever go to Oxford. To study, no less."

Something about that melts his body and makes him smile. His palms creep up my back. He pulls back my hood, freeing my hair, and his fingers curl around the strands, playing with them. The gesture is so cozy that something squeezes in my chest.

"So? Did you find someone else in New York?"

"To do what?"

I almost rip out the grass in embarrassment but somehow, it's imperative for me to know this. "To mess with? Like you messed with me?"

Maybe it's crazy but I have to know.

In reply, Zach's hand spreads over the line of my neck. Gently. Only he knows how to be tender with fingers as rough as his.

"No," he rasps as he sifts his other hand along the strands of my hair. "There's only one shade of blue unlucky enough to catch my eye."

I can't even stop the sigh that escapes my lips and I grow heavy. So heavy that my chest lowers itself of its own volition. Up until now, our upper bodies were kind of floating within touching distance. But my sigh makes me go flush with him.

My breasts smash against his chest.

Zach groans and it's so rough and needy. It's... erotic.

So erotic that I'm not even ashamed to shift and drag my breasts across his hard chest.

Turning his face to the side and staring at my hair, he asks, "So what shade is it? It's different than what it was back in school."

It is.

Three years ago, I had a gentler shade of blue. This one is louder, pops out more. Suits me more, too.

"Bad Boy Blue."

His fingers stop sifting and he glances at me. "No shit."

I shake my head. "No."

I changed colors just after he went away. I went to the store and as soon as I saw the label, I bought it.

"Fuck me," he mutters to himself. "Bad boy blue, huh? You're obsessed with me."

"In your dreams."

"What was the other one called?"

I narrow my eyes at him because I don't trust where this is going. "Voodoo Blue."

He laughs.

And the sound of it is unpracticed but so free and light that I have to bite my lip. I will *not* laugh or smile.

"Don't tell me you bought that after the whole emo shit went down."

So, yeah. In ninth grade, there was this rumor that went on strong for about a month or so that I was a devil worshiper. I was the only – as they say, 'emo' or 'goth' chick – at St. Patrick's.

Of course, his minions had fun with that.

I elbow his side hard and he jerks, grimacing. "Fine. I won't tell you. And neither will I tell you that I had a voodoo doll with your name on it. I used to stick pins in it."

His smile goes back to being lazy. "Oh yeah, you're definitely obsessed with me."

I elbow him again and jerk up from his body and he's loose enough to not be able to stop me. But apparently, he still goes after me.

Even drunk, his reflexes are better than my clumsy retreat and he winds his arm around my waist and rolls us on the ground, until he's hovering over me and his body is settled between my spread thighs.

"Told you I'd snatch you up and get you on your back," he muses, slurs actually, the syllables thick and bleeding together, and I shudder under him.

"What? We had a deal." I fist the grass. "I didn't throw myself on you. You *pulled me* down."

"Eh. Whatever."

Now that the positions are changed, it's like the spell has broken somehow. I remember where I am. I remember what I am. A maid, and he is for all intents and purposes, my boss.

I glance around. The cottages are still dark. Mrs. S's cottage is directly opposite to where we are lying on the ground, all entwined with each other. If she happened to look out the window, she'd see us.

"Zach, I'm serious. Let me go. What if someone sees us?"

"Everyone's sleeping."

"What if they wake up?"

"What then?"

I frown at him. "They'll see us. Mrs. S has very strict rules about that, okay?"

"What rules?"

"The staff can't... fraternize with the family or their guests."

Zach shifts in between my legs and settles his lower body over mine, his pelvis locking where the juncture of my thighs is. His hard stomach is pushing into my soft belly.

"And this looks like fraternizing?"

"Yes." I'm breathing hard. "I can't lose my job. I need this job. I *need* my house back."

He studies me. Studies my panted breaths, my flushed face. The sweat on my upper lip, my frown. I'm freaking out right now, I know.

If I lose my house, I'll lose everything.

But at the same time, I don't want this to end. Whatever this is.

It's so fucking confusing.

Over me, Zach moves. Somehow, he makes himself bigger, broader. He spreads his arms on either side of me and stretches his back. He shifts up my body and aligns his torso with mine.

"What are you doing?" I ask, fisting his shirt.

"Hiding you."

"What?"

He looks down at me with serious, intense eyes. "No one would be able to see who's under me. If they look, all they'll see is my back and nothing else. So you won't lose your job or your house."

I want to laugh at his asinine logic. He's drunk. Clearly.

But he's also so... sweet to do this for me. And that just makes me want to grab onto him and never let go.

It makes me want to hide under his body forever.

"Thank you," I whisper.

His eyes go down to my parted lips, and I do the same. I watch as he licks his own lips. God, they are so soft looking, so dusky and thick.

Without a thought, I stretch under him, rubbing our torsos together, and his eyes jerk up to mine.

"You're not, are you?" I ask.

"I'm not what?"

"A-a virgin, I mean."

He shoots me a scorching look at that and my back arches skyward. Toward him.

"What do you think?"

I guess that's his reply to my question.

"When?" I whisper, squeezing his sides with my thighs.

Zach sneaks a finger under my hoodie and touches the bare skin of my waist. He flicks it, like strumming my nerves, stirring them. "Fourteen."

He might as well be, the way my body's reacting. My nipples bead up, become bullets. Achy and itchy. "Who?"

"A tutor."

"What?"

"She was boring. I was bored. So I shut her up."

"What'd you do?"

He scoffs. "Again. What do you think?"

My thighs won't stop their rhythmic squeezing and my back won't go down. My pussy is aching, *aching*, hurting so badly. And I realize that his dick is right there, right against my clit and maybe, if I get to move a little, I can relieve some of this pressure.

"Kissed her?" I guess.

He shakes his head once.

Something about that and his finger on my waist that has escalated from strumming my skin to almost scratching and digging into my flesh, makes me undulate against him and realize what he's talking about.

I gasp at that realization and he smirks slightly.

His dick. That's what he meant, didn't he? He shut her up with his dick.

And I feel it pressed against me so tightly, that big, heated thing.

Before I can say anything to that, Zach lowers his chest onto me. My eyes flutter closed before opening and focusing on his.

"What's the blue in your eyes?" he asks, shutting up all my questions. His fingers curl up in my strands. "It's different than your hair."

My entire scalp tingles. "T-turquoise."

"Like the ocean."

"Yes."

"That was the first thing I saw. After I got out of here. The ocean," he tells me, sounding almost wistful. "Reminded me of your eyes. Reminded me I was free for the first time ever."

"Free from what?"

"From this place. From them."

Yeah, I wasn't paying attention before, back in school.

Zach was lonely. He was so, so lonely.

Just like I was. In that school.

I unfist my hand from around his t-shirt and slowly, carefully reach up. I sweep the strands of his hair aside and rake my nails down his scalp.

"How long were you down there, in the hole?" I ask.

"All night."

Horrified, my gaze flies to his. I think Art was in there for an hour and I shake every time I think of those sixty minutes.

Right now, I'm frozen. Can't even breathe. Can't even think.

All I can do is look up at him in a dull sort of panic.

"B-but they came for you? Right? They pulled you out."

"Nora found me. But no, they never came."

They.

His parents. They never came.

"I was jealous of the kid, can you believe it?" He chuckles humorlessly. "I was jealous that everyone came for him. When..."

No one came for *him*.

"How could they not come?"

His lips stretch into a cold but also self-deprecating smile. "Because I've been expendable. An afterthought."

I feel a blast of heat in my chest. It takes me a second to realize that it's anger. On his behalf. It has a different flavor than the anger I've felt at him. It's a little more potent, more explosive than any other kind of anger.

How can he be an afterthought for anyone?

He's been my very first thought, my last thought, my *only* thought, for years. For years, all I've done is revolve around him.

Round and round and round.

"You're a lot of things, Zach, but you're not an afterthought. You can *never* be an afterthought," I tell him fiercely, honestly.

He's always been my nucleus of everything.

I look at him, his face, the sky at his back.

Yeah, he's a lot of things but he's not an afterthought.

A second later, he grips my wrist in an unflinching hold. With a clenched jaw and brutal eyes that bore into mine, he takes my hand off his face.

I'm confused as to what happened when he stands up. It was all so sudden that I crash back down to earth and my mind is reeling.

Zach takes a stumbling step away from me and I manage to sit up. "What are you doing?"

"Getting out of here," he says in a brusque tone, stumbling again.

I come to my feet and catch his arm to steady him. He shakes off my hold and begins walking again.

"Zach," I call out, following him. "What the fuck are you doing? You can't even walk. Let me help you."

"Leave me alone."

Two steps before he stumbles once more and I have to grab hold of him again.

"Jesus, what?" he snaps.

"Hey, I'm trying to help you. Do you want to fall to your death?"

"Are you saying you want to save me if that happens?"

We both stare at each other in mutiny. I have no clue how we got here. One second, he was okay, just lethargic, and now, he's as mean as he is when he's sober.

"I'm saying that I'm not selfish and cruel like you. You never helped me but I'm going to because I'm a nice person." He opens his mouth to argue, I'm sure, but I put my hand on his lips to stop him. "And the sooner I help you to your room, the sooner I can get back to sleep."

Three breaths.

That's how long he takes to clench his jaw and acquiesce.

I feel it all on my palm. His puffs of air, that hard clamp of his bones, his rough night-time stubble. And from my palm all of it goes down to my belly, making it tug and ache.

It takes us a few minutes to make our way back to the mansion's service entrance. I enter the code to get access.

The nightlights illuminate the empty hallways. I know I'm courting danger but I couldn't just leave him there.

Thank God for the sleeping staff.

Zach has enough presence of mind to grab the bannister with one hand whenever it's time to climb the stairs.

Finally, we're at Zach's door. As soon as we enter, he loses all energy and all but face-plants on the floor. Grunting, I push him toward his bed so if he wants to fall, the mattress will be there to break it. When he goes down and crash-lands on the bed, I breathe a sigh of relief and stretch my back.

I cover him with his blanket and then go ahead and take off his dusty, grass-stained boots, too.

As I set them by his bed, I notice his book is lying sprawled much like him, pages open and folded at the ends.

I pick it up and smooth them down. There are pieces of a broken pencil, just a few inches away from the book. I pick them up, as well, rolling them around in my palm.

So weird, these broken pieces.

Did Zach break it? Why would he? Why would anyone?

Just as I'm about to close the book and set aside the ruined pencil, I see something.

His name. On the front page.

It wasn't there the last time I saw the book. Meaning, he must have written it recently. Probably a few days ago.

But why does it look like it was written years ago and not by him but by someone much, much younger?

Actually, no.

I'm wrong. I'm so fucking wrong. Age has nothing to do with it.

It's written by someone who mixes up uppercase and lower. Someone who wanted to use cursive but a few letters later, changed their mind and started writing in print.

It's written by someone who has difficulty writing.

It's written by him.

The guy who's sleeping now, but who drunkenly stumbled out to my cottage, and watched the stars from under my window.

Chapter 16

The Dark Prince

I'm dreaming.

Usually, my dreams are of my bike and the endless road while I'm riding away from this hellhole.

But tonight, I smell sugar and I see blue. Both the color and her.

She's on top of me and her curly, cloud-like hair's all around us, making a curtain. And then, I roll over and trap her under my body. Hiding her from the world.

She can't get away now and neither can anyone see her.

She's safe. Her job's safe.

But then, she's laying me down on my bed and covering me up with my blanket, *caring* for me.

What the fuck?

I feel her taking my shoes off. I want to tell her to get away from me and leave me the fuck alone but I don't have the energy.

I never should've drunk this much. I don't even drink anymore. Maybe occasionally but nothing like I used to. I don't know what I was thinking.

Jesus.

If drinking makes me dream of her and these *nice, warm things*, then I'm quitting tomorrow.

Fuck.

I need a cigarette.

Why am I not smoking? Why am I suffering through headaches and intense cravings when I can take the easy way out?

Oh, right. Because of her.

She wants me to suffer. She wants me to not sleep, to go through withdrawals.

Of all the people on this planet, I *had* to be an asshole to one girl who wouldn't take my shit lying down. Who wouldn't leave me alone.

Fucking excellent, Zach.

Even now, her fingers are in my hair.

They're running through the strands, caressing my forehead all the way down to my jaw. Everything pulses on my face, My jaw, my cheeks, my teeth, even.

"I can't believe I'm saying this but... I'm sorry," she says. "I mean, I *think* I'm sorry, Zach."

Everything goes black before I can ask her what she is sorry for.

Chapter 17

I know how it all started.

The years of misery and hate.

Or at least, I think I know. I have a theory. And if it's right, then everything I've believed in my entire life will turn out to be a lie.

Okay so, that might be a little too dramatic. But still.

I'm freaking the fuck out.

It's been twenty-four hours since I saw the drunk version of Zach, followed by his book with his name on it and the broken pencil.

Ever since then, I can't stop the flood of memories.

Zachariah Benjamin Prince.

There's something so powerful about his name that things that I had buried inside of me are rushing back to the surface. All of them about St. Patrick's.

But for the first time, I'm not thinking about how Zach and his minions made my life miserable. I'm not thinking about their pranks. I'm thinking about my retaliations. The things I did. The things I said.

I'm thinking about our first meeting.

I spent the entire last night thinking about it, digging out memories, trying to remember everything that I can about the very first time we met.

By morning, one thing was clear in my head. So, so clear that I'm surprised how I ever forgot it in the first place.

His twelve-year-old handwriting and my ten-year-old reaction to it.

Now I remember that I saw it.

We were supposed to do lines in detention and I caught a glimpse of the ones he did in his notebook. And because he was such a jerk to me, I taunted him about it. I got so mad that I thoughtlessly said the first thing that came to my mind at the time.

It's like ants crawling all over your page. It's gross. Your handwriting is the grossest thing I've ever seen.

I can hear my voice in my head and it sounds mean. It sounds hurtful.

The following day, after lunch, I found my notebooks torn up and destroyed in the school hallway. And then, smirking, he walked up to me and looked at me like he wanted to crush me under his school boots. As another one of my retaliations, I punched him in the face.

Over the years, when his gang called me names, I called them names. I called Zach an imbecile. An illiterate, aimless leech who'd forever suck on his father's bank account. I called him a burden to society, a waste of space.

When they hid my homework, I smiled at them and told them that they should at least thank God that they chose me to pick on. If they had chosen someone like Zach, they wouldn't even have any homework to hide. Because everyone knew that he hadn't turned in a single project since he started going to school.

Does he even know how to read? Highly doubtful. I bet he never learned.

And that's just one example.

For years, I've ridiculed Zach's intellect and his lack of focus in school. Both to his face and privately.

What if it all started with one little comment that I made? What if the years of vendetta and hatred could've been avoided if I hadn't said that one thing?

I'm not going to go all martyr and say it's all my fault. But I've always blamed Zach and maybe, just *maybe*, I'm not entirely blameless myself.

"Blue! Look!"

Art's voice brings me out of my thoughts. I'm at the kitchen island, prepping dinner, when he comes rushing in.

I'm so glad he's over what happened to him last week. These days if I'm watching him, he doesn't get to go anywhere further than my front yard. Where I was flung over Zach last night, to be specific.

"Look!" he repeats, spreading his arms wide, grinning.

Shaking all thoughts of last night, I round the island and lean against it. "Oh my God!" I exclaim. "Look at you, dude. Where did you get all this?"

He's wearing his usual jeans and a black Batman t-shirt, but he has a motorcycle jacket on and a pair of sunglasses. The sleeves of his jacket are adorned with little balls of flames and gosh, he looks like a badass.

"Zach gave 'em to me," he squeals.

His name makes me go still and look up to find him at the door. At the very threshold. He's wearing the same leather jacket but no sunglasses and no balls of flames. I guess he doesn't need them.

He's kind of on fire already, with his bronzed skin, rough stubble and intense gaze.

I can't take my eyes off Zach and I'm not even going to try. This is the first time I'm seeing him all day. He wasn't working out this morning, nor was he in the kitchen like he usually is, with Maggie doting over him. I assumed he was sleeping off his hangover.

Does he even remember that we met last night?

"He said I could wear it to school," Art says while I'm still looking at Zach.

"Oh yeah?"

"Yes! He says I'll look super cool in it. No one would mess with me."

Art makes a fist and growls and I throw out a broken laugh. I reach over and pat his cowlick. But when I speak, I'm looking at Zach. "Zach's right. No one would dare mess with you. You're gonna show everyone how badass you are."

I've always been expendable. An afterthought.

My eyes get watery when his words echo in my head. His eyes, however, get hard, unflinching and opaque.

Nothing in them suggests that he remembers what happened last night.

A second later, he breaks the stare and takes a step back from the threshold as if leaving.

"Wait," I call out.

He stops and throws me a glance.

"Are you leaving?"

"Looks like it."

"Don't." I rush to explain, "I mean, we're just going to have dinner. Art and I. Tina's not here. And then, we're going to just hang out until Doris comes back from her shift. So, uh, you could stay if you wanted to."

And fuck whoever sees him here. We're not doing anything wrong. It's just an innocent dinner.

His frown is more like thunder than the mere crease of muscles, but I'm not afraid of it. And neither is Art. He dashes over to Zach, grabs his hand and pulls him inside.

"Yes! It's gonna be fun. Blue's making pancakes. It's breakfast for dinner day."

"It is. To cure the Monday blues." I nod, staring at Zach.

"She makes the best pancakes ever," Art informs Zach as he brings him closer.

"It's true. I do. My dad taught me."

A somber expression passes over Zach's face at the mention of my dad. I can't believe I mentioned him so casually when I make sure to never talk about my parents. If I don't talk about them, then I don't miss them.

But I guess I can talk about them with Zach.

Step by step, he comes closer and my ability to think shrinks to only one thing: does he remember?

Does he remember last night? Does he remember what I said to him the very first time we met?

He stops a few feet away from me, still being held by Art, who's talking excitedly. I can see him hopping on his feet but I can't really tell what he's saying.

I grab the edge of the counter and breathe the fresh scent of blueberry pie wafting off Zach.

Zach's eyes drop to my lips. "I like 'em extra sweet."

I find myself nodding. "Yeah. Okay. I have syrup."

He looks up. "You do."

"Yes. All kinds of them. Chocolate and maple and strawberry. You can have whatever you want."

I realize I'm talking kind of fast and kind of breathily, like I can't get enough air just because he's sucking me dry with his eyes.

"Whatever I want, huh?"

Oh, and I also accidentally said the same exact thing as I did the night I snuck into his room.

My reply is different this time, though.

Against a pounding heart, I nod again. "Yeah. Whatever you want."

Zach roves his eyes over my features, probably trying to gauge my feelings, and I give him a small smile.

Before he can react to it, Art pulls him away.

After that, I get to work. I mix up the pancake batter, adding in chocolate chips to make them extra sweet. I'm not much of a cook but this is going to be the best damn meal Zach's ever tasted. I'll make sure of it.

I hear their chattering in the background. Mostly it's inconsequential, but then I hear Zach's low voice and I move closer to the edge of the kitchen so I can hear him clearly.

Art's sitting on the couch, his legs dangling, and Zach's kneeling on the floor before him.

"You know what bullies are?" Zach says. "They are cowards. They are afraid of everything. They are afraid of themselves. They are afraid of you."

"They are not afraid of me."

"You kidding? They are *terrified* of you. You probably haunt their dreams, buddy."

Art giggles. "No, I don't."

"Yes, you do." All traces of amusement go away from Zach's face as he continues, "That's why they pick on you, Art. Deep down they know that this is it. This is the best fucking time of their lives and when it's over, *they're* over. If they are tall, they know that's it. That's all they are ever gonna be and that's why they pick on people shorter than them."

"When am I gonna get tall?" Art mumbles.

He chuckles. "You'll get tall. You'll get taller. That's the thing about the bullied, Art. The bullied, they know they'll change. They know things will get better for them. Your bullies know it too. They're terrified of you because they know your time is coming. One day you're gonna be taller than them and you won't even need this." Zach wraps his big hand around Art's fist. "You won't need your fists, your jacket, nothing. And you know what else?"

"What?"

"When you're taller, they won't mean anything to you. They'll mean nothing. Less than nothing. You won't even remember them."

"Are you sure?"

"Yeah. For bullies, their whole life is about you. Their whole life revolves around you, about putting you down. That's how they feel better about themselves. But for you, they don't even exist. They don't even matter. You're gonna forget them and move on, but they'll never forget you. That's your power."

"You mean, like my superpower?"

"Fuck yeah, your superpower."

Art giggles again. "You're not supposed to say that." Then, he leans over to Zach. "Blue doesn't like bad words."

"She doesn't, huh?"

"Nope. One time, Tina said the F word at dinner and Blue freaked out. She thinks I'm a kid and I'm not supposed to be around bad stuff."

Zach throws a lopsided smile. "Yeah? Well, she does freak out easily, doesn't she?"

Art nods his head enthusiastically. "But she doesn't freak out on me. She told me once that I was her favorite person ever."

"No shit."

"Yeah. I think I'm gonna ask her to marry me."

So far, I've been super quiet. Super-duper quiet. Even though there's this weight pressing down on my chest. My tears are clogging my nose, my throat. They are clogging my very breath.

But I've managed to stay undetected.

At Art's words though, I snort in pleasure and Zach looks up.

His eyes are liquidy, not like mine though. Mine must be a mess right now. Red and swollen, probably. His are as dark as ever but with undercurrents of some pretty intense emotions.

He's always been the bully and I've been the bullied.

But maybe I'm a little bit of a bully too.

Don't be like me.

No matter what I am, my life revolves around him. It always has.

"Well, good luck with that," Zach replies to Art's earlier cutesy statement that melted my heart. "Blue's pretty hard to catch."

Not if I don't run.

I wish I hadn't run that night – the night I went up to his room to confront him about the date. I wish I'd stayed and... kissed him. I wish I'd touched him some more.

I stare at his eyes, his dark hair, the cut of his face, his lips. The way he's kneeling down on the floor, being all tender with Art, and yet he looks so powerful, the tallest guy I've ever met.

The guy I might have hurt for years and years, without knowing.

"D-dinner will be ready in ten minutes," I say, clearing my throat.

When it's ready, I tell them to go wash up while I serve them each a huge stack of pancakes. With all the syrups that I could find in the fridge.

Dutifully, they both sit on the bar stools and dig in. Well, at least Art does, and when Zach simply picks up his fork without even glancing at the food, but keeping his attention on me, I turn away.

I start cleaning up, avoiding his gaze. I can't eat with them.

The truth is that this is the very first time I've done anything remotely nice for Zach. I've never even smiled at him. And every time I hear my own voice from years ago, it all gets too much.

Art's making yummy noises but Zach is silent. I'm not sure if he likes the food and I want him to. I want him to like it. Very, *very* badly.

After dinner, I rinse the dishes in the sink but before I can put them in the dishwasher, they get snatched away from my hand.

It's Zach. He has them in his grip and I go to protest but he slides them all in the rack, shuts the door and hits start, whirring the magic appliance to life.

"You didn't have to do that," I tell him.

He shrugs, his jaw clamped. "It's nothing."

"Um, and thanks for talking to Art," I begin. "About everything. I just... I've tried to teach him a few things myself. And Doris, she talked to the teachers about the bullying and it was okay for a while. But no one can watch these kids 24/7. So, I'm sure he appreciates that."

He traces my face with his gaze before stopping at my parted lips for a beat. Lifting his eyes, he says, "If the kid needs to learn, he should go right to the source, shouldn't he?"

I go to say something but Zach doesn't wait. He spins on his heels and walks away, only to come to a halt by the island.

Giving me his profile, he says, "You should eat something, too."

Again, he doesn't wait for my acknowledgement. He takes off but I'm not ready for him to leave yet so I follow him out of the kitchen.

But Art beats me and insists that Zach stay some more to watch a movie with us. God, I love that little guy.

I'm not even going to lie and say that I know what's happening on the screen. I don't. I'm more interested in how Art seems to lean toward Zach with every passing scene and how Zach throws his arm on the back of the couch as if to remind Art that he's there to catch him if Art ever tips over in his excitement.

Doris texts saying that she'll be a little later than usual and that she'd be grateful if I'd put Art to sleep. She'll come get him after work.

I agree. Art's stayed overnight in my room before so it's not an issue at all.

I'm tucking Art into bed when he says, "Can Zach read me the story tonight?"

I freeze.

It's like all of these feelings inside of me that were churning and expanding and ballooning, all of them come to a sudden halt, pressing against my chest in a painful way.

"Please?" Art says again, turning on his side and cupping his hands under his cheek. "It would be so much fun."

I'm so rattled that I don't know what to say. Or how to say it.

I can feel Zach, again, standing at the threshold. As if this is a different world from his and he's not allowed to enter.

I cover Art up with the blanket and decide to make an excuse. "Uh, you know, Art, Zach –"

"Not tonight, buddy." Zach's voice cuts me off.

"Why not?" Art's face is about to crumple and that pain in my chest intensifies.

For Zach.

"Because I gotta go."

"Oh." Then he beams sleepily at Zach. "Next time, maybe?"

"Yeah." Zach clears his throat. "Next time."

He's lying; I know that. I can feel it. In fact, I think he's been evading, lying, avoiding this thing for a very long time. Probably all his life.

A second later, I hear him leave. Third time this evening and all I can think is *not yet*. He can't leave yet.

"I'll be right back, okay?" I tell Art, who looks kinda surprised at Zach's abrupt departure.

I rush to the dresser, pick up the first book I see, and all but throw it at Art. "Read this until I come back."

I run out of the room and find Zach at the door. "Wait!"

Zach stops before slowly turning around and facing me.

It's a little scary to say the things I want to say to him when he looks like that. By that, I mean his usual self. Arrogant, cruel and like he wants to crush me with his bare hands.

"Oh!" I jump in my spot. "I've got something for you."

I run into the kitchen and with shaking hands, I open one of the drawers and retrieve what I want to give him. When I turn around, he's right there. In my personal space, trapping me between him and the counter.

This is the closest he's been to me tonight. But he's not close enough.

Not like he was last night.

I extend my arm toward him. "Here. I bought this for you."

He doesn't even look at what I'm offering him. "You bought something for me."

"Yes."

"When?"

"A few days ago."

"A few days ago."

"Yeah."

"What is it?"

I glance down at my hand. "You can look for yourself."

"I want you to tell me."

Keeping my head down, I set my offering on the counter and fold my hands in front of me. "Chewing tablets." I stare at my bare feet and his booted ones.

"Chewing tablets."

His boots are big, large. I wiggle my toes. They feel small and vulnerable against his boulder-sized shoes.

I feel small and vulnerable.

"Yeah. Tobacco chewing tablets. I stole your pack and so I kinda wanted to replace it. But then I remembered that I'm against smoking. So I bought these. It's supposed to help you with the cravings."

I'm still looking at the floor, fiddling with the hem of my loose, off-the-shoulder t-shirt, tucking the strands of my hair behind my ear.

"Are you saying you bought me these because you wanted to make my life easier?"

I nod. I heard that he was going through some pretty intense headaches and I wanted to... help him.

But that's not the reason I stopped him from leaving just now, obviously.

Okay, Cleo, ask the question. Ask him if he remembers. Stop wasting time.

I'm almost done gathering my courage to just come out with the question that's been bugging me since last night, when I feel his hands on my waist: bare waist, and I jerk my head up.

Then my feet leave the floor and he's sitting me up on the counter.

"You need to stop manhandling me," I pant but there's no heat in my words.

Zach keeps his hands where they are, under my shirt, on the naked skin of my waist, and wedges his hips between my spread thighs.

"Start talking," he growls and it goes straight to my lower tummy.

We mirror our position from yesterday. His hands on my waist, mine on his shoulders. My thighs around his hips and our chests punching each other with every breath. Only we were horizontal and he was drunk, and today we're both in full possession of our faculties.

"About what?"

His jaw ticks. "You smile at me. Then, you invite me to have dinner with you. I eat the food. It was fucking delicious so I eat some more. Meanwhile, you're blushing. You can't look at me. But every time I try to leave, you stop me. So I'm asking you why the fuck are you acting like a bad rash I can't get rid of?"

He liked the food.

I want to smile but I bite the inside of my cheek to stop. Instead, my fingers become claws at his neck. "That's incredibly mean and offensive."

"I *am* incredibly mean and offensive. Always have been."

"I don't –"

He digs his fingertips into my flesh. "Start talking, Blue."

"Do you, uh, remember the first time we met?"

My ankles are crossed at his back again, and I tighten them when he frowns. "What about it?"

My fingers begin to move and I curl the soft strands of his hair at his neck. His nostrils flare and my mouth dries out.

I clear my throat. "I don't... expect you to remember the whole thing, of course. It was a long time ago but, uh, we met on my first day at St. Patrick's. And we both were in detention. The teacher asked us to do lines, I think. I can't remember what we were supposed to write, though. Anyway, we were sitting like, two seats over or something because I could see your –"

"One."

"What?"

"One seat over."

"Oh."

"Yeah. And we were supposed to write *I'm sorry for being bad* about a hundred times. Fucking Mrs. Pennyweather."

Right.

It's very old-fashioned and outdated. But now I remember that the teacher, Mrs. Pennyweather, assigned to us was older than dirt. And she'd make us do lines every time we ended up with her.

I move my body even closer, my thighs and my ankles cinching up around him.

"What else do you remember?" I whisper.

Zach practically lifts me up and forward, until my breasts are plastered to his chest. "Everything."

I shudder against him. "You remember everything?"

"Why don't you just get to the point?"

The point.

Um, okay.

Drawing up all my courage, I look into his eyes. "I didn't remember it until last night and I..." I bite my lip before blurting out, "Zach, I've always wondered why you picked me of all the people at school. I thought that it was because I'm from the other side of town and I was new and because we didn't have anything in common and I didn't belong with you guys. And because people like you, you know, rich and rolling in money, think they can do whatever they want. But now I'm... I'm wondering something else."

I can't feel him breathing. His chest isn't moving and his lack of air is making me dizzy. As if even his organs are connected to mine. His lungs don't breathe so mine don't either.

"Zach?"

"What happened last night?" he asks, his grip increasing on my waist.

"Huh?"

"You said you didn't remember but now you do. What happened to make you remember?"

I can't possibly entwine myself around him any further, but I try as I answer him, "You don't remember, do you? About last night?"

"Tell me."

"I saw something."

"What?"

"I was going... I know you told me to stay away from you but I was going to your room anyway. Because I..." I swallow. "I just had to. But then, I saw you outside my window. You were drunk and you fell. I ran to you and, uh, we talked. And then, I helped you up to your room. When I was tucking you in, I saw your book."

His hold on me is punishing and I know later when I look in the mirror, I'll find the red prints of his hands. I also know I'll touch those fingerprints with my own.

"And?"

His words have a dare.

He's provoking me to say it.

"Why did you refuse to read the story, Zach?" I whisper, grasping his neck, touching his taut vein, crackling with electricity. "Why'd you lie about it?"

He remains silent. Not that I was expecting him to say anything. But his silence is answer enough.

Zach is dyslexic.

And from what I saw, he also suffers from dysgraphia. Meaning he has difficulty reading and writing. It's pretty common for people with dyslexia to struggle with their writing as well.

I know very little about it but my mom used to tutor a few kids who suffered from it. She'd say that suffering from a learning disability almost always comes with a certain type of stigma. A certain type of shame.

She'd say that such kids are always more sensitive than the rest. Even if they do work hard and learn how to read and write, they always have this little part in them that makes them doubt themselves. They might not always show it but every little failure cuts them deep.

If it's true, then I've cut Zach, slashed him, made him bleed as many times as he's done me. All without knowing.

"For years, I've been... I've been saying all those things to you. All those barbs and insulting comments and I had no idea," I say, my voice laden with guilt, my fingers caressing the dark stubble on his jaw. "I can't stop hearing my own voice. All the things that came out of my mouth. All the hate and I always thought you deserved it and it was your fault. But maybe, I'm not so pure and good as I thought I was. I was cruel to you too. And I've been wondering if all of this could've been avoided –"

My words cut off on a gasp when his thumbs hook into my belly button. The pressure of them is exactly what I sometimes feel for him.

It radiates down, to my lower abdomen, my core, my thighs and I'm all charged up. Just by his one touch.

"Nothing," he growls again, and I feel it down to my toes. "That happened between you and me. Could've been avoided. Not one thing. Because *I* picked you. And I picked you because you were different. You stood out. You stood out to me. And I couldn't stop watching you. Not for a single second. Your crazy pigtails that grew into your crazy blue hair. Your socks that grew into knee highs. Your dirty, smudged uniform, exactly like mine. The detentions you used to get for talking back to teachers. Your little outbursts, your little retaliations. And even though I never, *not ever*, came to your rescue, you still looked at me with your blue fucking eyes. There used to be this... this tiny ray of hope that Zach would probably do something. That Zach would be better this time. That he'd save you."

Shaking his head once, he flexes his grip on my waist. "It used to make me mad. It used to make me feel fucking... *protective* of you. Like I wanted to crush everything harmful around you. And it used to make me feel bad about myself when I wouldn't."

He scoffs. "You don't know the first thing about being cruel. Cruel is what I've done to you just because you made me want to change. Because you made me want to be better. And I didn't wanna be better. I didn't wanna change. I didn't wanna be a different person. A person who'd save someone. A person who'd stand up for what's right. I'm not that person. I refuse to be. I don't care about the world. I don't care about anybody. I don't care about you. So nothing that happened between you and me could've been avoided. I would've found you and hurt you and let you get hurt, anyway."

His words sink into my bones. Into my very marrow, and I'm burning with them. With his inflammable, incendiary tone.

With his pyrokinetic stare.

I'm burning to tell him that it's not true. He saved Art, didn't he?

"And you know something else?" he continues.

I shake my head, or at least, I think I do. I'm not very aware of anything but him in this moment. About the things he's saying.

"Cruel is what I'll do to you if you don't stop sticking your nose where it doesn't belong," he whispers, threateningly. "Do you *finally* understand?"

When I don't nod my head like he wants me to, the press of his thumbs increases and I swear, I *swear*, I feel it down to my core in a straight line. That pressure.

Maybe there's a nerve going from behind my navel down to my pussy and he's found it without even looking.

"Do. You. Understand?"

He articulates every single word like I can't hear him. I can. I'm just not comprehending anything.

Still, I jerk out a nod.

His reaction is to clench his jaw and let go of me. He steps back and away from my closed thighs and I've never, *ever*, in my life felt colder than I do right now.

It's like he took away all the warmth with him.

I slide down the counter and watch him leave.

He takes lunging steps to the door but stops with his hand on the knob. He gives me his profile like he can't be bothered to turn around and look at me, and I see his hard, angled jaw and his high cheekbones.

A prince through and through.

"And eat your fucking dinner."

chapter 18

I'm working a dinner party tonight.

It feels more like a tragedy, however.

It's an intimate affair, with only a handful of people: Mr. and Mrs. Prince; Mr. and Mrs. Howard, Ashley's parents; and of course, Zach. Ashley isn't here; she's away at college.

Thank God.

Now for the tragedy. I don't think anyone else notices this but I do. So they're all seated around an antique-looking dining table with an ornate filigree along the edges and curved-at-the-bottom legs.

That's not the tragedy. The tragedy is that Mr. and Mrs. Prince, along with Ashley's parents, are seated together, as if in a huddle. They look like a nice group, men dressed up in tuxes and women wearing designer dresses.

And Zach, he's seated all the way at the other end of the table.

It feels like there's a line between him and his family and their friends. Not to mention, he's the only one in this group with no fancy clothes on. He looks more like us, the staff, with his dark, threadbare t-shirt and spiky hair, than one of them.

I'm serving wine and trying to be invisible to them. So far it's been successful. They are all absorbed in themselves, except Zach.

Zach has been staring and *staring* at his dad's hand over his mom's. Yup, they are holding hands – Mr. Prince has his fingers wrapped around Mrs. Prince's wrist – and sipping their drinks from the free ones.

It's all very lovey-dovey, but for some reason, it doesn't feel like it. It feels like there's something wrong in the way Mr. Prince is dominating almost all of her hand.

"So, Zach, how long are you here for?" Mr. Howard asks.

This is the first time anyone has included him in the conversation. Mr. Prince's eyes snap to his son and something crackles in them. Something very close to annoyance.

Zach looks away from his parents' entwined hands and focuses on Mr. Howard.

"As long as it takes," he drawls and glances at his mom.

Lowering her lashes, Mrs. Prince dabs her lips with a napkin and clears her throat, smiling slightly. Mr. Prince's hold on her hand increases. I can see his knuckles turning white as I pour wine in his glass.

"Take to do what?" Mrs. Howard asks, taking a bite of her steak.

Zach toys with the stem of his wineglass. He hasn't taken one sip or even a bite of his food. All he's done is watch his parents with anger.

"To forget this place."

The scratch of a chair dragging on the floor sounds and it's Mr. Prince. He looks like he's going to stand up or say something, I don't know, but Zach's next words stop him.

"Because I miss them so much when I'm gone." He's looking at his dad. "England's a cold place to live after the heat of our town."

Ashley's parents laugh like it's the funniest joke ever. There's a chuckle from Mrs. Prince and a cold smile from Mr. Prince that matches so beautifully and spookily with Zach's.

"You must be very proud, Ben," Mr. Howard says to Mr. Prince.

"Yes, very proud."

Mr. Prince's voice is lashing. It almost cuts the air in two, if possible.

Zach's jaw clenches.

Mr. Howard carries on like there's nothing wrong. "We all remember how much of a troublemaker Zach was back in school. You definitely would've had some sleepless nights."

This is addressed to Mrs. Prince, who hasn't spoken a word in ages. She clears her throat and I see her wrist flexing under Mr. Prince's hold as I top up Mr. Howard's glass.

"Yes. But you know, kids. Besides, he's at Oxford now and so I think it turned out okay." She leans over to her husband and kisses him on the cheeks. "It was all Ben."

I round the table to go to Zach and top up his glass. Although, there's nothing to top up. He hasn't been drinking; I just needed to be close to him.

His knuckles around the stem of his wineglass are pretty much the same color as his father's. All leached out and white. Bloodless.

He doesn't even spare me a glance. I wish he would. Because my eyes would drip the same anger that his gaze holds. They're all talking around him like he doesn't even exist.

I hear Mrs. Howard's airy laughter. "Everyone's a troublemaker when they're at school, George. He was just being a boy."

Mr. Prince takes a sip of his wine. "Troublemaker or not, Zach is a Prince. And every Prince is born with a certain set of traits, a certain intelligence, a certain intellect. Going to Oxford is just a part of it. I went. My father went. My father's father went. And if Zach hadn't, then he wouldn't have been one of us."

Then, he smiles at the table in general as his eyes remain pinned on his son. "And that was just unacceptable to me. And to my wife." He turns to Mrs. Prince and kisses the back of her hand.

More chuckles go around the table.

Fuckers.

Every single one of them.

I can bet anything that Zach's father wasn't supportive of his dyslexia. Which is so unfair and archaic.

It's not Zach's fault that he has a learning disability. Not to mention, it's easily treatable. This is the twenty-first century, people.

Zach was right.

He's expendable. An afterthought. To his dad, at least.

Because according to his dad, he isn't a Prince. He's defective.

He's a reject.

Isn't that what bullies say to you? You're too fat. You're too short. You're a nerd. You're a loser. You eat too much. You eat too little.

It's not Zach. It's his dad. He's the bully.

I can almost see him bullying Zach into believing that he doesn't belong in this family. The family of perfectionists and architects who build estates and palace-like mansions and are town-founders in their spare time.

I can almost see Zach as a little boy trapped in a tower with a glass window, where he can see the stars but never touch them.

Because he was made to believe he couldn't.

---

fter dinner, I see him.

Zach's walking down the winding pathway that cuts directly across the cottages and along the side of the woods.

I'm in the kitchen, cleaning up. But at the sight of him, I wash my hands and say my goodbyes. And I run out after him.

Ever since he came back, almost every night I hear him take off on his bike. I don't know where he goes. Maybe he just rides, feels the wind in his face, but after what happened tonight, I don't want him to be alone.

My running ability is kind of hampered though, because I'm wearing two-inch-heeled Mary Janes instead of my best friends: my leather combat boots.

But I follow him, nonetheless.

I want to call out his name but something is preventing me. Probably it's the tightness in his posture. His fisted hands and the fact that I know he wouldn't like it if I called out his name and asked him to let me be with him so he's not alone.

In fact, I'm sure he would downright hate it if I stuck my nose in his business.

Cruel is what I'll do to you if you don't stop sticking your nose where it doesn't belong.

Whatever.

I'm sticking my nose in his business and he can't stop me.

But then, my next thought brings me to a halt. I realize what his destination is.

Damn it.

I should've thought of it sooner. He's going into the garage, the main garage at The Pleiades. The staff members also have a garage, right across from the main one, but it's smaller. I've been in there once and I have no inclination whatsoever to repeat that experience.

Zach punches in the code to his own garage and the stupid gate whirrs to life and pulls up.

Okay, so now is the time to call out his name. If I want to stop him, this is the moment. Because if he gets on his bike, all my good intentions will be for nothing.

But the moment is gone in a flash and I'm left standing there, feeling queasy.

Maybe I should go back. I can't follow him in my car. I'm not going to.

Nope.

I haven't dealt with my issues yet, okay? I haven't had the time. I've been busy and I can't... I just can't.

But if I don't do it then who will?

Definitely not his bullies of parents.

Before I can even think my plan through, I break into action. I run to the garage door, punch in my code that I remember from six months ago when they gave it to me.

The smell of gas and leather seats has invaded every inch of the space and if I paid attention to it, I'd throw up.

So I don't.

I don't pay attention to anything but my little blue car, parked in between an SUV and a truck. My house keys are in my pocket and my car keys are attached with them. I've thought about throwing them away a million times but I always back out. I always think one day, when I have my house back, I'll deal with my fear.

Well, I guess today's that day.

I'm facing my fear. For Zach.

I beep the car open and slide into the seat. My thighs are clammy and so is my entire body and I feel like I'm glued to the leather and that I'll never be able to get out. The thought makes me so dizzy that I'm about to climb out when I hear the roar of his bike.

Fuck it.

I don't have the time to be queasy. I shut the door and start the car. It occurs to me later that there was a chance that it might not have.

I pull out and get the automatic garage door going and peel out after him.

Everything feels claustrophobic and yet familiar at the same time. So familiar that I feel like I was driving just yesterday instead of being on a hiatus for about a year.

I catch up to him just as he turns at the bend of the road and merges with the highway. It's been ages since I took this road. It runs parallel to our town and I've had nights where I'd just coast along it with all the windows down.

Some nights, I'd find Zach riding along too. I always made it a point to stay out of his sight but I remember feeling jealous of all the wind on his face, all that freedom of being out in the open. The thrill of it. It felt like flying.

Soon we're leaving the highway and taking the exit into a neighboring town. I think we've been driving for about thirty minutes when we come to an area that's more or less deserted, with several warehouses and chain-link fences.

It's kind of spooky but we don't stop here. We keep going and going, until the buildings fall away and the trees crop up. We go through the woods and come to a clearing.

A big, wide clearing full of lights and music and people.

God, there are so many people and cars and bikes and trucks. All of them are parked haphazardly, with no system at all.

I stop the car at the edge of the field and take in the scene before me.

The people are shouting and dancing and writhing. But mostly, they are gathered around something deep but huge.

A hole in the ground.

Only this isn't a hole, it's more like a canyon and Jesus Fucking Christ, a bike is racing toward it right now.

I grip the wheel tightly as I hear the roar of that unknown bike, louder than the ruckus of the people. It's hurtling right toward it, gaining speed until the ground is no more, and then it arcs over the gap. I swear for a second no one speaks, no one makes a sound and it's all dead-silent.

Oh my God, he's going to die.

But the bike somehow manages to lunge across and stomp back onto the ground. But I guess it's not a smooth landing because the guy slips and loses control of the death machine he's been sitting on.

He gets thrown off and the bike skids away from him.

I know I should be more concerned about the guy who was riding it. But he has a circle of people gathered around him and I have a bigger problem.

A bigger, badder problem. Namely, Zach.

While I watched that unknown biker trying to kill himself, I completely lost track of him. Every cell in my body is telling me that Zach's going to do it. He's going to jump across the hole in the ground.

I would've laughed if I could at the irony of it all. He fell into a hole when he was a kid, so now he spends his nights lunging over one. With his fucking bike.

I leave my car where it is and stumble out. I don't even have the time to shut the door before I go straight down. I fall on my knees, busting them over the dry hot gravel. The heels of my palms skid and the skin scrapes.

"Oh fuck!"

They're bleeding slightly and I feel so weak. I don't think I have the strength to even sit, let alone get up.

But I have to.

I've come this far. I can't turn back now.

I'm going to kill him after I save him. He better watch out.

Somehow, I drag myself up and shut the door of my car. I take a few deep breaths that do very little to settle my stomach, but at least I can walk.

I cross to where the people are gathered, all the while looking for Zach. Most of them are drunk or high or are *getting* drunk or high. Half of them look like bikers and all of them look like criminals to me.

Hey, I'm not judging. I'm just extremely scared as to what this place is and how is it that it's not crawling with cops. None of this looks even remotely safe or even legal.

But then, I don't have the time to ponder over the legal repercussions because I hear another bike revving and cheers have definitely made me deaf this time.

It's not Zach, the guy on the bike, and I'm both relieved and disappointed. Where the fuck is he?

From this close, I can see the wheels of the bike churning the gravel. I can even smell the gas, the leather, the freaking sweat.

This biker does the same thing as the last one. Charges to the canyon, and when I think he's going to fall off and break his stupid neck, he launches into the air, makes the huge lunge and lands on the other side.

Again, the landing isn't smooth. In fact, it's worse than the other guy's. People gasp and holler when he curls into himself and grabs his foot while his bike careens away from him.

Okay, enough.

I have to find Zach.

And I do. As soon as I turn, I see him.

He's on his bike, revving it, and he's in the woods, straight across from where he needs to make the jump.

Under the moonlight, I can see that he's staring at the canyon with a single-minded focus. His black-as-night eyes are pinned to it as my eyes are pinned to him. To his frozen, rigid frame. He's straddling his bike, but somehow, I've never found him taller or broader than at this moment.

And then, he puts the helmet on before doing the turn-thingy with the handgrip, throttling the bike and hurtling toward the hole.

The drunken crowd parts and I try to get closer to him. I cut my way through the people, jostle them, bump into them to get close to the edge.

"Zach!" I call out his name but he simply passes me by, blowing up the strands of hair in my face.

I stand there panting as I watch him zooming close to the canyon, and when he arcs the bike in the air, I shove a fist in my mouth to stop screaming.

While he's in the air, he heaves his body up and basically stands on the footrest thingy and the girls in the crowd go wild.

Fucking show-off.

I can't stop myself from running to the edge of the big, wide hole that I think is going to kill him tonight.

Jesus Christ.

It's deep and it's black. I don't even know how far down it goes. Maybe to the center of the earth where all the fire is, where the quakes come from and shake the ground.

Every single person is watching him streak through the air like he's a shooting star. A black, dark star that's sucking off all my oxygen and making my heart beat and maybe even bleed.

All I know is that if he dies doing this stupid thing, I'll somehow resurrect him, kiss the fuck out of him – yes, I'm going to kiss him, bite him and eat him up, only to kill him myself.

I'm biting down on my fists when it's time for my dark star to come down. And come down he does.

On his downward arc, Zach sits back down on his bike and leans forward. Even though he's too far away for me to notice these things, I still feel the muscles in his shoulders and back, even his biceps bunching up.

There's an answering tightness in my muscles.

I want to scrunch my eyes closed but I can't. I have to see this. I have to see him land.

As soon as his wheels touch the ground, I bite my lip. Hard. Until I feel the blood oozing out.

The dust flies off every which way and as if in slow motion, I see the tires bouncing with the impact.

Any second now, he's going to fall. This is it.

My eyes fill with water and my head starts shaking.

But Zach's still on his bike, blasting through. I see him put his foot down and dig it along the dirt until he spins the bike around and comes to an abrupt halt.

The crowd erupts in cheers but I'm too dumbstruck to even move.

Too dumbstruck to even loosen my fist or my body. I'm still a tight mass of nervousness and dread.

Zach's seated on his bike like he's some sort of prince. A dark, *dark* prince with his black leather jacket and huge boots planted on the ground.

I come unglued when he parks his bike on the side. A few people surround him, thump him on the back, shake his hand. He takes his helmet off and rolls his neck, running his fingers through the strands, and I take off.

I run around the wide gap, my Mary Janes stumbling through the dirt.

"Zach!" I call out his name when I reach the other side and he's across from me, still standing among the group of people.

This time, he hears my voice and his eyes snap up to me.

He appears surprised, but slowly it leaches off and all that remains is his big frown and a pulsing on his jaw.

Oh please.

I'm mad at him too and I'm not going anywhere.

We stand there, staring at each other across the width of the hole he just jumped. The spotlight is glaring and I can see his sweat-soaked t-shirt. His jacket is gone – he probably took it off in the minute or so it took me to run across – and sweat is dripping down the side of his neck.

When Zach begins to move toward me, my breathing stutters. He's striding over, strong thighs bulging in his jeans and his long legs eating up the distance.

Behind him, I see another biker making the jump and people are cheering all around us. But it doesn't matter.

Not to me and definitely not to him.

He doesn't even bat an eyelash or give any indication that he knows we're in the middle of a crowd.

Zach needs to get to me.

I know it like I know that I wouldn't be anywhere else but here, in this moment. I'd drive that car all over again and bust my knees and scrape my palms.

I'd do it all over again just so I could be stared at with his black eyes, stalked by his equally black intentions.

When he reaches me, I crane my neck to look at his sharp and stunning face. He's breathing through his mouth, his chest swelling under the dust-covered t-shirt.

And the first thing out of my mouth is, "You idiot."

Chapter 19

Zach clamps his jaw at my words.

I want to call him all the rude names in the history of the world for scaring me like that but he shuts me up before I can even open my mouth.

He bends down and heaves me up in his arms.

Somehow, I knew he'd do that. I knew it. Manhandling me is his favorite pastime. Not that I'm mad about it.

I guess I need to touch him just as much.

So I hike up my thighs around his hips, wrap my hands around his neck and fist his damp hair.

I hug him tightly and he hugs me back.

And then I can't stop talking. Everything I'm feeling needs to come out. It's the adrenaline, I think.

"What were you thinking? What's wrong with you?" I grit out my words as I tuck my face in his neck and he walks toward something – I don't even care what or where.

"You're crazy, you know that? I can't believe you put yourself through this. I mean, I know people with dyslexia have other things they're wickedly good at; I've been reading up on the internet. But what the fuck? You could've died. You could've broken your neck. You could've paralyzed yourself. Did you see all those people? They couldn't make the landing. They couldn't…"

My breath hitches, thinking about all the botched-up attempts to land smoothly on the ground and I hold onto him tighter. I rub my lips on his pulse, tasting his skin, the salt of his sweat. It soothes me. It makes me believe that he's alive and he's taking me somewhere with him.

"Do you have any idea how scared I was? Any idea at all?" I continue, tugging on his hair, crossing my ankles at his back. "I was going out of my mind, watching you fly through the air. Newsflash, Zach: it's a bike. Not a fucking plane. And is this even legal? I don't think so. I don't. Fucking. Think so."

I bite his pulse slightly; his taste, his smell explodes on my tongue, and his hold on me goes even tighter.

"I can't believe this is where you go almost every night. What if you get caught? What if the cops come and arrest you? You wanna go to jail, Zach? Is that your plan? Is that –"

I stop talking when my back thumps against something – the door of a rusted, white truck – as Zach deposits me against it, and we come apart.

We're far away from the crowd and roars of flying bikes and all I can hear is our roughened breaths.

"What the fuck are you doing here?" he growls, leaning into me.

His hands go down to my butt and squeeze the flesh over my skirt, and I bite my already-torn lip at the pressure.

"I followed you."

"What?"

"After that dinner... I didn't want you to be alone. I didn't –"

Another squeeze of my ass. "Who said I wanted your company?"

God, he's rude.

And big and bad.

He hasn't changed. He's still the same as he was back at St. Patrick's.

I, however, have changed. I have changed the way I look at him. His rudeness doesn't bother me. It just... fits. Fits him like armor.

He probably needed it for all the wars he has fought, living in that glass tower.

I tug at his hair with equal pressure. "Me. *I* said you wanted my company so here I am."

His nostrils flare. "Is it going to take a restraining order for you to keep away from me?"

"Try me. I dare you."

Zach bows his body toward me even more. It's like the clouds are obstructing the moon and the world has gone dark.

It's okay.

I'm wrapped around darkness; I'm not afraid of it.

"Remember the line, Blue. You're very close to being on the side of stupid," he warns.

The strands of his hair graze my forehead and my nose bumps against his. Even that slightest touch is enough to make my back arch and dig my nails in the nape of his neck.

"You're stupid too," I whisper, thinking about the tattoo on his wrist. "Look what you're doing. Jumping across canyons. Even though, it was... a teeny, tiny bit magnificent."

It was.

Now that I'm not scared out of my mind, I can admit that he looked really, really sexy and invincible. A daredevil.

Zach's eyes rove over my face. "You *are* obsessed with me."

"No." I flinch, then, "Kinda."

He presses me into the truck with his body. His torso is pressing into my belly and his chest is flattening my heavy, throbbing breasts. His weight must be crushing me but all I can feel is a sense of freedom.

A sense of life.

So much life that I might die from it.

"Didn't your mom teach you to stay away from your bully?" he rasps.

It's so reminiscent of all the things he said to me when we first met that it takes me a second to gather my breath.

In that second, I imagine him when he was twelve, all angry and arrogant, and I was ten, all indignant and annoyed. I imagine what would've happened if he wasn't so screwed up and we hadn't fought that day.

Maybe we would've been friends. And maybe one day, we would've become something more.

Instead of a hate story, our story would've been one of love.

I look into his eyes as I cradle his hard cheek. His stubble is rough under my fingers and his skin is hot and that expression – the one I've been chasing after ever since I saw it when he cornered me in the hallway.

It's regret.

I can't believe it took me so long to figure it out. He's regretful. Probably of all the things he did to me and put me through.

"If you're my bully, then I'm the bullied, right?" I begin. "Well, I'm moving on. I have the power. So I'm choosing to forget. I don't remember the guy who bullied me. Who stood by and watched me get humiliated over and over. Who I hurled insults at. Instead of him, I remember the guy who came to my rescue when I cut my palm that first night at the party. I remember the guy who gave up cigarettes because I wanted him to suffer. And who ate that custard even though he knew what I was up to. I remember the guy who sent Ashley away and defended me. I remember the guy who pulled a five-year-old kid out of a hole and who made that kid feel better about his situation. Instead of my bully, I remember the guy who said he wanted to protect me and when he didn't, he hated himself a little more every day."

This is my catharsis.

Tina was right. I have to let go and I *am* letting go, of old anger, the past, the sense of injustice.

I just didn't know it would be like this, wrapped around the guy who hurt me.

But I guess it makes sense. He's been the center of my universe. Why wouldn't he be with me when I take this step?

"And to answer your question, my mom taught me to stay away from my bully but she also taught me to never stand by if someone was getting bullied."

Zach's breaths are harsh and halting and I can feel them down to my bones. I can feel his pain, his anger, his outrage and torture, *everything*.

Maybe this is what they call telepathy.

This, right here, is transcendence.

"I'm sorry but..." I squeeze his sides with my thighs. "Your family's fucked up. Like, really fucked up. Your dad?" I shake my head and fist his t-shirt. "He's a bully. Do you understand? You don't have to go to Oxford or whatever to be a Prince. It's all bullshit. Don't let him tell you that you don't belong. Don't let him make you believe all the crap about you, Zach. You don't deserve that. You —"

Zach pushes his hips into me and rubs up against my core, making me shut up.

"Yeah? What do I deserve?" he asks roughly, staring at me with a breath-stealing intensity.

God, he's so close.

And hard, and I'm wrapped around him so shamelessly.

But I won't let him distract me. He needs to know that his dad is an asshole. That he doesn't deserve to be treated like this because of something that's not his fault.

"I'm serious," I tell him.

"Me too." He rolls his hips against mine, making me shiver. "Tell me what I deserve, Blue."

"Not this. Nobody deserves to be treated like this."

Clenching his jaw, he uncurls my hand from his shirt and grasps my palm.

A sharp pain flares in the center of it, reminding me that I fell the moment I got out of the car. Zach's thumb is pressing on that wound. It's the same palm I'd cut the night he came back, my left one.

Frowning, he looks down. "What happened?"

"I fell. Because I was dizzy. When I got out of the... c-car."

The scrapes on my knees pulse as well. It's like the mention of the car is making all my injuries flare up.

Still holding onto my hand, he looks up. There are a few seconds of confusion on his face but then it clears off.

"You followed me in your car."

"Y-yes."

He shakes his head once. "I'm giving you a ride home."

He goes to move away from me but I tighten my legs around him. "No."

"What?"

"I don't want to go. Not yet. I want..."

"You want what?"

His eyes are intense. They glow in the dark. Like beacons. Except, a beacon is supposed to be safe, but his eyes come with a danger of drowning.

"I-I want you to kiss me."

Gosh, did I really say that?

The sharp inhale of his breath says yes. I did say that and he's surprised.

Well, why wouldn't he be? I ran away from him last time when he made me feel something.

But I guess I was lying then. To myself and to him.

I think I've wanted him to kiss me for years. Even when he was just my bully.

Maybe it's pathetic and I'm the girl in horror movies who dies right in the beginning because she just can't stop herself from checking out the basement.

So be it.

I'm that girl.

I'll go down in history as the girl who courts heartbreak and hence, deserves tragedy.

"I make you bleed," Zach murmurs in a low tone, rubbing his thumb over the seam of my lips. A tone laced with regret.

"Yeah."

His thumb traces the torn skin of my lip in the middle. "I make you cry too."

I blink and a tear slips out; I didn't even know it was hovering at the edge. "Yes."

Wiping off my tear, he whispers, "I won't stop. I don't know how."

He will stop. I'll *make* him stop.

This cycle of bullying that started with his dad. It ends with us.

I'll change our story.

If he's a false prince, then I'm his street Cinderella. I don't need glass slippers or a pretty gown to change our stars. I can do it in my quiet leather boots and my gray uniform.

"It's okay," I whisper.

His nostrils flare at my answer, as he watches me with a strange possession. It's dark and scary and thrilling. It makes me hold onto him even tighter.

But he easily shakes off my limbs and steps back.

Suddenly I'm adrift and my legs come down on the ground, my spine sliding along the metal door of the truck. They are shaky and numb, and my feet are bare. My Mary Janes fell from them a long time ago and I've completely forgotten how to stand on my own.

"Zach?"

And to my shock, he comes down on his knees – falls, almost – and grabs my hips to keep me steady. His face reaches up to the bottom of my breasts and he buries his nose in the valley. It doesn't matter if they are covered with clothes, Zach has a habit of destroying all the barriers between us.

Wrapping my hands around him, I whisper, "What are you doing?"

He lifts his head and stares into my eyes. I notice all the dirt smudges on my white shirt, how twisted up and stretched out my buttons are, straining against my heaving breasts.

Zach doesn't answer me. Not until he sits back on his haunches and lifts my right leg, draping it over his shoulder.

"Kissing you," he says simply.

"What?"

"You heard me," he says, dragging the hem of my skirt up.

I stop him and try to push it down. "Zach."

"What?" he bites out.

"Aren't you supposed to be closer to my lips, if you want to kiss me?"

It's a wonder I can balance myself on one leg because he's not letting go of the one he holds captive, and he isn't letting go of my skirt either so it's banded mid-thigh.

Slowly, Zach smirks. "I'm trying to be."

"You're what?"

"Trying to get close to your lips."

I fist his hair. "What... I... Whose truck is this?"

That's the only question I can come up with right now.

He shrugs, like he doesn't care. "The fuck I know."

I look around; it's all deserted even though there's a large crowd behind us. "What if someone comes?"

Zach chuckles.

His hands are much larger than mine and he uses that to his advantage and pushes the skirt up and up, exposing my panties.

"That's always your first concern, isn't it?"

"Well, yeah. I don't want anyone to see us, see me half naked."

He glances at my simple cotton boy shorts and fingers the seam of them, making me shudder. "You know, I thought I was dreaming the other night. When you were sprawled all over me. You wanted me to kiss you that night too, didn't you?"

"I was sprawled because you pulled me down, and yes. But." I exhale out a shaky breath. "I don't know how this is kissing."

He smiles, and then his thumb gets inside my panties and makes contact with the outer edge of my core, making me jerk.

I gasp out his name when the blunt pad of his thumb flicks it. So casually, like it's mundane, him touching the edge of my pussy.

"It's kissing because I'm gonna put my lips on your lips."

At this, his thumb gets further inside my panties and rubs along the center of my core. Finally, I get what he means and it makes me blush like I've absorbed all the heat from the air around us.

"I didn't mean that kind of kissing."

Zach's smile is still in place, a lopsided, horny smile. "Not my problem. This is how I kiss, Blue, when..." He trails off and leans in, like he just can't help himself. He can't help himself from taking a sniff of my covered core.

It makes him groan and my head falls back on another whimper.

"When what?" I manage to ask anyhow.

His lips are right there, right on my clit, separated by just cotton underwear. "When my dick's pissed off."

I look down, grabbing the side of his face. "Your dick?"

"Uh-huh." He nods, dragging his nose up and down my pussy.

His stubble feels even scratchier under my fingers right now. In fact, everything feels scratchier when it touches my body. His soft t-shirt, his velvet hair, the air around me.

"Why?" I breathe out, shifting restlessly on one foot.

He's still rubbing the center of my core with his thumb, sniffing my scent. "Because of you."

"Me?"

"Yeah. You're pissing off my cock, Blue. You've been pissing it off for days now. The way you move in that tight little uniform of yours. The way you run around, your blue braid flopping behind your back. You're inviting trouble, aren't you?"

"No."

"No? Your tits bounce when you walk, baby." I shudder at his casually thrown endearment, like he was waiting to say it all his life. "Did you know that?"

"I don't." I arch my hips, trying to get closer to his mouth. "I don't do it on purpose."

He chuckles and somehow, it hits me right in the clit. In my slippery, *slippery* clit.

God, I think I'm creaming my panties in front of him. I think he can see it. He can see how my pussy is salivating for him.

"You don't, huh?"

"No."

His head goes in and out of my vision as I blink and try to keep my eyes open against the onslaught of all the lust and hormones.

Zach drags his lips along my lower belly and the ache I always feel for him flares up. It punches me on the inside like it knows him. Knows the source of its existence is near, right there, talking to it, talking to my skin.

"It's just that they are so big, aren't they? Your tits. They're so fucking big that you can't help being a good little maid for me," he rasps, painting his crude words on my flesh.

"Y-yeah."

My tits are heaving now. The nipples feel like bullets. They need him. They need his hands and Zach brings out his thumb from the inside of my panties, reaches up with both hands and cups them.

Giving me his eyes, he kneads the flesh. "Are you being a good little maid for me right now?"

I nod, turned on out of my mind. I think I even orgasmed a little too, with the way my inner muscles are fluttering.

"You gonna soothe my pissed-off cock, baby?"

I nod again, this time with a moan.

"Yeah? You gonna let me French kiss your virgin pussy, even though anyone might walk up to us and see you riding my mouth?"

My breaths are turning into hiccups, into sobs, and my nails are raking down the side of his neck. "Yes."

He pins me with his gaze, his thick lashes giving it a mysterious look. "It's okay. I won't let them see anything. I'll hide you. I'll always hide you away from prying eyes. Anything worth seeing, Blue, is gonna be in my mouth."

I haven't even gotten over the current those words of his sent through my system when he pinches my nipples hard before letting my leg go. He makes quick work of my panties, dragging them down with needy, stabbing fingers and pocketing my underwear.

And then, there's nothing left to do but kiss.

It occurs to me then that I should be embarrassed by the fact that I haven't shaved down there in ages. Back when I was still a normal, albeit irresponsible and rebellious teenager, I used to shave it regularly. But after my parents' death, it never even occurred to me to do anything about the downstairs business.

Zach doesn't mind, though. If his groan is anything to go by, he likes it. He takes a quick whiff of my untamed curls before covering me with his mouth.

He was right; I was worrying for nothing. Anything worth seeing is going to be in his wicked, sucking mouth.

Draping my thigh over his shoulder, he gets in there. He parts my lips with one hand and licks the center of me, like he's licking the juicy part of a fruit.

"Zach," I moan, digging the toes of my other leg in the dirt.

The pebbles hurt me but his mouth is giving me enough pleasure to suffer walking through shards of glass.

He curses at my pussy and I feel his *fuck* in my chest, making my heart go haywire. Don't even talk about the butterflies. They are everywhere. Even in my calf that dangles from his wide shoulder, making it buzz.

I thought him licking up the juices of my core, circling my tight, untouched hole, would finish me off. I thought if he did that for like, five more seconds, I'd explode. My fingers would flex in his hair and I'd shout out my orgasm to the sky.

But then, I didn't know that his lips would close over my little clit at the top. And if the electricity that shoots through my body is any indication, she was horny for him. For the long sucks of his mouth, the scrape of his teeth and his grunts.

Jesus. His grunts.

They are taking up all the empty spaces of my soul. I'll hear them until the day I die. I'll sleep to them. I'll wake up to them. I'll imagine them day in and day out.

That and his rippling shoulders and his shuddering back.

I had my eyes closed up until now; don't know when I shut them. I open them and look down.

I look at the obscene picture we make. My fingers buried in his hair and his mouth buried in my cunt, moving this way or that, up and down. My thighs are open and his shoulders are jammed in between them. My skirt is somewhere around my waist and my blouse is all wrinkled and bent out of shape.

But that's not the most shocking thing.

The shocking thing is that Zach, the guy who's eating me out, is humping the air. His hips are moving and he's kneading his dick.

His pissed-off dick.

He's tugging it with one hand while his other hand holds my pussy open. It's all happening inside his pants. He hasn't even taken it out, and yet he's abusing it.

The taste of my pussy is making him abuse it.

"Z-Zach... I..."

I trail off when he grunts the loudest at the sound of his name on my lips and his hand moves. It trails away from my pussy and kneads my bare ass that was stuck to the heated metal and I hadn't even realized it.

I guess I haven't realized a lot of things.

Things like how, standing like this, one leg flung over him and the other slightly bent, opens up something else.

Something that I never – not in a million years – thought that someone would touch. That other hole, pleated and dark.

Zach kneads a globe of my ass before dragging his fingers down along the seam before grazing that uncharted part of me.

His fingers there and his mouth on my clit, making my vibrating channel soppy, make me come.

My hips jut off the car but Zach keeps me balanced with his body and his mouth that's still sucking on my clit while lapping up all the juices from my core. His fingers are still buried in my seam, pressing against my dark hole that won't stop clenching.

"God..."

I moan and claw at his neck and chant out his name over and over. My entire body clenching and releasing until there's nothing left.

In the background, I'm aware that he's shuddering too. That Zach's moving, shifting, and his grunts crescendo to a long, masculine moan.

It makes me want to smile.

I wish I *could* smile though. But all my energy is gone. I'm half slumped over him and half leaned against the truck, and I want to crumple to the ground.

Then I feel arms around my waist and I open my eyes. Zach's eyes are lazy and his lips and jaw are covered with me.

I hang from his arms, limp and sated. "I think I'm dead."

He reaches up with his other hand and wipes me off his lips. "Yeah? Then how are you still talking?"

I chuckle drowsily. "You killed me."

Amusement crinkles the corners of his eyes. "Uh-huh."

"You came too, didn't you?"

At this, he looks away from me. He straightens my clothes with no help from me whatsoever. I just keep staring at his face, his beautiful sharp face.

"What? Are you embarrassed that you came? It's okay. I came too. Like a fucking train."

When he's done he lifts his eyes to me. "I know. You flooded my mouth."

I bite my lip, smiling like a lunatic.

"You always get drunk after an orgasm?"

I wind my arms around his neck, letting him take all my weight, and reach up to kiss his jaw. "Maybe." My eyes go wide. "Oooh! I have an idea."

"Why don't you try keeping it to yourself for once?"

I tug at his hair. "How about you give me another orgasm and we can find out."

Chuckling slightly, he tucks my flyaway strands behind my ear. "Right now, we're getting you home. I'll get someone to drive your car back."

"Thank you," I whisper.

Without acknowledging my thanks, Zach bends down and heaves me up in his arms for the second time tonight. Although, this one's bridal style.

"Oh, you don't have to carry me."

He's silent as he begins walking.

I nuzzle against his collar bone. "I'm heavy."

"If you say that one more time, I'll drop you right here and leave. You can find your own way back home."

I don't know why but I can't stop my smiles tonight. Maybe orgasms do make me drunk. Or maybe it's orgasms given by him.

"You wouldn't," I mumble.

Growling, he squeezes his arms, thereby squeezing me to his chest. I snuggle against him as we walk through the still charged-up and noisy crowd. Zach stops by a few people and tells someone to drive my car back.

Then he walks to his bike and sits me down on it. When I touch the heated metal with my bare feet, I realize I left my Mary Janes somewhere back by the truck.

Eh, it doesn't matter. I have my prince, I don't need shoes.

Zach fits his helmet over my head and straps it closed, getting in front of me. "Hold –"

"I know."

I wind my arms around his waist and plaster my cheek over his back, holding on to him.

"This is stage five clinginess, you know that, right?"

Closing my eyes, I reply, "Whatever. You like it."

I feel his short burst of laughter as he kickstarts his bike, puts his hand on my arms and gets me to tighten my grip around him. The bike comes to life beneath me, vibrating against my sated core.

As we take off into the night and I breathe in the air of freedom, I decide that no matter what he thinks or says, I'm saving him.

I'm going to save him from his glass tower and I'm going to save him from all the cruel people in his life.

And while I'm saving him, I'm also going to kiss him.

On his mouth.

chaqter 20

The Dark Prince

I was six when they diagnosed me.

It started with ADHD that led them to figuring out that I had dyslexia.

My dad wasn't happy, but I guess he accepted it. He thought extra lessons, special tuition would make me good as new in no time.

But by the age of seven, they found out that I had dysgraphia too.

That pissed him off, I think.

But I can't be sure.

All I remember was me working hard and my dad not being happy about it.

I remember him finding faults. Tearing up the pages of my book. Every night he'd come to my room and demand that I read to him. When I struggled to spell out words, he'd leave frustrated. He'd tell everyone to not let me go outside or have any play time.

He'd fire tutors left and right when he thought they weren't doing their jobs.

Then I made them that fucking card. And that was when I realized that my dad, all his anger and aggression, was because he was dyslexic too.

"It didn't take me that long to learn how to write."

That's what he said to my mother that night.

I asked Nora about it and she told me.

So my dad, Benjamin fucking Prince, was dyslexic himself. Maybe all his frustration was due to the fact that his son was imperfect like him. Maybe I reminded him of his childhood days. Maybe he hated me because I was too much like him.

Talk about a fucked psychology. I'm pretty sure a shrink would love to figure him and his self-image out.

I quit figuring him out a long time ago.

All I care about is making him as unhappy, as miserable as he made me all my life. If that means never learning to read and write like a normal fucking person or unlearning whatever I'd learned, then so be it.

Blue thinks I've been bullied into believing all the crap about myself. She couldn't be more wrong.

The thing is, I don't care what they made me believe.

All I care about is my revenge.

My hatred for the man who gave me life.

My bully.

Chapter 21

I'm in Zach's room.

It's nothing illegal. I'm just here to clean. Actually, Grace was supposed to do that, but I switched towers with her.

She smiled at me a little but other than that, she didn't say anything.

It's okay. She's good at keeping secrets. Not that anything secretive is going on here. I'm just doing my job.

Among other things.

The only kinda iffy thing is that the door was locked and even after knocking, he didn't open. But I got in anyway via a hairpin; I had it on good authority that he was home.

And he is.

He's in the bathroom, taking a shower, and I'm out here, making his bed.

Over the gentle hum of the water and trying *not* to imagine him naked, I straighten out his pillows, tuck his bedding the right way and pick up his strewn-about clothes. Even with that, I think his is the cleanest room I've *cleaned*.

His book is nowhere to be seen and I wonder what he did with it. I wonder if he still has it.

Then the shower's turned off and a shadow falls across the room – as crazy as that sounds – and I know he's out.

He stands at the threshold of the bathroom, a towel wrapped around his slim but muscular hips, and he's drying his wet, *extremely* wet, hair with another one.

His eyes are trained on me but he doesn't look surprised to see me. I might be losing my touch there.

I might also be losing my mind and all my senses because all I can do right now is stare at him. Stare at his gorgeous cut body.

I'm not one of those girls who go all crazy over a good physique. Nope. I mean, I enjoy it but I don't make it my wallpaper. But I'd make *him* my wallpaper and I wouldn't even be ashamed of it.

Take his neck, for example. It's something so innocent and mundane, but not on him. On him, neck takes on another meaning. Long, graceful, tendons rippling, veins standing taut.

There are drops sliding down and I'd lick all of them, snaking down his prominent, beautifully sculpted collarbones, his chest.

Oh God, one goes to his tight, dark nipple.

And the ridges of his abs. Six. I count like an idiot. He has a six pack and that V. Now I know why everyone's so crazy about the V.

I get it.

It's all about where that V leads to. It's about…

"My face is up here."

I snatch my gaze up, feeling flushed all over. "I know." I bat a wayward curl off my forehead. "Are you planning on putting on some clothes any time soon?"

With a dark sort of amusement, he looks me up and down, making my uniform feel tight, tighter across my chest. My *tits*. "Not particularly."

I swallow. "Do it. It's good for the environment."

He's setting the room on fire.

"Can't say I care about the environment very much." He smirks, giving my chest one last glance. "But I do care about how flushed you look. And the state of your nipples. They're trying to punch holes through your uniform."

With that, he gives his hair one last rub with the towel before dropping it on the floor and walking away.

"You asshole."

He goes to his dresser, his back rippling, and I swear I hear him smile.

"I take it you're here for something," he says as he fishes a pair of jeans out and then casually drops the towel from his waist.

I slap a hand over my mouth to stop the squeak.

His ass. Jesus Christ.

I'm not an expert but holy shit, I think that's how all asses should be. Tight and hard and firm and round and *oh my God*, I don't know how he got that part as bronzed as the rest of him but yup. It's bronzed and tempting and corded with muscles.

I watch him put his jeans on with an open mouth and a thundering heart that's on the verge of giving out.

As soon as he turns around though, I force it to close. Quickly, I look away from him too. Can't give him too much indication that I'm perving over his body. Though I do notice that he hasn't buttoned up his jeans. They're just hanging around his hips with... nothing.

I clear my throat. "Yes. I'm here..." I approach towel number one by the bathroom and pick it up. "To clean." Then, I make my way to where he's standing and kneel to pick up towel number two at his feet.

Our eyes clash, me on the floor and him hovering over me like the sky.

It messes with my breathing, so I get up and stand before him. "My job, remember? I take it seriously."

"Do you?"

"Yes."

His eyes are all intense and burning up as he murmurs, "A good little maid, huh?"

My thighs clench. They literally spasm at his low tone. The place between them throbs and pulses like a wound. A wound that needs his tongue and his teeth and his long rough sucks.

I lick my lips and clear my throat again. "That reminds me that I'm here for something else too."

Zach frowns and folds his arms, flexing his chest and biceps. "And that something else is?"

I take a deep breath and hug his damp towels to my stomach. "I don't want you to go." His frown intensifies and I explain, "To that place with all the bikes and the stupid gap in the ground."

"*You* don't want me to go."

I tighten my features into something stern, something that means business. "Yes. It's dangerous and it's illegal. I mean, you look sexy as hell. No question about that, but *I* don't want you to die or get arrested."

Zach cocks his head to the side and scratches his jaw. It's stubbled and rough-looking and I want to scratch it too, run my fingers through it.

"Correct me if I'm wrong. Weren't you just a maid a second ago? Who died and made you the boss?"

I ignore his harsh words. "I won't let you go."

"Excuse me?"

"I'll stop you from going."

His next breath is long as he slowly unfolds his arms and takes a step toward me. I know I need to be a little brave right now, what with him staring down at me like he wants to throttle me, and his muscles look up for the job, too.

But like a chicken, I take a step back.

"You'll stop me from going," he repeats.

I nod and watch his bare feet advancing on my leather boot-covered ones. It gives me a... thrill. I'm not afraid, exactly, or I'm not *only* afraid. I'm bursting at the seams with excitement and arousal.

"And you're gonna do that how?"

I look into his eyes and threaten him exactly like he did the other night when I broke into his room. "I'll call the cops on you."

His jaw ticks. I know it's the anger and it's also the memory of that night. "You'll call the cops on me."

"Yes." I lick my dried-out lips and watch a stray droplet shake off his messy, spiky hair and travel down the left side of his chest. Exactly where his heart lies. "I'll tell them that you're involved in something illegal. They'll throw you in jail and –"

"Tell me where we live," he murmurs, cutting me off.

"What?"

"Tell me the name of the town we live in, Blue."

We both come to a stop.

"P-Princetown."

Zach smiles coldly. "Yeah. The Princes own this town. The cops won't touch any of us. Not even me. Even if I'm a bad one, I'm still a Prince."

He's right.

The name of our town is Princetown. The town with the heat of hell, with holes in the ground, with lines, with the north side and the south side, with The Pleiades.

The place filled with bullies.

The birthplace of me and Zach.

I sigh and resume walking back. "Well, then, I'll fuck up your bike."

He resumes chasing me, as well. "You'll fuck up my bike."

"Yup. I'll cut off the brake thingy and scratch it with my hairpin. Actually, my keys. I think that'll be more effective. And, uh, I'll mess with the throttle or something."

There's a hint of a twitch on Zach's mouth and I get hit by the fact again that he's the most handsome guy I've ever seen.

Like, *ever*.

"Do you know anything about bikes?"

"No. But I can learn. YouTube has everything. That's where I learned how to pick a lock."

That twitch graduates into a lopsided smile. "Stage-five clinger."

"Call it whatever you want. You're not going there. *Ever*."

"Then how do you suggest I make money?"

That makes me stumble a little. Did he just say money?

"What?"

"Money, Blue. How do you suggest I make it if I don't do my job? Ever."

"This is your *job*?"

He shrugs. "Last night wasn't. But yeah, they pay me for this. So this is my job. You know, the thing responsible people do."

I swallow roughly at the reminder of what I said to him on his first night back.

For some reason, it never occurred to me. I've always seen him as this rich, bored guy who got everything handed to him.

But no. He's far from it.

"Was this your job in like, New York?"

"Yeah."

"But this is dangerous."

"I'm good at it."

There's no doubt about that. But even so, I'm scared for him. "How did you even learn to do that?"

"People taught me." When I frown at his vague answer, he elaborates, "There was this guy on the staff a few years ago. I got started on his bike. He taught me. He'd take me to the hole sometimes. He quit and went to New York. He hooked me up with people when I showed up at his door out of the blue."

In this moment, Zach seems so worldly to me. So experienced and daring and brave.

"I'm scared for you," I whisper when I have nothing else to say to him.

"You don't need to worry about me," he replies with a blank look.

But I am worried.

"Is that all?" he asks, curtly.

We've been dancing around each other for quite some time now and when my back hits the wall, I know it's over. This dance.

I need to come out with the other, the bigger reason for my visit.

Plastering my spine on the wall, I tilt up my neck. "And I want you to come to my cottage. Tomorrow."

"What?"

"Yeah. Tina won't be home; she's working the night shift and I'm not babysitting Art. So I'll be free."

"Free to do what?"

He's too close and his eyes are too scorching. Blazing. I want to look away but I can't rip our gazes apart. I can't be a coward and leave him alone when I ask this question. "Where's your book? The one you had. About the stars."

The tendons on his neck move in agitation. "I threw it away."

"Why?"

"Not into reading."

"Well, that's still not a reason to throw away a perfectly good book."

"It is for me."

I lick my lips and his eyes follow the gesture. "Well, tomorrow. At my cottage. We're going to read."

He frowns. "Excuse me?"

I don't think I've ever seen him this deadly and this angry before. And I've seen him angry plenty of times.

"Yes. Because, Zach, you promised a little boy that you'll read him a story. And I swear to God, you're going to read him one."

He leans down, his palms on the wall, caging me in. "Is that so?"

"Yes." I inject every scrap of courage in my tone. "Dyslexia is a learning disability. Meaning, it makes it difficult to read. Not impossible. Lots of people have it. And I realize that it's not convenient and I'll never be able to fully grasp the difficulties associated with it, but damn it, Zach. You're going to read. You should've been reading all along. I can't believe your parents never made the effort. It's just so ancient and archaic that I can't even –"

"They made the effort."

"What?"

"I had tutors. They taught me. Or tried to."

Okay. That's good, right? I mean, I thought he never received any help, judging by his handwriting. "And?"

"I didn't want to learn."

"What? Why not?"

I'm so exasperated and confused right now. Why wouldn't he want to learn?

"What is this? Twenty questions?"

Gah.

I'm so mad. Why does he have to make everything so difficult? I'm trying to show him that he can do it. That he can read and rise above whatever bullshit his dad has spewed on him and made him believe about himself.

But he *has* to put up a fight.

"Do you know Art has no parents?" I begin instead. "His parents died when he was two. In a car crash, like mine did. Maybe that's why I feel so connected to him. Not to mention, he's being bullied at school. My sweet guy has no friends except you and me. And his grandmother is getting on in age. On top of everything, he had an accident. Do you know how lonely he is? Do you? How can you not come through for him? How can you live with yourself, Zach? He's the cutest little guy with blond hair and green eyes and he worships you. Are you going to let him down?"

"Are you done with your sob story?"

I glare at him.

Then, with a long-suffering sigh, he asks, "What time do you want me there?"

"What?"

"I'm not going to repeat myself."

"Seven," I blurt out on a relieved breath.

"And what about if someone sees me going into your cottage? What'll happen to your little job?"

I bite my lip because holy shit, he's right. People might talk if they see him going in and out of my cottage. I mean, once was okay. Art was with us but if he continues to visit me, people will talk. And rumors are how these things start.

"Didn't think about that, did you?"

I shake my head guiltily.

Another sigh. "You've got a back door that leads out to the woods, yeah?"

"Yes."

"I'll be there."

That just makes me smile. That makes my whole body smile. Him taking care of me like that.

He goes to move away. "Now, get lost."

"Wait. One more thing."

"What?"

There's tension in his frame. His shoulders appear tight and his stomach looks like a hard slab of rock. A rock with ridges and all.

I've upset him. I've made him agitated.

But I want to smooth out his rough edges now.

Under his burning gaze, I drop the towels I've been clutching onto the bed by my side and step closer to him so I can touch him.

With my chest.

My breasts press into his ribs and a sigh of relief goes through me.

Even though the front of my uniform is kind of damp from holding on to the towels, the wetness of his chest still seeps into the fabric, beading my nipples. It's remnants of his shower and the heat of this town. Heat of us being together.

His pecs move with a long breath and I breathe with him.

My hands find purchase on the hard globes of his shoulders. "You didn't give me what I wanted last night."

I'm looking at his tense face; it has become dark with lust and his cheekbones jut out.

"You came. Like a fucking hurricane while your cunt was spasming on my mouth, trying to catch my tongue. You didn't want that?"

I blush and my lips part with a stuttered breath. I drag my breasts along his body as I go on my tiptoes, my eyes fluttering shut at the friction.

"I wanted you to kiss me," I say to his lips.

Perfect and thick, bisected in the middle with a cupid's bow. They are mine. I'm taking them today.

"And I did."

I glance up into his eyes, swimming with lust. "On my mouth."

"I don't kiss on the mouth."

"Why not?"

"Let me rephrase that: I don't kiss *you* on the mouth."

A week ago, this would've offended me. I would've retaliated with cutting words and maybe even a prank.

But now, all I can see is that Zach peeks out his tongue and traces his lower lip, as he watches mine. Like he's imagining kissing me but for some reason, he won't do it.

So my retaliation's going to be a little different.

Namely, this:

I push to my tippy-toes, my nipples scraping against his chest and get close to his lips. "Tough luck, Zach. Because right now, I want to kiss *you* on the mouth."

And then, I do it.

I kiss him.

I pucker my lips and start with a dry one. One smack dab in the middle of his mouth. The second one on one corner and the third on the other.

Slowly, my hands creep up to his wet hair and I fist the strands as I keep kissing him, giving him little pecks.

Just when I gather enough courage to taste his skin with my tongue, his hands grip the uniform at my waist. He hauls me toward him, clashing our fronts together, and forces my mouth open with his.

He isn't like me. He isn't shy. He doesn't start me off with dry pecks.

Nope. He simply invades my mouth with his tongue like it's his God-given right. Like my mouth was made for him. For his tongue to invade and abuse and make love to. And my lower lip was made for him to suck on.

But a second later, he fists my braid and wrenches our mouths apart. And all I can do is clutch at his neck, rub up against him to get back to me.

"You fucked up, Blue," he growls over my mouth.

"What?" I pant.

"Now, you're fucked, baby." His scans my face. He looks like he's memorizing it. He's committing me to memory.

"Why?"

His eyes, black and threatening and so beautiful, come up to mine. "Do you have any idea how long, how *fucking* long I've wanted to kiss that mouth?"

I shake my head.

"A thousand years." He studies my parted, blue-painted lips. "Or at least, it feels like it. I've wanted to kiss it ever since you first put on your lipstick in eighth grade."

Oh, I remember that.

I got my highlights too. Tiny strips of navy blue in my dark hair with a sparkly dark blue lipstick.

"I knew the moment I tasted your lips I'd become a fiend for them. And now you've fucked up," he keeps growling, jacking up my heartbeats. "Because you're mine now, Blue. *Mine*. And you've got no idea what I'm gonna do to you."

His words are a dose of electricity. A shot of vodka. And maybe even a hit of cocaine. Everything in my body buzzes and vibrates and clenches.

Even my soul.

"I've wanted to kiss you too," I admit. "Maybe just as long as you have."

Shuddering, he grabs my ass and drags me up his body. I wrap my thighs around his waist as he all but falls on the bed with me in his arms.

Suddenly, I'm inundated with him. His warm, hard body over me, his smell on the sheets even though I just put on fresh ones, and his mouth on mine.

He's kissing me over and over.

Actually, it's all one long kiss where he sucks on my mouth as a whole before forcing it open with his tongue. He sweeps it over my teeth, tangles it with my tongue and gorges on my taste.

It's exactly the way he smelled me that night.

He was eating my smell, and now he's eating up my mouth. He's eating up our first kiss.

Something breaks loose in my chest at the thought.

This is our first kiss.

I've known him nine years and this is the first time I've known his mouth. It's a tragedy. It's a travesty. It's outrageous.

We should've been kissing the very first moment we met. We should've been kissing for years, for ages, for eons.

We were made for kissing, he and I.

His hands are roaming all over my body, dragging the fabric of my uniform up and up, until my thighs are all bare and open and he can knead the flesh.

My own hands can't stop touching him, feeling his shoulders, his back, grabbing his ass. The blunt heels of my boots rub against his jeans, slide along the bed as I kiss him back.

I do what he tells me with his mouth to do. I open. I let him in. I let him play with my tongue. I let him taste me.

And in all of that, I'm tasting him. His blueberry pie taste mixed in with something that's only and irrevocably him. I'm sweeping and sucking and pulling at his mouth. And I'm moaning.

I'm moaning so, *so* hard. I can feel the vibrations running up and down my limbs. I can feel my moans wetting my channel. I can feel his dick too because it's hard and it's rubbing up against my core.

We're writhing on the bed, humping against each other, making noises in each other's mouths.

I feel like I could come like this. I could go off like a firework, even better than last night.

But Zach shifts my world again.

He wraps his arms around my waist and pulls me up. Our teeth clack as we change positions and our kiss gets broken.

I'm panting into his mouth as he spreads his thighs and maneuvers my body, making me straddle him.

My uniform is pooled around my waist, baring my blue panties. There's a dark spot there that makes me undulate against his erection.

His erection that's peeking out of the open fly of his jeans.

I can't look away from it, from the broad head of it, the purple color. The pissed-off color of his cock. Surrounded by dark, mysterious curls. I want to touch them, touch the head of his dick that has a drop of pre-cum oozing out of it.

"Show me your tits."

His rasped words force me to look away from his erection and at him.

He's breathing heavily, too. I guess he was doing his own watching. While I was ogling his cock, he was staring at my chest. A button has come undone, stretching the gray fabric obscenely over it.

Swallowing, I ask, "What're you going to do to me, now that I'm yours?"

Maybe I should've asked this *before* I stepped into his room and so brazenly kissed him. Yeah, that would've been the smart thing to do.

But that ship has sailed.

Zach thrusts my dress up some more, until my ass is bared, before grasping the cheeks in his hands and massaging them. He pulls them apart before pushing them together and every time he does that, my clit grinds against his dick.

"You afraid?" he asks in an abraded voice.

"No. Maybe a little."

He leans down and places a soft kiss on my lips, making my heart melt. "I'm gonna use you up."

"What?"

He nods, his nose rubbing up and down my own. "Yeah. Why shouldn't I? I hate this place. I hate every second of every day that I'm here. I deserve this. I deserve something good, don't I?"

I cup his jaw and say with everything inside of me, "You do."

"I've decided that you're it. You're what I deserve."

"Me?"

"Uh-huh." He kisses me again, softly, in such contrast to all the harsh, possessive things he's saying. "So I'm going to use you up as long as I'm here. I'm going to kiss you, bite you, suck on your tits, play with your cunt. As much as I want. *Whenever I want. You're my prize, Blue. You're my prize for all the fucking suffering.*"

Prize.

I'm his prize.

The rush of his words feels sweeter than the orgasm last night. *So much sweeter.*

I've never been a prize for anyone. No one's ever wanted me as a reward, as a trophy for all the suffering, for all the misery.

Yes, I'll be his prize.

I rub up against him and bare my neck so he can kiss me there. He does.

"What do I do? As your prize," I whisper.

He puffs out a breath on my collarbone. As if in relief.

It sinks into my skin, his breath, making me moan.

"You show me your gorgeous fucking tits when I ask you to."

I swallow and work on my buttons, lust pricking every inch of my skin. My fingers shiver but Zach helps me. He covers them with his hand before undoing the buttons for me.

He groans lustfully when my breasts come into view, cupped by a simple blue cotton bra. "Jesus. I think this time you killed me."

I chuckle. "Then how are you still talking?"

Zach's bent over me, his abs flexing and curling, like in worship, rubbing his open mouth, his nose, his entire face in my cleavage. Making me feel... beautiful and pretty and not overly large and heavy.

I'm his prize.

"God," he groans again as he pulls down my bra and sucks on my nipple.

I jerk in his lap and clutch him to me. If this is what takes away his suffering, then I'll show him my tits every chance I get.

"You're gonna pull down your uniform every time I ask, aren't you?"

I rock against him again because he read my mind. "Yes."

Groaning, he gives a long, tight suck before letting go of my breast. "Fuck yeah, you will. You'll bare your tits for me. Every day. Multiple times a day. Whenever I'm hard up for it. You'll come to my room and make my bed. And then, I'll throw you down on it, tear your clothes off, get out your tits and suck on them. You'll writhe for me, won't you?"

I nod, almost whimpering.

"You will. I'll keep sucking on it and sucking on it and you'll make a mess on the bed. You'll cream my sheets. You'll leave a wet spot, yeah?"

"Yes. For you."

Anything for him.

Zach's hands have gotten rough on my ass, both desperate and reverent. I'm actively humping against him now. I can't help myself. I'm rocking against his dick. His pre-cum is sliding down, mixing in with my own cream.

We're both making a mess on each other.

"Yeah, you will." He can't stop kissing me and I can't stop kissing him back. "Sometimes, I'll get you on your knees, Blue. I'll put your ass up in the air and flip your skirt. I'll eat you out from behind and your tits will dangle like forbidden fruits."

"Zach..."

My eyes scrunch shut at all the things he's saying to me. All graphic, erotic, filthy things.

"Yeah, that one will be hard. I won't know where to go first. To your sweet pussy or your naughty tits. So I'll punish you then. For tempting me like that. For making me choose."

"H-how?"

He nips at my lower lip. "I'll play with your ass. You liked that, didn't you?"

I jerk out a nod, barely catching my breath. My body's so filled up with lust and his words that there's no space for air.

"Next time, I'll stick my finger in it. I'll lube it up real nice using your pussy juice. And when I'm kissing you, shoving my tongue down your throat, I'll finger your ass, Blue. I'll finger it until you come all over my bed. All over my sheets."

Our movements are frantic. I'm almost jumping up and down on him, making my tits bounce. Zach's eyes go from my lips to my eyes to my breasts.

Nothing, nothing at all, has ever made me feel so desirable.

"But then... I-I'll have to change your sheets."

Chuckling, he moves to my neck to lick up a drop of sweat. "You'll do it. I have faith in you. As soon as I'm done with you, you'll get up and make my bed again. You'll straighten out your dress, re-braid your hair and walk out of here and no one will know a thing, right?"

I'm so close. So fucking close and he won't stop talking and I don't know what to do but to keep moving against him and say yes.

"Yeah, you will. It's a shame, isn't it?"

"Why?"

"It's a shame no one will know what a good little maid you are. How dedicated to the job. How you serve me. How you take away my suffering. My pain. No one'll know that."

"It's okay."

"Nah, I'll put in a good word for you, baby." Zach grips my ass hard and pushes back against me and I come.

With his rumbled words in my ears and his dick pressing against my clit, I'm shaking on his lap. Shaking like a leaf in the wind. Or maybe like the ground during an earthquake.

And then, it's Zach's turn.

He comes with a groan, his forehead pressing against mine, his breaths covering me in a sweaty, misty film.

He's juddering against me and I notice the drops of his cum spilled on his stomach, his jeans, in my panties. It's the sexiest thing I've ever seen.

Still panting and sweaty, he lowers me on the bed, half-dressed and indecent. From this angle, the sun glares down at me but Zach blocks it with his big body.

He wraps his hand around my neck and growls, "Who are you?"

Even though I have very little energy left, I still arch my back. As if his voice is a call from my master.

"Your prize."

His fingers flex around my throat in possession and he bends down to smack a hard kiss on my lips. "As long as I'm here."

I would've smiled, because really, I'm happy and I feel cherished.

Only there's one thing I totally ignored before.

I'm his prize, his most adored possession but only for now.

Only as long as he's here.

chaqter 22

The Dark Prince

Mine.

My prize.

She is my prize.

She. Is. *My prize.*

Chapter 23

I'm his prize.

I'm *someone's* prize. His.

I haven't stopped smiling ever since he said that yesterday, after he made me come so spectacularly. And then, he straightened up my dress and I washed up in his bathroom, redid my hair and smoothed the wrinkles out of my dress before leaving his room.

Exactly like he told me I'd do.

He's going to be here any minute. I'm watching the back door at the end of the hallway like it will burst open by itself and he'll emerge all tall and handsome.

It should scare me that I didn't even think of it, of someone seeing him getting in and out. I should have.

For all my rule-breaking, this job is important to me. This is the only thing I have that will get me back my house. The place filled with my parents' memories. I can picture them in the living room, at the island in the kitchen, on the stairs, in the backyard.

In that house, they are alive and I'm not an orphan.

So yeah, I should've thought of all the details before inviting him over. But is it crazy that I find it sweet that *he* thought of them? That he wanted to protect me?

At seven o' clock, the knock sounds.

He's here.

I can tell by his knock. It's loud and short. More like a pound. I rush to the door and throw it open.

Zach's face is bowed but he lifts his eyes to look at me. I give him a blinding smile.

"You came."

He takes a few seconds to check me out and my toes curl, his eyes moving up and down. I kinda dressed up for him. Nothing crazy. Just a form-fitting top that shows off my breasts and tiny shorts.

"Well, you did threaten to call the cops on me," he drawls, bringing his eyes back up to mine. "And fuck up my bike. And no one touches my bike. So here I am."

I chuckle. "Really? For the bike? Don't you think you love it a little too much?"

He's had his bike for nearly as long as I've known him. Numerous times, I'd imagine doing something drastic to it just to mess with him. A few times I even came close.

"I think I love *her* just enough."

Good thing I was holding on to the edge of the door or I would've toppled over. I swear his *love* went down to my knees, making them weak. That and the way he's been watching me ever since he arrived.

Like he can't get enough of me.

"Are we going to stand here all day or are you gonna invite me in?" he asks when I don't say anything.

I shake my head and step aside. "Yeah. Come on in."

His boots click as they cross over the threshold and something about that makes me flush. It also makes me restless and talkative.

"So you're one of those guys."

Zach turns around to face me as I shut the door. "What guys?"

"Who call their mode of transportation a she." I walk to the kitchen where I've set up all the books and things that we're going to use tonight as I keep babbling, "It's a little crazy, I think. It's just a bike. I mean, I have a car. I love that car even though I'm a little scared of it right now. But I don't call it a he. I just call it an *it*, you know. Oh, and the guys who name their cars? Ugh. How pathetic do you have to be to do that? Right? It's like –"

"I have a name for my bike."

My eyes almost pop out and I press my lips together, grimacing.

Why do I keep saying the wrong things around him?

I spin around and find him almost right behind me. "You do?"

"Yes."

"What is it?"

He takes a step toward me and I press against the edge of the island. "Blue."

"What?"

"I call it Blue."

Zach's crowding me now. His big, tall body is bent to the shape of mine. I feel his thighs pressed up against my slightly open ones and I hear my own pulse in my ears. Racing, *racing* and roaring.

"You call your bike Blue?"

"Uh-huh."

"But it's black."

"So?"

"I..." I frown and for some reason, he finds it funny. He finds it a reason to bend down and kiss my blue hair softly.

My eyes fall shut on a sigh.

"Speechless, finally," he whispers to my hair. "And all it took was one simple fact."

Narrowing my eyes, I put a hand on his stomach – the stomach that I was kind of riding yesterday – and give him a push.

He leans back and I say, "Very funny. Why do you call your bike by a name that you call *me*? And while we're on the subject, let's talk about why *do* you call me Blue?"

Zach throws a look at my hair and shrugs. "Yeah, that *is* a mystery."

"I didn't get blue hair until the eighth grade. You've been calling me Blue since day one."

"Your point?"

"Why don't you ever call me Cleo?" I burst out with a question that I didn't even know I had.

I've had it forever, inside me.

Suddenly, I have this great, *great* urge for him to say my name. It's not that I don't like the name he gave me. I love it. I've always loved it even when I never accepted it.

But I want to hear how my name will sound on his tongue.

I want to know what goes through his mind when he calls me by his special name for me. Why did he name his bike after me?

I want to know everything about him. *Every little thing.*

"But that's not your name, either."

"What?"

Zach leans over and whispers on my lips, "Cleopatra. That's your name, right?"

I swallow against the onslaught of emotions. I feel the savage flapping of the butterflies in my stomach and I press my belly against him to make him feel it too. Make him feel all these crazy, intense emotions inside of me.

"But hardly anyone calls me that."

A lopsided smile as he traces my cheek with a thumb. "Do you know Cleopatra was an Egyptian queen?"

I nod. "Yeah. My mom used to tell me that she was the most beautiful woman of her time."

"People are crazy, aren't they?"

I clutch his dark t-shirt at his waist. "Why?"

"They don't know what they're talking about. One look at you and they would've snatched away her crown and laid it down at your feet."

The shudder that goes through me is the biggest one yet.

He called me beautiful.

Beautiful.

I blink up at him. "You're being nice to me."

He smiles slightly and acknowledges my statement with a grunt.

I place a kiss on his jaw.

"So, is this it?"

He tips his chin toward the books scattered on the island and I nod. "Yeah. Art sometimes leaves his storybooks here but I borrowed all of them from Doris. So we have a lot of reading material."

His nod is short, barely there.

I can feel his reluctance. How much he doesn't want to be here. He doesn't want to read. He doesn't want to do this.

I bet it has to do with his dad and his bullying.

The man who should've nurtured Zach is the one who's made him wary of something so basic as reading.

How fucked up is that?

"Take a seat," I whisper to him.

He does, albeit rigidly.

I sit on the chair beside his and slide the books close. "So, uh, I thought we should start with Art's favorite story. And I want you to read it so we can see how far along you are."

I can hear him grinding his teeth, but he doesn't say a word.

Opening the book, I push it over to his side. For a few seconds, he doesn't make any move to reach for it. And my eyes fill up with tears as I watch him sitting here, looking all angry and lost.

I've watched him grow up, see. I can very easily imagine him as a kid, doing the same thing in classes, in his room, with his tutors.

Maybe even in front of his dad.

Perhaps this was a bad idea. I don't want to dredge up any bad memories for him. I just want him to feel good about himself.

I'm about to call this thing off when he grabs hold of the edge of the book like it's an explosive object.

Then, he begins to read.

We've been working on his reading for an hour now.

I asked him to read a few pages so I can gauge the level of damage his dad has done to him.

Turns out, it's a lot.

Because Zach isn't bad. He isn't bad at all.

Yes, he's slow and he's halting. He can't do some of the bigger words. Not right away. It takes time for him to read them, compute them. I've had to help him a few times, put my finger under the word and enunciate the letters.

But it's not something that's so terrible that it should keep him from reading.

That's the thing about bullying, isn't it?

It isn't confined to a single moment. No. Bullying has consequences. It creates ripples that span for years. Sometimes for an entire life.

They call you fat and so you stop eating. You watch what you eat until you die.

They call you a nerd and so you stop reading in public. You still look over your shoulder when you read on a park bench.

It destroys you, a vital part of you. It fucks with your mind, with your heart, with your soul even. It changes your beliefs, your lifestyle. It makes you anxious. It causes panic. It won't let you sleep.

But then again, the bullied are powerful, aren't they?

We're resilient. We're strong. We're a motherfucking force.

Zach's a motherfucking force – he can do whatever he wants. And I could throttle his dad for ever making him feel less. I could throttle myself for not seeing this sooner.

There's a frown on his forehead and as I watch him, his right hand with the tattoo moving across the page, I blurt out, "When'd you get this tattoo?"

He stops reading and lifts his eyes.

He's really, *really* been good ever since we started this. Not once did he make a casual comment or use sarcasm. I gave him a book and told him to read and he did.

"The first year I moved away."

"What does it mean?"

A lip twitch. "I can cross the line."

I roll my eyes. "Yeah. But what line, exactly?"

"Line between normal and me."

I feel a crack. Right in the middle of where my beating heart is.

"You've done it, Zach," I tell him fiercely. "In fact, there wasn't even a line. There's nothing separating you from anyone. Not one thing. I think all those lessons you had? Those tutors? They were fucking amazing. *You* are fucking amazing. I'm not an expert, of course. My mom used to tutor a few kids, but I think if you practice enough and if we can get some help from a professional, you're going to be golden. You could go to college. Can you believe it? You could be like a lawyer or a doctor or I don't know, an engineer. You could do whatever you want. You could –"

He stands up from his seat, cutting off my words.

I don't know when it happened but sometime during my whole speech, he took on a dark aura. His jaw became hard and his eyes are glittering, as they are trained on me.

Even though we've fooled around only twice, still I know what it means. It means he's turned on. Badly.

"Zach –"

Bending down, he swallows up my words with his mouth.

His kiss is ferocious, even more than it was yesterday, in his bed. His teeth are scraping and his tongue is viciously lapping across my mouth.

Finally, he rips away from me. He wipes off the navy blue lipstick from his lips and grates out the question, "Who are you?"

I almost go limp at the erotic aggression in his features. "Y-your prize."

A possessive, lopsided smile. "I think you need to touch up your lipstick. I ate it all up."

My thighs tighten as I lick my lips. "You did?"

"Uh-huh." Straightening, he pulls me up. "We can't have that, can we?"

Powerless, I give him my weight. "No."

He steps away from me and I have to somehow find it in me to keep standing. "Lead the way."

Stumbling and completely confused, I walk to the bathroom with him following me. As soon as we enter the teeny-tiny space, he shuts the door. My heart starts banging in my chest.

"What's –"

"Lipstick," he orders.

I look at him in the mirror; his eyes are roving over my body. My breasts look so big and swollen in this tight top and my shorts barely cover my ass, stopping so close to my horny core.

With trembling hands, I open the drawer and take out my lipstick. I look at him in the mirror again, as if to ask him what next.

"Put it on," he rasps.

I watch him take a couple of steps back before he sits on the closed toilet seat, as if settling in for the show. I dig my toes in the fuzzy rug and press my thighs together.

Then, I open the cap of the lipstick; it's a roll-on and I inch forward to get closer to the mirror before putting it on.

I'm actively avoiding looking at him in the mirror. I can't. This is too... intimate. Somehow, something super sinful.

I do this every day, bend forward and paint my lips, but this has taken on a new meaning completely.

Now, I'm thinking about the thrust of my ass and how my thighs are stuck together, and my calves are straight and straining. I'm thinking about the arch of my back and the pout of my mouth as I move the roll-on around.

I'm thinking about what he's *thinking* about, sitting there, watching me in the mirror.

I don't have to wait long to figure it out.

Just as I'm finishing up, watching for any smudges, I hear him. I hear his zip opening and my lipstick almost clatters down in the sink. I grab the edge of the counter; my breaths are too heavy, too fast.

"Now, come here," he commands.

I look at him in the mirror. He's sprawled on the toilet seat, his thighs spread wide. The space is so small and he's so large that his one thigh touches the ceramic bathtub and the other, the tiled white wall. His jeans are open, hanging limply around his cut waist, while his t-shirt is shoved up, baring his lower stomach and that V.

And he's stroking his dick, with his eyes on me.

"Why?" I ask him.

Not that I have the strength to refuse him. I'll go where he tells me to go but I want to hear it from his lips.

I want to hear him talk dirty to me. Tell me all about the things he wants me to do to ease his suffering.

There's a knowing light in Zach's eyes as if he's aware of my game. "Because I've been sitting out there, doing your bidding, reading a kid's story for God knows how many hours. I'm tired, horny and fucking pissed off." He gestures to his dick that he's still stroking, going up and down. "You see him? He needs you. He needs you to wrap your blue-painted lips around him and suck him like a goddamn lollipop."

I bend my knees while pressing my legs together. He's creating a ruckus in my body with his words.

"But what if I..." I lick my *blue-painted* lips slightly. "I smear my lipstick all over him?"

His fingers tighten around his cock, pinching the top. "I'm counting on it."

I bite my lip, imagining the length of him covered in blue lipstick. Suddenly, I can't wait to paint him. I can't wait to color his dick with my lips.

I turn around and walk to him in a daze. When I reach him, I kneel between his spread thighs.

The very first thing that hits me right in the gut is his scent. His musk is stronger than his blueberry pie smell and I lick my lips again as I watch his hand go up and down over his length.

"You like lollipops, Blue?"

"Yes."

I keep watching his cock. It's like a rod, hard and heavy, rounded at the top. Big, like everything else about him. Thick enough that I know there might be some discomfort when I put him in my mouth. I'll have to watch for my teeth, make sure not to cut him. He's going to be bumping against them, even against the roof of my mouth.

Like yesterday, the pre-cum is leaking down, making it sticky, making his hand sticky too. And I want to taste that stickiness badly.

So badly that I decide that I'll do anything, anything at all to suck him off.

"What's your favorite flavor?" he asks.

I look at his face, finally. He's breathing hard, through his mouth, his eyes drugged up, stoned, and I know he's dying for this as much as me.

We're both dying and my lips on his dick is the only way to keep us alive.

"You. You're my favorite flavor," I whisper, and he groans, throwing his head back, bumping it against the wall.

I splay open my hands on his thighs and, opening my mouth, I kiss the crown of his shaft.

And just like that, his hand falls away and he makes it into a fist, punching his knee. "Fuck."

That first kiss is all it takes.

For me to get addicted to it. Addicted to him and his taste. For my breasts to get heavy and my nipples to get hard.

I open my mouth then, and suck on it.

And again, that very first suck is all it takes for me to get so attuned to him that every little hitch in his breath as I move my tongue around, discover the roundness, the sponginess of his head, resonates in my core.

"Fuck, Blue," Zach moans and buries his fingers in my hair.

Those sticky, *sticky*, covered-in-his-lust fingers.

I don't know why that arouses me so much that I feel my own juice pulsing out of me, seeping into my panties. But it does.

I move one hand from his thigh and grip the base of his dick, rubbing my thumb over the vein that runs on the underside of it. I decide to look for it later, when I'm done smearing my lipstick and eating him up like he ate me out against that truck.

For now, I'm going to rub my lips all over that trunk of flesh and paint him blue.

I go up and down, my breasts bouncing, my knees grinding on the tiled floor of the bathroom as I smear my lipstick over the most intimate skin of his. I lash my tongue over the pin-prick hole from which his cum leaks out.

Panting, I ask him. "How does it look?"

At my question, he opens his eyes and his abs flex. He looks at his cock – it's smudged with blue – and then, at me. "Fucking perfect."

Smiling, I lick up that vein I've been thinking about and his hips jerk.

God, his cock is a miracle, I swear.

Thick and long and sturdy, and I need to get back to it. So I do.

Grabbing the base of it, I suck on the crown again, all the while swirling my tongue.

The more I suck it, the more my cunt spasms, the harder my nipples get. My breasts have become a source of torment. They're heavy, and as I kneel on the hard floor, almost on all fours, they pull and dangle and shake every time I take him in deeper.

I have about half of his length inside me now and I'm on a mission to swallow all of him up.

From the little jerks of his hips and his fist in my hair and his constant chants of *fuck*, Zach would love that.

Just as I'm about to try for it though, he pulls me away. He tugs on my hair and tilts my neck up and stares down at my face.

"You've made a mess, Blue," he says roughly, as his gaze moves over my lips and his thumb flicks at the corners of it.

"You asked for it," I whisper.

"I did."

"But I'm not done yet."

"No?"

"I think I missed a few spots. I need to be thorough," I breathe. "Besides, I-I'm still hungry. I still need to suck and suck and suck until I find what I'm looking for."

I reach up and sweep a few strands of his hair away from his sweat-beaded forehead.

He almost leans into my soft touch and my heart squeezes. But a second later, he's back with his harsh, mean tone. "And what's that?"

I softly kiss his jaw and whisper, "The creamy center of your lollipop."

I blush at saying something so out-of-this-world dirty and he growls.

Still growling, he presses a hard – the hardest ever – kiss on my mouth. "Bedroom."

A dark thrill courses through me at his tone.

"Now," he orders when I simply keep looking at him and don't move fast enough for his liking.

I stand up on shaky legs and Zach kisses me again. Still kissing, we make our way to my bedroom.

Somehow, we land on my bed.

Zach attacks my shorts, opening the buttons and shoving them down my legs, along with my panties. It's so frantic and desperate that I don't even think to ask him about his intentions. I kick them off and he maneuvers me over him.

He's lying on the bed as he spins me around until my mouth's on his cock and his is in my drenched and bare core.

Finally, the words blurt out of me. "What're you doing?"

"Need your pussy on my face while you're sucking me off," he mutters.

His words alone cause a mini-orgasm in me and I fall on the bed, on my elbows, my wild blue hair making a curtain around my lips and his cock.

Two things that are made for each other.

Then he takes a long, greedy swipe of my pussy and I lose my mind.

I burn and the only way to soothe it is to wrap my naked lips around his cock again.

Oh God, this is sixty-nine, isn't it?

Why does it make me feel so fucking dirty and turned on at the same time?

My sucks stutter when I feel his fingers rubbing up my wet slit.

It makes me moan, those blunt fingers playing with me while I'm giving him head. My nails dig into his thighs and my breasts press into his flexing stomach as I come up for air before putting him back in my mouth, trying to take him in even further.

"You're so wet, baby," he groans over me. "And you shaved for me, didn't you?"

My answer is to moan around his shaft because yes, I did. Besides putting on a tight t-shirt and short shorts, I shaved down there.

Maybe I wanted this to happen. I wanted him to lick me and finger me while being sprawled on him like this.

His hips are moving slightly. Not too much but just enough that I have to loosen my mouth and let him have his way. I jerk when I feel his fingers over the seam of my ass.

"I told you next time I'll stick a finger up there, remember?"

I moan again, and writhe my ass in the air, inviting him.

His chuckle is pained. "But I lied."

I bite him lightly for that comment.

He chuckles again. "I'm not only going to finger your ass, Blue. I'm also going to stick it up your pussy."

I gasp and almost dislodge his dick from my lips.

His words are slurred and halting like he's losing all control. His thighs are clenched up tight and I think he's going to come.

And I think if he does what he promised to do, I'll come with him.

I prepare myself for the invasion but I guess I'm so wet that I don't feel the pained impact when he inserts his thumb in my pussy. I feel a slight pressure and a little stretch when he moves it around a bit but it's not bad.

Not at all.

It's so fucking good.

The moment he slides that wet, lubed-up thumb over the crease of my ass and circles my pleated hole, I feel his cock spurting pre-cum on my tongue.

He emits a long grunt that reverberates through me, down to my toes.

Just as I come up for air, Zach slides his thumb inside my ass and I moan over the head of his dick. It jerks on my tongue and I latch on to it and suck on it like it's my job.

It feels weird and new and painfully erotic, his thumb in my ass.

But he doesn't stop there. He slides a long finger inside my pussy, which apparently goes pretty easily, and I almost swallow up his dick, sobbing over it.

"Fuck, fuck, fuck. Goddamn, Blue."

I feel him moving his fingers inside me, inside both my holes, and the pressure starts building. I know I'm close. I know he's close too.

"I can feel it, baby," he pants. "I can feel your cherry. It's there. It's tiny and it won't let me get through. Feels like it's taunting me."

The last part of his speech is less words and more grunts.

You should bust it then. Tear it open so you can get in.

Just as that thought flashes through my mind all bright and shiny like a star, I come.

I spasm around his fingers and that makes his shaft jerk inside my mouth. I let his head go and peek out my tongue so he can come on it like I'm coming on his fingers.

The tightness and convulsions of his body match mine. And so do our noises. Probably our heartbeats match too, in this moment.

I drink him down all the while he's milking me. His taste is just as I imagined it to be. Musky and spicy and him.

So fucking *him*.

So fucking Zach.

The guy I belong to. The guy who thinks I'm his prize.

Somehow, he also feels like the guy I should give everything to. Even my virginity.

Chapter 24

I'm dying.

Or at least, it feels like it. The pain is so intense and it came on so suddenly that I can't breathe.

I'm at the threshold of the kitchen, trying to catch a glimpse of Zach because I know he comes in for breakfast in the mornings, just after his workout.

We've shared a few meals that way. All he does is stare at me and all I do is talk up a storm with Maggie and try not to blush.

But this morning, he's not alone.

His hair's sweaty and delicious and he has his vest-type t-shirt on and there's a bowl of something sweet in front of him. I don't have the time to check out what it might be because I'm busy staring at him with Leslie.

It's not a secret that after Zach helped Art, he's everyone's favorite. The cooking staff can't wait to serve him. The girls can't stop eyeing him and giggling and gossiping about the magnificence of his body and that face and that smirk and how strong he is. His workouts by the pool are pretty famous too.

Leslie is doing what all other girls on the staff do. She's giggling and leaning toward him with her hip cocked out. Maggie's chuckling too, where she stands by the counter, close enough to be included in the conversation.

And Zach?

He's smirking up at her.

He's so freaking involved with whatever their conversation is that he hasn't even touched his food. He's absorbed in Leslie and her smiles and the way she's playing with her blonde braid. It looks like there's something between them. Like they know each other.

Like she knows all his secrets and struggles. She knows about his reading. She knows that the more he reads, the better he gets, and when I tell him this, his face closes up.

I haven't been able to understand that. Why wouldn't he be happy to see the progress he's making? Why wouldn't he want me to compliment him and flush with pleasure every time he reads a phrase correctly without confusing the letters?

Sometimes I think it's shame. He's embarrassed and angry to be making progress. Which is so weird that I think maybe I'm imagining things.

And every time his expression becomes cagey, I know what comes next. His kisses and his hands.

Jesus, his hands are always so desperate and horny, on the verge of tearing my clothes off so he can get to my bare skin. To my breasts, my thighs, my pussy. As if he needs it all like he needs the air. As if he needs to make me come and he needs to come himself while I'm spasming in his arms. And all I can do is give in to him.

Why wouldn't I?

I'm his prize, right?

Except, maybe those are simply words.

Maybe he says them to everyone. Maybe he said it to Leslie, the girl he's been flirting with so openly while he sneaks into my cottage like a thief.

It's crazy, I know. I was the one who wanted all the secrecy, even if I forgot to plan for it. He's just adhering to my wishes.

Never looking at each other if we ever pass by in the hallways. Not talking while having breakfast. Never saying a word to each other if I accidentally come upon him by the pool and he's out there, either working out or swimming.

It's me. I set the rules and Zach's been so careful about protecting me and this *stupid* job.

I realize that I don't like it.

I don't like the necessary secrecy and that he's touching someone else. I don't like that he's too engrossed in her to notice me.

A sound rises in my throat, a mixture of a gasp and maybe a hiccup. A sad, jealous hiccup and somehow, it reaches him.

Zach lifts his eyes and looks straight at me. His lips part and my own purse.

Leslie notices that she doesn't have his attention anymore, so she turns around and, finding me there, she beams.

Her smile is so enthusiastic that I can't even hate her for being close to what I want.

"Hey, Cleo. Come on in," she chirps.

"Ah, finally you're here. Come, I made the English custard again." Maggie smiles fondly at Zach. "It's Master Zach's favorite."

English custard.

I smile slightly at both of them before turning back to Zach. He's sitting there rigid, his jaw clenched in that angry, mean way of his.

What does he have to be angry about? I'm the one who's feeling betrayed.

"It's okay," I say, keeping my eyes on him. "If it's… Mr. Prince's favorite, then he should have all of it."

With that, I spin around and get out of there.

I'm in such a hurry that I bump into someone at the end of the hallway. It's Ryan.

He steadies me with his hands on my shoulders. "You okay?"

His gentle voice makes me want to cry but I hold on. "Yeah. Sorry. I should stop doing that to you."

Chuckling, he says, "I don't mind."

"How are you?" I ask, studying his handsome face.

He has always made me feel safe. *Always.*

And now that I look at him, I realize that maybe I wasn't made for safe. Safe does nothing for me. I wasn't made to be handled with gentle fingers and soft touches.

Maybe I was made for rough strokes, pulling hands and harsh stares.

"Good. You?" He frowns. "Is everything okay?"

I nod. "Uh-huh. I'm just, you know? Rough day."

"It hasn't even started yet."

I chuckle sadly. "I know. It's just going to be one of those days."

Nodding, he begins, "Listen, I, uh, wanted to tell you. I guess you already know though, since Tina's your friend and –"

I thrust up my hand to make him stop. "It's okay. I know. Tina told me you guys are going out Saturday and that's awesome. Really."

Tina took my advice and asked Ryan out on a date. I think he was shocked. She said he didn't say anything for about ten seconds as he kept staring at her.

I bet it was because he was staring at her with new eyes.

"You sure? I feel like such a, I don't know, a player or something."

I laugh loudly at that and bump my shoulder against his chest. "You are not a player. Not at all. You're one of the most decent guys I know, Ryan. In fact, you're *the* most decent guy I know. So no, I don't think that at all. I just hope you guys have a good time."

He smiles; grins, actually. "Okay."

I can see it in his eyes that he's really looking forward to it. As much as Tina.

"Okay." I nod and step back from his embrace.

Ryan bends down and kisses me on the forehead. It's a brotherly kiss. I can't believe we ever wanted to go out. Maybe that's why we kept putting it off, subconsciously. Our being busy and not finding the time might have been a sign in the first place.

Just as he leaves, I feel a prickling sensation in the back of my neck.

I know who it is before I even turn around.

Zach's standing at the threshold of the kitchen, staring at me with accusing eyes.

It feels like a night for wearing my mom's nightie.

After it got ruined, Maggie tried to clean it for me. She was partially successful. The stains dulled out but I can still make out the huge outline of it on my chest, just under the lace. I decided to fold it neatly and stow it away so it doesn't get damaged any further.

But tonight, I'm alone and sad and I want something comforting with me.

Zach didn't show up for our meeting this evening and I'm so angry.

So jealous.

I keep seeing him with Leslie and I'm filled with so many irrational emotions. Emotions only he can invoke in me.

God, that guy has always stripped away my sanity and left me a mass of craziness and passion.

Just thinking about him with her is making me want to cry again like I'm still in high school or something. I've been crying ever since I got inside the door after work and so I decide to find some ice cream. Tina and I, we keep it stocked.

I fish it out of the freezer, find a spoon in the drawer and go to my room. But as soon as I enter, I spy someone outside my window.

Putting aside the ice cream carton, I rush to it and see the flashes of the same elbow and thighs and shoulder.

Zach. He's rounding the corner, probably making his way to the back door of the cottage.

Sighing sharply, I move away from the window, shove my feet in my leather boots and run to the door, throwing it open before he gets there and marching outside.

He comes to a stop when he sees me.

Even though I'm a few feet away from him, I can still hear his harsh breaths. They are agitated and making his chest look infinite times bigger and broader.

Under his dark gaze, I walk up to him. "What are you doing here?"

He takes me in, his eyes moving as fast as his breaths and now, also my heart. What he finds on my features doesn't make him happy. In fact, it makes him downright pissed off.

"I told you," he growls.

"What?"

"I told you I'd make you cry. I told you that I'd keep doing it."

Anger rises inside me like a wave. I've been crying for this douchebag all evening and this is what he has to say to me?

"So?"

"So you can't fault me for that. You don't get to pout about it," he bites out.

"Pout about it?" My nails are digging into my palms. "Fuck you, Zach, okay? Fuck. You. Yeah, you told me. You told me that you'd make me cry and like an idiot, I didn't listen. But I'm finally listening. Are you happy now? Proud of yourself? Go home."

Zach steps closer to me and my heart takes an extra beat when his smell hits my nose. The night is hot as always but the heat coming off his tight body is like an inferno, and my pores sweat just by his nearness.

He drags in a long breath, his nostrils flaring. "I never lied to you. I never promised you anything. You've seen me at my worst, Blue. I've showed you my worst self. And when you begged me to kiss you, *I told you* that you were mine. And still, you let him touch you. You let him put his mouth on you."

His anger is as powerful as his body and I sway slightly from it. It makes me feel guilty and at the same time, it makes butterflies in my stomach wake up.

Damn it.

How does he always do that? How does he control every single thing about me?

"He's my friend," I say with gritted teeth. "I didn't *let* him do anything. He was being nice. And you're one to talk. You couldn't stop flirting with Leslie this morning. You didn't even touch your freaking custard."

Ugh.

I can hear myself being all peevish and childish but I can't stop myself. I can't stop this jealousy.

Another step closer and we're practically nose to nose. Or more like my face to his chest since he's so much taller than me.

"I want you to do something for me," he rasps.

"I'm sorry?"

"I want you to run."

Something in his tone, in the mean lines of his face makes me swallow. "W-what?"

"I want you to turn around and run. As fast as you can." He pauses to pull in another breath. "The way I'm feeling right now. The way I'm twisted up. I don't…"

There's hardly any space between us but still, I move closer to him. I've never seen him like this. All agitated and riddled with angst. Every breath, every word that comes out of his mouth is so tortured, so laden with harrowing things that all the instincts I possess make me want to comfort him.

Take away his pain, even though he's hurting me too.

"You don't what?"

Zach's eyes are swirling with a predatory glint. "I don't want to hurt you."

Oh, Jesus Christ.

I can't even say, *you won't hurt me*. Because I know he can. Not physically, no. Emotionally, yes.

He can hurt me. He *did* hurt me this morning.

As I watch him now, I realize how capable he is of destroying me. And I'm not talking about bullying or the past.

I'm talking about right now.

I'm talking about the way I feel for him. The way I disregard the rules of my job, the way he makes me proud when he reads, the way my heart swells when he's with Art, the way he makes my skin sing when he touches it.

Maybe what I'm feeling isn't childish at all.

Maybe it's the most profound emotion we as humans, can feel.

God, when did he become this powerful and when did I become so powerless?

"I –"

"Run," he growls, this time louder.

And I don't even stop to think about it. I do as he says: I run.

I take off into the woods. I run as fast as I can.

I'm not running from my bully. I'm running because he hasn't been my bully for a long time now. He's something else to me now.

Something more.

The light of the moon's beating down at me through the leafy branches of the trees. For some reason, even the stars are brighter.

The leaves are crunching under my boots. That's the only sound, except for the sound of my breathing. But then, another sound joins in.

He's running after me. Chasing me.

I knew he would.

Like Orion.

The thought makes me stop and, panting, I turn to face him.

He's right there, a few feet away.

"You stopped."

I walk backward. "I didn't want to run anymore."

He walks forward, toward me. "Why not?"

Because he is to me what sharp objects are to fragile things. What a flame is to a moth.

Destiny.

We are destiny, Zach and I. We're stars, aren't we?

You can't run from destiny. You can't outrun fate. You can't stop a moth from perishing in flames and you can't stop a sharp object from making a fragile thing bleed.

"Because I don't want to play games anymore."

"You think this is a game?"

"No. This isn't a game." I keep walking backward, unafraid because if something happens, he'll lunge forward to save me. "Who am I?"

He frowns, wiping his mouth with the back of his hand. "My prize."

My back hits a tree and I arch my spine, wrapping my hands around the trunk. "Then, you should claim me. But you should also know one thing."

"What thing?"

"This prize belongs to you but *you* belong to this prize just as much."

Zach finally reaches me and leans forward to put his palms on the rough bark of the tree. "Yeah?"

I lift my chin. "Yes."

"You know why I wasn't eating that freaking custard?"

"Why?"

"Because I was waiting for you. Because I thought like every day, you'd come and we'd…"

"Eat together."

Finally, I smile.

He moves his hands and buries them in my loose hair, tilting up my neck. "You know what belonging to me means?"

"What?"

His forehead drops to mine. "It means that you're the only thing in this world that I feel… responsible for." His frown is so deep that I feel it on my skin. "You're the first thing that's ever belonged to me. The very first thing and I don't… I don't want to hurt you."

My heart's gone. I don't hear it.

Slowly, it's falling out of my body and I know right down to my soul that if I don't stop it, it'll leave forever. It'll die.

Zach steps into me and I feel him on my stomach. His thick, hard cock.

It jerks against me and in reply, my core clenches.

And I know what he meant by his repeated words, about not wanting to hurt me. I know why he asked me to run.

"We're going to have sex, aren't we?"

"You're a virgin."

I grab onto his t-shirt. "And you're so big."

Groaning, he rolls his forehead over mine. "You're so tiny, I'll hurt you."

I feel a drop of cum leaving me and seeping into my panties. This is so reminiscent of that night when he asked me if I was a virgin or not.

"Yeah. You'll stretch me out."

He grinds his erection into me and I moan, thrusting my breasts at his chest. "No matter how careful I am."

It's okay.

Let my heart die. In its place, I'll make a new one. A heart that only beats for this lonely, *lonely* boy in front of me.

"And you know what belonging to me means?" I whisper.

Zach looks into my eyes. "What?"

I'm lonely too. My parents are gone. They took away my house. There's nothing in this world that belongs to me.

Except him.

"It means that I trust you. It means that I know you'll be careful. And it means that you're the only one I want to give my cherry to."

I lean up and place a kiss on his soft lips.

But Zach deepens it. He presses a hand on the back of my head and pushes open my mouth with his tongue.

Then, he's heaving me up and I'm wrapping my limbs around his body, and we're striding back to where we came from.

My cottage.

Chapter 25

Zach carries me into the cottage through the back door that I'd left open when I marched out to meet him.

In my bedroom, he lowers my feet to the floor and, kneeling, he takes off my boots.

The light's switched off but the window's open and the moon's strong. Somewhere up there, I have faith that tonight Orion has caught up with The Pleiades. At least tonight, he's resting.

When Zach's done, he stands up and towers over me. There's so much tension and lust in the air that I'm getting breathless.

I'm getting shy.

"You missed your lesson for tonight," I tell him, just to say something.

I see his lopsided smile in the silver moonlight. "Lesson?"

"Uh-huh." I nod, smiling too. "I'm your nerd tutor and you're the jock who needs to pass the test or he won't make the team."

He reaches forward and traces the lace on the neck of my dress, looking at it like it's the prettiest thing ever. "Yeah? What do I play?"

Shivering, I look him up and down. He's tall and broad and he looks like he's always bursting out of his clothes.

"Um, football?"

"Am I any good?" he asks, still fingering the lace like he can't stop touching it.

"Yup. You're the best. Only, you just can't focus in class."

He moves his fingers up my neck and grabs onto the curls of my hair, playing with them. "Why not?"

"Maybe because you're always watching me," I whisper, reveling in the tiny little ways he's touching me.

"So you're my classmate, too?"

"I am. I'm also very intelligent, ahead of my years, and that's why they want me to tutor you."

He chuckles. "So why do I watch you?"

I swallow and gravitate toward him. "At first, I think it's to intimidate me. To make me feel less than you. Because you're the prince of the college and I'm just… a blue-haired, weird girl."

He glances up from where he was watching himself toy with my hair.

Boring his eyes into mine, Zach lets go of the strand and wraps his hand over the nape of my neck in possession. "But maybe I'm watching you because I can't stop. Because you're the most beautiful girl I've ever seen. And because your blue hair reminds me of the sky and the ocean. Freedom."

Blood's rushing just under my skin, painting everything scarlet. I've never been so awake in the middle of the night, so colored and flushed.

"Is that why you watched me in detention all the time?"

More often than not, I'd end up with detention and Zach used to be right there with me. Somehow, we'd always sit in the same places where we sat the first day we met. And all the while I kept my head down and away from him because I could feel his eyes on me.

"Yeah," he whispers, flexing his fingers on my neck. "And to make you blush."

I lightly slap his shoulder. "That was a very rude thing to do."

Chuckling, he kisses me lightly.

This time, I'm the one who deepens it. I'm the one who invades his mouth and nips his lower lip, making him groan.

A second later though, he's taking over.

His hands fist my nightie before pulling it up and off my body. Just like that, I'm nearly naked, standing there in my blue boy shorts.

In my head, I knew we were going to have sex. But somehow, I didn't connect the dots that I'd have to be naked for it.

God, I'm naked.

I'm *naked*.

In front of a guy. In front of him. The most perfect specimen ever.

He's made of hard, sculpted muscles that, yes, I know he works for every single day. And I'm made of pillowy, doughy fat that I get from all the candies I used to steal from the kitchen cabinet when Mom wasn't looking.

I stare at my feet and try to picture myself naked. Big boobs, round stomach and wide hips with dimpled thighs. Oh, and all of it is whiter than the moon.

Zach takes in a deep breath and says, in a guttural tone, "Do you know how many times I've imagined you naked?"

I look up and remember he said something similar about kissing me. "A thousand times?"

A puff of air escapes him and he nods.

He looks mesmerized as his gaze moves from one part of my body to another. He seems like he doesn't know where to look first. His eyes are slightly wide and his mouth is parted.

I'm riddled with goose bumps everywhere. Everything on my skin is coarse and scratchy. Even my soft hair that brushes against the small of my back.

Zach puts his hand on the center of my chest, right in the middle of my heaving breasts. He splays his palm, touching both of them at the same time. "Jesus. The number of times I've jerked off imagining your tits. I can't even tell you."

He circles my left nipple with his thumb, shrinking it into a hard pebble. He loves playing with them; I know that. He loves waking them up, worrying them with his fingers, sucking them with his mouth.

His hand moves down and without my volition, my spine arches. He reaches my stomach and digs his thumb into my belly button.

Somehow, he's pressing into that vein again. The one that swells and becomes taut every time he's close, every time I think about him.

Zach's breathing has become harsh as he keeps going. His hand travels down, rough and enticing, and slides inside my panties. The moment he touches my drenched core my legs go taut and my heels leave the floor.

I'm standing on my tiptoes, hardly able to balance myself.

He moves toward me and our bodies meet, me naked and exposed and him still wearing his t-shirt and jeans, burning me with their friction.

Sliding his arm around my waist, he helps me maintain my balance as his other hand cups my entire pussy.

"Zach." I moan his name and he squeezes it like it's an object.

He pinches my swollen lips together, making me fist his shirt and keeping me on my toes. I don't know why it's so erotic but it is.

"Who are you?" he whispers.

"Your prize."

As if those words are a catalyst, Zach captures my lips with his.

I wind my arms around his neck, fisting his shirt in the back, pulling at it, tugging it. Impatiently. God, his kisses have made me so impatient for him, his cock.

He gets the signal, and taking his hand out of my panties, he shoves them down, completely baring me before going to his shirt and snagging it off his body.

I want to work on the fly of his jeans but he doesn't let me. He goes back to kissing me and I forget everything but his lips and his roving hands.

My hands are no slouches, either.

They keep making sweeps over his shoulders, the ridges of his back, the slant of his side. I don't know where to touch him, *how* to touch him to make this hunger go away. He's hot and cut and corded and I can rake my nails along the muscled slabs until the end of time.

We break off to breathe but even then, our lips are connected. We're breathing each other's air as Zach walks me backward and lays me down on the bed before looming over me.

It's happening, isn't it?

He's going to be inside me soon.

I can't wait.

His hands are on either side of my head, making a dent on the pillow, and his breaths are so stormy that they stir the flyaway hair on my forehead.

I reach up and kiss him on the lips, making his entire large body shudder between my legs.

"Hurry," I whisper, hugging his sides with my thighs, pressing his hips to me.

I thought now would be the time he'd shove his pants down and enter me. I'm ready, anyway. I think I've been ready for ages now.

But Zach moves down my body and snatches a nipple in his mouth. I thread my fingers through his hair, arching up to him, my head thrown back.

With a grunt, Zach comes down to his elbows and plumps my breast in his hand. He's working my nipple with his mouth and I'm rubbing up against him, restless.

I drag my lower body up and down, stroking my clit on the ridges of his stomach, probably making a sticky mess on him.

But Zach doesn't mind. He encourages that. Every time my movements get a little lazy, he squeezes my tits harder and bites down on my nipple, grinding against me, forcing me to quicken my rocking.

Just as I think I'm about to come, humping over his abs, Zach lets go of my nipple.

"Zach," I gasp, outraged.

"Shh. Don't talk."

I growl and feel his smile in between the valley of my breasts.

He runs his tongue along it, going lower and lower, until he reaches my belly button. Burying his tongue, he laves it, licks it, bites into it, giving me hickeys.

My very first love bites.

I smile slightly in the darkness, looking down at his dark head, his puckered lips, hard at work on my body.

My movements are frantic now. Frenzied and fast. And I'm undulating, rocking, writhing; my feet keep slipping on the bed.

"I think I'm..."

I'm so, so close to coming and just when I feel his breath on my pussy and his finger on the tight hole of my ass, I lose all control and come. He latches on to my folds with his mouth and I pour my orgasm down his throat, tugging on his hair, hugging his face with my thighs.

I'm still in a daze, panting and sweaty, staring at the ceiling when Zach comes up from the bed and shucks his jeans off. His dick bobs in the air, hard and thick. So thick. I know the weight of it, the taste, how I have to widen my mouth, stretch open for it.

And now, it's going to be inside of me.

Inside of my tiny little hole.

I should be afraid.

But as I watch him climb onto the bed and crawl between my thighs that just drop open for him, for his bulk to settle between them, I realize that I'll do anything for it.

Anything for this guy hanging over me, tightened up and darkened in lust.

Anything for his dick to bust through and claim me.

I hike up my legs around his hips and cross my ankles at his back, opening myself to him, wordlessly.

Zach fists the sheets on either side of my head, sweat dripping from his neck. "I don't have a condom."

"I'm on the pill."

"I could be crawling with diseases."

"You're not."

He lowers himself on me and his cock, hot and heavy, settles on my stomach. The feel of it makes me twist under him.

"I'm not. I haven't done it without a condom before," he assures me.

"Good." I snake my hand around his neck and bring him even lower so he gives me all his weight. "I'll be your first."

I catch his chuckling mouth in a kiss and rock against him. He rocks back.

His hand goes to my waist as he traces the outside of my body before stopping on my thigh and hiking it up even more. I dutifully do the same with the other thigh, locking my lower body with his.

"Keep 'em there, okay?" he instructs.

I nod.

With his other hand, he reaches down and fists his dick. I can feel his knuckles on my stomach as he strokes it lazily. I even feel the hot plop of his pre-cum on my skin and the vibration of his chest when he groans.

My stomach hollows out when he lines up his erection with my pussy.

He looks at my face and I fasten my eyes to his. There are lines of tension around his mouth as he watches me and I cradle his jaw, feeling he needs comfort as much as me.

I don't want to hurt you.

I know he was only talking about sex but as I look at his tormented, horny face, I think that maybe every predator, every sharp object, has a soul. A soul that cries out when the flame burns down a moth and the lion cuts a lamb open with its teeth.

Zach's eyes flutter slightly at my soft touch as he circles my opening with his cock. My lower body is both eager and a little rigid in fear at the impending invasion.

And it happens in one thrust.

Keeping our eyes connected, Zach enters my body in one go.

I moan and my back arches up at that. My eyes fall shut as I drag in a shocking breath. There's pain. A pinching.

It's everywhere but it's not excruciating.

What's more dominant and immediate is the fullness.

It feels like my pelvis is stretched and filled to the brim. My stomach is swollen, and my chest is about to burst.

I'm about to burst.

Zach's head drops down to my shoulders and I feel his gusty breaths there, pummeling me like his groans.

It's like we both climbed up a mountain and now we need a second to gather ourselves.

He's inside of me.

Our most intimate parts are touching. They're locked up together. He's the first human being, the *only* human being ever, to be this close to me.

I bite my lip in elation as I feel a pressure building up.

Every little sound that he makes fills me with even more lust. Every sweep of his chest and ripple of his back drives home the point that I'm his and he's mine.

Tentatively, I try to move under him, relieve this restlessness that's pulsing. Like it's alive, complete with veins and a heart.

Zach snaps his head up. "Stop."

"W-what?"

"It'll hurt more if you move," he says with clenched teeth and a somewhat agonized expression.

I palm his sweaty shoulder, breathing in hiccups. "It doesn't."

"What?"

I move under him again, rock against his pelvis, and I swear I feel his dick jump inside of me. "It doesn't hurt."

Zach's astonished and I could've laughed. But in this moment, I'm so restless.

Maybe the universe knew that our bodies were made for each other. So the nature took away all the pain. But I can't explain that to him right now. I'm too needy.

All I can say is: "Please, f-fuck me, Zach."

He watches me struggle under him, trying to get him to move, trying to rub my hypersensitive clit against his pelvis but he doesn't come to help me. He doesn't rescue me and I claw my nails along his biceps, his side, his back.

"Please, Zach," I beg again.

And then, he gives a grind of his hips. "This what you want, Blue?"

I nod, sighing in relief. But it isn't even complete, that sigh. His movements drive the need higher. The craving doesn't end.

I know it won't. Not until I come, and he comes with me. Inside of me.

I'm dying to feel that. That splash, that splatter of his cum that I've tasted so many times before. My favorite flavor of popsicle.

Zach begins to move. His strokes are slow but long. He goes out completely, leaving me empty, before coming back in.

I moan out his name and his strokes become jabs. Short and thrusting and faster. I squeeze my thighs around his waist, biting my lip.

"I thought you were lying," Zach pants from over me, his eyes trained on my face.

"About what?" I gasp as I start to push back into his thrusts.

"I thought you wanted my dick so bad that you were lying about the pain."

"I do want it..."

His pumps are harder now and my channel is slicker. I can't believe that we haven't been doing it all this time. How will I ever go back to the land of living when he's killing me so beautifully with his cock?

"I thought your pussy made you a liar, Blue," he rasps, sliding his lips over me; my tongue peeks out to taste him. "But I guess she only made you a horny little slut for me."

My stomach clenches at that word and an *uh* comes out of me. As if in agreement.

It's true, isn't it?

I am a slut for him. I am horny for him. I've *been* horny for him for ages. For centuries, even.

"You are, aren't you?"

"Yes."

"Yeah, you are. I'm an animal for you too, baby."

Shameless, I arch under him, feeling his pounds all the way to my teeth, and all the way down to my toes.

His hips are slapping against mine and his balls are hitting my ass. My legs are jarring up and down his sides as Zach hammers into me. I hold onto his neck and try to keep steady but it's useless.

The entire bed is shaking, hitting the wall, making this the loudest fuck in the history of fucks.

And hottest too.

We're sweating against each other, breathing hot puffs of air.

Him and me.

Two lonely people who belong to each other and no one else.

I caress his stubbled jaw and he tucks his face in my neck like he can't hold himself up anymore and I hug him to me, letting myself go.

My breath hitches as I fall over the edge.

This orgasm is hands down the best one I've ever experienced. It's different. It starts up in my stomach and radiates out to every little corner in my body. It's violent too. I'm shaking and twisting and arching, and chanting Zach's name over and over.

It's like my body can't contain the hormones. Can't contain the avalanche of chemical reactions within me.

When I come back down, Zach pushes himself up from my body.

Still remaining inside of me, he kneels between my open legs and pulls me up, seating my ass over his thighs. This way he can see all of me, laid out in front of him.

It should be embarrassing but it's not.

In fact, it's the opposite of that. It's thrilling. Because he's watching his horny little slut, and she feels him swelling up inside her cunt.

I arch up for him and press my breasts together.

Moaning, I play with them as he resumes his drives.

His face is a study of tight and beautiful lines as he pounds into me and watches me tweak my raspberry-colored nipples. They're hypersensitive after my orgasm and I'm spasming every time I pinch them.

His upper lip is pulled down, curled over his teeth, and he's growling with every stroke. He's never looked more ferocious, darker than this. More like an animal.

And I've never felt more wanton and shameless.

His breathing has changed, become desperate, and sweat is sliding down his chest and his abs. He's close to coming; I know that. I know the signs.

Just as I knead a bouncing breast and catch a droplet of his sweat at his belly button with my other hand, he tightens up. His jerks become uneven and his black eyes fall shut.

His spine arches, throwing the ridges of his torso into stark relief, as he moans out my name to the ceiling and comes inside of me.

I feel it in my slowly dying heart, that moan, that jerk of his dick.

I sit up and wind my arms around him, bringing us both down on the bed. Groaning, he falls over me.

I'm soothing his back, tracing it with my hands up and down as my channel absorbs his orgasm.

And finally, my body goes limp, listening to his heartbeats.

He's mine.

The thought floats in my head.

I should feel relief. I thought if I knew he was mine, I'd be happy. I'd be content.

But now that I know he's mine, I can't help but think for how long.

Chapter 26

The Dark Prince

I sneak out from her room at dawn so no one sees me.

She's lying on her side, her cheek pressed to the pillow. Her blue hair's spread all over and there's a couple of strands just lying there.

Creepily, I pick them up and wind them around my finger, kiss her forehead, before leaving.

I head back to the mansion through the woods.

In my room, I get out a notebook I bought for myself a few days ago. It was an impulse buy; I'm not proud of it.

In fact, sometimes it makes me downright angry that I have it in my possession. I keep it hidden, out of sight like I'm packing drugs.

I only fish it out when I'm feeling restless. When I'm... missing her.

I sit at the desk, a desk that I haven't used in years but I've been using it kind of frequently.

They say it's easier to type up words on a computer, recognizing the letters on the keypad rather than trying to make them yourself. Because dysgraphia messes with that.

But I'm not doing this because I'm interested in making my writing better.

I'm doing this because I can't stop myself. Because she's in my head. These days, she always is.

So, I pick up a pencil. The strand of her hair's still wound around the finger of my right hand as I open a fresh page and write:

Cleopatra Marie Paige.

Chapter 27

I'm having the worst day.

First of all, I overslept.

Sometime during the night after the mind-blowing sex, Zach and I fell asleep. I slept through the entire night only to be woken up by the sound of his bike.

Turns out it was in my dreams, but still.

It spooked me something real bad. I don't remember all of it, but I have a blurry picture of Zach leaving this town for good. And I don't even find out about it until I wake up the next morning and hear all the gossip. Exactly like it happened three years ago.

With a churning stomach, I arrived at work, which I was late for. Meaning, Mrs. S wasn't pleased at my tardiness and on top of that, I missed breakfast with Zach.

And then, I heard that no one had seen him all morning. He never came down for breakfast and his suite was locked when one of the girls went up to clean.

I couldn't ask more without the danger of raising suspicion, so I kept quiet and freaked out in private.

Which I hated, by the way.

I hated how he wasn't there with me when I woke up. I hated that he probably had to sneak out in the middle of the night to avoid running into someone on his way back.

He was doing it to protect me and my job; I know that, but I don't like it.

I'm starting to hate it more and more every day.

Anyway, it's lunch now and my appetite is nowhere to be found.

I'm anxious and jumpy and all I want is to see Zach. For him to come back.

God, please make him come back.

I'm in the kitchen with Grace, Leslie and Tina. They're all chatting Maggie up about the new guests who arrived this morning. Apparently, they have been here before and last time when they stayed over, there was this big scandal about some stolen china.

I'm not even paying attention. In fact, I decide to leave in the middle of it because I can't sit still. Thankfully, all of them are too absorbed to notice my exit.

Where are you, Zach?

Maybe I'm going crazy. Maybe losing my virginity has made me all emotional and girly. That's the reason I want to take the day off and cry in my pillow.

I've been thinking so hard about all the things that I don't watch where I'm going and I bump into someone.

Not again.

This time though, it's Zach.

"You," I say with wide eyes.

His dark gaze watches me intensely. "Me."

"I was…"

I should be relieved that he's back. That he didn't leave for good. But suddenly, I'm feeling restless. Breathless, even. My thighs clench and there's an ache in between my legs. Where he was last night.

"You were what?"

His rough, heavy tone makes my toes curl in my boots. "I was, uh, looking for you all morning."

"I went out for a ride."

I notice his wind-swept hair, then. The slight flush on his cheeks and the scent of outdoors mixed in with his own sweet, delicious smell. He must've just gotten back.

"Why?"

"Wanted to clear my head."

"Of what?" I ask, distractedly as I watch his lips.

"Of you."

I jerk my eyes up to him and I realize in the last few seconds, his breathing has escalated just like mine. He looks on the verge of something and I probably look the same. The verge of throwing myself at him, touching him, climbing his body, to reassure myself that he's really here.

That we really had sex last night.

"Of me?"

"Yeah." His eyes bore into mine. "But I couldn't."

God, I'm buzzing.

My breaths are rattling my lungs and there's a crackle under my skin.

I don't want to, but I break our stare and glance back. The kitchen hallway is empty and so is the main hallway. I can hear people chatting in the staff room but no one's up and about. Which is super rare and I know it's not going to stay that way. Someone's bound to come, scurrying for one emergency or another.

I grab his hand and pull him away from the mouth of the hallway. "Let's go."

Silently, he lets me drag him into the closet just by the kitchen, as if he wanted to be alone with me as much as I did.

It's the same closet I hid myself in the first night he came back. I hadn't even seen him yet and I could still feel him, moving around in my body.

He is under my skin. Always has been.

I shut the door and switch on the light, facing him.

There's hardly any space between us. The closet was small to begin with but with him inside it, I feel like there's not enough air for us to breathe.

And then, Zach eats up that bare minimum space by pressing into my body. My spine's stuck to the door and my front is flush with his.

"There was blood. On the sheets. I saw it when I left," he rasps, and I feel his cock, throbbing just under my ribs.

I thread my fingers through his hair. "I know. I saw it too."

Pain flashes through his features. Pain and regret. Probably for making me bleed.

"I'm..."

"I like it," I whisper when he trails off, craning my neck up to get closer to his lips. "It means I'm yours and you're mine."

He swallows as he scans my face. "Are you feeling okay?"

At this, I lose my breath and tighten my arms around his neck like he'll leave right now, right this second. I haven't been feeling okay all morning.

"Blue?"

Biting my lip, I shake my head once.

His expression goes alert and so does his body. All tight and big and clashing with the softness of mine.

"Do you hurt?"

"I, uh, it's not that."

His hands grab my waist. "Then, what is it?"

I caress his stubbled jaw with my thumb, grazing the seam of his lower lip. It's so soft and full. "Do you... where do you live in New York?"

A frown bisects his smooth forehead and I go to caress that with my other thumb. "What?"

I move lower and trace the arch of his strong brows. "I just never asked you. Do you have like an apartment?"

He takes a few moments to answer as he watches me. "I share it with a couple of guys."

I smile slightly, rubbing the peak of his cheekbone. "Your friends?"

The pads of his fingers dig into my waist. "Kinda. Just some people Scoot, the guy who worked here before, hooked me up with."

"They ride like you?"

"One of them does. We, uh, perform at shows and stuff. I'm not home a lot."

I still remember the night I saw him jumping across the gap in the ground. It was scary, so fucking scary. But he was magnificent, too. Brave and shiny like a star.

"You're really good at it, aren't you?"

Some emotion moves in his eyes, making them liquidy, and I clutch his face with both hands. "Yeah. Took me a long time to find something I'm good at. Something that others think I'm good at, too."

Zach has a whole 'nother life out of this town.

I mean, I knew that already. But this gives it a concrete picture. An apartment he shares with friends. A job he's good at. I bet everybody who watches him perform thinks the same way. That he's brilliant and breathtaking.

His eyes take on a distant look, then. "Took me a hell of a lot longer though, to realize that not every dad treats his kid that way. For the longest time I thought that this is how it's supposed to be. A father is supposed to be mean and angry and I'm supposed to... just take it and hate him. I'm supposed to hate him so much that I become like him." Finally, he focuses on me. "A bully."

"Zach, you're not..." I begin with a determined and fierce tone. "You haven't been a bully in a long time."

"It was you who made me realize it, you know that?"

"Me?"

He's looking at me with something so akin to affection that I feel like I'll burst out of my skin. I'm so restless and needy.

So hungry for this elusive guy.

"Yeah. What you said to me on prom night. How I change you and make you into a worse person. That's when I realized I'd been doing to you what my dad does to me. I've been turning you into me, angry and vengeful."

Don't be like me.

His words from long ago make sense to me now. I get what he was saying. In his own way, he was telling me to move on, forget about him, live my life. He was telling me to be a bigger person, a better person than him.

I grab the back of his neck and press our foreheads together. "You're not like your dad. You're better than him. You're *so much* better and amazing and –"

Zach moves his hand from my waist and clutches my face, arching my neck up. "What's with the twenty questions?"

His brusque tone makes something clench in my tummy. Something thrilling and delicious. And I wrap my fingers around his wrist, the one with the tattoo. For some reason, touching it sends a shot of current slamming into my core.

"Why'd you come back to this town?" I ask.

His demeanor takes on a dark turn, a mysterious turn. "Why?"

Ever since he came back, I've seen him climbing out of tower one, where Mr. and Mrs. Prince live. It's the only place in this mansion where the junior staff isn't allowed. There have been so many rumors about why, but no one knows for sure and *no one* dares talk about it above hushed whispers. Mrs. S is super strict about it.

Every time I see him coming out of there, he appears angry and agitated. I don't know why. But I know it has something to do with his dad.

God, I hate that man so much.

"You were free, Zach." I swallow with difficulty as his grip on my face increases in pressure and my neck stretches up even more. "Of this place. Of your dad. Why'd you choose to come back?"

The little twinges of pain brought on by his possessive hold make my core spasm with arousal. Hungrily and violently. My breasts are throbbing, and my stomach is trembling with the rush of savage butterflies.

"Why?" he asks me again, looking down at me with hooded eyes.

Just tell me what's going on so I can help.

"Th-this place isn't good for you, Zach. You don't like it here. You shouldn't be here."

I don't know what I'm saying because I don't want him to leave. Not yet. In fact, that's the last thing I want.

But if I don't say this, I'll probably end up asking him to stay. I'll end up *begging* him to stay here. With me.

And I'll never do that.

This was his St. Patrick's for the first eighteen years of his life. He doesn't deserve to be stuck here.

"Why?" he growls, pinching my chin. "What're you gonna do when I'm gone, Blue, huh? You're gonna find someone? A guy? Go out with Ryan?"

When he's gone, I'll still be here.

Unlike Zach, I'm stuck here. In this town.

It's not going to end with just getting my house back, is it?

I'll have to work to *keep it*, meaning more mortgage payments. And for that, I'll have to work here, at The Pleiades. Where he grew up, where he was bullied and where we became something more.

I shake my head. "No."

"No?"

I dig my nails in his wrists. "No. I don't care about other guys."

A humorless chuckle escapes him. "Well, that's not gonna stop them, is it? From sniffing around you like hungry dogs. That's what you do, Blue. One look at you and a guy gets reduced to his most basic self."

Happiness blooms inside me at his harsh tone.

Not because of other guys he just referred to but because of him. Because *he's* the guy who gets reduced to his most basic self with me.

Zach makes me feel beautiful. He makes me feel stunning.

"What about you?" I pant, fisting his t-shirt. "Are you going to find another girl to date?"

His smile is cold. "I don't date."

Something breaks apart inside of me at his words. Some sort of a dam and I'm flooded with emotions. So many savage, violent, *possessive* emotions.

He's mine. I don't care what girl comes after me, he'll always be mine.

His dick has been buried between our bodies and I rub against it, whispering, "I want you to do something for me."

Zach rocks back even as he watches me suspiciously. "What's that?"

It's like I'm sick.

I'm possessed. There's a demon inside me. I swallowed it up the day I kissed him.

"I want you to fuck me."

"Yeah?"

I nod. "Yes."

"Right here, in this closet? Where anyone can hear us."

I put my hands on his shoulders and twist against his erection. "The night you came back, I shut myself in this closet. Because I didn't want you to see me."

"You were hiding from me."

"Yeah. I want you to fuck me in this closet, Zach. Show me."

"Show you what?"

"That I can never hide from you. That I was stupid to do that."

A muscle jumps on his cheek. "That's the smartest thing you've done ever since I got back."

And then, he swoops down and kisses me like this is our last kiss on this earth. He kisses me like we're coming to an end and this is how he wants it to happen.

This is how he wants them to find us, our lifeless bodies entwined together, and our lips sealed.

I kiss him back with equal fervor. With all this chaos inside of me.

My heart can't keep up with it. Everything is untethered, loose and banging against each other. All my organs, my bones.

My soul.

Zach breaks our kiss to move down to my neck and I bite my lip against the rush under my skin. My fingers bury themselves in his hair and my hips have increased their tempo.

He reaches my chest and bites my nipple through my uniform, making me gasp. He's sucking it, making love to it with his mouth and I feel it, feel the lash of his tongue through the cotton of my uniform and bra.

When he moves to the other breast, I see the wet spot he left on my dress and I almost come at the filthy, erotic thing he's done to my body.

"Zach, please…" I beg, moving against him restlessly.

His hands get under the white hem of my dress and grab my ass as he keeps sucking on my nipple, like he's drinking from it. Like he's drinking my lust and hormones.

I'm coming apart right now. My whole body is drying out.

Just when I think I can't take it anymore, Zach steps back from me, his lips wet and shiny, and spins me around.

My palms smack at the door and the sound is so loud that it echoes inside my chest.

Panting, I look back. "What are you doing?"

Zach appears possessed too. In a trance as he watches me, my arched spine and my stuck-out ass. He grabs my hips and squeezes, making my eyes flutter with arousal and heaviness before pressing his wildly breathing chest against my back.

"You wanna get fucked in a closet, baby?" he whispers in my ear.

I jerk out a nod.

"This is how you get fucked in a closet. From behind. Like we're two animals so desperate and crazy for each other that we can't even bother to find the nearest horizontal surface."

His words are filthier than anything I've heard in my life. More erotic and charged up and life-giving than my pounding heart and the blood flowing in my veins.

And all I have to give him in return is my slutty moan and a sharper arch of my back, offering him my ass.

"You want that? You want me to fuck you like that?" he rasps.

"Yes. Fuck me like I'm your slut and you can't get enough of me."

I feel his smile down to my curled toes. He presses a soft kiss on my cheek before moving away and flipping my dress up, over my ass. His fingers are rough and urgent as he hooks them around the band of my panties and pushes them down.

I'm panting. My breasts are pressed up on the door and my palms are sliding with sweat.

I imagine him pushing into my body any second now. I'm anticipating it, dying for it like my next breath.

But I feel something completely different.

Zach comes down to his haunches and presses his face in between my legs, making me sway on my feet.

I turn around just as he swipes my core with the flat of his tongue. My taste makes him groan and one of my hands reaches back and grabs hold of his velvety strands.

He hums in my pussy, making it clench. "God, your pussy tastes even better now."

"It d-does?"

"Yeah." He takes another taste, his hands kneading and parting my ass. "Because she's mine now and she knows it." A long, deep suck of my lips. "She knows who made her bleed last night." Then he jiggles my clit with his tongue, making me rake his scalp with my nails and arch into his mouth. "She should be mad at me, Blue. I made her all red and puffy. But she's not." He closes his mouth over my lips again, entering my channel with his thumb. "She loves it."

"She does," I say, breathily, rocking into his mouth.

Very, very much.

Zach eats me out while drilling my hole with his finger, his tongue moving lightly on my clit. It doesn't take me very long to come because I've been craving it, craving him ever since I got up this morning.

I'm coming down from my high when I feel him stand up, his coarse jeans grazing my bare ass. I hear the sound of his zipper and like a trained bitch in heat, my pussy salivates. I can feel my messy, wet thighs tremble.

"I wonder if you'll be this horny when I fuck you in the ass," he whispers, sending me flying into the sky, another stratosphere altogether.

How does he *know* all my buttons?

Slowly, agonizingly carefully, Zach slides his dick inside. I moan with his invasion. Moan and almost go crazy.

His jeans make contact with my bare ass and I go up on my tiptoes, clawing at the door. He probably just shoved them down enough to free his erection and get to my pussy. Like a desperate animal.

The thought makes me unsteady on my feet, drunk and high on him and his slow but thorough strokes.

Zach wraps my braid around his wrist, pulling my body into him. "Does it hurt?"

Somehow, I gather my senses and open my eyes, looking back at him. He's watching the slow glide of his cock inside of me.

It lights me up like fire, the thought that he can see my pussy opening up and closing around his cock like that. I wish I could see that.

"No," I whisper. "It makes me feel full. Fuller than last night. You're so deep."

His eyes go to me first and then travel to my hanging breasts. The uniform feels scratchy, but I don't have enough energy to unbutton it.

"I am, aren't I?"

"Uh-huh."

"You like that?"

"Yes. I love it."

We're whispering as if we're in a church, and somehow that makes me even more desperate for him.

"Does it make you feel horny?" he murmurs softly, his eyes glued to my tits.

I look down at them and find that I'm kneading the right one. I can't believe I didn't feel that. My fingers pull on the nipple and I bite my lip, blinking up at him and whimpering. Showing him how much I need him.

"And slutty, too," I whisper.

His jaw clamps and his stomach tightens up. I feel it when my ass hits it as he bottoms out. Still, he pumps in and out slowly, lazily, like we have all the time in the world and our lust isn't driving us to the edge of insanity.

"God, Zach, go faster," I beg him, trying to push back my hips.

But he has such a hold on my body that I can't move if he doesn't want me to. And he doesn't. "No, not when it can hurt you."

"It won't."

"Shut up, Blue."

He keeps torturing me with his slow, long pumps when I want him ramming into me. I want him jamming his big dick in my tiny, swollen hole so I can feel it forever.

So I can feel him fucking me when he's gone and I'm lying in my bed, crying for him.

Because I know I'll cry. I'll pine.

I'll dream about him for the rest of my days.

Frustrated, I clench my internal muscles, try to grip him harder, tell him that I don't care about the little hurt.

All I care about is him and his cock.

Zach stares at me accusingly as his perfect rhythm stutters.

"Blue," he warns, slapping my ass.

Like I'm a bad girl.

Maybe I am. I am a bad seed. Possessive and crazy and desperate for him.

So I do it again. In fact, I do him one better.

With the last of my strength, I pull myself up and away from the door. I arch my spine and plaster my shoulders over his chest before winding my arms around his neck.

His dick seems even deeper this way, with me standing up and him lodged inside from behind. My ass presses into his pelvis and I grind my hips, and despite himself he grinds back with a grunting breath.

I turn my face and tell him, "You can't torture me like this, you know. You promised."

"Promised what?"

"That you'll fuck me like I'm your slut."

Zach grabs my tits in both hands and squeezes them so hard that the moan that comes out of me is the loudest yet. "Yeah? You want everyone else to think you're my slut too? Because if I fuck you like that, Blue, you'll be screaming the roofs down. Your Mrs. S won't be the only person to know what you do for me. How you serve me."

Why does that arouse me so much?

Why do I want him to make me scream when I know the consequences?

My brain is melting and so is my body. And right now, I don't care enough about it to analyze.

All I want is to get fucked.

"I don't care." I roll my head from side to side as I breathe out, "I know you'll cover my mouth when I scream. I know you'll keep me safe."

I hear him breathe out a sharp breath, his chest swelling at my back.

A second later, I feel the wrath of his hands.

They tear at the buttons of my uniform, stretching it over my chest. With furious fingers, he pulls down my bra, making the straps stretch over my shoulders and snatching my tits, spilling them over my half-open dress.

He pinches the nipple, angrily, erotically. "You asked for it."

And after that, there's no talking.

He doesn't say a word and neither do I. I couldn't even if I wanted to.

His thrusts are rapid and punishing, making me bounce against him. His thighs and stomach smack against my ass and if he weren't holding me captive with his arm around my waist and his other plumping my breast, I would be on the floor right now.

And I revel in it.

I revel in his passion, his desperation. I love the sting of our bodies slapping together. I love the slight burn in my puffy channel. I'm ecstatic when he twists my nipples, worrying them between his fingers.

Through all of this, he hasn't stopped fucking me. In fact, he's bent his knees and made a lap out of his taut, muscular thighs so he can drill me deeper.

Suddenly, his hand on my breast goes away and I jerk my eyes open. I hear his panted breaths and his growls in my ear, misting up the side of my cheek as I feel that hand go lower, cupping my pussy, pinching the lips, the lips he's beating into with his big, *big* dick.

God, so big. So fucking thick.

And when he pinches my clit, I come.

A loud scream builds up in the base of my throat and I would've let it out. I would've ruined everything that I've worked for, for so many months, if not for his hand.

As I predicted, he covers my mouth with his big, strong hand and absorbs my scream with his palm.

Zach grabs my hip with his other hand, the one that was pinching my clit, so I stay steady on my feet as I spasm against him.

When he comes, he buries his face in my neck, spurting inside me.

Each throb of his cock and lash of his cum makes me jerk and writhe. He fills me with so much of his cream that some of it slides down my thigh.

As I come down from my high, I start to crash.

I start to feel disappointed. Sad, even.

I wanted him to prove me wrong. I wanted him to just let me scream. Scream and scream until the whole world finds out what we are to each other.

And I wonder why.

chaqter 28

We're at a carnival.

Yeah, a carnival.

By we, I mean me, Zach and Art. The three unlikeliest of people to ever go on an outing.

Actually, no.

Not the unlikeliest. In fact, all three of us have a lot of things in common. All three of us have been bullied in our lives. All three of us have no parents. I know Zach's are alive but are they really good for anything?

Moreover, Zach is Art's favorite person right now.

Especially ever since he read Art the story. That evening was amazing.

Zach was brilliant, albeit a little halting. He paused at a few words but nothing major. Art couldn't keep the shine out of his eyes and grin off his lips throughout the whole thing. I had to excuse myself to go cry a little in the bathroom.

I was just so proud. So in awe of Zach.

Later that night, when he came to me, I showed him how much.

That's somehow become one of our things: him coming to me at night. But not every night. Only when Tina's on the night shift and the cottage is empty except for me and him.

After I asked about his life in New York and he fucked me in the closet in broad daylight, so close to where we could've been caught, Zach has been careful.

So careful that me and him, we're the best kept secret at The Pleiades.

I don't see him at all during the day, except for when he works out by the pool and eats his breakfast in the kitchen.

The guy who I thought would have me fired when he first arrived a little over a month ago is the one who's guarding my job like it's *his* goddamn job to protect me from everything.

As the days pass, I become more and more restless. I feel like he could disappear any day, any second. And I won't even know it until he's gone like one of those falling stars that I so like to wish upon.

Maybe Zach feels the same way. I can't say for sure.

But every time he knocks at the back door of my cottage and I see the black night and silent woods at his back, he seems so hungry. So passionate, a mix of heaving breaths and hulking form.

Growling like a bear, he falls on my lips, pushes me into my bedroom and climbs on the bed with me. He tears at my clothes without any words. His fingers leave marks everywhere. His teeth leave bruises on my tits, my thighs, so close to my pussy that it feels like he's really eating me up.

I'm the same way.

My desperation, my violent need matches his. I break his skin with my nails. I scratch his back, his ass, his thighs.

He rides me with such need that I'm always desperate to come but still reluctant because I think, orgasm will put an end to this.

And I don't ever want it to end.

I want to get fucked by him forever and ever.

But it does get over, and by the end of it, we both are a sweaty, slippery mess.

And then comes our second thing. I read to him.

It's not a secret that I've never been into reading. But I'm starting to realize that I like it. Maybe I ignored it before because I hated going to school. I hated the students, the teachers, and not reading was my way of rebelling.

But I read now because Zach asks me to.

I think he likes books, as well. But for some reason, he doesn't want to read them himself. And it's not because dyslexia makes it exhausting for him to read.

It's something else.

Something that makes him withdraw when I compliment him or ask him about it. The only time he'll ever read is when Art asks him to. And even then, I can see reluctance in every line of his body.

Right now, we're exhausted. All three of us.

Since it's Saturday, I took a day off. We rode the bus to get here and spent the entire afternoon at the carnival.

I used to go to these when I was a kid but I haven't been in a long time. We tried everything. The rides, the games. The cotton candy.

I asked for a blue one. But Zach and Art both refused.

"It feels like eating your hair, Blue," Art explained.

"Yeah, Blue," Zach echoed.

"It's gross," Art continued.

"Totally gross," Zach said.

"Whatever, dudes. I don't care. I'm eating it."

And to show them, I took a huge bite of the fuzzy candy and moaned. Art went *ew* but Zach watched me with a hunger that he usually keeps reserved for the nights.

Anyway, the sun's setting and the sky is purple, and I think it's time to head out.

Art's dragging his feet and so Zach heaves him up and sits him on his shoulders. My steps go unsteady for a second at seeing the cutest little kid on the shoulders of the most beautiful guy I've ever met.

My two boys.

We're on our way to the exit when Art spots a giant alligator he *has to have* or he'll just faint right here. It's to be won in a game and Zach approaches the counter.

Sighing, I begin to follow but my eyes get caught up at a different stand. The chalkboard by its side says, *Written in the Stars*. And there's a sketch of a mountain, a lake and a moon with twinkling stars.

The tent's navy blue with off-white stars all over, and wind chimes hang off the cloth ceiling.

It's a fortune teller.

I've never been a big believer but something makes me approach it. A lady sits at the counter and upon noticing me, she smiles.

She looks... normal, a little bit older than me.

I mean, no chains or beads or a million rings to show off that she can see the future. She is wearing a poncho though, and a purple band in her red hair.

"Hi there," she greets me.

"Hey," I say, feeling a little stupid. "I don't..."

"You don't believe?"

I hug the giant teddy bear Zach won for Art by throwing a ring around a bottle. "Do you?"

She sits back in her chair, still beaming. "I'm here, aren't I?"

"I've heard that you guys are just people readers."

"Yeah. But that's what fate is, isn't it?"

"Uh, fate's what?"

She shrugs. "About people. It's not something magical. Though there is some magic. But mostly, it's about us, what we want."

"Really?"

Smiling, she nods. "Yeah. Really. They say fate is unkind and cruel to them. But maybe fate's just doing what they want it to do."

Scoffing, I roll my eyes. "Are you saying that people want cruel things to happen to them?"

"No. But sometimes cruel things happen because you're forging your way into something wonderful."

Right.

It was a mistake. I'm stupid.

"Yeah, I don't think so." I'm ready to leave but something makes me blurt out, "My parents died last year. I don't know what could possibly come out of *that* that's wonderful?"

She nods her head somberly. "Death's cruel. No two ways about it. But with death, comes life. Maybe you'll find life one day. Down the road, I mean."

Life.

Something bitter rises up in me. I'm not proud of it but it's there. I can't ignore it.

The truth is that in the past few days, I've come to resent my job. I've come to resent my goal that I've been so passionate about.

And it scares me.

What do I have if I don't have that goal? That was the one thing grounding me, the one thing keeping all the sorrow at bay.

"Life? What does that mean?"

She's back to smiling. "Means something pulsing with too many heartbeats and too much breath. Something red hot and passionate."

My mouth parts at *red hot and passionate*.

There's only one person who makes me feel that way. Who's *always* made me feel that way. And currently, he's trying to win a giant alligator for a five-year-old kid.

"Looks like you already have it."

I focus on the girl. "Now you just saw my face and read me."

She shrugs, setting her elbows on the table full of crystal balls. "Guilty. But actually, I saw you with him."

"With who?"

"That guy over there. In the black t-shirt with that kid on his shoulders."

She's pointing toward him at the next booth and my eyes follow.

Zach's gaze turns at the same time and his eyes are hot. Blazing, even.

His eyes are hypnotic.

Somehow, I manage to wave at him and look back at the girl.

She's smirking. "Told ya. You can't keep your eyes off him. I saw you guys walk by." Then she lowers her voice and it comes out like I imagine it must when she's reading the palms of her customers. "You love him."

The prediction or observation, whatever it is, hits me in the chest. I even take half a step back like I've been pushed.

Maybe by the invisible hands of the universe.

Such a fanciful thought and yet, it fills me with... life.

Too many heartbeats, too much air, red hot passion.

I shake my head instead. "I don't... I can't..." A deep breath. "I can't love him."

"Why not?"

"Because he, uh." I sweep a few fly-away strands off my forehead. "Because I work for him. For his family."

"So?"

"So it's against the rules."

"Love doesn't care about rules."

I shake my head. "He's just visiting. And I don't even know why. He'll leave soon."

"That's unfortunate."

I sigh with relief. She gets it now. She gets that I can't love him. How unfair it would be.

"But that still doesn't mean you can't love him."

Panic grips me for a second. That and anger, and I blurt out, "He doesn't want to be loved."

It's true, isn't it?

He hates love. Hates the very mention of it. I don't even know if he *can* love.

Let me tell you something about love: it hurts.

I can't love him. I'm not allowed to.

"Well, that's not up to him, now, is it?"

"I'm sorry?"

The girl has a tender look on her face. "He owns your heart. He might even hold it in the palm of his hand. He might close that palm and crush it one day. But what he can't do is force it to not beat for him. He doesn't have that power. And neither do you, maybe. A heart can be a real pain in the ass. You never know where its loyalties lie. Hearts have their own kings and queens. Sorry. So, if your heart loves him, well then, it loves him. You can't do anything about it. He *definitely* can't do anything about it. You guys are just gonna have to suck it up."

I emit a broken laugh.

I love him.

I love Zach.

That's what this has been about, hasn't it?

All this frustration and restlessness.

The fact that we're a secret. The fact that he'll leave me behind to rejoin his new life and I can't go with him because I have a different goal. A goal I'm starting to resent more than anything in this world.

"Suck it up." I look at the purple sky. "He's not going to like it."

"Big deal. Besides, he can't take his eyes off you either. So I don't know. I think you'll be pleasantly surprised."

I want to latch onto that hope.

I do.

But I know reality.

I love the guy who hates love. Nothing could be more tragic.

"Uh, okay. Well, I'm going to go but thanks for talking to me."

"You're welcome."

"Oh, and how much was it?"

She waves her hand. "No need. I didn't read you your future. I just observed a little. No charge for that."

I chuckle. "Okay. Thanks. I'm Cleo, by the way."

She offers her hand to me. "I'm Dove."

I shake it. "You mean, like the bird?"

"Yup, exactly like the bird."

As I turn around, I remember what Zach told me about The Pleiades.

How Zeus turned those seven sisters into doves and they flew away to escape Orion. And how Orion never lost hope and still chases after them.

What a crazy coincidence that a girl named Dove just made me realize that I love a guy who thinks the story of The Pleiades is the most pathetic tale of love he's ever heard.

I can't sleep.

I'm too amped up. I need Zach.

After the carnival, we rode back on the bus and parted ways just outside the gates. I didn't say a word and Zach kept giving me glances. I didn't know what to tell him. I didn't know how to act around him. So I let it go.

Tina wanted to grill me all about my day when I got back but I told her I had a headache and shut myself in the room. Nothing new. I've been lying to her a lot, keeping my relationship with Zach a secret.

Since then, I've been crying. I've been soaking my pillow and using it to smother my sobs.

At midnight, I don my stealth mode clothes and put on my boots. Jerking the hood up to cover my blue curls, I set out in the night.

It's dangerous; I know that.

But the thing is, I don't care. I don't care about anything right now but going to Zach, and asking him to make this pain go away.

I can't be in love with a guy who can disappear any moment. I can't love him when he hates love so much.

It's too excruciating. Too unfair.

I'm almost halfway up to the main house, passing by the pool, when I hear a splash. A continuous splashing.

I spy Zach under the pole light. He's making wide, long strokes with those arms of his.

Changing directions, I head over. I'm not trying to be quiet or sneak up on him but he hasn't noticed me yet. Or if he has, he hasn't given any indication. He keeps stroking, lapping around the pool as if he's trying to outrun something in the water.

I keep watching him, watching his glistening, tight body, his dark head that punctuates his arm-strokes.

I love him.

I love you.

As I stand here and watch him swim like he has fins instead of legs, I have no doubt in my mind that I've loved him since the very first moment I laid eyes on him.

I saw a boy, looking out the window in the detention room, watching the water fountain. I saw him with his shirt untucked, his hair messy, his tie loose and flipped over his shoulders.

And I thought: *him.*

I thought we could be friends.

But when I found out he was an obnoxious, mean jerk, I was hurt.

I was hurt that the guy I'd chosen for myself was such an asshole. That he wouldn't be nice to me. He hurt me by rejecting me and I hurt him back, and we kept going.

Until now.

Maybe hate is just love wrapped up in a barbed wire. Or at least, mine was.

I love you, Zach.

Abruptly, he stops in the middle of the pool with his back to me as if he heard me.

"You gonna stare at me all night?" he asks, plowing his fingers through his wet, slick hair.

With a pounding, bleeding heart, I walk closer to the edge. "You're not sleeping."

Zach turns around to face me. Water's running down his lashes, sluicing down the hard features of his face, and he scrubs a hand over it.

"Neither are you."

He looks tense, agitated, water lapping at his defined pecs. Probably like me but I don't know his reason. He's not in love, is he?

"So what did she tell you?" he asks.

"Who?"

"The fortune teller."

Oh.

I lick my lips. "She told me that everything happens for a reason. And that something is going to happen to me."

Zach frowns and drifts closer. "Something like what?"

The pool is illuminated by underwater lights, making it look like a soothing blue. A tempting blue. A blue I'd like to dip into someday. Tonight, maybe.

I take a few steps back and Zach tracks my every movement. I pull off the hood and unzip it. "Something like life."

"What?"

"Something with too many heartbeats and too much air. Something red hot and passionate."

I shrug off my hoodie and toe off my boots.

He looks like he wants to say something, but I cut him off. "Zach?"

"Yeah."

"I'm scared."

His frown gets even bigger. "Of what?"

Of you.

I grab the hem of my t-shirt and pull it off my body, leaving me in a navy-blue bra. "Of the water."

"Why?"

Because you make my heart bleed.

My hands go to the buttons of my shorts. "Because I don't know how to swim. I never learned. My dad tried to teach me when I was a kid but I just got so scared. I thought I'd drown. I couldn't stop crying so he brought me back home."

Zach's all alert now. He looks like he's going to come out of the pool. "Blue. Stop whatever fucked up, crazy thing you're thinking."

Bending, I shove down my shorts and step out of them. His eyes run up and down my barely-clothed body and I say, "My dad's dead, Zach. My mom too." At this, he comes to a pause, watching me carefully. "They're not here anymore. I don't have anyone in my life that I could turn to."

"Blue –"

"If I jumped into this water, they won't come and save me. They can't. Because I'm alone."

I probably look insane to him. Suicidal.

I'm not.

I'm just in love with him. And I know that if I tell him that, he'll break up with me. He'll probably call me pathetic or something and this secret affair will be over.

I know it in my stupid, fucking heart.

"You're not jumping in the water. I swear to fucking God, Blue –"

I cut him off again. "Will you save me?"

"Don't –"

"Tell me. If I jump in the water, will you save me?"

If I fall in love with you, will you catch me?

Again, a little too late to ask questions, right?

I've already fallen.

His shoulders move up and down in jerky breaths. His eyes are burning, scorching my body with his intensity, attention. It feels like he knows what I'm asking. The real question. Not the bullshit one I just made up.

It feels like he's going to say no.

"Yes."

Relief spreads through my limbs. Relief that I can do this. I can jump and he won't let anything happen to me.

Maybe this is my way of falling in love. Literally. Maybe this is my way of telling him. And by asking him to save me, I'm pretending that he'd say *I love you too.*

He calls out my name again but I don't heed it.

I just run and jump.

The splash that echoes, sounds like it's coming from inside a tunnel. The water punches me right in the chest and I feel a second of panic before his strong arms wrap around me. His big, strong, life-saving body collides with mine and I hold on to him, gasping for breath.

I don't think I was submerged for more than two seconds. Still, it feels like my lungs are full of water and starving.

Zach hugs me to him, smashes me, his arms wrapped around me like tight steel bands. Actually, his embrace is making it harder for me to breathe than what I felt when I jumped into the pool.

"Can't... b-breathe," I gasp, hanging on to him like a spider monkey.

At my warbled request, he loosens his hold, but then his hand is free to get tangled up in my wet hair and he pulls my head back.

I burn with his fury as he looks down at me. "What the fuck are you doing? Are you fucking crazy?"

His growled words settle in the vicinity of my heart and curl themselves like fingers around my lovesick organ.

"I wanted to find out."

He almost shakes my head by my hair. "Find out what?"

"What it feels like. Falling, I mean."

My answer doesn't please him. Not in the least. He squeezes my waist roughly. "You will never – *not ever* – do this again. Do you understand?"

I want to ask him how he will ever know if I take another plunge. He's leaving soon.

But I'm not that cruel.

I lick my lips, bobbing in the water even though I'm plastered to him. "I promise." Then, a tear leaks out and I whisper, "I just miss my mom and dad a lot."

Agony washes over his features and he hugs me again. I tuck my face in his salty and yet sweet-smelling neck and cry.

That's all I need.

A shoulder to cry on. I don't need any platitudes or any false consolations. Just him and his strong chest.

Sniffling, I turn my face and talk to the vein on his neck. "You know my house? The one I'm trying to get back?"

He hums, telling me that he's listening.

"I don't think I want it back for the right reasons." I finger the droplets on his collarbone as I continue, "I think I'm just afraid that if I don't have it, all the traces of my parents will be gone."

Zach squeezes me to him again and kisses my forehead.

"And there's another thing, I think," I continue.

"What?"

"I think if I don't want it back, then I have no reason to stay here," I confess. "Before my parents died, I wanted to leave town and go on a cross-country trip in my blue car. But when the time of it got closer, I started to feel panicked. I felt like, if I left this place, then no one in this entire world would know who I was. You know what I mean? Like, no one in this world would know what my name was. I'd be so, *so* alone. And then, they died and I was like, I can't go now. If something happened to me, they wouldn't know who to call."

I nod as if confirming my own words. "Yeah, so this is it. Maggie told me to quit my job and leave. Even Tina. But I've been using it as an excuse to just hide out here because no one in the world would know my name outside of this town, if I left."

His Adam's apple bobs with his swallow. I watch it happen and for some reason, it's so fascinating to me. It's so fascinating that the water is cool but the heat of his body is so thick that I'm sweating with it.

"I would know," he says gruffly.

"What?"

"I'd know your name. I'd be out there and I'd know who you were."

I smile, even though another tear leaks out. And something flashes across my brain.

A thought.

Such a fanciful thought: what if we're together? Him and me?

What if when he leaves, I leave with him?

What if he puts me on the back of his bike and we ride out into the sunset?

I move away from his chest and look up at him. His eyes are intense and sad and I realize, it's for me. He's sad for me.

His lips part as we stare at each other under the night sky, studded with a million stars.

"Someone could see you with me," he murmurs.

"I don't care."

"You need to be more careful," he insists.

"I don't. Not when I have you. You'd protect me," I reply confidently. "You've *been* protecting me all this time, right? Keeping us a secret. You don't want people talking about me. You don't want them to paint me as a slut, right?"

He's silent but his jaw flexes.

"This is another one of your ways to make up for what you did. Back at St. Patrick's. You never came to my rescue then, so you're making up for that now."

"You talk too much," he says roughly.

How can I not love him? This guy who repents in the sweetest and most caring of ways.

I wonder if I can ask him to take me along.

"I'll miss you when you leave," I whisper instead.

He stiffens against me. "I don't want you to."

"It's not up to you."

His answer is a hard clench of his jaw.

"Will you miss me?"

Zach's never given me any indication that he wants more than what we have right now. We've always had an expiration date on us.

But more than that, I wonder if he'd even want to take anything along from his old life when he leaves to rejoin his new one?

No matter what that thing might be. No matter if that thing is me.

"I don't want to."

I thought his denial – and I knew it would be a denial long before he uttered those words – would feel like an explosion.

But maybe some souls shatter in silence. They don't make a noise or even a rattle. They die quietly. Silently.

"I want you to do something for me," I say those words again.

The ones he spoke to me the night he told me to run, and then, I used them a day later because I wanted him to out our secret.

"What?"

I flex my hold around his body. It's weird being in water. I feel untethered. Lighter and heavier at the same time. At my flex, he squeezes me in his hold too.

"I want you to kiss me." I smile slightly. "Right here in the water. Under all the stars in the sky."

His thumb caresses my cheek for a beat before he bends down and kisses me.

It's hard at first. A forceful press of his mouth on mine, and then he begins moving his lips. And the kiss comes alive.

Wet and hot and burning.

In the background, I feel Zach moving. I cling to his body as I drown in his kiss. We drift across the water, and then I feel something on my ass. A cement step.

Zach has floated us to the end of the pool and he's sat me down safely on one of the steps, flanked by a silver railing that leads into the water.

Now that I'm on steady ground, Zach breaks the kiss to stare down at me. He's blocking all the light, casting a shadow over me in the shape of his big body. "You'll never do something like this again, yeah?"

"I p-promise."

I give him the answer he wants but even so, the angst on his face doesn't go away. It leaches out when he bends down to kiss me again.

He isn't as careful or slow as he was before. He slams his mouth over mine and I open under him. Both my lips and my legs to allow him in.

Above water, I can feel my nakedness. I can feel his nakedness too. He's wearing black swimming trunks and I'm only in my bra and panties.

His hard wet muscles feel like a perfect combination. They shift and bunch under my roaming hands, stoking up my need for him.

We kiss and kiss until we can't kiss anymore.

Until we need something more.

Zach makes quick work of our clothes, pulling down my bra to get to my tits and shoving my panties aside to expose my hole. I help him with his trunks and in a flash, he's inside me. He plunges in and out as he sucks on my nipples and places sucking, noisy kisses all over my chest.

I scratch his shoulders, his back, his biceps, whatever I can get to as I rock against him, fucking him with all these emotions in my heart.

I realize what I feel for him is too intense, too passionate, too heartbreaking and sad to be called love.

Maybe it's a tragedy.

Or maybe it's the blues.

I've got the blues and that's why I can't stop crying.

Zach lifts his head to find my tears tracking down my cheeks and his features are pained. I cry harder when he licks them up with his tongue.

I don't stop crying even when I hear the water splashing around us and our bodies feel buoyant. They're bounding and bouncing more than usual, making everything doubly erotic.

And when I come, I cry then, too, pouring my sadness on Zach's tongue and my climax on his cock.

Yeah, it's the blues.

Because I love a guy like him.

Chapter 29

He's walking up to tower one.

This never happens. *Never.*

For the past month, I've always caught Zach climbing down the stairs but never climbing *up*.

Oh my God, this is my chance. A chance to find out what's going on.

On second thought, it's none of my business. He's never revealed anything to me. I mean, if he wanted me to know he would've told me.

But then, on third thought, maybe it's a sign.

Maybe what's happening to him up there is just so horrifying that he can't talk about it and this is my chance to find out. I bet whatever it is, his dad is definitely involved.

And if I'm right, then I'm going to fuck him up and I'm not even kidding.

He's the reason Zach has felt so rejected all these years. He's the reason Zach is filled with so much resentment and anger.

Mr. Prince is a bully and isn't it my duty to stand up for Zach against him? Stand up for what's right?

My legs start moving before I've even finished my thought.

I'm supposed to get to tower three and tend to guests, but Tina's up there now and she can hold down the fort a little longer without me.

I quickly climb up the steps lest anyone pass through and ruin my plan.

The hallway with its flanked rooms looks much the same as any other tower. Although I will say that it's awfully white. And the overhead lights? They are glaring.

It's a harsh hallway. I instantly dislike it.

Of all the rooms, there's the second one on the right with its door ajar, and I walk up to it.

Through the slice of an opening, I see someone.

A woman.

She's small. Rail-thin and weak. She has a peach-colored gown on and her head's wrapped up in a beige scarf. She's propped up in the bed, blankets covering her lower body.

Something about her is so familiar and I don't realize what it is until she takes a breath, smiles slightly, and then begins coughing.

It's Mrs. Prince, Zach's mother.

It starts with a gentle cough that becomes harsher and more violent until she has to come off her pillows and cough into a napkin.

A napkin given to her by Zach.

I almost fall into the door with shock but thankfully catch myself. Although I do push at it gently so as to widen the gap so I can see clearly.

Zach's bending over her, his hand on her back, rubbing in circles, soothing her, and his mom's fingers are clawed over his other wrist for support. A few seconds later, her coughing fit goes away and she lies back down.

I can hear her ragged, noisy breathing as she tries to relax.

Zach throws away the napkin in an unseen trashcan, I think, before coming back to the bed with a glass of water. His mom dutifully takes it but still, he keeps holding it. Maybe because he thinks she can't handle it. And from the looks of it, she can't.

I still can't believe what I'm seeing.

Didn't I see her all made up and *healthy* at that dinner party with the Howards a few weeks ago?

Right now, she looks run-down. She's still beautiful but her cheeks are sunken. There are dark patches on her skin. Her lips are chapped and there's a bony, diseased quality in her demeanor.

"You okay?"

That's Zach.

He asks me the same question in that same low voice of his. It's concern.

"Yeah."

He puts away the glass and drags a chair to the bed, taking a seat. "Where's Dad?"

And just like that, his concern is gone and is replaced by hardness.

"Meeting," his mom replies.

"Of course." He picks up the TV remote from the nightstand and begins to fiddle with it. "A movie, okay?"

His mom nods.

"Was he here when the doctor came?" he continues but his eyes are on the TV. He's staring hard at it but I have a feeling that he knows nothing of what's happening on the screen.

"Don't start, Zach."

"He wasn't here, was he?" Running his teeth over his lower lip, he shakes his head. "Fucking typical."

"Zach."

Somehow, her voice gets stronger and she looks stronger too. Like a trick of the light. But maybe that's how she's fooling everyone. She's the kind of woman who can put on a face when the occasion calls for it.

"What?"

"Let it go. Your father has other duties. He has a company to run."

"Yeah, his fucking company. It will all fall apart without him, won't it? He can't even stay home to find out how long does his wife have left to live."

His mom glares at him. "Stop being so ungrateful. And stop using bad language in front of me. Where are your manners?"

He scoffs.

"Your dad's done everything for this family. He did everything for you. He's always wanted what's best for you."

"Only I threw it away."

A curt nod. "Exactly. Do you know how much it hurts him? The kind of son you are. Ungrateful and a troublemaker. But let's not dwell on such things." She lifts her chin and pats his arm. "I like this movie. Reminds me of how your father was when I first married him."

There's a slight smile on her face as she watches whatever the hell movie's playing. Zach's jaw is ticking though.

"Your father was such a handsome man back in the day. You take after him, you know," she says to Zach lovingly. "When you were born, your dad was so happy. So happy. He looked at me like I was his queen. I can never forget that look."

A few seconds of silence.

Then, "And neither can I forget the look in his eyes the day he found out that you're defective. I thought he hated me. You brought on such bad memories for him, you know. Of his own childhood."

Zach's grip on the remote is so tight, I can see his white knuckles from here. I'm afraid that they're going to bust out of his skin.

A few moments pass and she suffers from another coughing fit that Zach helps her through. He gives her the water again. And again, he holds it for her.

When she's done, he asks, "How's the wrist?"

"It's fine. Nothing but a scrape."

"What'd you tell the doctor?"

She grows stern again. "There was nothing to tell."

"Bumped into a doorknob, again?"

His mom sighs. "Seriously, Zach. What's eating at you this morning? Why can't you let it go? It was simply a harsh grip. Sometimes he loses control. He's stressed. He has a –"

"A company to run, I know."

She huffs. "Yes, and a sick wife. And a son who doesn't mind him." She looks him up and down. "Why don't you wear some nice clothes? At least wear them for the parties. Your father hates it when you run around in such tattered clothes. You look like one of the staff."

"I don't care what *father* wants, *Mother*," he replies back caustically.

His mom looks at him in outrage. "For the love of God, Zachariah, stop being such a brat. I can't believe I made the case with your dad to let you stay. Especially after what you did to him. Especially after all the times you've let *me* down through the years. Don't make me regret letting you stay."

Zach chuckles harshly. "You made the case for me to stay, Mom, because you knew that your husband wouldn't stay by your side now that you're not pretty and shiny anymore. Now that you're sick and it takes an army to make you perfect for his little parties, Dad doesn't want you anymore. He won't even come home because he doesn't want to see what you've become. The man you love doesn't want you, okay? Isn't that why we keep it all hidden? Like cancer is some sort of a crime. So you made the case for me to stay even after everything because you don't want to die alone."

His mom looks at him with a trembling chin and so much hatred and heartbreak that my eyes fill with water.

"But let's not dwell on such things," Zach repeats, sarcastically. "I think I like this movie too."

And just like that, all conversation is gone.

Even if I stand here for years, I know they won't talk anymore. All the things they could've said to each other, they already have.

This is it.

This is the whole reason why Zach hates love, isn't it? This is the whole reason why he'll never love anyone.

A self-absorbed mother who probably didn't care when her son was getting bullied. A hateful dad who should've supported him but chose to beat him down, instead.

How can Zach want love – any kind of it, really, either familial or romantic – when he's seen things like this?

I wonder how many times his parents rejected him before he realized that love hurts. Before he stopped trying and became a cynic.

They say love is the most powerful thing in the world.

But even love dies when you stomp on it enough. I don't think it is capable of living through something this toxic and dysfunctional.

Something this violent.

My eyes go to Mrs. Prince's wrist again, the one Zach asked about.

It's the same one that Mr. Prince was holding on to the night of the dinner with the Howards.

The night I found out how fucked up Zach's parents are.

chapter 30

I'm waiting for him in his room.

I asked Mrs. S to put me on the night shift tonight and she did because one of the other girls couldn't do it. So it's not really breaking and entering. Although I did use a hairpin to unlock his room.

I'm lying in his bed and watching the stars, still looking for Orion, when the door opens.

Zach steps inside and I sit up, wearing my mom's nightie. The one he likes with pretty lace around the neck.

For all his hardness, he likes feminine things. My curly hair, my sweet smell, my soft stomach and heavy breasts. The lace around the neck of my nightie.

His eyes find mine as he shuts the door.

"Hi," I whisper.

He tugs his white earphones off slowly as he walks in further. He's wearing a sweaty vest-like t-shirt that's stuck to his body, clinging to the curves of his muscles.

"Have you been running?" I ask.

He nods, dropping his cell phone on the dresser. "Have you been waiting long?"

I come to my feet and nod. "Yeah."

I've been waiting for him for years. But that's nothing compared to all the years I'll wait for him even when I know he'll never come to me.

"Did someone –"

"Nobody saw me," I say, cutting him off.

We meet in the middle of his room. He looks down and I look up and there's a rush inside me.

A shivering. A quaking. A landslide.

I take his hand and put it on my ribs. "You feel that?"

Zach stares into my eyes before glancing down where our hands are joined on my stomach. He presses his palm in my softness, grabbing onto it like he can't help himself. Like a starved, dying plant latches onto the sliver of sunlight.

"You're shaking," he says.

"Yeah. It's the butterflies."

His brows crease up. "Butterflies?"

"Uh-huh. You give them to me. You always have." I swallow, goose bumps waking everywhere. "Ever since day one."

Zach moves his fingers slightly. Going back and forth on my stomach as if trying to soothe them, the savage butterflies inside. I can hear the rustle of his rough palm over my nightie in the quiet of his room.

"I didn't know," he whispers, sweat dripping into his brows.

I use my thumb to wipe it off. "I used to hate them but not anymore."

His jaw flexes and his eyes get darker. More intense.

I wish I could say I love them, the butterflies, I mean. But I'm afraid.

I can't be, though. Not tonight. I need to be brave.

I need to confess.

Not about the love I have for him but what I did this morning. How I violated his privacy and watched him with his mom.

Widening my smile, I grab hold of his t-shirt and give it a tug. "Come on, let's go."

"Go where?"

"To the bathroom."

"Why?"

"So I can murder you and dump your body. It'll be easier to clean up the blood," I repeat his own words to him, tugging at his shirt again.

He shucks it off, dropping it on the floor. "Yeah, I don't think you'll murder me. You need my dick too much."

And your heart.

"You got me there." I pull him toward the bathroom. "So we're really just going to take a shower. Because you stink."

I hear his chuckle behind me.

"*We* are going to take a shower because *I* stink?"

Stopping in the middle of the bathroom, I face him. "Yup. That's the plan. I'm going to clean you up. Soap you up real good."

"Yeah?"

His voice is dark and sensual, just like the rest of him. His body glistens under the overhead lights and I can see every ridge and line of his muscles.

"Yes."

He tucks a finger in the neck of my nightie, first rubbing it over my skin and then tugging the fabric and using it to bring me closer.

I rest my chest over his, both of us breathing together, and tilt my neck up.

"Shouldn't you be naked for that?" he rasps, playing with my lace now.

I nod, biting my lip.

Zach fists my nightie at the chest and pulls it over my head before I can even draw my next breath and pushes my panties down.

Like always, he seems mesmerized by my body. My collarbones, my nipples, my belly button. The jut of my hips. That slit in between my legs. My toes.

Everything small and curvy and soft on my body is his favorite thing to see.

And I show him.

In fact, I move closer to him, to his sprung-tight, aroused body. I massage his shoulders and rub his chest. "You work so hard for this body, don't you? Every morning," I whisper, circling his collarbone, rubbing his nipples. "Push-ups, pull-ups. Squats. Planks. I don't even know what else."

I'm at his ribs now, bronzed and strong. I push my thumbs in, twist my knuckles over the ropy muscles. I feel his hips thrust. Gently, slightly, just a whisper of movement, grazing my bare belly.

"You sweat and gasp and pant. Every muscle in your body vibrates. Your veins stand up. I notice it all. In fact, by the time you're done, I'm panting. It makes *me* lose my breath from what you put this body through."

I clutch his sides before making my way down to his tight stomach with all the grooves. "When you grunt, I feel it between my legs, I swear. I get all swollen and horny just watching you. Watching how hard you work."

I thread my fingers through the tuft of his dark curly hair that leads down to his dick. Which is straining against his sweats right now.

Looking back into his hooded, slightly wild eyes, I whisper, grazing my needy nipples over his abs, "Can I make you feel good? Please? I want to make you feel good, Zach. Treat you like a prince for being such a hard worker. Let me show how much I love your body."

Let me show how much I love you.

At my words, he fists his hand in my hair, pulling my head back. His cheeks are jutting out, his jaw rigid and square. His neck is flushed with lust.

He's a guy at the end of his patience, at the end of his rope.

"Who are you?" he growls.

A girl who loves you.

"Your prize."

His other hand comes up and wraps around my neck, feeling my racing pulse. He's harder than ever, hotter and darker and completely wild.

"Take off my pants."

My hands fall to the waistband of his sweats and, swallowing, I do. He probably feels it under his palm, the jerk of my throat.

I manage to get them down to the tops of his thighs, exposing his hard cock that springs out like a weapon and slaps against his abdomen. Zach does the rest of the work, shoving them down and off his legs.

Then he walks me backward, his dick grazing my upper tummy. I feel its wetness rubbing over my skin.

Letting go of my neck and hair, he grips my waist and picks me up and puts me inside his ceramic bathtub before getting in himself and closing the shower curtain in one go.

Now we're all enclosed, cornered and hidden inside this tiled space, him and me. He casts a shadow on the wall, covering me completely and leaving no space for me anywhere but inside the contours of his large body.

Zach simply stands there, staring down at me with intense eyes, and in this moment, I'm filled with a purpose.

He wants me to serve and I will.

Clenching my thighs, I grope the wall behind me for the shower knob. When I find it, I turn it on and water rains down on us.

I step into him and push back the hair that is slick on his forehead. Taking his hand, I change our places, getting him under the spray of water. It's hard to look away from him, from the water sluicing down his muscles making him look so magnificent, but I do it.

I find the bottle of soap, squirt it on my palm before lathering it up. I start at his neck, going up and down the column of it, before moving down to his shoulders and chest. I make his skin all slippery and soapy and scratch his nipples, causing him to fist his hands on his sides.

Bending down, I soap up his torso. Stunningly hard and tight and defined.

Then I come down to my knees and soap up his cock. It's the most delicate, intimate and powerful thing on his body. Long and thick and proud, it stands as I stroke it. My fingers slip in the soap and I graze my thumb in the slit.

I hear his groan and glance up to see him throwing his head back into the water as I work him.

My entire body feels swollen with my lust and my love for him. This towering dark prince.

He told me once that if he wanted, he'd make me his slave and I'd fall down to the ground so fast, my knees would bleed.

I think this is it.

I'm his slave now, kneeling on the ceramic tub, serving him. Even though there's no blood on the outside, on the inside, I'm bleeding with his love.

I work his sac next, flexing them, rolling them in my palms.

It makes his cock jerk. A pearl of a drop leaks out from the top of it and mixes in with the bubbles of his spicy-smelling soap.

As much as I want to play with him, give him the relief he needs, I move lower. I need to pamper him first, spoil him before giving him his climax.

I soap up his thighs, my fingers sifting through the hair on them. Slowly, I move down and work on his calves. The muscles on them, Jesus. I never thought calves could be sexy but they are.

They *so* are.

When I'm done, I come to my feet and his nostrils flare. His eyes look stoned. They are dark and drunk, completely wasted.

Before I can turn him around, he grabs the back of my neck, pulling me flush to his soapy body. "What are you doing to me?" he whispers, turned on and angry.

Our chests slip against each other because of the soap and goose bumps wake up on my wet skin. "Serving my prince."

His grip stutters at the word and I know it means something to him. Me taking care of him like this when probably no one ever did.

When he presses a hard kiss on my mouth, I know it means *everything*.

I get him to turn around and his arms splay open on the tiled wall, his head bowing down.

I get more soap from the bottle and keep going, massaging and lathering up his shoulder blades and his spine. I poke my fingers in the dimples at the small of his back, soap the taut cheeks of his ass.

Once I'm done, I turn him back around and position him under the spray. I get all the soap off, go on my tiptoes to massage his scalp. I circle and rub his muscles until the water runs clean.

Zach opens his eyes, water rivering down his face, and he pushes his hair back, all sparkly and washed.

Looking into his eyes, I come down on my knees once again.

His chest swells as he stares at me with dominance and possession. Something about that makes me so horny for him. So hungry to bring him relief.

I take him in my mouth. He's been hard all through this, hard and leaking and I can't let him take it anymore. His shaft looks pissed off and I need to soothe it.

Balancing my hands on his hard thighs, I suck his dick.

His clean, musky taste makes me want to close my lids and savor this but I don't want to lose our contact. The connection.

But what I *can* do is moan over his length so he can feel the vibrations. And I do that.

I moan and suck and blink up at him with needy eyes. I open my mouth wide, wide, wider until I'm inhaling almost every inch of him.

And over me, he's tensing. His abs flex and he shifts on his feet, restless. His groans are louder than the splash of water against his back and the tub. His fists are getting tighter in my hair and over my shoulder.

Before long, he's thrusting inside my mouth like he'd thrust inside my cunt.

He's taking his pleasure from me instead of me giving it to him. And that's the highest kind of pleasure I can grant him: letting him take from me.

I rake my nails down his thighs, up his juddering stomach. I go back and dig my nails in his hard ass, making the globes twitch.

Then, I do something that I never thought I'd do in a million years.

I trace the crease between his hard, muscular cheeks, finding that dark hole.

Zach stiffens over me, his thrusts in my mouth losing their rhythm. But I take over the job again. I move my mouth, taking him in and out as my thumb circles his tight, clenching hole.

With my other hand, I palm his balls again, squeeze them, tug at them and rub my finger over the delicate perineum. It makes him go up on his toes and palm my right tit.

My heart's beating against my chest so hard at the illicit way I'm touching him. The way he's tightened up and twitching and grunting.

God.

It's the hottest thing ever.

It gives me the courage to pop my wet, slippery thumb inside of him, inside his tight hole, while vacuuming his cock in my mouth with a long, harsh suck.

And with a big jerk of his body, he spurts on my tongue.

But if I thought he'd let me set the pace, I was wrong. He grips my hair and pulls my mouth off with one hand while the other grabs the base of his spasming dick.

Zach aims at it at my chest and I arch my spine and push my breasts for him to come on. His hand circles his cock and he strokes, strokes, *strokes*, spilling his cum all over my tits.

White creamy ropes cover me and slide down the slope, plopping over my nipples. I don't know what to watch, his orgasm on my body or him, panting and vibrating.

When he's done, he opens his heavy lids.

Our eyes connect again, mine submissive and in love and his mean and dominating.

Clenching his jaw, he picks me up and forces me to stand. Panting, I look up at his harsh face.

"You think you can touch what I didn't give you?" he growls.

I hold on to his shoulders. "I just wanted to make you feel good."

He studies me for a beat and presses a short, hard kiss on my mouth. "Yeah? Well, I hope you're ready then."

"Ready for what?"

"Ready to really see what it means to serve me."

Zach doesn't give me the time to absorb his words before he changes our positions, then spins me around.

I'm facing that tiled wall now, the stream of the shower running down my back. I turn around to look at him when Zach grabs my hips and pulls me back, grinding his dick in the crease of my ass.

"What're you going to do to me?" I ask with a tinge of trepidation and a whole lot of excitement.

He runs his open mouth along the column of my neck. "I think you know."

I arch up against his dick that hasn't gone soft even after his climax. "Fuck me?"

"Yeah. That's for sure."

Something makes me ask him, "Where?"

His hands rub over my stomach, go down to cup my pussy in one sweep before traveling up to squeeze my breast. "In your ass."

I shudder against him and bring my arms up and back, fisting his drenched hair. "Okay."

"Okay, huh? Is that why you pulled that move on me, Blue? Was that your way of telling me? You wanted to get fucked in the ass."

I rub my thighs together. "I don't know. Maybe."

Pinching my nipple, he warns, "But then, this isn't about you now, is it? You're here to serve me. Take care of me."

Biting my lip, I nod. "Yes. It's about you. Whatever you say goes."

"It does." He kisses my cheek lightly, so in contrast with how he's humping my ass and twisting my nipple. "So I say that I'm gonna fuck you in the ass. But I'm also going to fuck your tight snatch."

"Oh God..." I moan out when he utters that word.

That dirty, filthy, nasty word. The word that really makes me feel like his slut, a maid hired just to serve him and his base needs.

As if they're paying me for this. So he can have a body to slake his lusts in.

They are all fools, then.

They don't need to pay me. I'll be his, body and soul, for free and forever.

Zach gives a hard thrust of his pelvis. "Are you ready for that? Are you gonna let me bang all your holes tonight, Blue? Both of them."

The shower is wetting my skin but I still feel like my pores are parched.

"Yes. Anything you want."

A harsh breath escapes him and he drops his forehead on the crook of my neck on a groan. "Christ, you're driving me crazy, baby."

I turn my face and kiss his hair. "You drive me crazy too."

He looks up then, his eyes hooded. Kissing me, he steps back and away from my body.

Keeping our eyes connected, he searches for the soap, finds it and squirts it on his palm. He lathers it up, breathing wildly. But unlike me, he doesn't wash my entire body.

No, he goes for my butt.

"Thrust out your ass," he commands.

Looking away from his intense eyes, I do it. I'm staring at the tiled wall when I feel his soapy fingers on my crease.

I gasp when he goes to my tight, clenched-up hole and circles it with his fingers. I feel him pulling the cheeks apart to get better access to it and I barely suppress my groan. My nails are clawing on the wall when he asks me to relax.

Still working on my hole, he presses his chest to my back and sucks on my earlobe. I moan, dropping my head back and resting it against him.

Maybe I'm relaxed enough now because he pops his finger inside, swirling it.

"Zach, I…"

"Shh, relax. I won't hurt you. I'll never hurt you, okay?"

"Okay."

"Push back."

It takes me a second to realize that he means push back, not with my body, but with my internal muscles.

I burn with embarrassment as I obey him. As if by magic, his finger slips inside even more.

It's weird, the fullness, but I don't hate it.

In fact, it makes me want to rub my clit. It starts up an ache somewhere deep in my core.

Zach kisses my cheek softly and brings one hand to play with my nipple. That gets me going even more.

My pussy is juicing up and I shift on my feet, lodging his long finger inside my ass even deeper.

"You like that?"

"Uh-huh."

"Thank fuck," he mutters.

I don't know how I can smile at a moment like this, when he's working his finger inside my butt, but I do.

He starts up a rhythm, in and out, loosening me up somewhat, and I rock against him. A second later, I feel the pressure doubling up and I realize Zach has managed to pop in another finger. He's scissoring them inside me, stretching me out for his cock.

I don't think anything can prepare me for his thick, long erection but I love him for trying. For making me like it.

Lustfully, I cover his hand on my breast and press it. Zach moves his down then, leaving me alone to toy with my mound, and goes to my clit. He strums it, making me moan.

My orgasm takes me by surprise. It happens so quickly, so suddenly, as soon as he touches my clit. It's not explosive though. But it's enough to clench all the muscles in my lower body and relax me.

I miss his body heat when he moves away from me.

With heavy eyes, I see him soaping his dick and I know this is it. This is the moment he'll enter my ass. He was just waiting for me to relax.

Looking up at me, Zach bends me forward even more and positions his dick. "Relax, okay? And push back."

I nod. "Okay."

Something somber washes over his face. Something that looks like gratitude. "I won't hurt you, Blue."

He's said it to me before but this time, I feel it down to my soul. I know he means now. He means he'll go slow. But I pretend he means emotionally, and he means forever.

"I know," I reply. "Now put it in."

A lip twitch.

And then, I feel the pressure. I have to turn away from him and rest my forehead on the wall.

Maybe I'm clamming up in fear because I feel Zach trying to enter but he hasn't breached me yet. I feel him come forward and play with my clit again. It makes me jerk with how hypersensitive I am.

"Push back, Blue," he whispers. "Let me in, baby."

Something about the cajoling tone of his words and that wicked finger on my clit loosens me up again, and he manages to stick the crown of his shaft in.

"God," I groan, panting.

Zach drops his forehead on my shoulder and bites at the skin. "Fucking Christ..."

His hips move, only a short jab but we both feel it too much with the way we're moaning.

"You're so tight. So, so tight. I can't..." he rasps.

I hear the agony in his voice. It reminds me so much of the night he took my virginity and was so worried about hurting me that I reach back and caress his hair.

And I push back more, welcoming him deeper.

Zach curses, his hips slowly, very slowly, rocking into me. In and out. It's barely there, the rhythm but still, I feel like I'm bursting at the seams.

I feel like I could come like this. With his fragile, careful pumps and his finger on my clit.

But then, he leaves my clit to grab my hips and keep me steady. Until then, I didn't realize that I was swaying, that my legs were too weak to hold me up.

With his hands on my hips, Zach finds a better rhythm. His pumps are longer now, deeper, but still gentle and slow.

I can hear his raspy breaths. He's strung tight like a bow. The pleasure is too much for him but he's holding back for my sake.

That purpose I'd felt when I started washing him up floods over me again.

Resting my forehead against the wall, I play with my slippery nub, trying to loosen myself up for him. So he can go deeper, faster. So he can fuck my ass like he wants to.

It works, I think.

The more I play with my clit, the looser I become. The pain is bearable. The stretch doesn't feel like it will bust me open any second, and his movements inside me are easier.

I can't believe this is happening. I can't believe that I'm taking him this way but everything about this feels right.

So, so right.

I was made for him. Every part of my body is his for the taking.

Zach groans with every inch he gains inside of me and his needy, horny sounds are pushing me over the edge.

My entire world is centered on him right now.

At his breaths, his sounds, his fingers digging into my hips, his dick inside my ass, forcing the parts of my body open that I never thought possible.

Panting and gently moving inside of me, he says, "I'll never forget this, Blue. I'll never forget how it feels..." He pauses to emit a groan and splay his palm open on my lower stomach. "How it feels to be inside your ass. So hot and tight and how you're letting me in even though it's hurting you." His thumb tucks into my belly button and he finds that vein again, the one that binds us, making it swell up. "I'll dream about this, Blue. I'll miss this when I'm gone."

Just as his words die out, I come.

My cunt gushes because he said he'll miss it. He'll miss being inside of me. It might be pathetic to some, but to me, it's everything.

He'll miss me. Even though it's only my body, but he will miss me.

I come so hard and violently that I don't even notice when Zach gets in completely.

His entire cock is buried in my ass as I spasm around him. And it's too much for him, I think. Because he comes too.

His erection throbs inside my ass. I feel every lash, every jerk of his dick as he empties himself inside of me.

When he's done, he wraps his arms around my waist and plasters his wet, panting chest to my back.

Good thing, too. Because I really have no energy for anything right now.

Gently, Zach detaches himself from me and turns me around. Blinking, I look up at him just in time to notice his lips coming down on mine.

He kisses me under the shower.

Kisses me and kisses me until my lips go numb and I grow sleepy. Then, he washes me up like I did him and carries me to bed.

Zach lays me down, all drenched with the shower, and comes between my thighs.

I open them wide and wind my arms around his neck.

"I don't want to tire you out," he says, settling himself over my body, his cock hard and ready again, nudging my core.

"You won't," I tell him, sleepily but surely.

"Blue –"

Reaching up somehow, I kiss him. "You said you'd fuck me in both my holes. Can't go back on your promise now."

Zach sweeps his gaze all over my face before shaking his head once and entering my wet channel.

It's a slow, sweaty fuck.

Actually, it's not a fuck at all. It's love.

We're making love.

Slowly, gently, thoroughly.

He's rocking into me like a soft wave and with every stroke, I'm drowning.

As I look into him, I realize that everything about him is heartbreakingly beautiful. His intense eyes, that strong forehead, his stubborn jaw. That masculine body flexing and rippling over me. His heat, his smell.

I can't stop feeling him everywhere.

In my pussy, my stomach. My womb, in my very femininity.

I want to keep looking at him but I'm so lazy and lethargic that my lids fall shut.

And I smile.

I love him so much.

So, so much.

If this is the only way I can tell him then, it's okay.

I can live with that.

I love you, Zach. But I'll never tell you.

The thought makes me come once again. I don't even know what number orgasm this is. I've lost count.

As Zach shudders inside me with his own climax, I realize that I also lost the secret I wanted to tell him. I can't remember what it was.

A second later though, I can't think of anything except going to sleep.

Chapter 31

Even though I don't remember falling asleep, I jerk awake in the middle of the night.

I'm in Zach's bed, naked and feeling like a noodle, lumpy. The room's dark, the only light from the bathroom.

There's a sheet over me, courtesy of Zach, I think. But he's not by my side.

I look around and find him in his armchair by the big glass window. The night's dark with bright stars and I guess it's way past midnight.

"Hey," I whisper, sitting up and clutching the sheet at my breasts. I can still feel him between my legs, him and his body.

Zach's naked too, the muscles silhouetted by the silver moonlight. His thighs are wide, and his elbows are resting on them as his gaze rests on me.

Actually, no.

His gaze isn't resting. There's turbulence in it, a strange intensity that shines brighter in the near-darkness.

"You love me," he says.

My languid, warm, thoroughly-fucked body feels cold at his words. Cold and dead and numb.

"What?"

"You. Love me," he repeats. Like, he's trying to taste the words in his mouth, roll them around between his teeth and tongue.

What comes out is not something he likes.

His frame gets angrier. His elbows dig even harder in his thighs.

I feel like a criminal, the way he's watching me. Someone who's committed a crime.

I don't know where I get the courage from but I raise my chin and fist the sheet on my chest, nodding. "Yes."

I swear I can hear the gnashing of his teeth. I can hear the grind. The angry rush of his blood.

"Since when?"

My heart should be racing right about now. I should be panicky. I should be trying to salvage this. But after the initial icy blast of shock, all I feel is relief.

He knows now.

It's out there. My horrible secret, or at least one of them, is out of my system.

"Since forever," I reply. "Probably since the first day I saw you."

I watch the impact of my words on his body. A deep breath. Flaring nostrils. The tautness of his veins and clench of his muscles.

Before he can grill me some more, I ask, "How'd you know?"

"You're not very good at hiding things."

That's when I realize that I might have said it out loud. The thought that made me climax and lulled me into sleep.

God, I'm stupid.

"Actually, I'm pretty good at hiding. It's just you I can't hide from."

"And isn't that the real fucking tragedy?"

My sinuses sting.

Yeah, this is a tragedy. It always was. Knowing that doesn't make it easier to live through, though.

"What about the second day?" he asks, all calm-like.

But I know it's all a lie. He's seething inside, getting ready to blow up.

"Second day of what?"

"When I destroyed your notebook? Did you love me then, too?"

"I –"

"Or the third day, when I asked one of my friends to trip you on your way to class? Or the fourth? And the fifth? Did you love me through the years of humiliation and pranks I pulled on you? All the times I could've saved you with just one flick of a hand and I didn't. How much did you love me then?

What about when I ruined your prom, huh? You loved me that night when you came here to give me a piece of your mind? Was that love when you told me how much you hated me and how I made you worse every day? A worse version of yourself?"

I thought I could be unaffected through this. I could go out with dignity as he interrogates me and not cry once.

But I'm already spilling tears.

They're streaming down my cheeks, silent but ever-flowing and Zach's watching me without a twitch on his face.

"I... did." I nod in reply. "I did love you through all of that. I didn't know it back then, but I loved you. Every time you or your friends pulled something on me, it hurt me. It made me angry. I used to cry a lot. I used to plot revenge. And I thought it was because I hated you. But it was because I loved you and the guy I loved was incapable of loving me back. So yeah, I did love you through all of that. My hate for you was just a kind of love that was angry and lonely and bruised."

It's hard to look at him after confessing all these feelings inside of me. All the things that made me so confused all through the years. That made me feel agitated whenever he was around.

But somehow, I keep looking at him.

I keep watching him, but then I regret it because I see something on his features that I've never seen before. Never in my context, at least.

Disgust.

Zach's *disgusted* by me.

"Jesus Christ." He licks his lower lip as he shakes his head. "You get even more pathetic the longer I know you."

I flinch.

I knew he'd say that but still I flinch.

"Do you know how pathetic it is to love someone who's hurt you? Do you realize how weak it makes you? How stupid?" Zach goes on, staring at me like I'm a stranger, like he doesn't even know me. "I admired you, Blue. I fucking respected you. I respected your hate for me. I admired that you wouldn't let me walk all over you. I admired your strength."

He plows his hand through his hair in agitation. "I don't want your love. I don't deserve your love, don't you get that? Even though I haven't been your bully in a long time, I was your nightmare once. What the fuck is the matter with you? What the fuck is wrong with you that you love me? How fucked up and weak do you have to be to fall in love with your bully?" He shakes his head once again. "You know what? I can't even look at you. Just get out."

Stunned, I don't move.

I'm glued to my spot.

"Out," Zach orders again.

"No."

I'm surprised to hear my own voice. I thought I'd never speak again.

He frowns dangerously. The thick fringe of his lashes covers his eyes, lending them a deadly look. "Excuse me?"

"Is that what you think you are?" I ask. "Weak?"

"What?"

"Do you think you're pathetic, Zach? Fucked up? Is that what you think about yourself?"

"What the fuck are you talking about?"

"I came to your room tonight because I wanted to confess something," I begin. "I saw you today. Going up to tower one. I followed you. I know I shouldn't have but I did. And I saw you with your mom. Y-you were taking care of her. She's sick. That's why you came back, right? To be with her? I –"

My words get cut off when Zach comes on me in a flash and his threatening fingers wrap around my jaw, pulling my neck up.

He's tall and big and naked.

Somehow, his nudity makes him even more menacing. Maybe because I can see what fury does to his body. The effects of it aren't hidden by clothes. Every muscle is set tight like a trap, ready to snap open and cut me in half.

"If you *ever* run your mouth about this –"

I shake my head, making him stop. "Never. Your mom's health isn't my business. But you're not worried about that, are you?"

I grab his wrist and pull it off my jaw. I stand up for good measure too.

If I'm going to have this discussion with him, naked no less, then I'm going to gather my sheet around me and stand up.

I'll come out shorter, but at least I'll get back my dignity.

Because everything makes sense. Everything is crystal clear now.

I know why he won't talk about his reasons for coming back. It has nothing to do with his mom's sickness but everything to do with him.

"You're not worried about me saying something about your mom. You're worried that I *know* why you came back. You're worried that people will find out you came back to take care of your dying mom. You don't want them to know that you spend your days with her, locked up in her room, helping her through her coughing fits. Keeping her company."

"Shut up."

I witness his face getting angrier, tighter, but I don't stop. I can't.

"That's what you do, don't you? You sit with her and watch mindless TV just so she'll have someone by her side. Why do you do that, Zach?"

He bends over me like a black cloud. "If you don't shut your mouth right now, I'll shut it for you. And you're not gonna like how I do it."

His threats mean nothing to me.

I'm not afraid. Maybe I should be but I can't be scared when I've discovered such a simple thing about him.

"You do it because you love your mom." I squint up at him. "And you hate that. You hate that you love a woman who's never put you first. Who's never loved you. Isn't that right? Your dad's a bully. By what I saw, your mom doesn't care and you *hate* that you're here for her."

And now that I've connected all the dots, I can't stop talking.

"All this time I kept thinking that you're too damaged for love. Either to want it or to give it. I thought the way you grew up, you lost it. That ability to be open and vulnerable to someone, and I wouldn't have blamed you. You had a shitty childhood. But somehow, that's not the problem. Is it, Zach? The problem isn't that you can't love. The problem is that you can. You *can* love. You're not damaged. At least not to the extent that you're incapable of it."

"That's why you won't tell anyone why you're here. You don't want anyone to know how after everything, you still love your mother. Why? Because you think it makes you weak, doesn't it? It makes you pathetic."

I shake my head as I see him in a new light. I can't believe I didn't figure it out before. I didn't realize how much of a victim he still is.

"God, Zach. Your world still revolves around your bully. You're still so wrapped up in what they did that you haven't been able to move forward. You're still so angry and hateful. You have to move on, Zach. You're ruining your life because of them. You can't –"

My words come to a screeching halt when Zach moves.

He marches over to his dresser, still naked but somehow so powerful, his muscles rippling. He fishes something out, spins around and throws it at me. All in jerky movements.

It's a t-shirt.

I don't even have the time to realize my confusion when he strides right back and grabs my arm in a harsh grip, his eyes manic and his breathing wild.

"Zach –"

Pulling at my arm, he starts walking, dragging me behind him.

"Zach, what are you doing?"

I'm stumbling; my feet are getting caught up in the sheet. I want to pull it up but my hand is fisted around it to keep it in place, along with the t-shirt he gave me.

A second later, that's not what I'm thinking about, the tangled-up sheet, because he opens the door and delivers the harshest pull, shoving me out of his room.

Did he just...

Kick me out?

I whirl around to find him at the threshold.

"Put something on and stay out."

He shuts the door with a bang, leaving me wrapped up in his sheet and clutching his t-shirt.

Panic claws at my throat, my stomach. I'm shaking. Frantically, I look down at myself and then at the empty, dimly-lit hallway.

I think I'm going to throw up.

I'm so cold and the only thing warm in my hands is the garment he gave me.

I don't know how long I stand there, trembling, staring at his door, still in shock. Humiliated to my very soul.

Then I hear a crash and a bang and a deep growl.

It somehow wakes me up, gets me moving.

I clutch his t-shirt to my chest and by sheer muscle memory, locate a powder room a few doors down. I get in, let the sheet drop to the floor and put his shirt on.

There's a mirror to my right but I'm afraid to look at it. I don't want to see my damaged, vandalized body.

Bending down, I pick up the sheet and wrap it around my shoulders.

Then I start walking, looking at my feet. I jump when I hear more crashes, a glass breaking.

They match the sounds of chaos inside my body.

I don't remember climbing down the stairs or walking through the sleepy mansion, until I find myself in the servant's wing and a light comes on.

It's harsh and I squint my eyes against it.

"Cleo?"

It's Maggie.

"What happened? Are you okay? You weren't in your room."

Still shaking, I look at her with tear-clogged eyes. "I was in h-his."

Her eyes go wide as she realizes what I mean by his. "Master Zach's?"

I nod.

She grabs my shoulders. "Did he… did he do something to you?"

"He broke my heart."

Suddenly, I remember what that fortune teller, Dove, told me. He might close the palm holding my heart and strangle it with his fingers.

I think he just did that.

He murdered my heart with his bare hands.

"What?"

"But I guess I broke his rules first."

"What? What rules? What are you talking about?"

I look at Maggie. "I fell in love with him."

Her face crumples in sadness and pity. "You stupid, stupid girl."

Then, she walks me to the on-call room I was supposed to be in tonight.

With each step, I keep thinking, *I'm a stupid, stupid girl.*

Chapter 32

The Dark Prince

I snatch the notebook buried under the mattress, the one I've been writing her name in, and throw it against the glass, growling.

The thump isn't satisfying.

So I throw the chair against the wall next.

Then the desk.

The dresser, my backpack, the pillows, the sheets, the lamp.

She doesn't get it, does she?

If I don't have anger, if I don't have my revenge, my hate, then what do I have? Where's the fucking justice for all that they have done to me?

I'm both the witness and the victim of all the crimes they've committed. If I move on, then all of the bad shit I went through, all of it would just go away.

They're off the hook, then, for fucking me up. For making me feel small and worthless and miserable.

Right?

Wrong.

They'll never be off the hook. I'll never forgive them.

Fuck moving on. Fuck being the bigger person.

I throw anything and everything that I can get my hands on until all that's left is destruction.

And her smell of sugar.

I've always loved you...

Her voice causes a pain in my chest. It's so intense that I come down on my knees.

I don't want her love.

I don't.

Then why the fuck does it hurt so much?

Chapter 33

He's smoking.

I don't think he's smoked ever since I stole his pack. He finally accepted the tobacco chewing tablets I'd bought for him. Though I haven't seen him use them more than a couple of times.

I haven't ever seen Zach in a suit before, either.

He's wearing one now.

It's black and crisp, those pants and that jacket, with a white shirt underneath. The collar is open and probably a couple of top buttons too.

It's hard to tell from here. There are a lot of people between him and me.

The ballroom is packed.

It's another party; it's Mr. and Mrs. Prince's anniversary. A real celebration of love, what with all the red roses and crystal hearts for décor.

They have been planning this party for weeks. So it wasn't a surprise, but still, I feel like I've been sucker-punched with all the love that's being blatantly displayed.

Funny, how one night can change everything.

One phone call might mean your parents are dead and three little words could get you kicked out of a room, in the middle of the night, all naked.

I spy Mrs. Prince in the distance, chatting with a group of heavily decorated ladies. Heavily and expensively. She herself is sporting a rose-colored gown, again the color of love, looking like a million bucks.

Looking new and shiny and most importantly, healthy.

Apparently, make-up can hide a lot of things. Though it can't hide how frail she looks. How bony and how, when she smiles, her artificially made-up eyes appear glassy. But I guess these people are not looking.

No one here cares about a woman who's shrinking and disappearing with every event, and a girl with blue hair whose eyes might look a tad bit puffier than what's normal for human beings.

To my credit, I've managed to be calm and not break down in the middle of the room like I want to.

My legs have the strength to carry me and my brain has enough sense that I smile and stop and present the tray full of champagne flutes at appropriate times.

Maggie wanted me to call in sick. She said it might be good for me to get some sleep and just rest, after the night I'd had. You know, with all the sobbing and crying like the world was ending.

And maybe it has.

Maybe it's the apocalypse. The sun has scorched the earth and all life is dead, except for some unlucky ones like me.

Who are alive to see the love of their life transform back into the bully he used to be.

I've been making circles of the room, carrying my tray, and so far, I've avoided going over to Zach's side.

He's tucked away in a corner by the French doors that lead into the grassy grounds and the starry sky.

And he's not alone.

He's with his old gang.

Like the prince he is, Zach stands in the middle of the circle, his back propped against the wall. He keeps looking out the French doors every now and then, smoking his lungs away and drinking champagne.

Ashley is to his right, standing super close. So close that with every breath, her breasts are touching his arm. I want to tell her that he's a fiend for big tits – a typical guy with simple needs. But I won't. Let her find out the hard way.

To his left is Rob. He used to be the most vocal of the group and he's also the one who tripped me on my second day at St. Patrick's. I've never seen Zach be close to anyone, but if I had to pick, I'd say he was closest to Rob. Or at least, Rob saw to that because he never left his side.

Then there are Chase, Alex and Samantha, forming a semi-circle of sorts. I honestly had forgotten about them.

Samantha used to follow Ashley's lead. Chase would repeat whatever anyone said and Alex would just snigger.

And Zach was the quiet one. He'd watch everything but never say anything.

Now, seeing them together, all grown up and decked out in million-dollar clothes, they all seem replicas of one another. Tall, blond and beautiful and made of the same fabric of cruelty.

Zach's the only one who's dark, filled with an innate darkness.

The darkness that I met last night.

Or maybe I met that darkness a long time ago. I just thought it didn't matter.

I thought that when he called me his prize, he would at least give me the courtesy of putting on some clothes before kicking me out of his room.

Anyway, I know now.

For the next hour, I continue to serve drinks and zig-zag around these people, successfully managing to stay on this side of the line, away from Zach and his grown-up minions. The moment someone calls me over to the other side, I know my time's up.

I know I'm going to have to face them. They'll *make* me face them.

No sooner than I've served the drinks to a bunch of old ladies that tsk at my blue hair and lipstick, I hear my name called in Ashley's very nasally and chirpy voice.

I take a deep breath, clench my fist before letting it all go, and swallow down the bile. It's okay. I can do this.

I *have* done this, a million times before. Except it feels like all of that happened in another lifetime.

Turning around, I walk toward them.

Or rather, I walk toward him. He's the only thing that I can see.

There are no outward signs on him of what happened last night. He looks the same, stunning and mean. Kind of dashing, even, in his suit that hugs his body like a glove or a lover's hand. *My* hand.

His midnight hair curls over the collar and sticks up in places, lending him a lazy, sexy look. I can almost see him at future parties like this, wearing suits, sipping champagne and breaking hearts.

With his black eyes, he watches me approach their group.

My body, stupid, *stupid* body hasn't caught up at all. It still flashes with heat at his stare. The flashes I've been getting all evening, making me think that he knew where I was the entire time, like I did him.

Reaching them, I stand at the edge of their group.

"Hey, Cleo," Ashley chimes in, wrapping her hand tightly around Zach's arm.

Like she has something to prove.

I look away from her hand and focus on her face. "Hey."

"Have you been avoiding us?"

"Something like that."

"Come on," she says with a mock frown. "We're old friends."

The group chuckles at that. I do, too.

That's such a blatant lie.

"Yeah, definitely."

"So aren't you going to serve us, while we refresh your memory?"

I give her a look but then I step forward, kind of including myself in the group. Then, Ashley starts the introductions like I've never met them before.

"This is Samantha. But Ms. Bridges for you, of course."

Ms. Bridges picks up a glass and giggles.

I want to pull out her tongue and wrap it around her throat just to get her to stop that high-pitched sound, but all I do is shoot her a tight smile. The sooner Ashley gets the satisfaction of humiliating me, the sooner I can get out of here.

Because her insults are not what's getting to me. It's him.

He's getting to me.

Standing there like a dark, silent specter. A ghost from my past. I can feel the blast of his hot stare on me, watching me, watching for my reactions as Ashley reintroduces me to the group of people who made my life hell years ago.

And he's not doing anything.

I could've stopped them with the flick of a hand.

Did you still love me?

Did you love me through all of that?

This is his response to my love.

He knows that I love him, and now he's doing everything he can to kill that. To crush it, to stomp on it. To bully it out of my heart.

What choice do I have but to stand tall?

To stay rigid and fight back. To be brave, even though I'm feeling sick to my stomach. To tell him that I do, in fact, love him. I loved him and *will* love him, despite everything.

Despite his coldness, his cruelty, his abuse.

Despite the fact that he's thrown me to the wolves once again.

As Ashley comes to the end of her introductions, Mr. Simmons, Mr. Brandt and whatnot, I wonder if Zach would still save me if I jumped into the pool like the other night.

Will he catch me or leave me to drown?

Finally, she re-introduces me to the love of my life. She waves a magnanimous hand at him. "And *this*, of course you know who this is. This is the guy you work for: Mr. Prince."

He takes a drag of his cigarette before blowing it out of his soft lips.

"Yeah, I know who he is," I say, looking at him but addressing Ashley.

To Zach, I say with my eyes, *I know who you are. I know you're better than this. You just won't admit to it.*

Before I can read his reaction, Samantha jumps in, "Is that your old school uniform?"

I look down at myself and realize, yeah, it could pass for it. White blouse and black skirt. Only the tie is missing.

Ashley chuckles. "Right? I thought so too. She seems to be... bursting out of it."

Ah, the body jokes. It never ends.

"I happen to like the visual," Rob says.

Chase repeats the same thing in different words and Alex sniggers.

In my peripheral vision, I see Zach coming off the wall. I'm not sure for what reason. It could hardly be to defend me, so I take matters into my own hands.

I turn to Rob. "Was that a compliment?"

"What do you think?" he replies, looking at my chest, smirking in an obnoxious way.

"I don't know. I can't decide whether to say thank you or knee you in the junk."

The smile vanishes from his face.

I'm ready to head back after that, secure in the knowledge that they're happy and content in humiliating me so they'll leave me alone now.

But I guess they still have more in them. Because suddenly, I hear a slow puddle forming at my feet. I look up to find the source. Ashley is sneering at me as she pours down her drink on the floor.

"Oops. I'm clumsy, remember?" She shrugs with wide eyes.

"Yeah and bit of a one-trick pony, too."

"It's okay, Ash. I think we can have it cleaned up?" It's Samantha's turn to shrug and make her eyes bigger.

"Right? I mean, I'm sure it's included in your job description?" Ashley adds.

I glance at her and then at the puddle at our feet. It's spreading, touching my borrowed Mary Janes and Zach's black leather shoes. Polished and crisp, like the rest of him.

Swallowing, I fish out a napkin from the small apron tied around my waist for just these emergencies.

Okay, Cleo, you can do this. This is just like mopping up any regular mess.

Biting my lip, I come down to my knees. The floor hits me hard even though I was anticipating it. My tray's empty now so I leave it next to me and get to work.

I spread the napkin over the puddle and hear chuckles from up above.

But I don't focus on that. It was never about their chuckles or insults or sneering. It was always about him.

The guy who wouldn't do anything to stop it. Like now.

I get the napkin to soak up the worst of it and then mop off the rest with the dry corner of it. My knuckles hit the pointed end of his shoes and I'm thrown back to the day when I found my books torn up and scattered in the hallway.

A twelve-year-old Zach came up to me on that day as well. I saw him, shoes first. He stepped on the pages and when I looked up, he smirked down at me.

He was so cruel that day, the boy I'd fallen in love with at first sight.

Tonight too, as I look up, I find him staring at me. But instead of smirking, his face is blank, and his gaze is burning.

Maybe he's remembering that day from long ago, too. Or maybe he's thinking about how I bathed him yesterday and how I sat on my heels and took him in my mouth, loving him.

He looked like a prince then, and he looks like one now.

I probably look the same too.

The lowly maid who serves him.

Slowly, I stand up, leaving the soiled napkin on the tray. "You were lying."

There's no indication on his face that he heard me but I know he did. I also know that he can hear my broken heartbeats.

"You're not mine, are you? You never were."

At this, his jaw clenches.

His eyes blaze and I'm doused with so much heat that I feel steam rising from my skin. I don't expect an answer from him. But he gives me one anyway.

"But you're mine, aren't you?"

I can't read his tone. The tone of the very first words he's spoken to me all night. Is it condescending? Insulting?

Is it disbelief?

Whatever it is. I'm going to tell him the truth.

I nod. "Stupidly."

"Stupidly," he agrees.

"And I'm done proving that."

I step back and take in the open mouths of all his minions. Sighing, I put my hands on my waist.

Then, I smile.

"Ashley, thanks for the re-introductions." I bend down and take off my Mary Janes, one at a time. "But it was totally not needed. I remember who you are. I remember all of you. You're the people who'll never amount to anything. You never did back at St. Patrick's and you don't now. Oh, and I also call you minions of the anti-Christ, in my head. Anti-Christ being Zach."

I address Samantha and wave at my boobs. "So these... are called boobs. It's hard to know what they are when you don't have them yourself." I unbutton the top two buttons as I keep talking. "But I'm sure if you ask your daddy nicely, he'll buy you a pair."

To Rob, Chase and Alex, I say, "Stop being pervs and stop hitting on the maids. Guys like you grow old to be the kind of creepy middle-aged men who force me to use the itching powder. You don't want me to use the itching powder on you, do you?"

They stare at me wide-eyed.

Finally, I turn to Zach.

Looking him in the eyes, I unbraid my hair. Slowly, methodically. With every knot that comes out, I feel like I can breathe again.

Once I'm done letting my hair loose, I give it a shake and throw him a tight smile. "I quit. Oh, and," I turn to a shocked Ashley. "the way you're rubbing onto Zach's arm? That's not going to work. He likes his girls curvier with bigger tits. You know, someone like me."

With that, I spin around and leave the ballroom, barefoot, with my long blue hair swinging against my back.

When I reach the exit, I spy a lonely glass of champagne and throw it back.

I might be a little bit in shock because I don't feel an ounce of regret. No regrets. Not one.

I'm not going to get my house back, and well, I don't want it. It's not going to bring back my parents and I have to cut ties some time.

I have to go find... life.

As I walk down the hallway, I decide that I'm going to take that road trip. I swear to God. No more excuses.

So what if no one knows my name out there? So what if I'm alone? I have myself and I have my blue car.

I'm walking down the hallway and I pass by a room when I hear a crash – not the kind of violent crash I heard back in Zach's room last night but still. It's a crack, I think. Because it's followed by a whimper.

I come to a halt and creep toward the door. I'm surprised to find it open when I turn the knob. For some reason, I feel like whatever's going on in there is something that happens behind locked doors.

And I'm right.

I open the door and stick my head in to see the supposedly happy couple whose love is being celebrated back there.

Mr. and Mrs. Prince.

There's a huge difference between their heights and right now, it shows in the most dangerous way. Mr. Prince is towering over her smaller, thinner frame and his hand is wrapped around the same wrist Zach was asking about yesterday.

He says something to her, but in a low voice that even I can't hear, and when she replies something haltingly, he gives it to her.

Oh my God.

He hits her, slaps her cheek and she hardly makes a sound. A whimper, that's it. Even lower than the one I heard.

How many times has he hit her for her to not make a sound? For her to be trained to go quiet?

It looks like he's going to hit her again and I burst through the door.

"Get away from her," I shout as I charge at him.

They both look startled at my sudden appearance. And unhappy. But I don't care.

"What the fuck is wrong with you, you old fuck?" I push at his chest when I reach him. "She's your wife! And she's sick."

Zach's dad is frozen but only for a second before he growls and charges back at me. He pushes me in retaliation and Jesus, it hurt.

My chest feels battered and he's only shoved me a few steps back.

Breathing with difficulty, I come at him again. Both with my fists and my words. "You're a bully, you know that? A fucking bully and I'm going to fuck you up so bad."

I punch him in the face to show him what I mean. His head swivels to the side but he recovers pretty quickly.

"You bitch," he snarls at me.

I hear Zach's mom screaming in the background. *Stop it, don't hurt him. Who said you could come in here?*

But then, my hearing goes to shit.

Zach's dad lays a hard slap on me that sends me crashing to the floor, busting my knees and jarring the breath out of me.

It takes me a few moments to recover.

A few moments to catch my breath and a few moments to realize that I'll live through the crippling pain.

Just as I gather enough energy to even think about sitting up and going back at it with Mr. Prince, someone's at my side.

It's Tina and Grace.

They are both sitting me up, asking me if I'm doing okay but I'm still a little disoriented. I don't compute how they can be here, by my side. They should be at the party.

I can't compute the noises that are coming from a distance.

Blinking, I try to focus, and I gasp painfully when I see Zach.

He's bent over his dad, straddling him actually, and he's punching him.

Repeatedly. Over and over.

His punches are ferocious and his arm ripples with his fury. God, he's scary like this. So angry and unhinged.

I almost feel bad for his dad.

Somewhere off to the side, I hear Mrs. Prince shouting. Some of the staff members are holding her back. And a few are inching toward Zach, probably to stop him.

"Zach," I whisper raggedly.

There's no way that he can hear me but I try again, anyway.

"Zach, stop."

His dad isn't moving and I'm sure he's killed him. Or if not, then he's going to.

I open my mouth to tell him again when he stops abruptly.

Panting, he grabs his dad's collar, who's alive, thank God, and growls, "Don't ever touch her again. Do you understand? Not ever. Because I'll kill you with my bare hands. Like I should've done three years ago. And this time, Mom's not gonna come save you."

His dad doesn't answer him; I don't think he can.

Zach lets him go with a jerk and stands up, before turning to me like a compass that always points north.

His eyes flash with fear and he takes a step toward me, but then all hell breaks loose.

The room gets thrown in chaos when cops barge in.

Someone must have called 911. They come in, check the state of the room, talk to a crying Mrs. Prince, start firing orders.

And before I can even stand up, they take Zach away.

It happens so fast that it leaves me dizzy and nauseated.

One of them approaches me and says that he needs me to make a statement once I'm through with the doctor.

"There's a doctor?" I ask, shocked, surprised and so many other things that I can't even fathom right now. "What... where did you take Zach?"

"He's been taken in for questioning," he says, casually. "You don't need to worry about that."

"But he was…"

I trail off when he turns away and then, I'm being flooded with hugs and sympathy.

Someone cries at my shoulders. Someone else sits me down in a chair and hands me a glass of water that I don't take a sip of.

"He was just trying to save his mom," I whisper to no one in particular, watching the door they took Zach through.

But someone answers. It's Tina.

She's kneeling in front of me. "No, he was trying to save you."

Chapter 34

I don't press charges against Mr. Prince.

They ask me if I want to, though.

But I think that it was just a formality. This is Princetown; I don't think anyone can touch the Princes.

They ask me what I saw and how it all came about. I tell them about Mr. Prince's slap and the suspicion I have about the abuse. Mrs. Prince's wrist, which apparently is marked up.

Mrs. Prince claims that I attacked her husband without any reason. But I guess when her husband started pushing me around, people were already at the door because of all the noise, rushing to my rescue, and they saw what happened.

Not to mention, there's another large imprint of his hand on her made-up cheeks.

It takes a few hours for them to question me and question me again before they let me go. The doctor had already cleared me, saying that all I had was a tiny busted lip and that I needed to take it easy.

Before I leave, I ask them about Zach and about what's going to happen to him.

One of them gives me a curt answer, saying that he'll be held longer for questioning and that's all I need to know. The cop who escorts me out gives me the real scoop – because he's young, a rookie, maybe, and when I tell him I'm from the south side, he perks up.

"He was violent. No question about it, and he said some things that might be used against him."

"Like what?"

He glances around and divulges, "He made threats against his father in front of witnesses." At my terrified look, he rushes to explain, "Look, as long as Mr. Prince is alive and kicking, I don't think anything's going to stick. There are people who saw you getting attacked and most of them confirmed that he was acting in your defense. It's just bureaucratic bullshit."

He was trying to save you.

"You said most of them. Why not all of them?"

He purses his lips.

"It's his mom, isn't it? She's insisting that he did it out of spite."

His silence confirms it.

God, that fucking woman.

Before I can talk further, I spy Maggie and Tina walking toward me. They both look concerned and as soon as they reach me, they burst out with all the questions.

They pull me away from the cop and help me out of the building. The building where Zach's being held for questioning.

Back at The Pleiades, Tina puts me in my bed and Maggie brings me tea. She gives me a pill for the pain, which honestly, I'm not feeling at all. But I take it, nonetheless.

I don't sleep that night. I toss and turn, thinking where Zach might be. If he got back or if he's okay.

In the morning, I find out that he's in the lock-up, and he's going to stay there through the weekend.

I'm at the kitchen island when I hear the news and I'm already off the bar stool when Maggie comes and stops me. "You're not going anywhere. You have to take care of yourself."

"But –"

"He's going to be fine. We went down to the station, all the senior staff members, and gave our statement about how Mr. Prince has been abusive for the past few years. They won't hold Zach for anything. They're just trying to throw their weight around."

I look at her in disbelief. "You knew about the abuse?"

Sighing sadly, she sits me down. "Yes. All of the old staff members. We knew."

"Why didn't you say anything?"

"Because we're just... the staff. No one would've believed us. Plus, Mrs. Prince never came forward and pressed charges. It's us against them. They own this town. This time though, there were witnesses, evidence. There are marks on her skin. I'm not sure if it will amount to anything but it will arouse suspicion."

Then something occurs to me. Something horrifying.

"Do you think h-his dad would press charges against him?"

Mr. Prince is in the hospital but they say he's going to be okay. I don't even want to think about what would happen to Zach if he weren't.

This time around, Maggie's smile is even sadder and that gets my tired and hurting heart racing.

"You don't understand these people, Cleo," she explains. "All they care about is appearances. When Master Zach came back, they threw a party when they were the ones who kicked him out. They lied about where he went. They've been lying about the abuse, Mrs. Prince's illness. They'll lie about this too. So it'll be Princes' word against the world. And this is their world."

She's right.

This is their world. They control it. They write the story. They spread the rumors.

I want to cross the boundary, the line that separates me from them. That takes me far, far away from this shitty town and its shitty people.

In all the craziness, I forgot to tell everyone that I quit.

When Tina comes back from her shift, I sit her and Maggie – she's been my babysitter all day while everyone visited me – down and tell them. They're both happy for me. They've been wanting me to go and explore. Do the things I wanted to do before I lost my parents. Only they didn't know that I've been afraid to do them for so long.

Only he knows.

I spend the night packing. Not that I have a lot of things with me, but still. When I go to pack the black t-shirt Zach threw at me when he kicked me out, I realize that my mom's nightie is up in his room.

Somehow, I forgot about that.

I thought getting parted from one last thing that belonged to my mom would devastate me. It'd be like she died all over again.

But I'm okay.

Her nightie is not her and neither is our house.

Besides, I feel kinda content knowing that Zach has something of me. His instinct would be to throw it away. But still.

When I'm done packing, I sit down and write a letter.

It's unplanned and impulsive. But when I start, I can't stop.

The next day, Sunday, is spent saying goodbye to everyone and collecting my last paycheck. Mrs. S is stern, as usual. But still, she says I did a very brave thing, coming to Mrs. Prince's rescue. She doesn't say anything about how Zach came to *my* rescue but whatever. She doesn't have a right to say anything anyway. I don't work for her anymore.

Leslie and Grace both hug me and fuss over me and tell me to send them pictures of all the places I visit.

"I always knew he liked you," whispers Grace.

Tears fill my eyes and I nod. "Yeah. He liked me."

Then the time comes to say goodbye to a little boy I'll miss the most: Art.

I spend my last evening with him. We watch movies. I make him his favorite pancakes. I read him his favorite story.

"Where's Zach?" he asks.

A lump forms in my throat and a tiny little gasp comes out that I manage to cover up with a cough. "He's out. But he'll be back."

"When?"

"Maybe tomorrow."

"Will he leave like you?" he asks, staring at me with innocent, sad eyes.

I can't stop my tears then.

Technically, Art's nothing to me. We don't share a blood relationship. I didn't even know him before last year, but I feel like I've known him forever.

He's my little brother. My baby. Orphaned and bullied like me. And like me, totally enamored with Zach.

I grab his hand and play with his tiny fingers. "Yeah. But you know what?"

"What?"

I kiss his first finger. "One day you're going to leave too."

"Me?"

I kiss his second finger. "Yes. You're going to leave this town and you're going to go somewhere real nice. Maybe a city or another town where they have lakes and mountains and there's just so much sky, and winter. Snow, maybe. Do you like snow?"

He beams. "I've never seen it."

"I know. We live in a hot place, huh?" I'm at his third finger now. "Well, then you'll go to a snowy town and you'll love it there. And you'll meet all these interesting people and you'll make all the friends."

"Will they be like the kids at school?"

I place a kiss on his fourth finger, then his thumb. "Maybe. Bullies are everywhere, you know. They come in all shapes and sizes and ages. But remember what Zach said? Bullies will never change but we will. We'll change and grow and one day, it won't matter to us what they do. We'll be ourselves. Our stronger, braver selves."

He nods, still smiling. "Yeah, we'll be so brave, they won't touch us."

Finally, I kiss the center of his palm. "Yup."

It's Monday.

The day I leave and the day they let Zach go.

I'm waiting for him outside the police station. It threatens to be a hot morning with a baking sun and sizzling humidity.

But then I remind myself that it doesn't matter. I'm not going to be here for that. I'll cross the line today and go north. Somewhere wintry and snowy so I can send Art all the pictures.

My eyes are nailed to the entrance as I wait across the street, and as soon as it swings open and reveals the guy I've been waiting for, I jump down off the bumper of my blue car.

Zach's eyes go immediately to me and he pauses mid-step.

He wasn't expecting me, I guess.

Oh well, I like to surprise people.

Once, he's over his initial shock, he begins moving. His long legs jump down the stairs and eat up the asphalt until he comes to stand before me.

"Hi," I whisper, rubbing my sweaty palms along my thighs.

I'm wearing my usual off-the-shoulder t-shirt and shorts along with my leather boots. And he's in his clothes from the night of the party, the white shirt that's smudged and wrinkled and half-tucked into his black pants, his suit jacket draped over his forearm.

"Hey," he rasps in a scratchy, barely-there voice.

"You okay?" I ask and he jerks out a nod, the thick stubble on his jaw catching the sun.

His eyes go to my lip. "You?"

I touch the little tender part on the corner. "Yeah. It's nothing."

The flare of his nostrils tells me that it's *not* nothing.

"Uh, there were witnesses who said that you came to my rescue. Immediately." I shift on my feet. "So, um, thanks for that."

He studies me a beat. "I should've killed him."

My eyes go wide and sweep the area for any lingering cops. "Don't say that. You're not even home yet."

"It's the truth."

I sigh, shaking my head. "Don't go around killing people because of me, okay? That's hardly a reason."

His messy hair ruffles with a very rare breeze. "That's the only reason there can be for me: you."

I shuffle back a step at that, at his roughly spoken declaration, pressing my thighs against the bumper.

There's a few moments of silence.

Awkward and heavy.

I hear his shoes shuffling on the sidewalk, coming closer to me. "Blue, I –"

"So your dad, he's not pressing charges?" I speak over him quickly.

I don't know what he was going to say but I don't want to hear it.

"He wouldn't," he scoffs. "This is scandal enough for him."

"Did you really beat him up all those years ago?"

A tiny nod. "I did. I got a few punches in before my mom stopped me and kicked me out."

"And now? Will she press charges?"

A bitter, heartbroken smile. "She won't do something that he won't do."

"Is it still a secret? That she's sick?"

He shrugs. "It won't be for long. They had to move her to a medical facility after that night."

"Yeah. They told me." Swallowing, I say, "I'm sorry. About your mom. I never... I never got to say that."

He accepts it with a nod. "My dad. He's, uh, always had anger issues, I think. Or at least, he had them with me. He wasn't very patient when I was a kid. Maybe because I reminded him of his own childhood – he's dyslexic too. I never met my grandfather; he died before I was born. But I can guess that maybe he wasn't a very nice father to my father. I don't know. The night he attacked my mom, I think that was the first time he'd hit her."

Shaking his head, he continues, "When I pulled him away from her and punched him, she said that it was my fault. That I'd always been a fucked up, rebellious kid and it was because of me that my dad was so stressed out. She told me to leave. I always wanted to leave, always wanted to run away but I never thought it would come about like that. Anyway, I left because I was poisoning everything. I was polluting you, tainting you with my hate. I was turning my dad into a violent man, apparently. And I never would've come back."

When he pauses, I add in a choked-up whisper, "But your mom got sick."

"Yeah. Nora called me and told me about my mom's cancer." He lets out a harsh chuckle. "I remember laughing. I remember thinking, *good; she deserves it*. My mom never came to my rescue when I was a kid. I think that hurt me more than my dad's behavior. She was always bothered about how stressed my dad got because of me and how that affected her relationship with him. And in the end, she was the one who kicked me out when I came to her rescue. I had no intention of coming back and taking care of her. But something made me jump on my bike and head out."

Something like love.

I bite the inside of my cheek until I taste blood to hold myself up and not crumple in front of him.

Zach's looking at me like he wants me to say something. I don't know what he wants me to say. All I have is what I wrote him in the letter.

Sighing, I tell him, "I have something to say to you."

He studies me a beat, his eyes intense.

Then, he swallows and nods. "Okay."

I reach back and fish out the envelope from my back pocket. "I wrote you a letter." Licking his lip, he stares at it. "Because I wanted to write down my thoughts before I told them to you. I know you won't read it. I know that. So, I'm going to read it to you. Is that, uh, okay?"

His hands are fisted at his sides and he clenches his jaw. "Yeah."

"Okay."

I open the envelope and bring out two thin papers. It looks so short for the amount of time it took me to write this, and yet so long, because now I have to read it to him.

Sniffling, I unfold the pages and plant my feet wide for better balance. I'm so shaken up already that one tiny poke and I'll tumble.

"Okay, so it's not poetry or anything but here goes..." I begin, *"Dear... you, I l-love you. I know you don't want to hear it. You don't even want it; you've said this to me enough times but I have to say it because it's my truth.*

It's been my truth ever since I was ten. Ever since I saw you that first time in the detention room. I was scared and hungry and I was on the verge of crying. But then, I found you sitting on one of the benches in the back. Your head was turned and you were looking out the window. You were looking at that big water fountain with such focus that you didn't even notice me when I entered. I don't know why you were watching it – although, now I know that you were looking at it because of the blue; you love that color. Anyway, I felt something. Right in my stomach..."

I have to pause at that because right this second, I'm feeling the same thing. The same buzz that I felt all those years ago. The butterflies.

I blink and get going again. *"I didn't know what it was, not until years later when I grew up and realized what desire or passion meant. All I knew then was that I wanted to talk to you. And I did. It didn't turn out that well. You were rude to me. And you were mean. For years, we fought. For years, we were cruel to each other. Sometimes you more than me. But nonetheless, it made me mad. It made me bitter. It made me sick to my stomach. I understand why now. Because I loved you and I wanted you to love me back."*

I sniffle and wipe a tear that streams down my cheek. I have to keep going. If I don't say it now, I'll never be able to again.

I don't know what Zach's thinking. I haven't looked at him. I've kept my gaze on the paper so far.

"But enough about me. I want to talk about you. I want to tell you your truth..."

The truth is that you love me, too. You've loved me as long as I've loved you. When you turned and laid your eyes on me that first day, you felt something too. Something that I felt in my stomach, you probably felt in your chest. For me it was the butter-flies and for you, it was a spark, maybe. A spark different than any other you'd felt.

That spark that made you want to be better. It made you want to save me from your friends and their pranks. You didn't, however.

Because you come from a place of hate. You come from a place that made you think love is a weakness. So every time you felt something for me, you smashed it with your own hands. You hurt me. You made me cry. You made me want to resent you. And in that, you resented yourself.

I want you to know that your secret is safe with me. I'll never tell anyone that you made the mistake of falling in love when that was the last thing you wanted for yourself. I'll never tell anyone that we're made for each other. That our souls are made of a matching fabric. Or that we're written in the stars. All I'll do is watch them. The stars, I mean. Every night from wherever I am. All I'll do is remember you and remember the time we h-had..."

I wipe off my tears again. They're plopping down on the pages, making big, watery drops, smearing the blue ink.

This is the last part. I have to get through it, and then I'll walk away. Forever. I'll start my life.

"It's every lover's wish to be with the one they love. But I'll never wish for more time with you. I'll pray that we never cross each other's paths. That this be our last meeting. Because this love that I have for you, I'm very protective of it. I know if I stay, you'll kill it one day. You'll take it away from me. And I can't let that happen. I want to love you till the end of time. Till the moon goes dark and the stars fade out.

"Yours, me."

My hands are trembling by the time I finish. My legs too. My voice, my breaths.

I've never been in this much pain before. It feels like dying. Or actually, it feels like... living.

Without him.

And I haven't even gone anywhere yet.

I'm still here, standing before him, looking at his shoes, crying like a stupid girl who fell in love with him when she was ten.

I crumple the pages in my hands and look up.

What I see nearly forces me to my knees.

I see a boy, a tired but handsome boy, who's staring at me like I'm his world. His jaw is set tight and rigid and his eyes, those dark, *dark* eyes are glassy and red-rimmed.

There's such vulnerability in them that I feel like our roles have been reversed.

Like I'm a sharp object, a blade maybe, and he's my fragile thing, a sheet made of gossamer silk.

I let the letter go in the light breeze that's somehow blowing today.

He looks like he wants to say something else, but I stop him, again. Because apparently, I'm not done talking. "Will you do something for me?"

"Anything."

I smile sadly, thinking about this magnificent but so cynical guy.

I think about all the times I encouraged him to read but he shut down. He would withdraw, become cagey like he was ashamed. I think about all the days he took care of his mom but kept it a secret.

I think about his anger, his hatred. His vengefulness.

"You know what your revenge is, Zach? It's to live a happy life. A life free of them and their abuse. A life where you're not ashamed or embarrassed about wanting more for yourself. A life where you take care of your mom or help a stranger on the street or pull out a kid from a hole. A life where you read a book and be proud about it. I want you to live that life, Zach, okay? Try to live that life for me. Because the alternative is just too painful for me to even comprehend."

And then, I can't take any more.

I have to leave or I'll drive myself insane, standing here, watching him. So broken and screwed and from some kind of dream.

I jog to the driver's side of the car, jump in and start it. I push down on the accelerator and peel out, all in one suspended breath.

I don't look in the rearview mirror, not until I'm about to take a turn and I know he'll disappear from my sight forever.

He's standing there, where I left him.

His suit jacket is on the ground and his hands are limp on his sides, and he's watching me hightail it out of there as his hair sways in the rare breeze.

After that last slice of a glance of him, there's nothing.

There's my life without him.

Just the thought of it makes me want to vomit. Though I know it's also my phobia of the car.

I throw the car in park and fall out of it and retch on the sidewalk.

All the while thinking that I stupidly didn't kiss him one last time.

Stupid, stupid *girl.*

Chapter 35

The Dark Prince

I'm going after her.

Not because she's mine but because I'm hers.

Because she knew that even before I knew it myself.

After she's gone, I lunge for those papers that she let go in the slight wind. I pick them up from the street, wrinkled and almost torn, and fold them up, reverently, before pocketing them.

I've always known, right from the moment I saw her, that she's beautiful. She's magnificent with her rounded cheeks, soft chin and those soulful blue eyes. She's soft in a way that I've always craved even when I crushed it with my actions.

But she's never looked more beautiful than she did then, with sun sparkling down on her blue, wavy hair, reading her letter out loud to me.

She's never looked braver, sweeter, more vulnerable and more like the girl I don't deserve.

But I can't leave her alone.

I won't let her go out in the world, thinking she's alone. That no one knows who she is or what her name is.

Her name is Blue and she's the girl I love. Ever since I was twelve.

I rush back to the mansion, pack up my clothes. I bring her blue sandals from long ago, still caked with her dried blood, and her nightie.

I bound down the stairs and run to the servant's wing. I find Nora in the staff room with probably every staff member there is at The Pleiades.

But that doesn't deter me from barging in and declaring, "I'm leaving but I want you to call me if Mom's condition gets worse, all right?"

I guess I've surprised everyone with my sudden entrance but I don't have time for shock. When Nora just watches me with an open mouth, I address the room, generally. "My mom, she has cancer. Ovarian cancer. She doesn't have a lot of time and, well, I came back because I wanted…" I swallow, words getting thick and clunky in my mouth. "I wanted to be with her in her last days."

There's silence.

I'll take it. I'll take the wide-eyed silence.

In my head, I always thought that if I told them I'm here for my mother, for the woman who kicked me out and never cared about me enough to even bother with my whereabouts these past years, people would look at me with pity. Especially the staff members who knew how it was for me while growing up.

I thought, to them, I would look weak. It *makes* me weak.

But for the two days that I was locked up, I've been thinking about how Blue loved me. How she told me that she was mine, even after I repeated my mistakes from St. Patrick's and didn't save her from Ashley's childish games. How proud she was while she was on her knees, mopping up the mess.

She's the strongest person I know and she forgave me my crimes a long time ago. She gave me her trust, her body, her love.

So maybe forgiving your bully doesn't make you weak.

Maybe it makes you brave. It gets you a little closer to being invincible.

Nora springs up from her chair and asks, "Where are you going?"

"I'm going after her."

She's still confused but I don't have time to explain. I turn to Maggie. "Where did she go?"

Maggie gives me a stern look from where she's sitting at the middle of the table. "Leave her alone. She's been through enough."

"Just tell me where she went."

"Why? So you can hurt her some more? She's been crying for three days now. I thought she'd pop her eyes out."

I rub a spot on my chest.

You felt a spark, probably in your chest.

"Tell me so I can make it better."

Maggie studies me with pursed lips. In fact, the whole room is studying me.

"Maggie," I growl.

"Fine. She said she was going north. She wants to go someplace snowy. That's all I know."

North.

"Okay, thanks." Then, I look at Nora. "Thanks for all that you've done for me." To Maggie, "You too."

After that, I'm running.

I don't stop until I reach my bike, and take off after her.

chapter 36

Someone's following me.

Or at least, it feels like it.

I'm losing my mind, I think. Maybe I *want* someone to follow me. Someone like him. It's insane.

I'm crazy.

First of all, how would he even know where I am? I never told him where I was going. That wasn't part of the plan. He's back at his mansion, probably sleeping or washing off jail before going to be with his mom.

And second of all, I don't want him to follow me. I want him to leave me alone, and die in peace, or at least, wish about my death in peace.

As it is, I've lost it, my peace, as soon as I lost the town limits in my rearview mirror.

I've been driving slowly and sketchily.

The highways are wide and the vehicles are wider. They're hurtling along like they're all out to get me and each other.

The first few hours, I take every rest stop exit and throw up all my organs.

Then I get hungry. Ravenous. So I stop at a food exit and load up on basically everything. Fries and burgers and slices of pizza and hot dogs. I have soda. I have water. I have juice. I have wafers and Funyuns and candies.

God, so many candies.

I have more food than I have luggage.

I sit in the parking lot and stuff my face with gummy bears while I watch people through my window. They all look happy, like they're on the best road trip ever. I guess they don't know what it feels like when you drive away from everything you've ever known.

The only person who can relate to that is the one I'm kind of running away from. And the funniest thing is, he won't even care. He won't even come after me.

Again, not that I want him to.

Or rather, this late in the day when I'm tired and exhausted, I can admit that I want him to, but I *can't* want that.

And that just makes me cry.

So I sit in that parking lot for about an hour, gorging on candies and sobbing my heart out, slumped over the wheel.

When I'm all out of tears, I realize that there's a prickling on the back of my neck.

So much prickling, it's almost an itch.

It sends me out of my car and I look around. There's miles and miles of road and infinite sky, and all the faces I don't recognize.

Sighing, I get back in, start the car and roll out of there.

I drive for the rest of the day, stopping here and there. When the sun's setting though, I'm done. I can't take it anymore. I find a motel on my GPS and pull in.

At reception, I get a room for the night and haul my luggage up the stairs. Without any obligation to save up for my house, I have enough money to get me through a few months. I'll need to find something after that, but I'm not worried about that right now.

Right now, I only want to sleep.

I slide the key in the lock and open the room. The walls are brownish beige and it has a queen bed with white sheets and a dark brown blanket.

I take a quick shower and put on a fresh pair of shorts and a soft t-shirt – fine, *his* t-shirt. I think it smells like him: musky and like blueberry pie. It covers me down to mid-thigh and sags around my shoulders and chest.

Even though I have more food than I can handle, I still decide to go to the vending machine I saw at the end of the hallway.

Only, the stupid machine is broken.

I stab at the buttons but nothing happens.

Glaring at it, I mutter, "You stupid piece of shit."

Then I growl and shake it.

"I want my fucking Twix, you idiot."

I kick at it for good measure.

"I don't think you get candy that way."

That voice makes me spin to my right even as I lose coordination in my limbs. I almost fall on the machine I've been abusing when I see him.

"You..." I breathe out, looking at him like he's a ghost.

Am I dreaming?

Did I fall asleep at the wheel? Or maybe I'm in that motel bed right now.

"Hey."

His rumbly voice makes me feel plenty awake, however.

Super, hyper awake. Like I can hear all the sounds, the buzzing of the overhead light, the low tones of television somewhere.

"What... how... you've been following me all day," I manage to say while my eyes can't stop gorging on him.

It feels like ages even though I only saw him this morning. In the same clothes.

Except, those clothes are even more rumpled. His sleeves are folded up to his elbows, exposing his tan forearms and his tattoo. His shoes are mud-caked and so are his pants. Don't even talk about the wrinkled shirt and messy collar.

"Yeah."

He's doing the same, gorging on me. His eyes going up and down, sweeping across my wet hair that's plopping droplets on the floor carpet and soaking the back of the t-shirt that I have on.

His t-shirt.

I grab the hem of it and he notices my nervous twisting. Lifting his lashes, he rasps, "Looks good on you."

I swallow, remembering how he gave it to me. "Is that why you picked it out?"

There's no venom in my voice but he still flinches.

"I picked it out because even then, I wanted you to have something of mine. Only, I'm realizing it now."

His words have always given me a rush. Sadly, a few miles of distance haven't changed that. I don't think even light years could change it.

I feel the first flaps of the butterflies in my tummy and it's very inconvenient when I'm trying to maintain my distance.

"How did you even know where I was?"

"Maggie."

"What?"

"She told me you were going north. There's just one highway out of our town and you drive really slow."

"I don't drive slow," I blurt out, the first thing that I can latch on to so I can somehow break the intensity swimming in his eyes.

I don't.

The intensity is still there when he answers, like he's aware of how I'm trying to just talk nonsense to diffuse this tension between us.

"Okay. Everybody else is just faster then."

"I'll have you know... that..." I clear my throat and tuck a wet strand behind my ears. "I've gotten tons of speeding tickets, okay? I used to be a menace on the south side."

His lips twitch at my asinine comment. "I don't doubt it."

How many times have I kissed that twitch in the past?

In fact, up until last week, I was kissing every inch of his skin.

What the fuck happened? Why are we standing so far apart?

Right.

Because I told him I loved him and he told me that I was pathetic.

"Why were you following me?"

"So you don't have to be alone," he replies in a grave voice with equally grave eyes.

"Alone?"

"Yeah." I watch his Adam's apple bobbing. "So you'd know at least one person no matter where you go. And at least that person would know your name."

My extremities, my toes and fingers, they curl. The weight of his statement is too much. It invokes too many memories.

The night I jumped in the water for him.

Seems like another lifetime. I was so brave, so reckless.

I thought nothing could harm my love, only to realize one thing could.

Him.

He could hurt it. The guy I'm in love with.

Sighing sharply, I say, "So what? You're going to follow me wherever I go?"

"That's the plan."

Zach says it so casually that it makes me mad. "It's a stupid plan."

"Well, it's the only one I've got."

"Look —"

"I know how it feels, Blue." His passionate voice cuts me off. "To be alone in a place, a big, unknown place, where no one knows you. It fucks with your head. It makes you cynical and hard. It makes you think that no matter where you go, who you meet, you'll always be lonely. It makes you miss home something fierce. It makes you feel like you'll never find a place where you belong. I'm not gonna let that happen to you. You're too sweet for that. Too good and shiny. I'm not gonna leave you alone in a world that's cruel and messed up."

He's stopped talking for a few seconds now.

I've counted his breaths, the long gulps of them since then. Seven. He's breathed seven times since he strangled me with his words.

My hands are fisted on my sides, my hair dripping water. I wish I could drip down to the floor like that, like water, and become nothing.

His stare, his words, his smell... him. Everything is too much.

It's pulling me in, making me feel homesick. Exactly like his words just now.

"I'm not..." I shake my head. "I'm not your responsibility."

"You're my life."

My thighs clench.

My entire body clenches.

In preservation? In love? I don't know. All I know is that I need to get away from him.

"Yeah?" I swallow my tears. "So you'll protect me from the world."

"Yes."

"But who will protect me from you?"

His reply is a wince and a clamp of his jaw.

Sighing, I leave.

A few minutes later, when I'm settling myself in the bed, I hear a knock; I know it's him. I don't open it. I clutch the sheets and stare at the brown, nondescript door.

Minutes pass but the second knock isn't forthcoming.

Slowly, I get out of the bed and turn the knob. He isn't there. No one is.

But at my feet is a brown paper bag and inside it, there's enough Twix to last me for days.

Chapter 37

He follows me every day.
Every time I look in the rearview mirror, he's there. Ever-present, with his helmet on, his body curled over his bike, making him look so freaking hot and completely masculine.

The first time I pull into a rest stop because I'm nauseated, Zach stops too. He follows me to the ladies' room and when I come outside feeling a little better but a lot tired, he waits for me with napkins and ginger ale.

"You're being ridiculous," I say weakly once I'm done wiping my mouth and sipping on a little bit of the soda.

He studies me with a concerned frown. "I think you need to take it easy today. Find a motel and just rest."

The sun's strong and Zach's directly in front of it, glowing like a star. He's back into his old clothes, threadbare dark t-shirt and washed-out jeans with gigantic boots.

I squint up at him. "And I think you should be somewhere else. In a different part of the world."

His lips smile slightly but his eyes remain stoic. "I'm exactly where I'm supposed to be."

Frustrated, I thrust the can of ginger ale at his abs, spilling a tiny splash in the process. "Fine. Be that way. In *this* part of the world, there are no maids." I gesture at his t-shirt. "You have to clean that up yourself."

Grabbing the can, he shrugs. "I think I can handle it."

I think he can.

That's the problem. He can do anything he puts his mind to.

And right now, it looks like his mind is set on following me.

When I stop to eat, he stops too. When I stop for gas? Yeah, he's there, as well. When I pull into a motel at night, he's right behind me.

The farther away we get from Princetown, the colder the temperature gets. The sun is always there but it's lurking in the background.

Like Zach.

He doesn't try to talk to me or approach me, except when I'm getting sick at the rest stops. Which seems to have abated altogether.

The smell of my car, the leather seats, the roads. They don't scare me anymore. I'm back to being myself before my parents died. I think I forced my phobia away.

Or maybe I'm afraid of something else now.

A certain tall, dark and handsome guy who won't stop following me.

After days of driving aimlessly, I decide to stop at a random place.

It's called Blue Dot.

Well, it has blue in the name so maybe it's not random at all.

It's further up north and it's located among the mountains. They say it snows there in the winter and the summers aren't as hot as Princetown.

We reach there a couple of days later. I say we because Zach hasn't left me yet.

It's been a little over a week since everything and he's been there like a shadow.

I don't trust him. I don't trust that he won't get bored and leave after a while.

Why would he stay? He has a life in New York. An apartment, roommates. A job that he likes and is good at.

You're my life.

I know he said that. I *know*.

But I can't believe those words. I can't. Not after everything he's done and how callously he rejected my love.

We stop at a diner to eat as soon as we arrive at Blue Dot.

I sit at one end of the bar and he sits on the other. The waitress is young and a chatty one, and she and I strike up a conversation.

When I tell her that I might be staying here for a while, she tells me that they are hiring. She also hooks me up with a bed and breakfast, a couple of blocks down from here.

The town is small, smaller than Princetown, but I like it. It's cold here. Winter is in full force. There's wind. Oh, and there's a lake, too. It's so blue that I fall in love with it the first moment I see it. Kinda like I fell in love with Zach.

The next day I arrive at the diner at seven and he's there.

God, doesn't he sleep? Take a day off or something?

The waitress who told me about this job walks me through everything and tells me which section is going to be mine for that day.

And whaddya know? Zach's already sitting there.

I walk up to him. "What are you doing here?"

He tips his chin to the menu. "I love the coffee here."

"You love the coffee." At his nod, I continue, "You've never had coffee here."

"I had some yesterday."

"No, you didn't. You had a hamburger and a slice of pie. I saw it."

When he smiles, I realize I shouldn't have said it. It makes me look like a creepy stalker. A stage-five clinger.

He folds his arms on the table and nods. "Yeah, you caught me. I'm just here for the pie."

I rest a hand on the booth and cock my hip. "Are you going to watch me work all day?"

The rays of sun enlighten his jaw and criss-cross through his hair, making him look so handsome that I have to take a deep breath and compose myself.

Don't cave, Cleo. Do not cave.

"No. But I can, if you want me to."

"You know what I want."

"Well, then I'll just come back at lunch."

Sighing, I stand up straight. "So what? Pie. Is that your order?"

"Uh-huh. And a cup of coffee with it."

I make a show of writing it down on my brand-new pad. "A piece of pie and coffee with a side of spit, coming up."

As I turn around, I hear him give a chuckle that melts like butter in my bones, and I know I need to be strong.

Much stronger, actually, than I had planned because after that, Zach shows up at seven every morning, orders the same thing and simply watches me bustle around.

It reminds me so much of when he first came back. He'd watch me run to the mansion in the morning or sometimes in the hallways, wearing my uniform.

He's doing the same thing here.

He watches me work, taking down orders, delivering food, chatting up the customers, all in my uniform of a red t-shirt and a black pair of shorts. And like at The Pleiades, I feel his gaze on me right from when he sits down at the booth until he leaves an hour later.

I hate that he's doing this.

I hate that he's making it so difficult to stay away from him.

Every day that passes makes it harder for me to resist him. Resist his intense eyes, his singular focus on me. The things he says even when he's not talking.

Damn it, I hate his fraught-with-intensity silences.

Sometimes I think I'm being stupid.

I love him, don't I?

What does it matter if he doesn't want that? What does it matter if he rejects my love at every turn and hurts me?

I'll take it.

I'll take it all if I can just walk up to him and touch those midnight, velvety strands. If I get to hold his hand or caress that hard jaw. If I get to kiss him, smell him, make love to him.

But then, what if he rejects me over and over and *over*, so many times that I become bitter? That I become angry and hateful. Exactly like I did back at St. Patrick's.

I can't do that.

I can't hate him when I know how it feels to love him.

I can't let him kill my love.

So I'm going to wait him out. He can't follow me around forever, right? He can't come to the diner every day for the rest of his life.

Turns out, I'm right.

After coming every day for about a week, he stops.

One morning, he doesn't come in. Worriedly, I watch the clock and jump every time the door opens up and a new customer arrives.

Zach never shows up though.

I spend the day alternately worrying over him, thinking that something happened to him, and being angry that he gave up so easily.

Which is just stupid. I wanted him to give up. I wanted him to go away and leave me alone. It's a good thing.

I can finally start my life now, without the past. Without him.

The next morning when he doesn't show up again, I decide I'm not even going to watch the door. Nope. I'm not going to act like a junkie, no matter how much I want to. He won't reduce me to that.

But then, I see him through the window.

He's on the opposite side of the street, striding down the sidewalk. Hurriedly, I walk to my boss and ask her for a five-minute break, even though I just started. I'm already out the door, pulling on my jacket because Jesus Christ, it's cold, before she even confirms.

I jaywalk to the other side of the street and follow after him. I don't know what I'm going to say to him when I catch up, but I have to see where he's going.

Asshole.

He's such a fucking asshole, isn't he? He made me think that he'd wait for me forever. That he wouldn't budge, no matter how I pushed him away.

But look at him now. Sauntering down the sidewalk as if he has no care in the world.

Okay, so that might be an exaggeration. He isn't sauntering but lunging, like he's in a hurry.

Finally, he stops at an autobody shop at the corner of the street.

Panting, I pause too.

That's when I realize the clothes he's wearing. A dark gray overall – a uniform.

Why's he wearing a uniform?

Slowly, I move forward, taking everything in. There's an office space with a board on top, saying Blue Dot Auto Body Inc. Right next to it is a large shed-like area with a few cars parked inside, along with a couple of bikes.

Zach stops by a guy who's drinking coffee, as he chats with him. He's wearing the same uniform as Zach.

Breathing in noisily, I watch them together. Until the guy spies me and alerts Zach of my presence.

He spins around, and immediately there's a frown on his face. "Blue?" He excuses himself from the guy and walks over to me. "What're you doing here? Is everything okay?"

There's a logo on the right side of his chest, spelling the name of the shop. "You didn't come to the diner."

"Yeah." He scratches his forehead with his thumb. "I got held up here all day yesterday. Apparently, they're slammed. A guy left and they didn't have back-up."

I simply blink up at him, at his explanation.

"But I was gonna show up for lunch today," he finishes, watching me carefully.

"I thought something happened to you. I-I was worried."

Zach smiles slightly. "I'm fine, Blue. Just working."

I look at the shop once again. The guy talking to Zach has left. It seems we're the only two people here right now.

Looking back at him, I ask, "You're working here?"

He chuckles. "That's what I said."

"Why?"

"Well, I figured I'm good with bikes. And they seemed really desperate. So why not. Besides, it comes with an apartment."

"Apartment?"

"Yeah. Up there, actually." He tips with his chin and I turn around to see an apartment on the second floor, across the street. There's a little coffee place downstairs.

"I was thinking," he goes on and I face him. "You could crash with me. The apartment is plenty big. I could take the couch."

"You'll take the couch."

"Yeah. It's a futon. It rolls out. It's gotta be better than the bed and breakfast that you're staying at and —"

"Stop talking," I tell him, finally coming out of my stupor.

Zach frowns like he's so confused.

He's confused? I am fucking reeling here.

Reeling.

"What are you doing?" I ask with gritted teeth.

"What do you mean?"

"What do you mean, what do I mean?" I say, hysterically. "Did you just ask me to live with you?"

"Well, yes. As I said, the apartment's got a lot of room."

"A lot of room. Right." Shaking my head, I look at the ground and gather myself. "Why do you have a job? Why do you have an *apartment*?"

"I can't stay at the motel forever. Where do you suggest I sleep?"

I throw my hands up. "In New York. You have all these things in New York. An apartment. A job that you told me you liked and that you're good at. Your life's in New York."

Throwing me a lopsided smile, he shrugs. "I don't have anything there that's not replaceable. And I told you."

"Told me what?"

The chilly breeze ruffles his spiky hair as he says, "You're my life."

His words have more of an impact this time. Maybe because now I can see what he means by it. He's showing me by re-arranging his life around me.

They hit me right in the gut and the butterflies go crazy. I feel their razor-sharp wings flapping, making everything bleed inside of me.

I wrap my arms around my waist, trying to quiet them down. "Why are you doing this?"

"Doing what?"

"Why won't you leave me alone?"

There's a slight flush on his harsh cheekbones. I think it's courtesy of the colder weather here. And he's not even wearing a sweater.

I don't know why I'm thinking about that when something much more important is at stake.

"Because I don't want you to be alone. Or afraid," he says with a clench in his jaw.

"I am not alone," I blurt out, looking up at him.

We've been standing a few inches apart from each other but while talking, we moved closer. I can feel his body heat, his smell, enveloping me, stopping the shivers brought on by the weather.

"What?"

I lick my lips. "I found a guy."

"A guy."

"Yeah." I nod. "He came to the diner yesterday. Sat in my section. He told me that I was beautiful and when I said that I was new in town, he offered to show me around. So we're going out this weekend."

It's a lie. Obviously.

And even telling it is making me want to throw up but I have to say it.

Zach's standing here, all taut and flushed with the cold. His black eyes watch me carefully.

"Are you going to ruin my date?" I ask when he doesn't say anything.

The vein on the side of his neck pulses. "Do you want me to ruin your date?"

I step closer for some reason, bringing the toes of our boots flush together.

"No." I shake my head once, boring into his eyes. "You want to watch me, right? You won't leave me alone. So I want you to watch me on my date. I want you to watch me as someone else makes me smile. Makes me laugh. As someone else holds my hand, kisses me goodnight at the end of the night. I want you to watch all of that, Zach."

His nostrils flare and the color on his sharp cheekbones deepens. I think it's from anger, rather than the cold.

"That's what you want, isn't it? To watch me. That's why you won't go away. What do you think is going to happen? Do you think I'll always be alone?" I scoff, "You're my first love. Sometimes, I think you'll be the only love of my life. But that doesn't mean that it won't get easier. That I won't find someone that I'll want to spend the rest of my life with. I want that, you know. Maybe I won't love him like I love you. Maybe he won't make my heart beat faster or he won't make the butterflies explode in my stomach. But it's okay. I want a home. I want babies. I want a future, Zach. Maybe it's okay for you to live in the past but I want to build my life. I want to belong somewhere. To someone."

To you.

Oh God, how I wish that. How I wish to belong to him. How I wish he belonged to me.

But I guess some stories are just doomed. They don't have a life, no matter how alive they feel.

Zach swallows and lowers his head. He watches the ground for about five seconds, the longest five seconds of my life.

In those five seconds, I think he gets it. He finally gets what I'm saying.

In those five seconds, I'm fraught with panic that he'll leave. And relief that it won't cut me every day to look at him, and not be able to touch him.

Then he looks up and his eyes are glassy. Vulnerable. Overflowing with emotions.

"I remembered something the other day," he begins. "When I was in that hole, I was scared. I thought no one would find me. They wouldn't even bother looking. I was a pain in the ass. Why would they look for me? So I lay there, watching the sky. It felt like I was somewhere deep. It was hot and muggy and the sky looked so far away. And then, I saw a shooting star. It was quick. Just a flash, but it was enough that I closed my eyes and made a wish."

He chuckles. "Goes to show how desperate I was. I didn't believe in wishes. Do you know what I wished for?"

Speechless, I shake my head.

"I wished for someone who'd care for me. Someone who'd love me. Who would put up with me and all the destructive things that I just felt compelled to do. I wished for someone soft. Someone shiny and bright. But more than that, I wished for someone I could be better for. I wished for you. And then, I found you but I was too fucking blind to see it. I was too angry and wrapped up in myself to realize you were it. That you were a star. No matter how much dirt I threw on you, you just kept shining. And I kept watching you do it.

"It'll destroy me to watch you belong to someone else. I'll die a little every day if you give your smiles to him. It'll fucking gut me to watch you build a future with him. A future I could've had with you but I was too fucked up to reach for it. But I'll watch you, no matter what. In your letter, you said that you'll watch the stars every night. Well, you're *my* star, Blue. I can't *not* watch you. I always thought that love makes you bleed. But I guess that's okay. I'll take it. If you're happy with some other guy, Blue, I'll take the bleeding. Because I love you."

Right in front of me, Zach grows taller. Broader. His body becomes tighter. The tendons on his neck stand out, that vein pulsing.

He's growing in front of me, becoming stronger somehow, and all I can do is witness it mutely. Tearfully.

And when he puts his hand on me, I can't stop him.

I don't want to. I've lost all my strength. I have nothing left in me but... him.

He's running in my veins and beating in my chest.

"I'm in love with you, Blue," he whispers, his thumbs working on wiping off my tears. "You were right. But it didn't start that day. It didn't start in that detention room. It started long ago, probably in that hole. Maybe even before I was born. I haven't just loved you for years, I've loved you for lifetimes.

Because I don't love you with just my heart. Heart's just an organ. It can be ripped away from the body, stomped on, squashed into a pulp. I don't love you with all my heart. I love you with all my soul. You're in the core of me. You're in my fucking essence. And no one can take that away from me. Not even death."

He drops his forehead onto mine and I'm outright sobbing.

I'm a mess.

I'm such a fucking mess that it's embarrassing.

It's so bad that Zach has to clutch me to his warm, hard chest, and I wind my arms around him, clinging to him like I'm drowning.

I have no idea how long I slobber all over him but finally, my tears have dried up and I move away to look at his face.

Tracing his cheekbones, I whisper, "It's cold out."

His lips twitch. "I know."

"Why aren't you wearing a sweater? A jacket."

He looks at my jacket. It's blue and puffy, the first thing I bought for myself the day we arrived. "I guess I forgot."

I fist his uniform. "You're an idiot."

"I am."

"I ruined your uniform."

He looks down at the wet splotch on his chest. "I made you cry."

"You're always doing that."

At my statement, he bores his eyes into me before stepping back.

And then, he takes my breath away as he comes down to his knees.

"What are you…" I ask. "What're you doing?"

Looking up, he says, "Making a promise to you."

"What promise?"

"I know I fucked up. I know I've fucked up a million times over the years. I don't deserve you. I don't deserve to breathe the same air as you. But if by some miracle, you give me a chance, Blue, I'll spend the rest of my life trying to prove to you that I can be better. That I'm the guy who wished for you on a night long ago and he realizes that."

This isn't the first time Zach's been on his knees in front of me. This isn't the first time I'm looking down at him.

But it feels like it.

All those other times were for sex, because he wanted to taste me, but this is… subjugation. This is role-reversal.

This is him asking me, *begging me* to give him a chance.

I take in his wind-ruffled hair and his magnificent face. The sun's bare minimum but still, his bronzed skin shines under it.

Even on his knees, he looks like a prince.

My prince.

"Okay."

His eyes flare. "Okay?"

A smile blooms on my face. "Yeah. Okay."

"Are you kidding?"

Something about that makes me laugh. My coat hits me mid-thigh and my bare limbs graze his chest as I step closer to him. "No. Get up. The ground's cold."

Still, he doesn't move. He's watching me seriously, like his entire life depends on it.

"I love you, Zach. I've loved you forever. I don't know how I lived apart from you when you were gone for three years. Maybe it was easier then because I didn't know I loved you. All I felt for you was this deep-seated passion that I thought was hate. But now? Now I know how it feels to love you and it's hard. It's so much harder to survive without you."

His hands come up to my waist. "I'll never put you through anything like that again. I'll never leave you."

Bending down, I kiss him lightly. "I know. But you gotta get up. My break's over and you have to kiss me thoroughly."

"I have to?" he teases.

"Uh-huh. I'm dying here."

Chuckling, he presses a kiss on my mouth before getting up and heaving me in his arms in that typical way of his.

And then he kisses me. Thoroughly.

Epilogue

They call him the Dark Prince.

Rumor has it that he has the blackest pair of eyes anyone has ever seen. And equally black hair.

Although, no one can say for sure because he always has his helmet on – it's a big, black thing that hides his entire face, and he leaves right after the show. He isn't much for the fanfare or stuff like that.

Nope. He's all about the bike.

The bike he calls Blue.

He can do a wheelie with his eyes closed and he can fly over holes. When he's in the air, he flips his bike like it weighs nothing. The crowd goes wild over him, chanting and screaming out his stage name.

Tonight, he's going to take a ride on the wall of death.

It sounds ominous and I swear it is with the way I'm shaking at just the thought of it. It's a well type thingy where the bikers start at the bottom, slowly gaining speed as they circle and circle. Until they gain enough momentum to ride parallel to the ground.

It's supposed to be based on a very simple principle of physics but I wasn't into science much back in school.

It all feels like magic to me. A magic that can go wrong at any time.

Although, Zach's been practicing for it for weeks now. I've seen him do it and he does it beautifully.

Even so, I'm nervous.

I guess I'll always be nervous when he goes on stage. He's the most precious thing in the world to me.

He's the love of my life.

And I'm waiting for him at the rink, hanging over the railing, getting jostled in the crowd, impatient for him to come out. He's the last one to go on and it feels like I haven't seen him for days. When I only saw him a few hours ago at the house we're staying in for the next few weeks.

We're in Vegas for the carnival where he's performing. His friends from New York tipped him off and now, we're sharing an apartment with them.

They are a good bunch; I met them a couple of days ago when we arrived. Although, Zach gets a little territorial when they talk to me. He's asked me to stay away from them and be by his side all the time.

I usually roll my eyes at him when he gets this jealous and tell him he isn't the boss of me. And he proceeds to prove me wrong by playing with my body like he owns it.

He does. I've no shame or reservations in admitting that.

I own him too.

And now, I'm getting all sorts of turned on, standing in the middle of the crowd. I can't wait for him to come out and be done with it so we can go back and be alone.

He gets all sweaty and impatient after one of his shows.

Although, in all fairness, this is only the second one I'll see him perform for a crowd. Last time was at a carnival like this in New York. That show was wild. We were there for about a week and every night was amazing.

I still can't believe how popular he is with the crowd. How people chant for him and how girls go crazy.

That, I don't like and I'm glad he isn't interested in fame or whatever.

He's only interested in me.

He shows me that every day. He's been showing it to me for the past six months, ever since he got down on his knees and asked me to give him a chance.

We decided to stay in Blue Dot because we both love the place. The cold weather, the mountains, the lake. There's so much sky there and everything is so wide and open and blue.

It feels like freedom.

We live together now, in the same apartment he got through his job at the shop. In the beginning, I thought it would be a little awkward. Moving in together when we've never even really dated.

But it wasn't.

Nothing with Zach is ever awkward. It's always filled with passion, yes. Intensity and an in-born heat. But it's never weird. Even when we clash, we clash so gloriously and naturally, like two celestial bodies meant to crash and burn and yet, still somehow orbit around each other.

Anyway for the first few weeks, I took the bedroom and he slept on the couch. We were sort of roommates.

Roommates who were irrevocably in love with each other.

We went on dates, explored the town, made some friends. It was Zach's way of making me feel cherished, doing the right thing by me. By the end of his courting though, I was bursting out of seams. I wanted his hands on me, his lips, his teeth. I wanted to be able to dive into his arms whenever I wanted and I wanted him to sink into my softness whenever *he* wanted.

Good thing, he was about to combust, too.

So, we graduated from being roommates to being girlfriend and boyfriend a month after we moved in.

Zach doesn't like that term: girlfriend and boyfriend. He thinks it's childish. But whatever. I like it. It makes me think that we're young and in love and the time we lost fighting and hurting each other wasn't as long.

In reality thought, it was close to a decade.

A decade of hate and screw ups and misery. When we could've been there for each other, through years of bullying.

I could've told him that he was amazing when his Dad beat him down and his mom didn't care enough. And he could've made me realize that it didn't matter that I didn't possess a society-certified body or if my hair was blue or if I came from the other side of town, I was still beautiful to him.

We could've saved each other so much heartache.

But I'm glad we're together now. Us against the world.

I'm glad I was with him when his mom passed away a couple of months ago.

Mrs. S called him with the news and we headed back to Princetown the very next day for the funeral.

We saw everyone: Maggie, Mrs. S, Grace, Tina, Leslie and Art. He's doing great and he's gotten so big. I can't wait for the day when he's the tallest kid in his class. No one will have the guts to pick on him.

Zach's dad was there at the funeral too. He met with Zach like the whole prison incident never happened. Like, Zach never punched him and Mr. Prince never slapped Mrs. Prince.

As expected, nothing came of that incident, anyway.

I don't know what's wrong with rich people but I'm glad we're out of that town. I'm glad Zach's moving on.

He did the eulogy that he wrote himself.

I've never been prouder of him. Not even when he brought home books and notebooks and told me that he wanted to learn.

He wanted to be better. For himself.

Every night before going to sleep, we read together. It feels like a dream, where we're naked and sweaty, wrapped up in a sheet, reading about love and passion.

Who knew reading could be so hot? Who knew I'd want to do it for the rest of my life? Maybe even get a degree in literature. But I'm not thinking that far ahead right now.

Right now, I'm in love.

I look down when the announcer introduces Zach aka The Dark Prince.

It's a mini-version of a stadium with the well at the bottom and spectator area up top. I'm two floors up and the bottom looks way deeper than it did a second ago. Swallowing, I scan the wall that Zach will be riding on, going in circles.

God, I don't want to imagine how far up the top is from the bottom and how hard the ground looks. Why can't they have safety nets or something?

Why do they have to make it so dangerous?

I grip the railing in tightly when the door on the far side of the well opens and Zach emerges from it.

He has his helmet on and his outfit is all black. Hence, the name.

He rides out to the middle, churning gravel in his wake and the sounds are deafening. I just stand there like a mute, on shaking legs as I watch him revving the bike and looking so invincible down there.

But he's not invincible.

He's just a... guy. A layered, beautiful guy I'm in love with and I'm so scared for him.

Blowing out a breath, I look up at the sky. It's studded with stars.

Our stars.

They feel like ours now, mine and Zach's. We watch them night after night, through the window above our bed. Sometimes, I watch them when he moves inside of me. Fast and furious, or slow and lazy.

I look to them now and ask them to keep him safe.

Please, keep him safe.

I whip my gaze down when the roar of his bike rises higher than the chant of the crowd. And then, he's taking off. He rides toward the wall at a speed that steals my breath and before I can even blink, he slides up.

He's there, on the wall.

I lean over the railing, hang my body out like so many other people as he circles the wall. He circles and circles, inching higher, gaining speed.

When he reaches the top, I bite my lip so hard I taste my blood. It's metallic and full of nerves as I watch him finally go parallel to the ground.

In this moment, my nerves abate a little.

They're there, of course but something else creeps in.

Something like adrenaline.

I feel like it's coming from him. Just as he hits the top-most part of the wall, he feels elated. He feels like he's conquered the world. He's touching the sky because in this moment, he's a star himself. Dark but still, bright.

And I smile even as my eyes sting.

It's like I can feel him, his emotions through the space. I can *feel* how much he loves it. How much he revels in it.

This is freedom for him.

Butterflies flap just under my ribs and I put a hand on my stomach. I'm shaking but not just from the nerves.

I'm shaking from watching him go round and round. I'm shaking from watching him go down this man-made hole and come back up. All in a blink of an eye.

He's light as air, and gravity doesn't mean anything to him.

Zach doesn't follow the basic laws of nature. He's above that.

He is the dark prince.

He's my prince and when his act is over and he brings his bike to the middle of the well again, I turn around.

I make my way through the chanting crowd and rush down the stairs. There's a staff entrance at the bottom of the stadium and I flash my visitor pass to the guy standing guard.

The inside is bustling with activity and people. The crew has their headsets on and they're running around like the entire world depends on them. Well, at least the act does so I'm happy they seem so dedicated.

It's a big space that breaks off into a tunnel, leading to the bottom of the well. I reach the mouth of the tunnel and see Zach getting off his bike. He takes his helmet off, followed by his jacket.

Even when he's practicing, he's always super-heated and sweaty after his stunt.

His black t-shirt is sticking to his muscular chest and his hair is all mussed up and spiky. There's a dark hue on his cheeks from the rush, I think.

A crowd is gathered around him, a couple of staff members and his friends from New York, and even though, I'm impatient to get him alone, I don't mind waiting until he finishes up.

But as it turns out, I don't have to wait long.

He looks at me as soon as he's done throwing the jacket on his parked bike. Back when I hated him or I thought that I hated him, this connection between us used to bother me. But now, I'm thankful for it. It makes me feel special, the only girl for him in this world. In this entire galaxy.

His stare is dark as always, and hungry.

He seems ravenous and my skin breaks out in goose bumps when he starts to walk toward me, in the middle of the conversation.

Breathing hard, I stand there, watching him approach me.

The first thing I notice when he gets close to me is his smell. It's musky mixed in with his favorite: blueberry pie. When we were in Princetown, I got the recipe from Maggie. I'm a disaster in the kitchen but somehow, I've learnt to perfect it for Zach.

"That's very rude," I tell him, craning my neck up. "Walking away in the middle of a conversation."

He leans over me. "I've always been rude."

Shaking my head, I smile at him and reach up to wipe off an errant drop of sweat, snaking down to his brows. "You were amazing down there. Like, really, *really* amazing."

"What happened?"

"What?"

His hand reaches out and he traces my lower lip with the rough pad of his thumb. "Have you been biting your lip?"

Oh, I forgot about that.

I nod, clutching his wrist and rubbing the end of his tattoo on his wrist. "Just a little. I was nervous."

"I keep making you bleed," he murmurs.

I step closer to him and his chest grazes mine. "It's not you. I'm just a chicken shit about these things. I keep thinking something will happen to you."

"Nothing will happen to me."

Then, he bends down and kisses me softly. He sucks in my lower lip and runs his tongue over the torn-up skin, soothing it. Apologizing for making me worry over him even though, I've told him a hundred times before: I'll always worry, and he doesn't need to apologize for it.

I wind my arms around his neck, going flush with him. Just as our bodies connect with each other, Zach puts his hands under my ass and heaves me up.

My legs go around his narrow hips and he begins walking, without breaking our kiss. I hear a few hollers in the background but I don't care.

Zach's kissing me. The world can catch fire and I still wouldn't mind.

He takes me out through the door, where a crowd has been gathered, probably waiting for the bikers to come out. I hear someone call out Zach's stage name and going all speculative if it's really him, but he keeps walking until we get far away from them. He finds a secluded spot between two trailers parked on the far side of the ground.

Propping me against the metal wall, he breaks off.

"No, don't stop," I breathe out, lifting my chin to go after his lips again.

His strong body shifts between my thighs, his pelvis rubbing against my swollen clit. "What are you wearing?"

Zach's frowning down at my t-shirt and I realize it's the first time he's noticed my attire. My *unusual* attire for the night.

He's focused on my bare midriff. It's pale and soft and right now, dimpled in the shape of his fingers that are clutching me.

"Uh, it's a t-shirt?"

He looks up. "Why isn't it hiding anything, then?"

Even though I'm a little nervous at his reaction at such a bold outfit and a lot turned on, I manage to chuckle. "What? It's hiding everything."

He digs his fingers into my flesh, and I stretch my spine, trapped between him and the trailer. "Not your stomach."

"I wanted to dress up a little." Then, because I can't stop myself, "Do you think I... you know, look weird? I mean, I'm not built like a leaf and –"

"Do you want me to drop you right here and leave?" he growls, getting up in my face.

His words remind me of the night I followed him in my car and found out that he can fly bikes. In fact, this whole encounter is making me remember how he put his mouth on my body for the first time ever and kissed me. Down there.

I punch his shoulder. "Stop being mean. I'm genuinely worried. I've never put on something like this."

"And you won't put on something like this ever again because you look sexy as fuck and only I get to appreciate that. You're mine, remember?"

God, why does he have to so sexy and possessive?

How am I supposed to stop myself from jumping his bones and falling in love with him every second of every day?

Smiling, I peck his lips. "I know. It says so on the shirt."

I gesture to my chest and confused, Zach looks down.

Across my breasts, it says: *Dark Prince's Cinderella*. And there's a picture of leather boots at the bottom.

I got this t-shirt custom made for tonight. I knew he'd love it. And he does. Unwrapping one hand from around my waist, he fingers the letters on my chest. It heaves like crazy when he brushes against my left nipple, going back and forth, waking it up.

I stretch my spine again, rubbing our lower bodies together.

Keeping his face dipped, Zach lifts his eyes up. "Cinderella, huh?"

"Yes," I whisper in a low voice, rocking against him once. "And you're my prince. Although, you act like a mean beast most of the time. But I can take you."

A lopsided smirk and then, his eyes move over my hair. "Did you do something to your hair too?"

Biting my lip, I nod.

"It's a different color."

I don't know how he can tell when my new color that I especially got for tonight is so similar to what I had before. There's a very subtle difference between the two, but if anyone's an expert on my hair, it's Zach.

He's obsessed with it. More so than he's obsessed with my breasts that he's still running his fingers over.

"It's Royal Blue," I tell him.

"For your prince?"

"Always."

An emotion flickers across his face that makes him clench his jaw. I recognize what it is; it's love.

Sometimes it's so intense for him that it borders on painful; I go through the same thing.

I know he's feeling that spark in his chest. Just as I'm feeling the buzz in my tummy.

I caress his jaw and whisper, "I love you."

Zach remains silent but his grip on my waist goes tight and his thumb hooks into my belly button.

One time I told him about the vein that runs just behind my navel. I told him how I feel something move inside my belly whenever he's close, and how when he presses against it, my body goes crazy. I didn't have to tell him the latter because he's spent countless hours kissing and licking that spot himself but still.

Now, it makes me moan, the pressure he's putting using his thumb.

"I have something for you too," he rasps, instead of saying *I love you too*.

He doesn't say the words often. Or at least, not as often as I do. I say it all the time: before going to sleep every night, rushing out the door for work in the morning, when we finish a phone conversation. When he's inside of me.

And every time I say it, I feel him absorb those words. I feel them move through his body. I feel *his* love radiating back in the way he presses a kiss on my mouth, in the way his eyes turn glassy.

So, I guess, he doesn't need to. He shows me.

I caress his harshly angled jaw. "For me?"

His Adam's apple bobs as he nods. Then, without taking his eyes off me, he reaches back and fishes something out of his pocket.

It's a piece of paper, folded once.

"I wanna read it to you," he says and my heart jumps in my chest.

Zach's reading has improved so much in the past months. His writing, as well. He puts an effort into it every day. In fact, we're thinking about him getting his GED soon.

And I know whatever he wrote for me, it's important to him. It's probably more important than all the words he'll ever say to me, and maybe that's why he wrote them down.

To impart their gravity, their worth.

"Okay," I whisper, fisting his damp t-shirt.

Frowning and clearing his throat, he begins,

"Blue,

I know I've fucked up a lot. I haven't wronged anyone the way I've wronged you.

No amount of Sorrys will ever make up for that fact.

But still, I'm sorry. About everything.

For all the times I could've saved you but I didn't. For all the times I made you cry and wasn't there to wipe off your tears. For all the times I made you bitter and angry enough that you started to hate yourself a little bit.

Words have always been hard to come by for me. I'm not good with them. I probably never will be. But I want you to know that I feel it.

I feel you.

Right in my chest, with every breath I take.

You saved me when I least deserved it. And I'll spend the rest of my life proving to you that you did the right thing in choosing me.

But more than that, I want you to know that I'm gonna marry you one day. I'm gonna give you your future.

When I'm wiser and better and not too much of an asshole.

When I'm really the prince you think I am.

Yours,

Prince."

It takes me a long moment to catch my breath after he's stopped reading. I probably look like a mess, crying like someone has died.

Whereas in reality, I don't think a night has been more alive. More fraught with electricity, emotions and energy.

I forgave him a long time ago for everything. He didn't need to apologize but I'll forever carry his words in my heart.

I'll accept them and keep them safe, just as I'll keep him safe inside my chest.

"W-When did you write this?" I manage to ask after a while.

Zach's wiping off my tears and tucking my newly-colored hair behind my ear. "I've been writing it a long time. Probably when you decided to give me a chance." My eyes go wide at his answer. "Earlier versions sounded dumb."

I snort. "Oh please. Nothing you say to me can sound dumb. Except, one thing."

"What?"

I kiss him first and cross my ankles at the small of his back. "You've always been the prince I think you are."

He smiles against my lips. "Yeah?"

"Uh-huh. You know what that means, right?"

"What?"

"You're going to have to marry me now."

"Is that right?"

"Yup. You promised. I have it in writing."

He kisses me again, pressing our bodies so close together that we breathe as one. "Stage-five clinger."

"You like it."

I deepen our kiss, then.

His taste floods my mouth and all I can do is hold on to him. When his lips move to my jaw, traveling down to my neck, I tell him, "I want you to kiss me. The way you like it."

He groans into my skin and lowers my feet to the ground.

Staring into my eyes, he comes down on his knees. "Be careful what you wish for, Blue."

He doesn't wait for my answer as his mouth falls on my bare belly and he starts working on my buttons.

Moaning, I arch my neck up and look at the stars again. They are beautiful and breath-taking, as always. But like every night, I search for the brightest of the bunch.

When I find them – two of them, in fact, I name them: Zachariah and Cleopatra.

After that, I close my eyes and lose myself in his kiss on my core.

The Dark Prince

She calls me a prince and herself, Cinderella.

I agree.

She's my Cinderella. Except in our story, Cinderella saves the prince.

I meant every word that I wrote; she saved me when I least deserved it. She saved me from my past and my anger. She made me realize that I was powerful enough to move on. That the past doesn't define me. I define myself. I make my own future.

She made me believe that I can break the chains and fly out of my tower.

Yeah, she made me a believer. Of love.

And now, I'm going to spend the rest of my life slaying her dragons.

Because she's mine.

My Blue.

My prize.

THE END

BONUS SCENES

Want to read first-hand Zach and Cleo's first meeting and prom night? Get your BONUS SCENES for free here.

Would you like to be notified when Saffron releases another book or when a sale is happening? Please sign up for her newsletter here.

For signed paperbacks & BBB merchandise.
Visit Store here.

AUTHOR'S NOTE

Thank you so much for reading Zach and Cleo's story. I'm usually very happy when I finish a book but this one made me cry. Saying goodbye to these characters was very hard. Perhaps because their experiences are very personal to me. And I know that they will forever inspire me to be strong in the face of adversity.

Bullying, as we all know, is a sociological problem. It's a disease, really – a rampant one at that. And my aim in writing this book is to make people aware of its effects.

Bullying has consequences and repercussions that can last a lifetime. Even one thoughtless, cruel comment can break someone's spirit to a degree that it takes years for them to put it back together. Not to mention, bullying is not confined to a school or a classroom or a playground. You can find it at your workplace, at your dining table and in this social media age, definitely on the internet.

As bullied, we always think that if we keep our head down and not react, things will stop. The torture will stop. The taunts and ridicule will disappear. The bully will disappear.

However, I can assure you that running away is not the answer. The answer is to stand up to your bully. The answer is to fight back. The answer is to do the right thing and take away your bully's powers.

Without you and your fear, a bully is nothing. A bully isn't even a bully. He's simply a coward and an insecure human being with a very small life.

As I said before, many of the characters' experiences and emotions are very personal to me. Meaning, I've gone through them myself. I've gone through the ridicule, the anxiety of it and the panic that it causes. The complete description and what inspired me to write this book can be found here: BAD BOY BLUES AND BULLYING [Insert Link].

As always, I'm very grateful for your time and your support. It is my sincerest hope that reading this story gave you the strength that I gained while writing it.

xoxo

Saffron

ACKNOWLEDGMENTS

My husband: He is and will always be my number one supporter. He has more faith in me than I have in myself. I don't know how I got this lucky but thank you for everything, baby.

My sister: I wrote this book while I was visiting her and she became such a champion of Zach and his character. I had such a great time with you, sis. I love you to the moon and back.

My parents: They're the best and most supportive parents a girl could ask for. Thank you for being so proud of me.

Sophia Karlson: You've been with me since the beginning and your advice, your counsel and the courage you gave me while I was terrified of so many things, is why this book is out there today. I hope you know that you mean the world to me.

My fearless team: My PA, Melissa Panio-Peterson and my publicist, Danielle Sanchez from Wildfire Media Solutions Inc. You guys are one of the most professional, dedicated and smartest women in this industry. Thank you for being on my team and thank you for your invaluable support and guidance.

My friends: Bella Love, Autumn Davis, Heather M. Orgeron, Mara White and Stephanie Rose. You all know the hardships I went through with this book and how it almost overwhelmed me. Thank you for being there and for believing in me. Book world or not, you're one of the good ones and I'm so proud to know you.

Purple Hearts and my readers: Thank you for being there for me. Thank you for your enthusiasm and your love. You guys are my happy place and I love you all!

ABOUT THE AUTHOR

Writer of bad romances. Aspiring Lana Del Rey of the Book World.

Saffron A. Kent is a USA Today Bestselling Author of Contemporary and New Adult romance.

She has an MFA in Creative Writing and she lives in New York City with her nerdy and supportive husband, along with a million and one books.

She also blogs. Her musings related to life, writing, books and everything in between can be found in her JOURNAL on her website (www.thesaffronkent.com)

www.ingramcontent.com/pod-product-compliance
Lightning Source LLC
LaVergne TN
LVHW041619060526
838200LV00040B/1353

9 781088 075456